ADVANCE PR

MW00353318

"...an impressive display ⌄. ...⌄⌄⌄⌄y ⌄⌄⌄⌄⌄my, mixing ancient Tibetan philosophy into the trappings of a police procedural. Those expecting a conventional mystery should be surprised— and thrilled—by this original take on the noir genre."

—BlueInk Review

"With enriching and thought-provoking lessons and deeply reflective prose, Ringel keeps readers' fingers on Lama Rinzen's pulse at every twist as he races to recover the lost dorje—in a hell that he himself is lost in—before his time runs out."

—US Review of Books

"The core murder mystery, unusual detective hero, complex world-building, and flowing dialogue make for an enjoyable read."

—*Foreword* Clarion Reviews

"Jim Ringel's sharp, witty *49 Buddhas* illuminates the mysteries of both Buddhism and murder."

—William Haywood Henderson,
author of *Augusta Locke*

49

BUDDHAS

49
BUDDHAS

LAMA RINZEN in the HELL REALM

JIM RINGEL

49 Buddhas: Lama Rinzen in the Hell Realm
Published by Black Bee Publishing
Niwot, Colorado

Copyright ©2018 JIM RINGEL. All rights reserved.

No part of this book may be reproduced in any form or by any mechanical means, including information storage and retrieval systems without permission in writing from the publisher/author, except by a reviewer who may quote passages in a review.

All images, logos, quotes, and trademarks included in this book are subject to use according to trademark and copyright laws of the United States of America.

Library of Congress Control Number: 2017917201
RINGEL, JIM, Author
49 Buddhas
Jim Ringel

ISBN: 978-0-9995398-0-4

FICTION / Mystery & Detective / Amateur Sleuth
PHILOSOPHY / Buddhist

Photography by Bruce T. Martin

QUANTITY PURCHASES: Schools, companies, professional groups, clubs, and other organizations may qualify for special terms when ordering quantities of this title. For information, email Info@BlackBeePublishing.com.

All rights reserved by Jim Ringel and Black Bee Publishing. This book is printed in the United States of America.

To Connie. For all your support.
You read like you mean it, and care like it too.

GARCIA AND HOLMES

SNOW. ICY SIDEWALKS. FRIGID AIR.

But not so frigid maggots don't crawl over Sonny Heller's sliced corpse.

Sonny roped in a Shaker chair, in a warehouse on 33rd and Josephine. Not far off Denver's Colfax Avenue. Twenty blocks, or so.

Maggots crawl where Sonny once had skin.

Inside a warehouse that had once been a Catholic church.

Over Sonny Heller who had once been an insurance man with bus bench celebrity and a slogan: Life is Hell. You're gonna need insurance.

Two uniformed patrol cops find him. Part-timers Garcia and Holmes. They knock off early from directing morning traffic beneath the burnt-out red-amber-green hanging at the intersection of York and Colfax. The city can't afford traffic lights anymore, and the way they staff the police force with part-timers these days, it's cheaper to cover drive time on an hourly basis. Pay per go. Nickel-and-dime cops.

That is the way Denver is anymore. All patrol cops part-timers. All the detectives freelance.

Garcia and Holmes knock off early and head to the vacant warehouse on 33rd and Josephine, where it's cold, but not as cold as outside.

Garcia, the veteran of the two by three or four days, unlatches the door. He's a new hire. Like all part-timers. Laid off, hired back, paid entry level wages over and over again. All so the politicians can keep promising tax cuts, tax cuts, tax cuts to the citizenry.

Holmes pushes Garcia to get inside. "Come on already. It's frosty out here."

The door latch kerplunks. Garcia shoulders it open. Inside the air breathes damp, with the stench of something sour.

"God, Jesus and Joseph." Holmes snorts. He stomps his boots on the floorboards. The warehouse is shadowed in the dull cast of light leaking through stained glass. Cracked shards missing in the glass, giving the windows a jigsaw design.

Holmes stomps his boots atop a scattering of 8x12 glossies, black and white, strewn about the floor. Porno glossies.

He pulls off a mitten and picks one up. "Jeese. What's her story?" A large naked girl, curvy, her back to the camera, knife in hand. She faces into an oval mirror, full length, but her reflection's dimly lit and the back of her blurred in gauzy mystery.

The room around them holds a sour smell.

"Dios mio." Garcia looks over Holmes' shoulder at the black and white. "Is this from a...what do you say... snuff film? A snuff film they make maybe here in the warehouse?"

"It's art, man. Pure art." Holmes picks up other photos from the floor. The exact same shot. All of them, copies of one another. He blows his fingers for warmth. "You see how nicely done they shot them? Perfect lighting casting long shadows down her back-side. The way they framed her. Mysterious. That big ass right up front in the camera. What do you think? A size ten maybe."

"Jesus, do not say that," Garcia says.

"It's a porno shot. What else you going to say?" Holmes' breathing fogs the air. "Maybe a size twelve, huh? A big girl."

"Yes, a big girl." Garcia points to her in the glossy. "But that is no way to talk about a woman. Even one with a tattoo on her ass."

Holmes sniffs. "That's no tattoo, pal. It's a birthmark of some sort."

Garcia looks at the photo. "Birthmark? No. Tattoo. Can you imagine, birthmark ..."—he scratches his ass— "en sus nalgas. Never seeing it, behind you all the time. No, God would not do that to a woman. Have a birthmark on her ass. That is a tattoo. Put there on purpose. Not by accident." Garcia sniffs. Twice. "What is that smell?"

Holmes unbuttons his too tight pea coat and slips the photo inside. "Well, I say it's a birthmark, but I'll check later when I get home."

"Don't take it." Garcia says. "We are not supposed to be here."

Holmes scuffs the floor, kicking the other copies. "Take them all if you want. Except they're each the same." Then he deflects his attention deeper inside the warehouse. And although stuffed too tightly inside his pea coat, rendering his arms un-liftable, he nudges a shoulder toward the warehouse's back nave. "What's that?"

Garcia is already looking. A packing crate tipped over on its side, empty. Next to the packing crate, rows and rows of statues, seven by seven, forty-nine total. Each no more than three feet tall. Each identical, one to the other. Little smiley fat men. Buddhas, like Chinese restaurants keep up on dusty shelves next to the por-celain cat waving how-do-ya-do.

Goosebumps roll down Garcia's arms. Something about this warehouse is not right. Even a part-timer can see that. Maybe they shouldn't have come. The Buddhas wear a coat of frost on their molded plastic bodies. Their plastic bodies wear draped plastic robes, except where their naked bellies hang out. Each statue molded the same. Every one of them laughing.

Garcia walks among them. He lifts one. "Doesn't weigh much," he tells Holmes. He drops it back to the floor. The statue kerplunks, hollow sounding.

He looks beyond the statues into the back of the warehouse sanctuary. "What's that smell?" He sees something undulating, strapped and slithering in a Shaker chair. A glimmering slither. Non-specific in form. Arms trussed. Body slouching.

"What's that moving back there?" Holmes asks.

Garcia squints. "Shit, hombre. That's human."

"Alive?"

"I don't think so."

Holmes clenches his mouth and nose and gags. He tries not breathing. Garcia pulls a bandana from his pocket and fixes it bandit-style over his mouth and nose. He steps toward the slumped body—blistered and puffed and Christmasy green, like a man turned inside out. Dead a long time. A day maybe. Maybe a week.

Holmes buries his nose in the crook of his sleeve. The strapped man's skin has been stripped loose from his body. It hangs in strips down his waist. His feet have been chopped into stumps. Around the stumps, ten shriveled fingers and ten curled toes stand up on end. Plus, two plucked eyes, two hacked ears, and a flap-fallen nose. All on the floor, none holding much shape.

"Don't touch it," Holmes gasps.

"Touch it? Shit, man, we got to call this shit in."

"No. We're not supposed to be here, remember? Not for this shit, we're not."

Garcia squints at the corpse. The way its lips are cut away leaving its gums to resemble a hollow Halloween grin.

A business card needled to the man's chest. What had been his chest.

"Jesus Lord." Garcia makes the sign of the cross. He reads the business card. "It's the bus bench insurance dude. One of the brothers, Sonny Heller." Next to the stumps that were once feet, a briefcase with its lid opened rests on the floor, with stenciling in its leather. Life is Hell. Get some insurance!

With all the police layoffs and the part-time patrol force and the detectives all confined to working freelance, there are deaths in Denver that go unexplained. But not Sonny Heller's. Anybody could tell you why Sonny Heller was killed. He's an insurance man. This day and age, who wouldn't want to kill him?

Holmes coughs, eyes bleary. "Heller?" Because Sonny Heller is a man you hear about in Denver, but never see. Successful. Enviable. Someone you'd like to be like.

At least up until now.

"Got to call this shit in," Garcia says.

"No." Holmes tries not breathing. "We're sandbagging. We left the job early." He stomps his feet to distract himself, to get some circulation going. "No."

"Sooner or later, they will find him. We got to call it in."

The body squeaks. A mouse caked in bile pokes its head from one of Sonny Heller's carved openings and twitches its nose, sniffing the part-time policemen.

Holmes doesn't hold back. Behind clenched teeth, a sudden eruption of nausea burns up his throat. The mouse turns and circles back inside the carcass. Vomit splashes onto Sonny's slumped body and splatters the photo Holmes is holding. It pools atop the insurance papers in Sonny's briefcase.

Once fully expunged, Holmes flaps the photo in his face, fanning himself.

"Shit." Garcia says, his partner gasping, hunched over, hands to his knees. "Now we got to call it in."

LESSON 1

After dreams, we awaken.
After death, we are reborn.
After rebirth, a new beginning.

MEANWHILE, ELSEWHERE IN DENVER, I—LAMA Rinzen, a Buddhist monk of the Kagyu lineage—awake from meditation and am reborn.

More than awake. My meditation is interrupted, and when it is I see I am reborn on Denver's Colfax Avenue. At the tender age of twenty-one years.

As my eyes open. What to see?

The composition of the room. A darkened apartment. Paper window shades. An altar with a Buddha statue in the center. The smell of gas fumes leaking from heat vents. A nylon jacket slung across a chair back. *Spurtz Gra*—the folds make the jacket lettering hard to read.

Pool balls break beneath the floor boards.

And a telephone rings.

These are the events that interrupt my meditation and awaken me.

What to see, what to hear? That once again, I am reborn into the Hell Realm.

Can I never escape?

The air feels pinched and cold. I see a baby crib in the corner. Beneath the baby crib a telephone rings.

Interruption.

Candles burn atop the altar. I awake, tired. Exhausted. How many lifetimes have I been in Hell? I sit on a cushion in this apartment, in this city. Denver. That's what the neon outside the window says. Denver. *The Aim Straight and Shoot Saloon. Best Billiards and Beer in Denver.*

My only hope, that this is the lifetime I find the dorje.

That is my mission: to find the Most Precious of Objects. To embrace its beauty, its long golden tube gorged into orbs at either end. Its tube embedded with jewels and gemstones. The dorje—pronounced *door-jay*—if only I touch it, immediately I will achieve enlightenment. Poof. Not just *my* enlightenment. Enlightenment for all. Every creature in the world, enlightened. This is my gift to all, as a bodhisattva.

As taught in the Shedra. A bodhisattva exercises utmost compassion by accepting to only be enlightened once he has succeeded in bringing all other beings to enlightenment. Such is my mission. Such is my duty. Such is the reason I suffer in Hell. To find the dorje, and touch it, and in a single instant—*boom*—all beings transport to the Pure Lands, where I then join them.

I close my eyes. With my nose I sniff, with my tongue I taste the sweetness of the dorje's delicious promise. I crave sweeping my hands down its length of gold and jewels, and touching its orbs that curl like grasping hawk claws.

The telephone rings again, interrupting my reverie. I look about the room. Wallpaper hangs from the apartment's walls. Incense burns upon the altar. I sit upon a gomden with my legs crossed. A

Buddha statue smirks at me from the altar, from between vases of evergreen sprigs, alongside a photo of my teacher, Daidyal.

The Buddha says hate and desire tumble together in Hell, and of the six Buddhist Realms, Hell is the lowest, and longest, and loneliest of them all.

The telephone rings. I stand to unfetter my red-saffron robes flowing in front of me, and I reach behind to smooth them with the back of my hand. In my other hand, I hold a mala, its string knotted, its beads slipping from finger to finger clacking one another while I pray. Until the knot frays, and beads slip from the string to the floor like raindrops falling upon stone.

Like in a dream.

All dharma are dreams. Dreams of emptiness. The Buddha taught that. That and a lot of other stuff. Sometimes I wonder if the Buddha was not just crazy, and people only listened to him because, what else could they do? Beneath the crib, the telephone rings. I reach for it. I lift its handset between ear and shoulder.

"Who's this?" The caller speaks quickly. I hear his voice and his accent and language and the abruptness of his words.

"You called me," I tell him. "Perhaps I should ask who are you."

"I'm looking for Rinzen Naraka. You him?"

My name. Never having been formally introduced, he knows my name. A display of Western efficiency, I presume. Without secrets?

"Yes. I am."

The voice sighs with relief. "Thank goodness. Police headquarters here, detective. Thank goodness you answered. Good news. Your number's up."

"Number?"

"Yeah. A crime down in the warehouse on Josephine and 33rd, and your number's up. You're a detective, right? Freelance."

"I am a lama."

"Well, Detective Lama, today's your lucky day. You caught

a live one. You fuck it up enough, job could carry you through Easter."

"I am not a detective," I confess. At least I cannot recall being a detective. Not this lifetime. Not any other.

From the other end of the phone the sound of paper shuffling, and the breath of exasperation. The caller recites a string of numbers. "That's you, isn't it? That your phone number?"

I look at the phone's cradle where the number should be. It shines black. Nothing else, no writing. "I do not know."

"Rinzen Naraka, right?"

"Yes."

"Well, I called you. Must mean something. Listen, work with me here. This is a big case, and I'm under a lot of pressure to get it placed. Big shot insurance guy goes and gets himself sliced up. His company carries the paper on the precinct, so the bigs want it solved. I been calling detectives on the freelance list all morning, and I'm not getting any answers. Finally, you pick up. That's got to count for something. You gotta be a detective of some sort, picking up the phone like you did."

I hear his urgency, his fear and bureaucracy—American characteristics, all—but I do not recall ever speaking English before. Its hurried breath and clipped understanding. "Insurance?" I ask.

"Yeah. Heller Insurance. The Heller brothers. Big shots. Gave a bunch of basketball hoops to the downtown parks. Patronizers of the arts. Brought over some Indian dance troupe last year. Nice costumes. Now one of them's dead. Politicians are scared. The politicians got the police budget in their hands, so the police are scared. Me, I don't give a shit. I just dial my way through the freelance list till I hit somebody. And lucky you, you picked up. It's your gig, if you want it. And believe me, you want it. Thing's a money-maker. This guy's insurance. Who wouldn't want to shiv him? Cast of thousands you could play out, one side against the other. Work it till the 4th of July, if you want. Fricka fracka, firecracker. Work it through Christmas. Next year's Christmas—not this year's, next year's. Fuck, work it all the way to retirement and shove it up their asses. That's the only reason we work anymore, right? To shove it up their asses? So what do you say? You in, you out? I got to keep dialing if you're out, and I got a second job over at another precinct I got to get to. So what, yes or no? But before you answer, consider this—I got to piss. Then I got to get in the car and drive, and I'm late already. Maybe grab a cruller on the way. Cup of soup. I don't know. What do you say?"

I feel a bit lost. "Why call me?" I ask. "I do not know why Americans kill one another."

"They cut him like origami, detective. International intrigue, okay? The insurance guy insured some trinket shipment from Asia, then gets killed. If you're like me—and I know I am—I'd take that action."

I shift the receiver from one ear to the other. "Trinket shipment? From *where* exactly in Asia?"

He *harrumphs* slightly. "I don't know. Asia. How big can it be?"

In a relative way, yes, I understand what he means. "What kind of shipment?"

"Statues of little fat men. Stand about yay high," he tells me.

"Budais? These statues, they are Budais?" I look at the Buddha on the altar before me. "Laughing Buddhas?"

"Laughing, I don't know. Happy, maybe."

"Where are they?"

"33rd and Josephine. Look, you go there, you ask for Inspector Gus Fernandez. He's the full-timer working it. I'm marking you down *yes*. You're going to thank me, Lama. Name's Fusco. You remember that? Maybe cut me a little spiff at the end, huh? Cut old Frankie Fusco some spiff."

"Fusco?" I say the name, tongue to my palette, lips circling the O in it. "Let me ask, Fusco. Does the shipment include a dorje?"

"Dorje? Detective, I don't want to tell you your business. Find who killed Sonny Heller first. Then you find your dorje. Start at the beginning. Work your way through it, like a detective might. Yeah. Sure, there's a dorje, I don't know. Why not?"

Start at the beginning. Find the killer. Because a shipment came in from Asia, and the killer probably did what he did to get his hands on the dorje.

Of the ten negative actions, killing is the worst. Worse than Wrong View. Worse than spreading gossip or having bad sex.

"Look. Go down and talk to Inspector Fernandez. 33rd and Josephine."

I do not know this place, 33rd and Josephine. I do not know anyone named Fernandez.

All I know is my mission in life. In all lifetimes. To be a bodhisattva. To bring all beings to enlightenment.

That is how I get out of Hell.

LESSON 2

When the student is ready,
the teacher appears.

I STEP FROM THE APARTMENT out onto its vestibule. Three identically-shaped doors stare at me from across the landing, each shoved into its own corner. No one comes out. No one goes in.

A wooden, designed handrail runs down a dimly lit stairway, its carving caked with dust.

Rebirths occur like this. Specifically detailed, yet obscure. What to see? I close my eyes. The immediacy of the moment washes over me–the smell of cooked cabbage, the heated stink of a light bulb filament burning out. A televised sports game scratching up through the walls from the Aim Straight and Shoot Saloon below.

Halfway between this landing and the next, a body slumps against the wall.

I step past, and its hand reaches for me, clutching my robe. I try pulling loose. The slumped figure lifts its face to me, and I see now my teacher, Daidyal.

"I thought you were dead," I tell him.

"Why would you think that?"

"You smell dead."

"Ah. *Smell dead,* yes. Good one. You thought I was dead because you killed me once, in some past life. Is that not why you thought me dead?"

I do not answer. "I have someplace to go," I say.

"Tell me, lama. If I am dead and non-existent, do you mourn for me?"

"Is that why you followed me here? To this apartment building? So I might mourn for you."

"Me, followed you? The teacher following the student? That's an odd twist. I hear you are a detective now." Daidyal wraps his fingers deeper into the hem of my cloak, holding me fast. "I'd like to see that, you as a detective."

"Why?"

"Because all appearances are empty, lama, and I am your teacher. I enjoy knowing what my students are up to."

"You *were* my teacher. No more."

"Yes, *was* your teacher. You fired me, I remember now. What have you learned since?"

"To stay away from you."

He laughs again. "Funny. Cheap shot, but funny. Let me be more specific. Why come here to Colfax? Such a dreary place?"

"It is Hell. Where else would I be?"

He holds one palm above the other, and then each palm side by side forming an imaginary box into which he is trying to fit my answer. "You know what I am asking. Your intention, what is it?"

"To find an insurance man's killer."

"That is why you've returned? For an insurance man? How boring."

"You know why. I have returned for the dorje. So I might bring all to enlightenment."

"Ah, now there it is. That is a familiar ambition of yours, is it not?" He scratches where a line of pink skin encircles his neck, where once he'd worn a necklace. "The dorje. Your mission. Have you forgotten what I taught in the Shedra? How each lifetime has a purpose? Each purpose unique and different from the last. Let me ask again. What is yours? Here. Now. In this lifetime, what is your purpose?"

"To find the dorje. And you will not divert me from it."

"Yes, yes, I understand. To find the dorje." He mulls it over. "But, no. You miss the point. The purpose of any lifetime is to learn the lesson of its realm. You for instance, in Hell. What will you learn?"

"That you put me here."

"Let me ask a different way—and since you are now a detective you should be able to clarify easily—I did not hear Fusco mention a *dorje*. What makes you think it's here?"

"Why be such a diversion, Daidyal? This trick of trying to lure me from my path?"

"A diversion? I merely ask why you seek the Most Sacred of Objects."

"To benefit all sentient beings."

"And what will you do with the dorje once you find it, for the benefit of all sentient beings? This object you seek. With its magnificent form? Will you cut it up to share among others? Melt it into trinkets for each of us to hold? Pulverize it and cast its dust to the wind?"

"It is sacred. Imbued with powers that I, a lama bodhisattva, and only I, can harness to bring all others to the Pure Lands. Do not pretend you cannot understand. This is the very reason you have kept it from me all these years."

"And the reason you tried ripping it from my hands in Drepung?"

"You were corrupted. Seduced. You could do no good with it."

"Your niru brigades attacked. We Drepung monks in meditation. *You* stole the dorje from *us*. Tried to anyway. And so I ask again. I did not hear Fusco mention the *dorje*. And trust me, I was listening. So what makes you think it is here?"

"Is this why you followed me? To claim it as your own?"

As a young monk I was taught to scrutinize my teachers. Examine their strength for guiding me along the path. Daidyal, I should have scrutinized him a bit more.

"We rode upon Drepung," I tell him, "to liberate the dorje. Enough of your slippery contrivances. Fusco most certainly did mention it."

"Did he? You are certain of that?"

I pull my robe from his grip and proceed down the stairs. "The lesson I learn is that I am in Hell once again because of you, my teacher. I should have chosen more wisely."

"Because of me?" he calls. "Is that how you see me. As an excuse for closing your eyes? Consider it like I do, lama. Who in their right mind would ship an object as sacred as the dorje to a warehouse here in Denver? How does one transport such a thing?"

"Diversion," I tell him. "You are simply a diversion. When I find it, even you will be enlightened thanks to my efforts. Even my enemies will benefit from my being a bodhisattva."

His elbow bangs the wall as he struggles to stand. "But suppose you do not find it?"

His words wash over me. I need not listen. I need not allow them to land atop me. I push against the iced glass door at the bottom of the stairs that opens outside into the cold.

"You are not my teacher, Daidyal," I call back. Then I step out that door onto a street, where everything looks familiar without being so. Like 33rd and Josephine, a place I do not know. Nor do I know which way I should go to get there.

All I understand is that life is a mundane affair, until I find the dorje.

Once I find the dorje, all that is mundane will then snap apart.

LESSON 3

With our thoughts,
we build a world.

EARLY MORNING BUSTLE, CAR TRAFFIC, Colfax pedestrians wrapped thick inside store-bought, label-laden clothing, scarfs to their noses, stocking caps pulled tight down their scalps.

Across the street an elderly pedestrian carries a metal canister upon his back, neck to buttocks. He teeters beneath its weight. "Hot buttered tea," he rasps. "Two dollars a cup." In a gloveless hand he balances an upright stack of Styrofoam cups. He lifts the cups to passersby, but they are not buying.

I see his lips move. *White devils.* I see he is Tibetan, cursing how Westerners forever hurry without even lowering their scarves nor lifting their face masks to smile at him. He is elderly, and he struggles beneath the burden of the tea sloshing on his back. Its saltiness snaps the air. A cure against the chill of the Tibetan Plains. There are others just like him on Colfax. Tibetans. I see them now, mixed amongst the gweilos.

They say America is a melting pot, and that émigrés are the burnt sludge crusted to its bottom. They say hard work can make you into anything you desire, and that émigrés belong if they will just behave like everyone else.

It is for beings such as these that I seek the dorje. Such as this tea vendor, these Tibetans. Surely any and all will benefit from my laying hands upon the Most Sacred of Objects. I pray this may be the lifetime I find it, for beings such as these. The gweilos, too. A warmth flushes over me. The tea man appears oddly familiar, until a bus pulls to a stop and blocks my view of him. The bus deposits riders. Its LED displays minus four Fahrenheit, its readout blurred from missing pixels. Then the bus jolts forward pushing farther down Colfax, opening up my view once more. So many Tibetans on Colfax. What better sign that the dorje is here than this vast array of believers.

In the morning mist of December gray, I cross the street. Snow hangs in the sky waiting to fall. I scurry beneath it, trying to catch up to the tea man. Surely one such as this must know something about the Most Sacred of Objects. Or at least he could tell me where I might find 33rd and Josephine. I see him walking past a Laundromat window ballooned with comic-colored lettering, puffed-up red, scribbly blue—*Fluff n Fold, 24 Hour Surveillance*. In front of the Laundromat doorway rides a curved, muscly man in a goggle-eyed bicycle helmet, lavender spandex, and a silken turquoise jacket that reads *Spurtz Granola Snax* on its back.

A bicycle courier, no doubt. Gweilo shaped. A *fungtow* trooper astride a fat-tired bike, slipping along the icy streets of Denver.

Calling to the tea man in front of him. "Somebody new in town?"

The tea man keeps walking, ignoring him. The courier pedals faster, one-handing his handlebars and in his other hand dragging a bicycle chain along the sidewalk. "I'm talking to you, tea man." The chain scratches like pebbles over ice. When close enough the courier jumps off the bike, letting it roll to the curb. He cups the tea man's shoulder and spins him so they face one another, tea sloshing in its canister. Other Tibetans around them make way for the intrusion.

"You listening? I asked if there's somebody new in town. Another émigré landed?" Warm air breathes out the courier's neoprene mask.

"Why ask me?" the tea man says. "If there is someone new, I am sure the Hellers have already closed in, trying to sell them insurance."

From his delivery satchel the courier pulls a fat-handled spike. Ribbons and baubles hang from its hilt. The courier leans the tea man against the Laundromat glass, placing the spike into the fleshy fold of the tea man's cheek. "We don't need any more émigrés coming over." Blade to cheek, he turns the tea man's face so his other cheek flattens against the laundromat's lettering. *Buck fifty a wash. Buck and a quarter on Tuesdays.* "So why don't you tell me. Somebody new in town?"

What the courier fails to realize, I—a monk of the Kagyu lineage and a bodhisattva as well—I am newly arrived, and come specifically to prevent this sort of thing. I come up behind the courier, tap his shoulder. "Why not ask me?"

The blade loosens in his grip. He turns and eyes my robes, hem to hood. "Who are you?"

"I am new to town, here to solve a murder."

Through the eye slits of his woolen mask, I see him pause with suspicion. "Solve what? A murder? Who? A Tibetan murdered? Who cares?"

"Not a Tibetan murder. An insurance man." And although I find it hard to read the courier's expression through his goggles, I sense his face growing limp and flaccid and weak as his hold on the tea man slackens. "An insurance man from Heller Insurance," I say. "Know anything about it?"

He pushes off the tea man, toward me. "Why tell you?

Investigating an insurance man getting killed, you expect me to believe that? That's not why you're here."

"Please, lama," the tea man says. "You must not get involved."

I do not look at the tea man. Instead I tell the courier, "Sonny Heller was killed. Of the ten wrongful acts, killing is the gravest. Wrong View, yes, that is bad as well. But killing is the worst. I, a Buddhist monk of the Kagyu lineage, have come to confront this killer with his transgression. So I might find the dorje, and you, me, all of us may be enlightened." I state it succinctly. I state it in a manner he might understand. "And you, I see you carry a knife. Perhaps you killed him."

The courier's cheeks raise, as if smiling inside his mask. "Yeah, right," he says. He behaves with all the superstition of a Westerner. Puffed up with self-appointed authority. False might. A pushy type of chumminess about him, hiding his nervousness. "You're not here to find a killer. How do I know you didn't kill him? Like maybe you're an assassin or something."

"I am a bodhisattva. Come to bring all to enlightenment, and denying my own Nirvana until all other beings achieve theirs."

"Yeah? Well, you know what I say? I say the Hellers shouldn't sell you émigrés insurance. Shouldn't try and make you feel like you belong."

The courier wipes his blade with a bandana he takes from his back pocket.

I watch him do so. I tell him, "You realize of course you are doing nothing more than projecting your own hate upon current circumstance, and then assuming your interpretation as fact. The insurance man was not killed because of selling to Tibetans. More likely his murder is linked to a shipment he insured."

The cyclist stops wiping. He lifts his eyes but not his face. "Shipment?"

"From Asia."

"What's in it?"

There it is. The curiosity of Westerners. It is how you reel them in, then make them wait. I nod at his jacket. "Spurtz Granola Snax. Do you work for them?"

"I asked you a question, émigré. What's in that shipment?"

I further ignore him. "Your uniform?" I point at his jacket. "Spurtz? Do they work for the Hellers?"

He rolls his shoulders, twists his head back, reading his jacket's lettering. "My colors, man. Club colors. Not a place I work. So what's in the shipment?"

Impatience. Belligerence. Obsession. Western ways, all. "Do you know where it is?"

"You're wasting my time." Then the courier springs forward, a burst of fire, slamming me into the laundromat glass. He places the blade tip to my eye. "You're not here to solve any murder. Whatever it is you think you're doing, you don't know the West." He flicks the blade, slitting a sliver of skin above the top ridge of my cheek bone.

I do not flinch. I do not wince. I look at him, wink once to ensure he has not obscured my vision, and then, a quick jab. I snap the cyclist back to the curb, down atop his bicycle in the gutter. He stumbles and falls. His knife clangs to the pavement with the peal of a struck bell. I stand over him. I paw a smear of blood from my cheek. "Pedal off," I tell him.

The cyclist clenches his knifeless hand in the other. "You broke my wrist," he whines. He tries standing, but does so deliriously. He swipes at the hem of my robe to pull himself up.

"Paragat-e." The tea man bursts from the crowd now, throwing his skinny frame with its back-strapped tea canister into the reeling cyclist, knocking him back to the curb once more. "Do you not see? You are no match. You, a gweilo. He, the lama liberator of Drepung?"

The tea vendor, covered too deeply beneath clothing for me to recognize, or to understand how he might know this about me.

"The lama liberator who, in service to the Great Fifth Dalai Lama, freed the Monastery of White Rice from its Gelugpa heretics." He points at me. "The niru captain Lama Rinzen Naraka himself. Come now to liberate us." He kicks the courier. "Come to liberate even you, silly gweilo." He yanks the attacker's face mask off, his helmet and eyewear, revealing the fattened baby-stare of a man-child with chubby red cheeks.

The tea vendor knows me. He recognizes me as the liberator of Drepung. How? Had he followed me here? I wipe my eyeglasses with the sleeve of my robe and I squint putting them on. The courier stares up from the sidewalk, his arm blocking what little sun burns upon him. "You think you can hide it from us?" He spits. "Why are you here?"

The tea vendor lifts the courier's bicycle and throws it back down upon him. "You heard the lama. Pedal off."

The cyclist stumbles to stand. He lifts his ride, straightens its handlebars, straddles himself over its seat. "You think he's here to liberate you?" he asks the Tibetans in the crowd. "Well, he's not." He clips into his pedals and begins riding, one-handedly gearing his way up through the bicycle's gears. Someone balls up a fistful of snow and throws it at him. Others buy hot buttered tea from the tea man and rain it down atop the courier. Its steam rises from his spandex.

While dispensing his wares, the tea man tells me, "You should not mess with those cyclists, lama. They ride the streets of Denver like they own them." His voice snaps like taut wire. He hands me a tea, urging me to drink and stay warm. It tastes bitter. I rattle with the taste of its bitterness, and at how this gaunt fellow could possibly know my name and that I rode to liberate Drepung. It must be that he desires happiness. He desires enlightenment, just as we all do. I see it in his eyes. I see how he fears being a stranger in such an incomprehensible place. Do not we all? The tea's salt crackles down my throat.

"You are bleeding," he says.

I wipe my cheek where the cyclist cut me, leaving a thin blotch of pink on my fingers.

"We are pleased you have returned, lama," he says, and he lifts my bloodstained fingers into the air. "Lama Rinzen," he announces. "He has returned."

A crowd now gathers. "Returned," they chant.

I pull my hand away. "No, not returned. I have never been to Colfax before."

"Never before," the crowd repeats.

"Never before, lama. Yes, indeed. Tell us," the tea man says. "When did you arrive?"

When? Bundled tight in their blankets and padding, I can see the sallow and worn faces of the gathered Tibetans. When indeed? How does one newly arrived even understand time? As a sequence of moments? Or as all things occurring at once?

"Not long ago," I say.

"Not long ago," the tea man repeats for the crowd to hear. "So new. So uncorrupted. Let us toast the lama with tea, shall we?" In unison they raise their Styrofoam cups to the air shouting Chiruu! as the tea man takes my arm. "Surely you recognize us, do you not? We who rode for you under the Banner of Yellow Light. Your lieutenants, archers and niru swordsmen, we—this crowd gathered on Colfax—we rode in your attack upon Drepung. A true bodhisattva, you were. A follower of the precepts and conqueror of aggregates, and now returned to lead us to enlightenment."

"Enlightenment," the crowd cheers, and then they murmur and mumble so that their words roll atop one another. "Lama Rinzen is returned. Returned to us," they monotone prayerfully.

What to hear inside their voices? Expectation and hope? A suggestion of more to follow? Promise?

"I am here, yes." I state it for them. Still, they cheer. "And for such effect, certainly there must be a notable cause," I say, because that is the way we explain things in Buddhism, for every effect a cause. Because if I have returned for the dorje and now encounter these gathered here, and if there is any magic in the world as they teach in the Shedra, would it not follow these here have the dorje and wish now to bestow it upon me? After so many lifetimes, and now this, the one lifetime I have anticipated, in which we will all be enlightened. "Have you brought me something?" I ask.

The tea man bows. "Of course we have, lama. And so honored we are you are among us." He nods to the back of the crowd. It stirs and wriggles in a serpentine wave of people, moving forward, as if they are passing something amongst themselves to give me.

So many lifetimes. So many years. And now, finally...

The passing moves with deliberation and reverence. Give and receive, hand to hand, light and small. I wet my lips, and in my first glimpse of what they pass, I see now it appears different than how I envisioned it. Rectangular in shape, white and flat. A young Tibetan lad who has pulled off his face mask accepts it from the woman behind him, and I see now it appears exactly as it seems. White and flat like an envelope. The young Tibetan passes it into the tea vendor's hands. The crowd's mood simmers. The tea vendor elevates the envelope in the air for all to see. For all to observe how it is barely large enough, barely bulky enough to hold an object as grand and magnificent as the dorje.

I scan the crowd to see if perhaps something else is following behind it. Like this is perhaps a pre-thing they are giving, to be followed by a true thing, more substantial.

"What is this?" I ask.

The tea vendor presents me the envelope. I lift its flap and leaf through its contents. News clippings. Obituaries. A stack of obituaries, held together with a rubber band. "What is this?" I repeat.

"Our dead," the tea vendor tells me. "Fellow émigrés, slain here by bicyclists and other gweilos. We would be honored, Lama Rinzen, if you were to sit in meditation with us. Sukhavati in honor of these who died. So they may pass to a better life. In two days' time, at noon, we sit. The day after the Great Contest, to meditate and drink chai in their honor."

What to say? I do not even like chai, or at least did not in any lifetime before. And I already sit meditation daily, performing *tonglen* for those recently passed. Plus, I am here to find the dorje. I do not have time to sit Sukhavati.

What to say?

"Yes, yes, of course, of course. Sukhavati. I would not miss it," I tell them while I pocket the envelope. "But first..."—and now I puff up slightly with solemnity, or gravitas, or whatever Westerners call it— "I am here to receive the dorje. Please, give it to me."

Silence. Then some laugh. Small at first, but then longer and louder. "The dorje." They push one another, repeating it over and over again. "The dorje. The dorje, he wants."

And although I would like nothing better than to laugh along with them, I find I am unable. "Yes, certainly. The dorje," I say.

"Ah, lama, you enthrall us with your presence," the tea man says. "The dorje."

"Wait, wait," one of the crowd quiets the rest of them, his arms flapping at his sides like a bird's in flight. He speaks with laughing solemnity. "The warehouse. On 33rd and Josephine. Where shipments of trinkets arrive. Perhaps the dorje is there." He holds the crowd quiet a moment, looking at them one by one until erupting in laughter, which they all join in.

"Yes," I tell them. "The warehouse. How can I get there?"

The tea man quiets the crowd. "The warehouse at 33rd and Josephine. Yes. I have heard of this place where shipments arrive from Asia." He places a hand on my shoulder. "I can take you, if you'd like. I, Choki, your lieutenant of archers and most trusted officer during our raid on Drepung, I will take you."

I look to see if he is mocking me. "Choki?" I ask. A name that sounds unfamiliar.

"Back in our niru days. Certainly you remember. Ah, but you are newly arrived, so maybe not. Take a moment, lama. Look at us. Surely you will recognize us."

I look the crowd over. How odd they appear. Unplaced in memory. "You can just tell me how to get there," I suggest. "I mean, why waste time?"

"You suggest going on your own?" Choki smiles with many teeth, a big, large biteful of a mouth. "Lama, you have taught us that we are all linked as one. Teacher and student. You and me, all these many years. How else would you know how to find 33rd and Josephine, unless I take you? As any teacher might expect from his student."

Whoever he is, no matter how old and feeble, at least he shows respect, this Choki. Even if he insists on glomming on like he is.

"I will take you to the warehouse. So you may find the dorje, which you have sought so many lifetimes, to bring us all to enlightenment."

The crowd cheers. They mutter incantations while their mala beads pass through their shriveled, cold fingers. Incantations in a language I do not comprehend, their words indecipherable except for their cadence and uncertainty.

LESSON 4

In the sky, east and west do not distinguish.
People create distinctions in their own minds,
expecting they are true.

ANY PLACE NEW, I SEE strangers. Their fear, their uncertainty, their wonder. I narrow them this way, objectifying them within the context of my own understanding. Relative truth. A way to discard what is for what fits. Choki here, for instance. He says he is my lieutenant. Is he?

I have not been a detective before, but I know its tricks. To see things as they are without expectation.

Choki leads me through the crystalline, icy mist of Colfax. We pass ancient women laden in rags pushing supermarket carts, and men kicking car tires angled into the same parking spot. I pull the neck of my robes up to my chin, and fold the burgundy cape from my shoulders up over my head. Choki walks in front of me, old and frail. He coughs the smoky cough of yak dung fires, all hack and spittle, and he walks stooped. Just as my mother walked in the money-less days after my father died. When my uncle came from across the field to abscond with her silver. *For safekeeping,* he said. Greed masquerading as care.

"Our raid on Drepung, so glorious," Choki calls to me. What the West calls small talk, this nervous chatter of his. "You have been an inspiration always, lama. Many thoughts. Such goodness. Still, I stumble to comprehend, why investigate the murder of an insurance man? All are born, and all die. What difference does it make to learn the cause of such things?"

How innocently he wonders. "Any good teacher delights in his student asking such questions," I say. "Not to learn answers. But to learn how to question, without expecting answers."

"Well stated, lama. I am blessed with such a lesson. So then tell me, what questions do you ask when chasing down a killer? And why bother doing so?"

"The West survives on uncertainty and suffering. Insurance men sell products to lessen fear of these natural occurrences. But the inevitable is never lessened, and so their clients feel cheated. Who has Sonny Heller cheated? That is the question."

"Yes, lama, you understand the West well. The way they sell promises of suffering's alleviation. Current payment for future re-lief. But why is it important we go to Josephine and 33rd?"

"It is not important *we* go," I explain. "Only that I go. It is my path. My way to proceed. You are here simply as a guide, giving directions."

"I see." He appears to absorb the lesson well, without rebuff. "You know, lama, they say the dorje hangs in a Lhasa museum. Our niru stormed Drepung once to rescue it, but now it simply hangs in display for tourists and curators to ogle. Behind glass, where no one can touch it. I hear there is a placard stapled to its frame saying DO NOT TOUCH. Perhaps the museum should in-sure it, against the future possibility of someone trying to achieve enlightenment."

"The dorje needs no insurance."

"Why? Because it promises more than its value, even if merely framed as art? Or because it hangs in Lhasa as a testament to our defeat by the People's Republic. You are a policeman now, are you not?"

"A freelancer," I correct him.

"You know the West well. But can you see the blackness inside a man's heart, and why Americans kill one another?"

Questions have no answers. Answers are ways to look outside the question for some sort of explanation, for some diversion from the path. A way of seeing other, and puffing up self. That is why men kill. They trick themselves into envisioning the world as defined and fixed, failing to see its emptiness and nonexistence. Not truly anything. Just a string of energy crackling and snapping and popping moment to moment into little bursts. That is the stuff of lifetimes.

Surely had Choki been a more attentive student during our raid on Drepung, he would know these things. "To find the dorje," I tell him. "Although it appears circuitous, this is why I seek the insurance man's perpetrator."

"Very nicely said, lama. So very…confusing in the way you say it. But suppose for a moment, the dorje actually does hang in Lhasa. Why search here on Colfax?"

He says it like someone hiding something. We pass a deli doorway stacked with palettes of Nantucket Nectar and Nehi.

"Being in one place does not disallow a thing from being anywhere else. The question you should ask instead, and perhaps answer for me … why do you follow me where I go?"

"For enlightenment, lama."

"Indeed." A proper answer. Still, a correction is needed. "But I mean instead, here, on Colfax, why follow me to this warehouse?"

"I am assisting you. As any good student would. Colfax is the longest street America owns, with many confusing neighborhoods and questionable storefronts. With bicyclists who ride as many as three or four abreast, who do not like Tibetans very much."

"You follow me because of what you fear?"

"Yes. Fear is how we survive. Fear and vigilance. Even now, walking as we are, I fear we should have brought others with us."

With this, I stop. Choki continues walking, I turn back to see the footsteps we have just trod in the snow, looking to ensure no one has followed. "We need no others," I say. Still, I see how empty this section of Colfax appears. Without pedestrians or moving traffic. Just cars at the curb parked bumper to bumper, a frozen procession of them buried in fallen snow.

Choki approaches me from behind. "No one here should venture alone, lama. Venturing alone only twists your view into something you think it is."

Snow and sweat wet my face. "Why do you follow me?"

"Because I know you. Your heart, and that you have returned for all beings, so we might escape this Hell, this Colfax Avenue, together. Because you are a bodhisattva."

It feels gratifying hearing him say so, this small recognition he bestows upon me.

"We rode once so you might rescue the dorje, lama. No matter that you failed. You rode for us."

"I hardly failed," I remind him. "The dorje simply slipped away. A simple miscalculation, which I come now to correct."

He lifts his eyes. They appear warm and glistening. "We appreciate this about you. Your persistence and way of sticking with us. There is so much correction we need here on Colfax." He points down an alley, where cars park haphazardly.

What to see? Snow. Frozen mounds of indistinct forms. Buried trashcans and recycling receptacles and children's pullcarts and sleds. Two forms larger than all the others, side by side. Rounded and windswept.

I approach those mounds that are larger and see they are human, lying on their sides. I kneel before them and brush off their top snow. Beneath one mound, a man frosted inside a nylon jacket and hardened denim jeans. Ear-flapped. Tibetan in appearance.

What's left of appearance.

The second mound, similar. Each lying in the repose of the dying Buddha. Their bone structure, their hair dark—yes, they were Tibetan once. A nick of skin stripped from each man's face, exposing frozen muscle.

"A gweilo attack," Choki says. "Colfax is no place for the newly arrived."

With my knuckle, I touch the shard of stripped skin. "Gweilos did not kill these men," I say. Standing, I wipe my hands in my robes. In the frozen gasp of the men's mouths, I see they died screaming deaths, foreboding their return to Hell. Unfortunates such as these...for them I seek the dorje.

"Westerners are a murderous people," Choki says. "You will learn this. You may think it easy to uncover an insurance man's murderer, but soon you may wonder why bother?"

I touch my fingers together over these men to recite a mantra so that they may pass unencumbered to their next lives. I murmur the Heart Sutra, so they are reborn strong. I pinch each man's right nostril, closing it, so life's energy may remain inside and assist them on their travels.

And while doing this, I observe necklaces ringing their necks where the skin has turned pink. Each necklace a golden chain, from which dangles a single charm. I lift one of the charms and study it between my fingers. Nicely carved. Colored glass embedded like jewels. A miniaturized dorje, it appears.

Standing over me, Choki says, "Gweilos too seek the dorje. Like you, they believe it is here on Colfax. They have their superstitions as much as we Tibetans. Their superstition is they believe the dorje is worth four point nine million dollars."

"Four point nine million?" I question. "So countable and specific."

Choki shrugs. "Perhaps not literally four point nine. But something close."

A line of snow drops from an overhead phone line like a rope falling to the ground, where it breaks apart. "We should call the police," I say.

"I thought you are police in this lifetime." Then Choki quickly adds, "No, no police. There are deaths in Denver the police don't care about." He unpockets a cell phone and dials, speaking in a dialect I fail to comprehend, until before hanging up he says the words *Colfax Avenue,* and then keeps walking.

"33rd and Josephine," he calls to me. "If you want to get there, we should go now."

I gaze once more at the fallen Tibetans. "We cannot just leave them," I say.

"Someone will come." Choki continues down Colfax. As I catch up, he asks, "Tell me, lama, a lesson, perhaps. You have sought the dorje so many lifetimes. Perhaps in Lhasa, perhaps here. How do you know it even exists at all? Cannot absence negate existence? Like this insurance man's murderer, or whoever killed the Tibetans in the alley. Does something exist if unfound?"

It is hard to say if he is serious with such drivel, or simply mentions it so that we talk. We pass a U-Store-It storefront rising tall, growing into the sky like an American façade of a medieval castle with turrets and stonework up top. Disney World looking. Inside the plate glass, bicyclists—some in Apache headbands, others with wires dripping out their ears— furiously pedal bicycles without wheels, lined in a row. They pedal straight toward us, without advancing. Frozen in place, lost in their own exertion. The plate glass has stenciled lettering. *Neighborhood Gym. Come in and man up. Discounts for women.*

Seeing me observe these cyclists, Choki raps the glass. "It's where they come to train. The Spurtz crowd."

"Train for what?"

"For self-absorption." Choki looks at me. "You're being here, we prayed it would be so. There has been chatter on the street about the dorje and how it might be found. And now you return. Perhaps it no longer hangs in a Lhasa museum. Will you find it this time?"

"It is my mission," I say. "My purpose."

"I understand such longing. Believe me, lama, I do. Even though you held it before it slipped from your hands in Drepung, I never saw it, but only heard of its magnificence. Sculpted gold, intricately formed out of the absence of space that surrounds it. Simple, yet intricate. Shining as one in a single moment. At either end, golden tentacles folding back in on themselves, like petals of a lotus in bloom, forming orbs of power. Like a hawk's talons snatching prey. Each end a reflection of the other, showing the sameness of things, teaching non-duality." Choki extends a clenched fist, knuckles up, fingers down, demonstrating how one might hold such magnificence. "Grasp it, it molds to your hand. Touch it, if only for a moment, and you can bring us to enlightenment, lama. You must."

He stands with one eye closed to block out the cold, and one eye open so he might see me as I listen to him speak.

"I will find it," I say.

"Will you?"

"It is my purpose. The intention that informs my existence."

"Nicely spoken." Choki turns to the U-Store-It storefront. "Look at these here. Bicyclists in training. Would you say they are cycling, lama?"

I watch the riders sweat and snuffle.

"The way they move, it resembles bicyclists, does it not?" he suggests. "Their stroke and lift. Yet they go nowhere. Each stays exactly where he or she sits."

I look down the line of their equipment, all weights and solder joints, wheels without tires.

"And so, in a relative sense, is bicycling a mode of transportation that separates where we are going from where we are, in which case they are not bicycling? Or is it pedaling atop something that resembles a bicycle, in which case they are? Does intention even matter? Does the dorje exist if we fail to experience it?"

"We will experience it," I assure him.

Choki looks down the line of pedalers. "Technically, I suppose, it is not bicycling. Spinning, they call it. Spinning their wheels without going anywhere. Besides…"—he taps the glass—"they have no place to go. The window blocks them."

"You do not believe I will find it?"

"We rode together in Drepung, under the Yellow banner. I believed in you then."

His response fails to sound like an answer. More a diversion. Choki continues walking, and I follow, an iciness now settling between us, broken only when Choki says we need to turn left onto Josephine.

Then again, further iciness. As if he, a minion, is challenging what I say. For another fifteen blocks I mull this over. Perhaps it comes from living so many lifetimes in the West. Which Choki has. You can see that in his stooped amble and hung-down face.

Eventually, we arrive upon a warehouse's front lawn, standing beneath a cluster of misshaped trees whose branches wildly scratch the sky.

"Here we are," Choki says.

"Where else could we be?" I ask, flipping his challenge back at him. "Other than *here*? Would it not be more proper to say, *we have arrived*?"

Choki blows upon his fingers for warmth. "Yes, lama," he says.

"Yes what?"

"Yes. We have arrived."

FERNANDEZ AND YOONG

INSPECTOR FERNANDEZ CHECKS HIS SHOES. Zelli Avianos. $700 a pair. He sidesteps bits of gristle and puke so as not to stain the leather.

What a mess. Art photos of a naked woman left behind. Corpse sliced and slicked to a wooden kitchen chair. The inspector barely able to distinguish the vic's sinew and muscle from the ropes holding them in place.

Who kills like this? With such Godliness? Such sheer brutality?

He braces his palms atop his knees and leans not too close into the face (what resembles a face) of what had once been Sonny Heller, insurance man. Or so the corpse's business card says, that the killer (so mockingly!) stapled to the exposed muscle of his chest. Heller's hands hacked off. Feet, too. He hardly seemed the artsy type. Why all the photos?

The inspector lifts his ball cap, tugs his bolo, smooths the sleeves of his duster. Where once Heller wore skin—cheeks, lips, forehead, temple—Fernandez sees it splayed back like a gutted jack rabbit. A crisscross of nerves, and a mouth torn down to its gums.

He worries that his soul should be exposed to such darkness. Fingers and toes and limbs scattered about the body like strewn rose petals. How does one wash away such darkness?

Inside the insurance man's opened briefcase, a cell phone rings. It vibrates atop a pile of papers. The phone display says CURLY HELLER. One of the brothers. Looking for Sonny.

Fernandez dares not answer. When the brothers find out… oh, Jeese, when the brothers find out, they'll ask how someone of their class, their caliber, their family gets killed in this way. They will ask how soon before bringing the killer in, and what the police owe in insurance premiums, and the number of claims the department files per year. When was their last rate increase?

Insurance men ask a lot of questions. Insurance men ask whatever they want.

But what Fernandez wants to know, truly wants to know, how does a citizen like Sonny Heller come to such a place? How did he get so hacked up? Did he resist? Was he drugged? Why all these Buddha statues? Why the porno photos?

Many questions. A lot to answer.

Not a proper case to be assigned a tag-along. Bad exposure for the city. Downtown politics, a newly-funded Better Policing Exchange program, so now Fernandez is assigned an agent from the People's Republic of China. Yoong? Is that his name? Yoong? He stands behind Fernandez rolling an annoying click clack of rosary beads through his fingers. With his free hand he hands Fernandez a cell phone.

"Downtown, sir. They want to speak with you."

Fernandez stretches upright, looking over the mess. Sonny Heller. Looking so much smaller than a man of his stature should.

"Sir." The Chinese agent waggles the phone.

"Identification confirmation," Fernandez replies. "We need an ID check. Confirm whether the vic's Sonny or not. Forensics. Lab work. See if there are drugs in his system. Wounds on his..." He doesn't know how to say it, or what's even left of the man to speak about. He takes the phone from the Chinese agent asking, "What's your name again?"

"Agent Yoong, sir."

Yoong sir. That kind of tag-along. Polite.

"Well, Agent Yoong. One thing to know about downtown." Then without fanfare or display, the inspector hangs up the phone. "They can wait. Now's a time for focus. Look around, see what we see." He points to the big wide door out in the warehouse foyer. "No forced entry. Not obvious, anyway. What does that suggest? The killer and vic met willfully. Maybe knew each other. Art shots on the floor. A girl with a knife. Beauty and violence, confusing those things as one. Need to get a timestamp on those photos."

"They will call back, sir."

"Who?" Fernandez bristles. "The time-stampers?"

"Downtown."

"Yes, well... we'll see." He points to Heller. "You ever seen anything like this on your side of the world?"

"No, sir."

He shows Yoong the photo. "Or this?"

The China agent takes it in his hand, scrutinizing it. "Quite professional," he says. "Nicely lit. Scrimmed lighting, creating a gauzy effect on the girl, dreamlike. On the mirror, the lights more barn-doored, harsher. And her reflection in the mirror blurred. Very high quality pornography you have here in the West."

Fernandez studies the photo. "Pornography? You think it's porn?"

"Oh, yes. Very professional. See how the girl fills the shot, her backside large and prominent. All the focus on her, yet her back to us, so we don't quite see her. She is hiding."

"What about the tattoo on her derriere?" Fernandez points to a darkened shadow of her upper right gluteal.

"Not a tattoo, sir. More of a lighting effect, I suspect. A shadow. Maybe a birthmark." He brings his thumb tips together and cups them beneath the curve of her ass.

Fernandez turns the photo to see better. "That's a tattoo, Agent Yoong. Finding a girl with a tattoo on her derriere, it makes the whole case a lot easier." Then he turns his attention back to Heller's corpse, hovering his finger an inch or so off the body, pointing at a slat of epidermal tissue that hangs limp. No wider than a razor blade. Long and flappy enough to cover the victim's genitals. What's left of his genitals. "And the skinning's not post mortem either. It's how he was killed. Killer who gets her kicks from inflicting pain." He studies the photo once more. "Watching her victims suffer. What do you even call that, this kind of killing? Why would she leave photos of herself behind?"

Yoong passes the beads through his fingers. Fernandez looks the beads over, sees they have no crucifix, and that they're looped together by a knotted string.

"Ritual slaying," the agent speculates. "Delivering a message, I suppose."

"To whom?"

"You, perhaps. A dare. Killers sometimes prod the police this way. A come-and-find-me taunt. You are one of the few full-timers left on the force, are you not? With all due respect."

That kind of agent. The kind that says with-all-due-respect, but doesn't mean it. Plus, he's puffy. In a puffy blue down jacket, like an émigré might wear. "You Tibetan, agent?"

"No, sir. Proper Chinese. Mandarin."

"That different than Tibetan?"

"China liberated Tibet. That makes Tibetans Chinese, but Chinese are not necessarily Tibetan. You appreciate the distinction, do you not?"

But Fernandez doesn't appreciate anything. Particularly a Chinaman agent looking like an émigré being assigned tag-along. Too many émigrés, if you ask Fernandez. And now he's assigned a Chinaman agent.

Lesson 5

If you meet the Buddha on the road,
kill him.

WEED TREES CREAK IN THE warehouse's front yard. Broken shards of stained glass slice up Old and New Testament lessons.

A golden Jesus rising on a cloud.

An elder sacrificing a child, holding a knife over his chest.

A blond gandharva blowing her trumpet.

I do not recall ever being a detective, but I know the job entails seeing what is. Refusing to imbue the world as we anticipate it, leaving us to wonder, *what to see?*

Choki is gone now. And although I can still picture his hunched frame and craggy, wind-swept face, he is no more than a memory, an abstraction.

Is this what the Buddha means by emptiness? Someone once present, now present no more?

Standing on the warehouse portico I try feeling the dorje's

energy. Nothing. No wisp of it being inside. Only a dull throb against my thigh, which I touch. Deep inside my robe's pocket a cell phone rings. I remove it. It resembles Choki's phone in the alley, only this one shakes in the palm of my hand, like a hatchling chinking from its shell out into the open sky.

I answer. "Hello."

Wind crackles. A woman's voice whispers staticky. The story pauses. She asks, "What do you see?"

"Who is this?"

"Do you see what you are looking for?"

"What am I looking for?"

"A murderer. A way to survive." A moment lapses. Then another. Then the phone clicks, and the story resumes. I look at the phone, now perfectly still in my hand.

Such is Hell. Delusion and uncertainty. One moment disappearing into the next.

I reach for the warehouse door. Its handle stings cold. I wrap my hand inside my sleeve, and thumb its latch.

The door opens.

Inside the warehouse, silence echoes beneath tall ceilings throughout a single large and empty room. At my feet there are photographs. Artful, sexy. I do not look at them.

What to see? Inside the warehouse nave, an unpacked shipment of Buddha statues standing seven by seven, fat and happy.

To the side of the statues, an empty crate tipped on its side. Beyond the crate, two men conversing in the warehouse apse using small gestures and quiet tones. One points at a chair.

No sign of the dorje. Not a sniff or whisper.

In the chair, perfectly still and cleanly severed, a human form sits bound and upright. Killed in a slow execution. A moment frozen in time.

As one might witness on the Tibetan plateau, in lifetimes past. Lingchi.

Who in the West could possibly know such a way of killing?

No gweilo, certainly. No killer of insurance men, most likely.

Had someone followed me here? Someone from some previous life?

A perfect execution on display. A thin blade slipped beneath epidermis, inside out, excising that sixteen percent of body weight called skin. Excising it from muscle, and then muscle from bone. A complete flaying. Connective tissue and blood vessels exposed to the sun, germs, and airborne pathogens.

What preserves a man, if not his skin? What defines him if not the shape of his form, now shaped no longer? His form stripped away. What distinguishes one being from another, or from its environ, if not the skin they wear?

Who in the West kills this way? Lingchi?

One of the men conversing—the taller of the two—stoops to pick something up from the floor. The other appears Chinese, but with an American haircut and a dowdy, *splooshed* turtle face stuck up out of a puffed marshmallow coat. Navy blue. The tall one talks, squinting at what he's lifted, studying it like a jewel.

What to see? A torso, with fingerless hands and lopped off feet. And I wonder—is a hand still a hand without its fingers intact? When does it stop being a hand, and its transition into *stump* begin? When the first finger's hacked? The second? The third?

Or are all parts that comprise a thing the actual thing itself? Is a hand still a hand without its fingers?

I look at my own fingers and see them wriggle. I sniff them, not smelling my scent, but more the things I touched. The apartment's telephone, Choki's packet of obituaries, the warehouse's door handle. I sniff and cannot smell the dorje on the chaired man's corpse either. Whoever killed him did so before he even had a chance to steal it.

I flex my fingers, still stiff with cold. Each barely feeling the other as they touch. I roll my hand around its wrist, turning its fleshy side up and stretching the fat between thumb and forefinger. Not a flabby stretch. Not like I myself am flabby. Smoother, with well-defined knuckles, as if should I lop it off—as Heller's hand is lopped—and place it outside beneath a weed tree on the front lawn, and then should I return inside—might I exist both here and there simultaneously? Twin extensions of myself in the world?

Is a part of the whole not the whole, only smaller? Is an acorn really just an oak tree in waiting?

And that is what makes me question, what to see? Hands, body, knuckles—all concepts of ourselves. A way of recognizing ourselves in a crowd. None of them true individually, only in the composite that makes up who we are. Just as who we are is not real, outside of the composite of how we interact in the world.

Is this what the Buddha's talking about when he talks about emptiness? Who we identify as. And could these men conversing in the back apse of the warehouse have found the dorje? Could they now be keeping it from me?

I step from the vestibule. The tall man stops talking. The Chinaman steps toward me. He wears a smile. "Hello, lama." He bows. He sounds pleasant enough, but only in the way sounding pleasant makes one suspicious.

"Do you know me?" I ask.

"From your robes," the Chinaman says. "You are dressed as a lama. A Kagyu, I believe. No? I am sorry, but you cannot be here. This is a crime scene." He says it with a kindness reserved for children, not somebody recently reborn with the wisdom of all ages. "A very unbecoming place for a man such as yourself."

The tall one watches, scrutinizing the Chinaman's talk.

"I was asked to come," I tell him.

"Asked?" The Chinaman looks at the tall one. "Asked by whom? What is your name?"

"What is your name?"

"I am Agent Yoong. From the PRC. Here on exchange to observe the policing methods of the West. Asked to assist the inspector on this case. The case of the dead insurance man." He moves among the Budai statues toward me, while the tall one remains back in the apse wearing an oilskin duster and long dark hair, watching me from beneath the brim of a purple Colorado Rockies baseball cap. Obviously, the one in charge, this tall one. He stands solidly.

I point to the corpse. "I am Freelancer Rinzen Naraka. I assume this is our dead insurance man."

"Freelancer? A lama freelancing on the police force? Such a pleasure to see a compatriot, a fellow Chinese such as myself, finding work in the freelance pool here in the West."

"I am Tibetan. Not Chinese."

"Ah." He looks at me doubtfully. "A plateau dweller. I see. A distinction you make, I am sure." He laughs. I do not. Instead, I look at the Budais with their dancing feet and chubby arms and molded plastic and sharp-edged seams. Machine Budais. Each the same as the other. Not a flaw between them, except how they were manufactured in such a crass and mass marketed manner. Why ship plastic Buddhas all the way from Asia?

The tall cop sways forward. His heels clunk each step, rattling the statues and shaking the stained glass. His shoulders squeeze tight inside the duster, and the hem of his duster floats atop the floorboards, unbuttoned so that beneath it I see his brown shirt and mauve bolo inside a cacao suit with coffee-cream pinstripes. He walks stiff-legged, his black hair shiny and bouncing.

What to see? Not the man's eyes, certainly. His eyes stay hidden beneath the shadow of his Rockies cap. A police detective's trait, to see without being seen. Only when close enough does he lift the cap, revealing his one eye as chestnut-colored, and the other milky.

"You a freelancer?"

"I am."

"Usually don't get assigned any freelancers when there's an international tagging along." He points his jaw at the Chinaman. "Budget restrictions. *Comprendez?*"

I do not answer. He wipes his thumb and forefinger at the edge of his nose, snorting off some speck of something that's settled there. "What are you doing here?"

"I am Lama Rinzen Naraka. I received a phone call. I was told to look for Inspector Fernandez."

"Fernandez?" The tall one pushes his tongue into his inner lower lip. He breathes his words more than speaks them, and from the gravel in his throat, I suspect he is a smoker or drinker, or had been once.

I stay focused. "You are Fernandez. Are you not?"

"Me?" He snaps his head to the side, as if catching one of the Budais making a false move. He nods at the statues. "You dress like them. What are you? A Buddha?"

"Not a Buddha," the Chinaman clarifies. "A lama."

"I'll do the asking here, Agent Yoong." Fernandez sounds like an impatient man.

"Inspector," I say, "the Buddha is an enlightened being. If I was enlightened, would I be in a place such as this? Colfax Avenue?"

He does not change expression or lift his hands in the air or anything, except to say, "I'm here. You saying there's something unenlightened about me?"

The Budais seem to get it, what he is saying. They keep their laughing expressions while the inspector continues, "What? You think you get enlightened and then you just don't have to come around Colfax anymore? Like poof." He snaps his fingers. "You're someplace else." He snorts a laugh, quick but unfunny, and he steps closer. "Who are you?"

"I am a lama of the Kagyu lineage."

I wait for his response.

Nothing.

"I received a phone call from a man named Fusco. He said my number was up."

Again, nothing.

"For a freelance assignment. Investigating the murder of an

insurance man. Killing is the most grievous of the ten violations. Wrong View, too. But killing, that is the worst."

"You think he was murdered?"

I look at the corpse. "Certainly. Because he insured a shipment from Asia."

"Asia?" Fernandez pulls a sheet of paper from inside his suit and unfolds it. "The statues, from Asia?"

"More than just statues."

"More than statues? You sure of that? Because I look around, that's all I see." He waves his hand in the direction of the Budais. "What? We're just no good at making plastic figurines right here in the USA, so they got to come from Asia?" He fingers down the paper in his hand, reading it line by line. "Kagyu, huh?"

"Rinzen Naraka. A detective."

"Freelance," Fernandez corrects me.

"Freelance. Yes."

"We're all detectives, Kagyu. Just trying to figure shit out. Being a detective doesn't necessarily make you a freelancer, though." He twists his jaw, cracks it against the air. "I don't have any Naraka on my list."

"I received a phone call."

"Yeah, me too. Get phone calls a lot. Got one just now I didn't even answer." He calls to the Chinaman. "Yoong."

"Yes, sir."

"Did I just get a phone call I didn't answer?"

"Yes, sir."

"See what I'm saying?" the inspector says. "Anybody can get a phone call. And we don't much go for people just wandering in off the street to investigate a murder. Now Yoong here, he's an international agent, so I got to work with him. But you?" Fernandez looks over his shoulder. "Downtown tell you who we have dialing freelancers this week, Yoong?"

"No, sir."

"Fellow named Fusco?"

"I do not know, sir."

Fernandez turns to Rinzen. "You see? Nobody knows any Fusco. And I don't know you. And I don't know what are you doing here, or your interest in one of our insurance men getting killed? *Comprendez*, Naraka?"

"Lama," I correct him.

"What?"

"My proper title is *lama*. Naraka is a name I was born to. Lama is a title of achievement earned over multiple lifetimes. Achievements of observation. Seeing things as they are, as the Buddha taught. Handy for detective work, I might add. For leading me to the insurance man's killer. And the dorje, of course. Which is the reason he was killed in the first place, and which in turn will bestow enlightenment on all beings. As you say, we are all detectives. Looking to do some good in the world."

But the inspector does not seem like a man interested in doing good, nor in understanding what I am saying. His face hardens. "Let me tell you something. This freelance system's a gimmick, okay? Made up by bureaucrats and accountants to stroke the pockets of the taxpayer. Me? I'm unconstrained by gimmicks. I give them short shrift. So go tell your buddy Fusco you're off the case." He refolds the paper, sticks it back inside his suit jacket pocket. "In fact, tell him you were never on it."

"Inspector, please. My mission…"

"I don't want to hear about your mission. I don't want to hear about any la-di-dah enlightenment, either. I'm here to do serious work, lama. I got a case to solve. Things get bozo'd up in life—and they get bozo'd, believe me they do—that's when I come in. To figure shit out. For all I know, you killed Sonny."

"I did not. You know this, inspector."

"Do I? Okay, well then maybe I did it."

"No, inspector, not you either. Trust me."

"So you didn't kill him and I didn't kill him. That's a load off my mind. So who did?"

I glance at the Chinaman. "He could have," I suggest. "A Mandarin, like him."

The Chinaman's smile grows dim. "Inspector, please. I am here on a mission of exchange and good will." He shakes his head, looking at me. "I do not know who you are or why you speak so presumptuously, lama. Listen to the inspector. You are not invited to work this case. Maybe another, but not this one. I am an agent of the PRC. As a guest in this country, both of us, we must show respect to our host."

Fernandez cuts him off. "Forget the friendly shit, Agent Yoong. And you, Naraka. You should just leave. I got a murder to solve here. An out and out... what do you call it? A hacking of some sort."

"Lingchi," I say. The word rings into the corners of the room like a struck gong, and then reverberates out again.

"I apologize for my countryman," the Chinaman says to the inspector.

Fernandez waves him off. "What did you call it?" he asks me.

"Lingchi," I repeat.

"Lingchi?"

"It is a Chinese practice, yes. Lingchi."

"A Tibetan practice," the Chinaman interrupts.

"I thought Tibetans *are* Chinese," the inspector says to Yoong, dismissively.

"We are not," I assure him. "And lingchi is a Chinese practice, thoroughly."

"A Chinese practice? What, like a form of assassination?" The inspector circles me now, looking me over.

"Not assassination, no. Assassinations are committed by those lowly upon the more superior. Lingchi goes the opposite direction, imposed by authority upon the weak."

"Lingchi?" Fernandez says. "What's that in English?"

"Death by a Thousand Cuts. Not exactly a thousand, but many." I zigzag my finger at Heller to illustrate the point. "The

Long Slow Climb to the Mountaintop. A Chinese ritual for punishing crimes against the state."

"Colorado? Wyoming? Which state? How do you know it's called lingchi?"

I hesitate. "It was practiced many lifetimes ago. The Chinese administered it against those they disliked. Slowly, painfully slicing a person's passage to the next life. Inflicting humiliation. I have come to stop such practices and bring all to enlightenment." The last part I say because it is true. The first part because I suspect it is something the inspector might like to hear.

"Awfully big of you," Fernandez mutters. "Except one thing. Insurance men aren't enemies of the state."

"Indeed," Yoong agrees. "More specifically, inspector, Lama Rinzen Naraka is not on your list."

The inspector ignores him. "Why would someone do it? Lingchi? Here on Colfax?"

Again, I hesitate. "To recover something sacred."

"Sacred?"

"Something lost."

"Lost? That what makes it sacred?"

"The dorje, inspector. Stolen from we Kagyus and the Tibetan people long ago. Some say it hung in a Lhasa museum, and that now it is shipped here, and missing. I have come to find whoever has the dorje, and in the process will find who killed your insurance man. It is why I am here."

Yoong steps forward. "Please, lama. Beliefs are one thing, but as you know the dorje does not truly exist. In a museum or elsewhere. It is a superstition among you Steppe dwellers. I have studied the shipping manifesto. Budai statues, yes. But no dorje. See the facts in front of you. There is no dorje here. It may not even exist at all."

Fernandez bites his inner lip. His throat rasps. "These dorjes. They use them a lot in art photography? Porn?" He shows me a photo. Scuffed with shoe marks. Like on the floor in the entrance.

A girl holding a blade. Much like the blade the bicyclist held on Choki. Except the girl is naked, and the bicyclist was overly dressed for cold weather.

I look away. "Nothing like that, no."

The inspector strokes his index finger through the crevice of his chin. "Yeah. Still, this lingchi you mention…"

Yoong steps forward. "Inspector, please. Who here in the West would even know lingchi, or be in so lofty a position as to impose it on an insurance man? Unless of course…" and here he looks at me "… you mean to arrest an émigré."

"A Chinaman," I suggest.

"A Tibetan," he corrects me.

The inspector breaks in, interrupting us. "All right, all right, let me tell you boys something. A story. Put it in perspective. When I was just a little chico, my father, every day my father sold burritos out of a cart. Twenty-eight years. Burritos, Pepsi, tortas. For our family, he sold these things. *Para mi madre,* a blessed woman born of saints. A simple man, my father. He worked his routine. Every day the same. Till one day. One day he drives home in a brand-new Coupe de Ville. Where had he gotten such a magnificent car? How had he paid for it? These questions my mother wore on her face, but did not ask. She saw the delight in my father's eyes instead, as he drove the Coupe de Ville. Very happy, a very happy day for our family. He drove the Coupe de Ville and he parked it at the curb in front of our house and he looked at it out the window, right through supper, and all that night as the rest of us watched TV. A small house, we lived in. A casita. The neighbors come… ah, the neighbors come over to say to my father, *oh, how lucky. So blessed you are with such un coche. It will bring you much luck*. But my father, a simple man, a hard worker, a man of routine who sees the true value of things, he tells the neighbors, *We'll see*. Just like that. *We'll see what luck it brings*."

"But, inspector," Yoong says. "If you believe this is lingchi, why not question Tibetans before the killer gets away?" He looks at me. "Or perhaps Westerners who are particularly adroit at knife work?"

"We'll see," Fernandez tells him. Then he focuses on me. "I like seeing what you say here, lama. Lingchi. I like it a lot. You may not be on my list, but why don't you make yourself available? Go down to the precinct. Find this Fusco fellow. Have him get you a desk. A pad. Paper. Pen. Coffee, if you want. Write down what you know about this lingchi. Every last word."

"I told you what I know. Better I stay here and search for the dorje."

"Agent Yoong and I will collect the evidence. Tell you what. When we do, we'll send it down for you to take a look at. Perhaps you'll find the dorje there." The inspector lifts his ball cap, pushes back his hair. "Take one of the art photos, too." He lifts his eyebrows at me. "See if you can make out what her tattoo says. What it might mean."

"No, no," I tell him. "It doesn't mean anything. I should stay and look for the dorje."

"Trust me, lama. You'll see." Fernandez rubs his palms together, for friction and warmth.

"But I do not even know where the precinct is," I tell him.

The inspector looks at me, stumped, as if he had not considered such a problem. Then he snaps his fingers. "I'll have a part-timer take you." He snaps his fingers like it is a brilliant idea that only now just occurred to him.

"Inspector, are you sure? Is this usual procedure here in the West?" Yoong asks. "He is not on your list."

Fernandez itches a sallow fold of his cheek. "We'll see," he says. "We'll see if I'm sure or not."

Lesson 6

Watch your thoughts, for they become words.
Watch your words, for they become actions.
Watch your actions, for they become habits.

OUTSIDE THE WAREHOUSE, SNOW WHISPERS from the sky. Two mismatched uniform cops now stand guard on the portico to either side of the door. Garcia and Holmes. That's how they call themselves.

I look at the photo the inspector handed me. A girl with the knife in her hand. The part-timer Holmes sneers, "What do you think, lama. Size twelve, or more of a ten?"

But to me, that just sounds like numbers. Abstractions Westerners use to confuse things.

"I could not say," I tell him.

"Come on, you're a detective, aren't you? I say size twelve. Tell the inspector that, how I say size twelve and if I'm right, I'd like to be a detective someday."

Yoong steps from the warehouse. "Part-timer Garcia," he says to the other cop. "The inspector asks you to drive the lama here to precinct headquarters. To an interrogation room. Provide him whatever he needs." He points to me. "We will send evidence for him to examine. He will be assisting us. For a while at least."

Then Yoong steps over and whispers to me, his lips barely moving, "Why did you mention lingchi, lama?"

"Why did you not mention it?"

"Watch what you say. We are guests in this country, not wanting to defy our hosts." Yoong walks me out of earshot of the part-timers. "Understand something. The West prefers procedure. Everything yes, no, black, white. They understand the truth of a thing by analyzing what it is not, not by what it is. Very dualistic thinkers here in the West."

"The inspector asked," I say. "He wanted to know about lingchi, so I told him."

"Yes. Well, the best success is the quickest success, understood or not. Westerners don't like failure, or being seen as one. It is far too difficult for them to accept. Power, cash, celebrity, the size of their Twitter following, these are the things that matter. A little word of advice. If you want to be a freelancer here, don't speak. Observe. Don't be showy. Meld. That is how the West likes it."

He points to the photo in my hand. "You are newly arrived, are you not? I am sorry you must see such a thing. But now that you have, find the girl, why don't you? Get her to confess. The inspector likes success, even when false. The more you look at a thing, the more you can change it. The more likely she will confide in you, and confess." He sighs.

I look now at the photo, holding my gaze on it. The manner of its staging. Its lighting.

Yoong steps past me and says to Garcia, "Take him now, please. It is cold out, and I am sure the lama might appreciate a nice, warm interrogation room." He smiles appreciatively, smiling at each of us. "The inspector and I will be engaged, so please, no further interruptions." With that, Yoong goes inside, just as a blustery whiteout of snow blows down from the roof shrouding the Chinaman in mist as he disappears.

Garcia takes my elbow, escorts me down the steps to a patrol car with cracked taillights and a glass back window pockmarked from bullet shots. He opens the rear door and pushes my head down as I enter. "Watch yourself." Inside the patrol car, Plexiglas separates the front seat from the back. Outside, Garcia's cell phone rings. He closes me inside and looks at the phone's display. He snaps it open. *Bueno, mi querida,* he says. *Como estas?*

From the back seat I hear Daidyal behind the Plexiglas. "Nice fellow, that Chinaman."

"He is some kind of agent. He works for the state."

"You dislike that about him?"

"I dislike their invasion of Tibet. Their enslavement of our people."

Daidyal shivers. "Don't be so political, lama. Things pass."

"They are keeping it from me. The dorje. It arrived to the warehouse. I know it did."

"Ah." Daidyal nods, shaking his head *no*. "That..."—he points to me— "... what you're doing there, it's odd reasoning. More desperation than fact."

"You are my teacher, Daidyal. Why not agree with me, just this once? Consider it. A shipment arrives. Forty-nine Budais. Plastic. So cheap they are not worth the price of postage. Consider it. Do you truly suspect nothing of more value shipped? The dorje, perhaps?"

Daidyal rolls his head. "Oooh. Reasoning, reasoning, is that what you are up to? Thinking things through. Tell me, have you ever counted the number of abstractions that comprise a single thought? What do you think you're doing here, lama? Why even come to Colfax?"

"They know more than they are saying."

"Of course, of course, they are police." Daidyal sounds impatient. "Secretive. So should you be. You crack a secret by entering it. Not by denying it, yelling at it. Play their game. Go along. Go to the precinct, write down this lingchi information they're looking for. See where it gets you. Poke around their evidence, oooh, so much to see."

"Do not make fun. Why do I even listen to you?"

"Why? This second-guessing of yours, very ego-clinging, lama. Not a proper habit for a newly minted detective. Did I teach you nothing in the Shedra? Pursue the girl, why don't you? It might be fun. You have already seen her naked."

"A photo, only. They can tamper with those things."

The part-timer Garcia taps the patrol car glass, signaling that I should buckle up. *Tu cinturon.* Then he re-cups his hand over the phone not to be heard. Up on the portico the other part-timer, Holmes, hikes his collar tight to his neck and lowers the ear flaps of his cap.

I tell Daidyal, "The girl is a distraction."

He leans against the front seat and shivers, causing it to rattle. "Life is distraction. Better to be distracted here in a sheltered patrol car or down at the precinct than out on the street. Look, this lingchi write-up, I can help you with it if you'd like."

"You?"

"What else have I got to do? I do not know anyone on Colfax. Besides, with what little you recall from my teachings, there are things I might remind you of."

Through the scratch of the Plexiglas and in the patrol car's rearview, I now see a limo approaching from behind. Its widely-spaced headlamps push dimly through the falling snow, until the limo pulls up alongside the patrol car. I wind down my window. The limo's rear driver's side glass whispers open as well, revealing a trim gentleman, elderly, with trimmed hair and moustache, in a trimmed suit and wearing no coat. A wave of warm air escapes from the limo out into the cold.

"May I help you, officer?" the gentleman asks curtly. He wears calf-skin gloves perched atop a marble-handled cane. He leans forward on the cane, stretching himself tall in his seat.

"Help me how?"

"Hah?" A raspy voice from the far, unseen side of the limo barks out. "How self-absorbed, Curly. Introduce yourself to the man. He doesn't know you. Why should he?" The distant speaker now leans across the limo toward me, looking gray like his fellow rider, and equally as pale, with a nose just as pinched, but bushier eyebrows. "Please excuse my brother, officer. We are looking for Sonny. We are supposed to meet him here. At this warehouse. If you could tell him, please, his brothers have come. Such a god-forsaken part of town, is it not?" While speaking, he eyes the warehouse's façade of stained glass. "Looks nearly Catholic."

"Sonny Heller, do you mean?"

"Yes. I make no de-*loo*-sions…" —he drags out the *loo* part of the word— "why he wanted to meet in this part of town, I couldn't fathom a guess. Allow me to introduce myself. My name is Huey Heller, and this gentleman beside me is my brother, Curly. And Sonny… well, you may have met Sonny."

"I am afraid I did not."

"Yes. Well, we believe he is inside the warehouse there. We don't know why, or if we even have the correct address. 33rd and Josephine? We received a call to meet him."

Heller. The brothers. Insurance men. "A call from whom?" I ask.

"Why, Sonny, of course."

"He called you? When?"

"Yes, he called. He said we were to meet him at the warehouse on 33rd and Josephine. He had something to show us. Do we have the right place?"

Just the entry I need. "33rd and Josephine. Yes. What did he want to show you?"

The brothers seem perplexed. "He did not say. Just that we should come and see for ourselves, because without seeing we might not believe. Is he in there? The warehouse? We would really like to speak to him."

"Yes." I say it slowly. "Yes, he is, so to speak. But, no. I am afraid you cannot speak with him." And then, I explain more succinctly how Sonny has now moved on to the Pure Lands, to enlightenment or yet another rebirth—maybe even moved to Hell once more, depending on what lessons he learned along the way. "I can show you the body if you like." Because if they like, perhaps I could peek around a bit more for the dorje.

But the Hellers do not understand. They fumble to make heads or tails of what I say.

"Dead?" the one named Curly asks. "You mean *dead* dead? Forever?" This is the way they think in the West. Death as finality. Everything extinguished.

"That is one way to put it, yes," I explain. And as a means of confirmation–that Sonny Heller is indeed who is tied to the Shaker chair inside–I show them the photo. "Perhaps he knew this girl?"

They stare at the photo a good long while. "What is this, a joke? All we see is her derriere. Where did you get this?"

"Inside."

"Inside? Sonny is in there?"

"Perhaps I could show you. Perhaps look around the shipment a bit. See what he meant to show you. May I ask, were you expecting a shipment?"

Oh, Jeese, Daidyal hisses. *So obvious, lama. Their brother has died. These men deserve compassion.*

The old teacher may be right. The brothers lean together, as if listening without wanting to hear. Leaning, broken. I see now the similarity in their bone structure and age.

"Dead why? Why here?" Huey asks.

"He may have been dragged here," Curly suggests. "Against his will. Was there a struggle?"

"No," I say, and then correct myself. "No signs of a struggle. Just a shipment of Budai statues. Was he expecting such a thing?"

"Buddhas?" Curly waits a beat or two, staring into the space before him. "Buddhas are not our persuasion, officer."

"Have you called the coroner?" Huey asks, an antsiness to his voice. "You need to call the coroner. We will need a death certificate confirming he is dead. For our Excess and Surplus insurer. You're certain he's dead?"

"We can go in and see for yourselves." As I say this, snow continues to slip from the sky. I step from the patrol car to move closer and lean down to the limo's window, seeing Huey's hand on his brother's knee, squinting past me to better see the warehouse and its street sign. Josephine and 33rd.

"Poor Sonny," he gasps. "It seems so much sadder with snow falling. This girl in the photograph, is she the one who did it?"

I look at the glossy. The fullness of her form. "I cannot comment on what we know about her." That is a true thing for me to say. Or I could say nothing. That would be true as well. "If anything though, we suspect she may have had a connection to the shipment of Buddha statues." That is not true, of course. "I understand Sonny insured the shipment." That part is. "Was there anything else in it?" That part, too.

"Good God, man. Find the girl. Did she stab him?"

"Stab him?"

"She is holding a knife." He shakes the photo at me.

"Not stabbed, no." I avert my eyes. "His death was a result of lingchi."

"What?"

"Not something a gweilo might understand. To be honest with you," I say, "I doubt the girl did it."

Curly shivers. "My God." Shock seems to overtake him. "My God, my God." He begins raising the window, wanting to end the conversation early, it seems. Its dark glass ascends, revealing my own dull reflection in its glass, and my dread that I cannot let them leave until they admit the shipment included the dorje. I flush. An ache creeps in behind my eye. The window freezes, suddenly ceasing in place.

I lean to the car and suggest, "Why do we not go inside so you can see him."

"I don't want to see him."

"Was your brother expecting a shipment of Budais?" I ask.

Curly fiddles with the window further, cursing beneath his breath, banging at the glass.

"No," Huey states emphatically. "He was not. Anything else, officer?"

"Anything other than Buddhas?"

"Anything else you want to ask us?" He asks with slow impatience, before stepping up the pace of his words. "Our brother is dead. Murdered, in fact. Curly, please." He slaps his brother's hand. "Stop banging the window like that. Wind it up, for God's sake."

"Who would want to kill him?" I ask.

Their eyes shift. "We are insurance men, officer. A dangerous profession." Huey folds back into the far side of the limo. "Threats. We receive threats, many. But we are insurance men, and not easily intimidated."

Curly fidgets more anxiously with the window, little red veins puffing at edge of his nose.

"Threats from whom?" I ask.

Huey speaks one word at a time. "We do not pay attention to threats. We do not let anyone keep us from the work we do. Insurance work. Please, officer, we now need be on our way."

Their manner of concern, it grows a bit snippy now. While Curly continues to fidget, Huey watches him, absently saying, "We will arrange for the body. I assure you that." He speaks with finality, not wishing to discuss it further.

I step away from the car, nodding at its window as I do. The window's ascent now resumes. It slips closed, and the limo pulls away down Josephine, a small gasp of exhaust following behind.

Cold seeps from the pavement into the soles of my mukluks. Garcia still speaks on the phone. Snow sprinkles from the sky. Daidyal steps from the patrol car and joins me. "All this talk, is it getting us anywhere, lama?"

"Why would they drive here like that," I ask, "only to just drive away again?"

"People in the West do not stay anywhere long. They are rootless and always on the go. Why not just go down to the precinct like the inspector asked you?"

"They know something. The precinct is just a diversion, but those Hellers know something."

"Precisely," he says. "The precinct is a diversion, and you should go there. Precisely because it is a diversion. And a step outside your own persistent mind."

Lesson 7

We need not understand objects.
Only our interactions with them.

A GOOSENECK HALOGEN SHINES DOWN on the interrogation room table.

I shield my eyes from its glare and consider what the Shedra taught me. That time swirls in on itself. That nothing arises of its own accord. Each *now* is a confluence of before and after, rendering time into a stillness which we glimpse while looking for eternity.

Each Hell I am born into is no different than any other. Except in this one I will find the dorje. I know I will.

I know I must.

Each effect grows from its cause. To know where the dorje is, first understand who committed this lingchi. Look in the warehouse, for whoever did it surely left a bit of himself or herself behind. Find what they left, there I will find the Most Precious of Objects.

The gooseneck lamp burns down upon me, and I sweat. The interrogation room is windowless. Except one window with its shade pulled down. The window to the observation room no doubt, where others watch me.

The wool of my robes feels itchy. In a notepad Garcia gave me I scribble, *All I Know about Lingchi*. Write something down immediately it transitions into something to be remembered, Westerners say. When really it is just a way to forget. To stash away in some drawer someplace and forget.

The Hellers, for instance. They come looking for their brother. I say he is dead. They leave the warehouse without seeing him, like his death is something to forget. Dead from lingchi. They do not even ask about it. What do they know that makes them not ask?

In a ceiling corner of the interrogation room, the red eye of a camera blinks. Someone watching. Following my every scribble in the notepad. How long since I have been reborn? The interrogation room has no clock. Its door rattles, then kicks open. A short dump of a patrolman waddles in carrying two cardboard boxes. He slaps them onto the table, their tops flapped shut, and he pulls out a handkerchief to wipe away his sweat. "You Naraka?" The boxes collapse a bit beneath their own weight, one on top of the other.

"What is this?" I ask.

The cop smiles. "You don't like answering questions much, do you? Yeah, you're Naraka. Picked that up about you on the phone. I should be a detective someday, the way I can pick things up on the phone when I'm talking." He sticks out a hand glistening with perspiration and meaty like yak scrotum. "Name's Fusco." He shakes my hand up and down. "I put you onto this gig. Moneymaker, huh? Work it slooow, lama. Listen to me now, work it real sloooow. A man like you, Asian, a holy man, you know what I mean. Work it dead-ass slow. So we make a lot of money. You're not forgetting my spiff, are you? Fernandez, he'll pressure you to wrap things up. Pin it on any old schmoe and close the case. Don't do that. See things for what they are. You're a smart guy, right? I see that about you. You're smart. You know how to work it slooow, rack up some overtime. More for you. More for me." Fusco scratches his index, middle, thumb fingers together like he is making the sound of money. "Treat us like they do, working shitty part-time, freelance jobs, make 'em pay."

How different the name sounds—Fusco—when spoken here in my presence, not over the phone. I imagined it sounding different. "You are the one who called me?" I ask.

"You bet your sweet bippy. Compadres, you and me." He shuffles his hand back and forth between us. "We got a lot in common."

"Fernandez says I am not on his list. I do not even know if I am working this case or not."

Fusco's face bends. "You listen to me. Screw Fernandez. We have a saying around here, at least I do. *Screw Fernandez.* Pompous jackass. I checked on you. You're the real McCoy. A detective, with military credentials, too. Some niru stint you pulled over in Lhasa. Believe me, Fernandez wants a guy like you. He's got some Chinese agent hanging over his shoulder, but he needs you. What did you do? Tell him it was lingchi? Good thinking. He likes thinking things can wrap up quick. But play it slooow, lama. Play it real slooow."

Fusco slaps the side of the top box he's dropped on the table. "Evidence from the crime scene. Just came in." Fusco draws two fingers up from alongside each of his hips, shooting them six-gun-style like a cowboy pushing into a saloon. "From down the warehouse. *Bing bing,* knocking 'em dead, lama."

The boxes appear long enough, perhaps wide enough that the dorje might fit inside. If it was placed on an angle. Top left, bottom right. "What is in them?" I ask.

"Oh, lots of interesting stuff. The dead man's suit. The one he wore when he got to the warehouse. Wasn't wearing, not after, because... well, you know. Plus, some porno shots. Pens, papers, portable stapler. Insurance looking stuff." Fusco rolls a chair out from the table and plops into it catty-corner. "No Buddha statues. The Buddha statues, they're too big. We sent a van down for them. Do you believe in that stuff?"

"Vans?"

Fusco nods. "Buddha statues. But yeah, sure, vans too."

I lift the top box down onto the table beside the other. I sense nothing special about it, except for my own anticipation.

"You're some kind of detective, huh? All the way from Asia. You an assassin?"

"I am a monk of the Kagyu lineage."

"Yeah, but you're from Lhasa, aren't you?"

"How do you know I am not from here? Colorado."

"Because in Colorado, everybody comes from someplace else." Fusco smiles, nods to me. "Besides, you don't look Coloradoan." Then less smile, no nod. "Tibetans get killed here in Colorado. Every day." The air hangs silent after he says it.

"Why is that?" I ask. "Who is killing them?"

"Anybody. Last group in, first group hated. That's how we think here in this part of the world. Bigotry's not something we're steadfast about. Just something we shift around from group to group."

The box flaps shred as I pull them. "You understand the West well, Patrolman Fusco."

"Ah, no, not *patrolman*. No, sir. Part-timer Fusco." He leans across the table on his hands, arms stretched out. "Work parttime. You know what that means. Means I don't give a rat's ass. Look, you find that dorje, lama, keep it for your own. Not like I'm going to say anything. You should know that about me. I don't give a rat's ass. And if you're an assassin, like you might be, well that's just something you did back in Lhasa once. That's all."

"I am not an assassin." My fingers squirm inside the box's contents.

Lozenges.

Gambling stubs.

A catalog. *All Things Asian.*

I take these things out and place them alongside the box.

"You led a raid on Drepung though, didn't you?" Fusco says it like small talk. Like what else is there to talk about. "Nasty shit, Drepung."

I dig deeper inside the box.

Pens.

Paper.

Stained glass shards nicking my knuckles.

"I only ask..." he shrugs, shoulder and belly, "because I'm a military man myself. Once led a raid on Abu Dhabi. That was the slop. Way I see it, Drepung, Abu Dhabi, they sound practically the same. Both have *d*s in their names. So, we got that in common, me and you. Dorje, too. That's a *d* word. You really think you'll find it?"

How easy for men like Fusco. Sniff and grab whatever's easy. I dump the box's remaining contents onto the table. Packets and potpourri and a broken lock from the shipment's crate.

No Sacred Object.

Fusco opens the catalog *All Things Asian,* flips through its back pages crammed with boxy ads. He points one out to me.

"Four point nine million, you know?"

That is what the ad says. *Tibetan dorje. The Most Sacred of Objects. Yours for just $4.9M dollars.* I lift the ad from him to be certain I am reading it properly. "An abomination," I say, this idea, selling such sacredness, for money.

"Looks like you're not the only one looking for it. That's all I'm saying. Four point nine million, you and me—that's quite a bit of spiff."

"The dorje is not for sale. Look at this ad. How crudely the dorje is drawn." I push the catalog toward him. "Nothing more than pencil and ink. Plain. Barely revealing its splendor."

"Yeah. And a Chinese phone number, to boot. A teaser ad, we call it," Fusco says. "Why advertise over here for a number you got to call all the way over to China? Whoever placed this ad, they're not selling the dorje. They're just trying to boost its price. The way we do deals here in the West, bleeding the other guy out of his money. Nobody wins until the other guy's bleeding."

I flay open the second box. A teaser ad, he calls it. Seeing a thing not as it is, but only as its value. "The Hellers insure this sort of shipment often?" I ask.

"The Hellers? Strictly medical insurance, lama. Health plans. That sort of thing. Maybe some life insurance on the side."

I pull items from the second box. A bloody billfold. Heller's ID. Business cards with his email and a slogan. *Life is Hell. Insurance comes from heaven.*

I find a stack of photos of the girl with the knife in her hand. I straighten them and place them in a pile atop the table. I lift the man's suit from the box, its jacket, belt, pants. A blue collared shirt and navy tie. Not tattered, nicely folded. No signs of blood.

Inside the jacket, in its inner pocket, something flat and slippery. A plastic packet. I open it. A pungent odor leaks out, and inside I find an insurance form splattered with vomit. The form written in English, but not an English I understand. Insurance English. Diversionary English, meant to throw you off the path. The only thing I understand is the signature page, where the policy is marked *Rescinded.*

"What does a policy like this actually cover?" I ask. "Do people actually read them to know?"

"Insurance policies? No. People just sign them."

Stapled at the back of the policy, I find a news clipping. Single column. Three paragraphs short, with short wording and peculiarly written. *Icons of Drepung to Vist Denver.* Peculiarly misspelled. Telling how Heller Insurance prides itself as a collector of ancient Tibetan artifacts, and is bringing a shipment of them all the way from China to display in the lobby of their business. For émigrés to come in and gawk at. Maybe buy some insurance while they are there.

An article in a newspaper, about what nice fellows they are,

Heller Insurance, bringing over stuff like that. Except the brothers said they know nothing about the shipment.

I page through the policy, uncaking one page from another. Name of the insured—*Abril* something or other. Her last name illegibly crusted in vomit. An address on Colfax. Seemingly familiar. Smudged handwriting scrolling the left column of the policy. A notation someone has made on the policy.

The notations says *Madame Sun's Olde Tibetan Emporium and Meditation Center. All Things Asian.*

Upon reading it, I drop the policy. From my hand to the table. From there to the floor.

"Find something?" Fusco asks. He bends and picks up the policy, reading the notation. "Madame Sun's. You know the place? A little shithole of a shop, down on Colfax. They selling the dorje, you think?"

"I could not say," I say, and I put the policy back into its envelope and pocket it inside my robe pocket. I stand. "I need air."

"Air?" Fusco looks puzzled. "What do you mean, like outside?"

I wrap myself inside my robes, pressing the insurance policy inside my inner pocket to my chest so that he might not see that I have it. I make for the door.

"You leaving?"

I do not explain. I just do so.

"You leaving? Taking a break? Good for you, lama. Working it slow? You're not going forget my spiff, are you?"

But I do not even understand *spiff* or what it is. Nor am I even thinking about it.

What I am thinking about is the emporium whose name is notated on the policy, and where I need to go next, even though I am uncertain how to get there.

LESSON 8

Delusion is the cause of our rebirth into the six realms.

- In Praise of Zazen, Hakuin Ekaku

I HAVE NOT BEEN A detective long, but I know how mysteries unfold. The past reappears. An emporium is mentioned, oddly named, from another lifetime. Someone follows me without my knowing.

The evidence boxes at the precinct tell me two things. The dorje arrived here on Colfax Avenue. That's the first thing.

Second, finding it will require untumbling the mystery of Sonny Heller's death. Who killed him? Who stole the Most Sacred of Objects from him? Who has it now?

But why should an emporium be named like it is? Why notate it on an insurance policy for me to read? Me, a bodhisattva destined to find the dorje once and for all, and bring all beings to enlightenment?

Is this what the Buddha talks about when he talks about

emptiness? The way the past buries itself inside the now, no longer existing, yet here?

Searching those boxes tells me I must be quick about it. The longer one looks, the more he changes what he seeks. I must find the dorje, unblemished, enlighten everyone, and be done with it.

I stand in front of the Aim Straight and Shoot Saloon. The address written down for the girl Abril from the policy. A familiar enough looking place. A place where I had come from only hours earlier. What to see? A building of faux brick painted true yellow. A Christmas wreath sagging from its front door dropping needles by the tens and twenties onto a waiting welcome mat. Not literally the tens and twenties, just needles falling sparsely. Half a building away, inside a glassed door, the stairway from the apartments I descended this morning. It all seems so familiar.

Down the street a clatter arises—*swish swish*. A peloton of masked riders. Cyclists in lycra wearing spider glasses. Club letters stitched glittery across their chests and down their pant legs. *Spurtz Granola Snax*. They swoop the corner while time slows for a moment. I step from their path so as not to be hit. The cyclists' snort past, their uniforms steaming, their bike chains gnawing. Other pedestrians make way as well. At the corner, the peloton leans right and disappears behind a noodle shop. I know this because its sign says so. It is called *Noodles*.

Pulling on the glass door to the apartments, it appears frozen shut. Perhaps locked. I read the names on the mail slots, straining to make sense of their faded ink. One says *Abril*. Like in the policy.

I turn my focus back to the Aim Straight and Shoot. I step over fallen needles into the bar's gaping darkness. Cold from the street whistles in behind me.

What to hear?

Billiard balls clacking. Carved elephant ivory colliding against one another, the tusks of a single elephant for one game set, sixteen balls. Crafted for the have-wants of the West.

My eyes adjust. No neon glows inside the Aim Straight. Very

little of the room is lit. The television is turned off. In its darkness, spindly shadows form. Dark outlines of flimsy-legged folding chairs leaning into flimsy-legged card tables. A flimsy stairway up one wall to a closed door. The stenciling on the door's glass reads, *THIS WAY TO THE APARTMEN S.*

In front of me a shadowy, unshaved bartender emerges in 40-watt dimness. He hunches over a newspaper and teethes the gum end of a pencil. His flannel shirt sags over a once muscular but now flabby chest. He does not look at me. On the other side of the room, pool balls crack in a cubby. A uniformed bicyclist steps this way around the pool table, stretching out long in spandex and knee socks. He lines up a shot. Tattoos strangle his neck and arms. His wool cap and bike shirt display the familiar emblem of the *Spurtz* gang. Who are these cyclists?

A second Spurtz man watches the first, looking the same. Same shirt. Same logo.

I announce to the roomful of them, all three, "I am looking for Abril."

The bartender straightens. The bicyclists too. The bartender tongues the pencil's pointy end. "What are you, coming here dressed all like a smart ass, in robes like that?" How they talk in the West. "What are you doing here?"

"I am Lama Rinzen Naraka, a monk of the Kagyu lineage, here to bring all sentient beings to enlightenment. To do so, I must find Abril. I think she may be able to help."

"Help? With enlightenment? You mean, like being smart, like you think she's smart? What are you, like a smart guy yourself? Tell me something, smart guy. An eight-letter word for pies in a field?" No *hello* to his voice, no *how-do-you-do*. "Ends in *T*," the bartender says, like that is the hard part—an eight-letter word ending in *T*.

The bicyclist who had been about to shoot now steps a step closer to me. "Whoa, wait just a second there, Kagyu. Don't answer that." He leans his butt against the pool table. "First, tell me what you're doing here? This is a Spurtz bar."

The other cyclist leans on his cue stick, chalking it while rolling his tongue over his teeth.

The bartender waves him off. "*Bullshit,*" he says. The word crackles in the crisp air. Cyclist 2 unfolds from his cue stick.

"Bullshit," he repeats. "Yeah, that's it. Pies in a field. Cow pies. Bull pies. Bull shit. That's it, right there."

"All right." The bartender tries flexing inside his flannel, stretching it so a button pops. "I got another. Starts with *B*, connects to the *B* in *bullshit*. To accomplish the impossible, it takes these."

"Brains?"

"Five letters. Fourth's an *L*."

"Balls?" number 2 says.

"Balls." The bartender mulls it over. "Balls, indeed."

As their game unfolds, I try to decipher how it answers my question about Abril's whereabouts. Then the bartender booms once more. "All right, listen up. Here's what we got. Five letters. *You hold it to create, but its creation you cannot hold.* Fourth letter's *J*."

Suddenly, I see the moment. Where it is going, and how instances reoccur and names come back familiar. Or at least their lettering. "Dorje," I say.

The bartender looks up. "*Dorje?*"

"You hold it, the Most Sacred of Objects, and it brings enlightenment," I explain. "Purified mind. Incomprehensible. Incapable of being held. Write it in. *Dorje.* It fits."

"The hell it fits," bicyclist 2 says. "Don't listen to him. He's Kagyu."

Bicyclist 1 spits at the floor. "Dorje, bullshit. Guy walks into a bar dressed in his colors and says *dorje*. A Spurtz bar he comes into, saying *dorje*. Screw him. *Banjo.* Write that in." He bends his leg up, knee in front, stretching his spandex, strumming his fingers at the air. "With a banjo on my knee. Pluck it, it's a sound. Can't hold sound. Something you touch, taste, smell or see—those things you hold. What you hear. That's sound. Sound's a bitch you can't hold onto. Sound always leaves you, sooner or later. That's the whole reason it's there in the first place."

"*Banjo.*" The bartender counts out the letters. "Yeah." He squints at me. "Shit better than *dorje.* Where'd you come from?" he asks.

"I am Lama Rinzen Naraka."

"Not asking your name," bicyclist 1 says. "He's telling you, this ain't a Kagyu bar. It's *Spurtz.*"

"I am looking for Abril."

"*Ooh la lah,*" bicyclist 2 catcalls. "Miss Desire. *Grrr.* Lives upstairs, Kagyu. Other door. Why come here?"

An overhead fan casts a chill down on the room. The bicyclists hold their pool cues like they no longer intend to play pool. The cold inside my fingers thaws out, itchy. The bicyclists step closer, and the cold feels like should I defend myself, take a swing at them, my fingers might shatter.

On the other side of the wall, where the stairwell climbs to the apartments, there is the sound of feet shuffling. Two sets. At the bar, the bartender scratches his neck, watching me and the cyclists. Down at my mukluks, little bug-like speckles ping up off the carpet onto the hem of my robes.

The cyclists keep approaching. The bartender runs stubby fingers through his scalp. "You boys take this outside, why don't you?"

Footsteps race the stairs on the other side of the wall, then stop.

Bicyclist 2 says, "Answer the man. What are you doing here?"

"I am here," I say, and then fall quiet. No further explanation necessary.

Bicyclist 1 swats his cue stick at me. A jolt surges through me. I step out of range of the cue stick's swing, cupping my hand, catching the stick mid-swipe.

It snaps. It drops in two pieces to the floor.

"I come to bring enlightenment," I say. The words taste bitter. Slightly metallic. I feel the jolt again. Bicyclist 2 approaches from behind. A kaleidoscope of butterflies flutters inside my stomach. My heart calms. My blood flows more slowly. Time crawls. The cyclists appear sluggish now, like a slow rock tumbling, or as an elephant walks among hummingbirds.

I have not been a detective before, but when outnumbered I know how to change the odds. Slow things down, so you can see them happening.

I spin on the ball of my right foot and lift the other to wrap around Cyclist 2's cue stick. It breaks, like the other one. Its top end pops off into the bone above cyclist 2's left eye, denting his forehead. Dropping him to the floor.

I spin on my left foot and now point at cyclist 1. A burst of funneled air explodes from my fingertips, knocking him back, sprinkling his nose into an explosion of bloody cartilage.

Behind the bar, the bartender reaches for a Louisville fungo. I see him. I shake my head *Don't*.

He doesn't.

With the cyclists floored, I scan the room, now floating with dust and quiet.

Except for the stairwell on the other side of the wall. Something cracks there. I hear voices again. "Screw you," a woman shouts.

"What are you doing here?" One of the cyclist grabs onto my robe hem. More for support than to come at me.

I lean over him. "Who followed me? You? Who sent you?"

They choke. "This is our place. Spurtz Granola Snax."

"Who do they work for, these Spurtz Granola Snax?"

"They work for everyone. They're nutritious."

From the other side of the wall, a second *crack*. Someone hitting someone. Someone being hit. I focus on it, but then back at the cyclist. "Where is it? The dorje, I want it?"

"Come on, man. Leave us alone. You're not even supposed to be here."

I straighten. I look down upon those cyclists. "Madame Sun? Did she tell you that?"

"Who?" Cyclist 1's teeth are outlined in blood, and his saliva pink when he talks. "I thought you were looking for Miss Desire. Over there, on the other side of the wall." Then I hear a third slap.

Abril? Whose policy had the article about the dorje shipment stapled to it.

"That is her?" I ask. Then I bunch up the hem of my robes and cross the Aim Straight to the stairs running up the wall. I hear a voice muffled. Not hers this time. More muted, with the distinct timbre of a building superintendent. I hear him say the word *furniture*, and something about a garbage chute.

It clogs. You do not get rid of furniture in garbage chute. It clogs. He sounds hollow, like words in a fish tank kerplunking against glass.

I make my way up the stairs and through the door separating the Aim Straight from the apartments. On its other side, a woman in a puffed up winter coat and leggings says, "I don't throw furniture down your poop chute, you poop chute, you." Her voice sounds like phlegm. Raspy.

What to see? The very stairwell I descended this morning. The super now descending it, huffing and puzzling over my sudden appearance. "What you do here?"

On the landing above, the girl's cheeks glow red, one redder than the other where he slapped her. She stands outside an open apartment, the same apartment from which I exited this morning. "Abril?" I ask. Perhaps not loud enough for her to hear me.

The super lumbers closer. "Lawn chair." He flaps his arms at me and turns back to the girl. "Lawn chair, in a garbage chute. What is wrong, such doings? Lawn chair"—he points up at her— "like you sit in up on roof in summer. In your bathing suit. I see you on roof in summer in your little beach bathing suit. In your lawn chair. Now stuck in my garbage chute. It is yours."

"You pervert." She rubs her cheek. "Watching me in my bathing suit. You're a pervert."

"No. Not watching. Seeing." The super taps a finger to his eye and shows it to me. "I never watch. I see. I see what goes on. I know."

"Do not touch her," I tell him.

"Touch her? She not touch me. Not touch my garbage chute." And I see now the super's cheek dabbled with chewed dots of blood, and I wonder if perhaps the girl had slapped him, and not the other way around.

From inside the apartment at the top of the stairs, a telephone rings. Familiar sounding.

"Hey." She calls down. "Bodhisattva? You here to do something, or what? Get up here and answer the phone, why don't you?"

Energy explodes out of her. Angry energy. "You know me?" I ask.

"You're here to help, right? Damn, I'll do it myself, have to do everything myself." She steps inside the apartment, picks up the phone and slams it down in a huff so that it rings no more. The entire display makes me wonder, a woman such as this, how could she possibly have the dorje?

I edge past the super, who appears smaller now. "I see," he says. "I see what goes on." He pokes his eyeball again, more crooked now, more nervously.

She reemerges onto the landing above. "Nothing goes on. He's a lama, for Christ sakes."

"You know me?" Again, the phone starts ringing.

"Oh, Jeese, answer that, why don't you, lama." She is yelling at me, disrespectfully.

I move up the stairs, trying to see her and match how her shape beneath her down jacket might fit the shape of the girl in the photograph from the warehouse. Wiry neck. Wiry glasses and hair. An odd resemblance, if any at all. Wide-shouldered. Her hips rounder. Her eyes dull like a hungry ghost's, crookedly staring, one eye larger than the other. Her lips bent.

"Are you Abril?"

The phone rings.

"Pretty please," she begs. "Answer the phone, why don't you. With sugar on top."

"Who is calling?"

"I don't know. You tell me. Maybe a nuisance call. Maybe someone important. Answer it."

I peek inside the apartment. The phone shakes beneath the baby crib where I left it.

"You are not on lease," the super yells up to us. "Your name, it is not on lease."

"His name is too on the lease," she says.

"No," I tell her. "I cannot be on the lease. How could I be?" I look around the apartment. What to see? The same as earlier. My cushion sunken from meditation. Candle wax dripping. "Are you Abril?"

She ignores me. The phone rings. She yells down the stairs to the super. "Yeah? Well, the place has bed bugs." She pulls off her coat, bares her arms, itching them, scratching up blood. "Bedbugs aren't on the lease either, you know." Her words smell of saline and sulfur. "And that lawn chair was a piece of garbage. It ripped my bathing suit, you pervert." She slams the door. The phone rings. She looks beneath the baby crib. "Answer it," she yells. Her neck is blotched and her face twisted with brown freckles and scabby red pustules dotting her temples. White acne scars on her jaw. "Answer the phone." She wears a loose-fitting sweater, black and gray, slumped off one shoulder.

The phone rings a half trill more and dies.

"Damnit, lama. See what you did." She stumbles into me, against my chest. "You missed the phone call." Then she lets out a long breath, releasing her tension into the space around her, leaning on me. "At least you've come." She clutches my robes in balled fists. "At least you're here with me now."

I lean my head back away from her, so I might see her better. "Are you Abril?"

She places her other cheek to my chest and coughs. "Yeah."

"And you know why I am here?"

"Yeah." She leans in deeper. "I know. You've come to help me."

"I have come to help everyone," I say. "Which I will do, once you give it to me."

She sighs. "Give what?"

"The dorje."

"No, no, lama." She places a finger to my lips. "Don't talk now. Relax. Let's take this moment together, because you've come a long, long way to help me. That's what's important. And that's why you're here. Let's start again. I say, *So you've come to help me?* And you say, *Yes.* That's all." She leans close. "Can you say that? Can I hear you say *Yes?* You have come to help me."

Lesson 9

The greatest wisdom is seeing through appearances.

SHE STUMPS ME.

So you've come, she says.

First, she stumps me with her obviousness. Yes. Certainly, I have come. How else did I get here?

Second, with her obfuscation. Her suggestion that I had come specifically with her in mind. To specifically answer her cry. Without understanding that as a bodhisattva I aid all manner of persons, animal, flora, and enemies. Not just her.

"You had a health insurance policy with Sonny Heller." I reach inside my inner robe pocket and pull out Choki's list of deceased Tibetans.

No, not that.

I reach inside my inner robe pocket and pull out her policy. I show it to her.

"It stinks." She leans back, not trusting it. "Besides, Sonny rescinded my policy."

"Do not make it more complicated than need be," I tell her. "It has a newspaper clipping attached." I stay focused. "Icons of Drepung to Visit Denver. Why is such an article as this taped to your policy?"

She takes the policy from me and throws it aside. She cups my elbows in her hands, pulling me close, "Stop it, lama." Her body feels feverish, her hair scratchy against my chin. She presses upon me awkwardly, unbudging, a little shorter than I am, and I consider all over again—she could be the girl in the photograph, judging from how she feels. Perhaps I should have looked at her glossy longer.

"You knew him, did you not?" I ask.

"Who?"

"Sonny Heller." I show her his business card. *Life is Hell.* She looks at it without concern, and then turns her cheek back against my chest.

"I don't believe that. Let's not talk about it, okay?"

About what, exactly? Her knowing Heller? His being killed? "I am not here strictly on detective business, if that is what worries you," I assure her. "Or at least I have never been a detective before. But I can say this. Avoidance is a form of attachment, and attachment a form of obsession. We escape from neither."

"Uh huh." She tilts her head back. "Although, you would think avoidance would be the opposite of attachment, no? From the way the word sounds."

"The Buddha tells us avoidance is suppressed attachment. Just another obscuration that keeps us from seeing who we truly are. Self-denial. Replacing self with an image of self, and someone we would prefer to be."

"No, no, no, lama. Don't make things so confusing. Avoidance keeps us from facing what's trying to kill us."

"No," I instruct her. "Avoidance is obsessing that everything might kill us."

"So then avoid it? Survive. That's why we're here. To continue being here. For survival. And you—you're here to help me. Right?"

Why ask again? "Yes," I say. "I am a bodhisattva."

"Good. Because I had insurance once. And then when I went to use it, I didn't have it any more. Sonny took it away."

"And you are angry because of it."

"Yes."

"So you stole the dorje from him. Committed lingchi?"

"Now you sound like a detective. I thought you said you weren't one."

"I just like seeing what is in front of me. Perhaps it was someone else, and you merely put them up to it. So you could take the dorje."

Daidyal's voice interrupts me, "Is that the most convincing you can sound? The best you can say to her?"

"Quiet," I snap. I focus back on Abril. "As a bodhisattva, my mission is to help."

She cups the nape of my neck in one hand, leans back snapping the fingers of her other hand in my face. "Don't get squirrely on me, lama. I don't know what you're talking about. Dorje? What's that?"

I pause. I innocently explain to her, "In the shipment at the warehouse."

"I was not at the warehouse. Listen. You sound confused. Let me explain. I had insurance, and now I don't. That's wrong. And you are here to right that wrong, as a bodhisattva should." She pokes my chest. "To help get me get my insurance back. *Capisci*?"

Capisci what? What is this language she speaks, this way of speaking to me? A lama. "Get you insurance? No, no. There is no need for insurance. Once I have the dorje, I can bring you to enlightenment. See it like this, see things as they are—insurance is just insurance. Something I know nothing about. But enlightenment, that is a freeing of self. For all beings."

"I didn't bring you here for enlightenment. I brought you here to get my insurance back. Life or death."

"Are you sick?"

"Sick? No, I'm not sick. But what happens if I get sick, or want to have a baby? Something like that? I pay for insurance, but when I need it, they rescind it. That's how insurance works. It shouldn't work that way."

"But you are not sick. You do not need it. And once you are enlightened, you will not need it even more than now."

"What are you talking about? You think I'm being unreasonable? I'm not being unreasonable. Help me get my health insurance back. Easy peasy. Bingo. That's why you're here. Enough said."

My voice cracks. "I would not even know where to start looking for insurance. I am not a bureaucratic kind of person."

Her jaw flexes, and her eyelids flutter. "We start by tearing this shit down, that's where we start. Tear this shit down."

I am taken aback. "I am a bodhisattva. I do good, not tear things down. How could I?"

"You know how. With black magic."

A low wave jitters through me. I pause to breathe, the story momentarily suspending, then resuming again. "I do not do black magic."

"You're a bodhisattva, aren't you?"

"Yes."

"So what? You're the good-doing kind of bodhisattva, even if the results are bad. Or are you a bad-doing kind of bodhisattva who makes results good? Cause and effect, right? Because if you're just the good-doing kind, that's not how you survive in this world. That's how you get run over. How your story doesn't get told, because you're dead. Like Heller. That insurance man."

"You knew him?"

"I didn't know him. That's not the point. You *know* black magic. That's what important."

Of course she knew him. Of course she knew about him bringing in a shipment of artifacts, plus the dorje, stapled right there to her insurance policy. The one that was rescinded.

I think of the emporium. Of asking about it. Until Daidyal interrupts.

"A bit of a pistol, isn't she, lama? Such gravitas. A survivor. I like that in a girl."

"She is delusionary," I say. But why even talk with him? No, I must focus on Abril. "I am here for the dorje," I tell her. "Plain and simple. The Most Precious of Objects. When you see it, you will rejoice for the betterment of all sentient beings and abandon this silly quest for insurance. Help me, why not? Help me find Sonny Heller's killer. If it is not you, if you are not involved, then help me and show me the purity of your existence. You will be blessed for being chosen for such a mission. A newspaper clipping about the dorje's arrival was stapled to your insurance policy. Why?"

"My rescinded policy."

"It means something."

"Nothing means anything, lama. You should know that."

"Still, we must stick to the path."

"What path? You're saying you came to Colfax Avenue for enlightenment. This shit hole? You're way off the path, pal. I ask you to be a bodhisattva, even in the teensiest little way, and you refuse? Because you're too busy trying to help everybody, instead of just me?"

"In rebirth, one does not choose where to be reborn, Colfax or not," I explain. "One simply arrives."

"You're like a Mars Rover, just roaming around up there bumping into things." Her head bobbles. "Listen. You're here because of *me*. Get that straight. Because I need you here. Because I need insurance. So bodhisattva up and do what you're supposed to do."

"Sonny is dead," I tell her.

"Sonny who?"

"The insurance man."

"What do I care?"

"A shipment arrived at the warehouse and he was killed."

"What, like a plane landed someplace with stuff in it? Big deal."

"A shipment with the dorje. And now the dorje is missing. And Sonny rescinded your insurance policy." I watch her reaction. "You look suspicious," I tell her. "The police are going to want to speak with you. If you have the dorje, just give it to me. So it may all be over with."

Daidyal materializes further now, full form, so that I can see him. "Interesting interrogation skills you exhibit there, lama. Tell me, as a detective, do you ever question your own mind, or only a suspect's?"

"Shut up," I tell him. I focus on Abril.

"Listen to her," Daidyal says. "She is very good. Perhaps she should be your teacher, now that you have fired me." He sits atop Abril's rickety kitchen table, his feet propped on a chair, chin in his hands. "Everyone can use a little guidance."

"Hey. You listening to me?" she asks.

Daidyal shushes me. "Quiet. She speaks."

But instead of speaking, she lifts her sweater over her head, pulling it and her shirt up while turning her back to me. From this stance, I observe how she appears curved and rounded, like maybe she could be the girl in the photo. "You know, those dead Tibetans in the ally…" she asks. "You know what it is to lose someone, lama?"

I change my focus from her naked back to re-focus on the baby crib behind her. "Is that why you are angry? Because you lost someone? Because you did not have insurance, you lost someone?"

"You can't lose what you don't have. Right? You studied black magic. You know that. And you know that goodness sometimes dresses up ugly, and that ugly's just something the other person sees." She faces me now, her breasts goose-bumped. "You said yourself, you didn't choose Colfax. Why not me? How about me choosing it for you and conjuring you here?"

"How could you do that?"

"You're Lama Rinzen Naraka of Tibet, famed for black magic

and for all the shit you pulled back in the day."

"I seek enlightenment, pure and simple. I do not practice black arts." My tone stays flat, unprovoked. Perhaps even convincing.

"But you did once. And what we once did is what we become."

"Lesson learned," Daidyal pronounces. "A lesson in karma. She is good, lama."

She shakes her head. "Google says you do black magic, and I'm going with Google." She hands me a computer printout. "You studied black arts at the Monastery of White Rice in Lhasa. Drepung Abbey."

"No," I tell Daidyal. "She is confused."

Although it is true, I raided Drepung once—just once—to re-trieve the dorje. I look at her printout. It appears as nothing more than a hasty compendium of my life's shortcomings. Over many lives.

"I am a Buddhist monk of the Kagyu lineage," I explain. "Black magic is an impractical and unprincipled craft, primitive in nature, and certainly it does not adhere to the great teachings of the Buddha."

"Been Googling you all week, lama. The Magician Abbot of Drepung, he was your teacher. You turned on him. Some argu-ment about some bullshit, or something—I skipped that part, it sounded boring."

"My, my." Daidyal gleams. "She has a direct way of knowing things, does she not? And so acutely accurate. And cutely stated, too. So naked she appears. Look at her, lama. She speaks to you."

"You were the scourge of Tibet," Abril says. "Everyone feared you."

I explain it honestly, so she might hear what I say. "Daidyal..." —the air chokes as I speak. The story pauses as I look for words, and then resumes— "the abbot was once a great teacher. Once. But he allowed himself to be seduced by a witch, living her life in-stead of his own. Instead of living his commitment to the Dharma. When he turned to her, he turned against me, his student.

Naturally, when a teacher turns on his student…he will excuse it as a lesson I must learn. But the truth is, he broke his vow. That's all it was. He stole the dorje from me, as the witch seduced him to do. Thusly, he was transfixed by her, and the dorje has been lost to we Kagyu ever since. There. I have laid it out. Certainly you can see what is in front of you, just as I have explained it."

Daidyal moans. "Oh, really, is that how to speak to a woman? Good god, man, she's nearly naked. Can't you think of anything better to say?"

"But why can't you say it, lama?" she asks. "You killed him. Everything dies. I have brought you here to do some good and tear this shit down. To bring us all insurance, as we deserve. As is necessary. Survival. This is what matters."

"The Buddha says we need not survive," I say, "and that we each exist in emptiness."

"Well, the Buddha's nuts. Stop listening to him. He's crazy."

Such a mind. I try a different approach. I bow and ask, "You say you lost someone. A child?" I look at the crib.

"I didn't lose anyone." She slips her sweatpants and undies to her ankles and hobbles across the floor to cup her hands atop my shoulders stepping out of them, kicking them aside. "I'm only asking you to do this for me. To do the right thing. Right now. All right? Seize the moment. Do that. That's what I do. You want to be here with me, you got to learn to do that. Like right now, be with me. Wait here and be with me. I need to take a shower." She lets me go. "But, yeah. Since you ask, I know what it is to lose someone. The bond between a mother and child. I know nobody lives forever. And when they die, they leave a little something behind so people remember them. Yeah, maybe a child. But if you want to have a child, you got to have insurance. Otherwise, hospitals charge you right up the yin yang."

She turns and walks to the back of the apartment. Naked, through dull lighting and dim candle glow. So dim, I am unable to decipher the shadow on her upper glute as either birthmark or tattoo. Or anything really.

"Why was your policy rescinded?" I ask.

"In the West, go see a doctor, they write it down. They call it a pre-existing condition. They tell the insurance companies, so you never know what's covered and what's not. Or what pre-exists."

"All conditions pre-exist."

"Tell that to an insurance man." She is all voice now, having disappeared into back bathroom. The cell phone inside my pocket rings.

I answer.

The phone asks, "You still looking for a dorje?"

A hard voice to recognize, or to discern as either male or female. Tibetan or gweilo. Or Chinese.

Nor can I figure who exactly knows I am here on Colfax? Who followed me? Whose story is this, or what number they called? Or how I even got this cell phone?

"You saw him, right?" the voice on the phone asks. "All cut up. And now you're looking for the dorje, aren't you? Meet me downstairs, outside the Aim Straight. Let's talk."

The phone clicks.

"Who's that calling?" Abril singsongs from the bathroom.

"I should go," I tell her.

"You can't go. I'm the one who brought you here."

"I have to meet someone."

"I'm the one who brought you here. Remember that, lama."

I step out of the apartment onto the landing and descend down the steps to Colfax. Abril steps out after me, wet and dripping and towel-less, watching my descent. "Your Buddha says life is empty. Do you know what he means by that? He means just because you go looking for something, it doesn't mean it's there. Things that are missing, for instance. Or why we do what we do."

My mukluks grate each step of my descent, scuffing dirt and sand and making little scraping sounds. The sounds keep me from hearing what she says, and from knowing what exactly it means.

LESSON 10

Intention tells the mind what to perceive.
Attention holds the mind on the perceived.
In this way, perceiver and perceived become one.

SHE SAYS SHE IS THE cause for my being here. Westerners do that—see themselves as the center of things.

She says I am here to get her insurance, but why? People cannot conjure people for insurance, any more than they can marry someone or take a thankless job, just to have their health care provided for.

I look up and down Colfax, first one direction, then the other. Pedestrians cross crosswalks. Cars bump along bumper to bumper. A slow-moving cyclist weaves the street, occasionally twisting his front wheel to stand-still in place waiting for the cars to move.

How do things occur? Sort through the evidence box, and I come across Abril's rescinded policy. Attached to it, an article about artifacts arriving in a shipment. Search the shipment, and see a photograph of Abril naked. Possibly Abril. There to meet the shipment. She says it is not so. But her name is on the policy. The address where she lives is where I was reborn.

Mysteries pursue a wobbly path, snaking through resistance and diversions. Once born, beings fight to stay alive. They put up with anything to stay alive. Once I find the dorje, I can change all that. All beings will rise above mere existence and succumb to enlightenment. What will death matter then?

How long have I been here now? A half hour in the cold. The Colfax crowd thinning. The cars unclog and leave the street. Only the cyclist remains, circling one way, then the other. At the intersection he turns back east, gray snow kicking up from his tires leaving a blackened stripe down his back that bisects his jacket's lettering. *Spurtz Gra… la Snax.*

A second cyclist comes out to join him. His jacket striped with snow and reading the same. At the east end of the block, they turn again. The icy pavement slips beneath their wheels, but they hold steady heading west now, as other cyclists pedal from alleyways to pedal alongside them. I look at my cell phone. Who called me? Who said we should meet here on the street like this? Bicyclists, setting a trap?

I hit the dial back number, waiting to hear if it rings in any of the passing Spurtz jacket pockets.

No sound.

Not a one of them stops pedaling to answer. Instead, they pass in front of me snorting warmth from beneath their face masks. They ride the street, their goggled faces turned toward me, looking at me.

A half block more, and now other cyclists join in their circling back east. Back east, others join, and then circle west. Where still more join and then circle back east. Only this time, pedaling straight at me. Jumping the curb, the whole peloton of them, pedaling straight at me on the sidewalk. Slipping close, they unclip and swing their legs to dismount. They clutch their bikes by the seat backs and walk them around me, their goggle-stares bug-like.

The lead among them leans his ride against a street lamp. He walks bow-legged, spandex leggings shining in the snow. "This him?" He points me out.

"Yeah," another cyclist wheezes from beneath his scarf, his arm in a cast. "Kagyu." Others surround me, carrying tire irons and swinging bike chains oiled and gunky with road slop.

The lead cyclist pulls down the wheezing cyclist's scarf. I see two blackened eyes, a purplish veiny web of a nose. "You do this?" the lead asks me. It appears to be cyclist 1 from inside the Aim Straight. "There were two of them," the lead cyclist says. "Theodore's still in the hospital."

In life, it is important we see face to face the results we leave behind. I try to think of the words to ask if they are the ones who called me on the phone about the dorje.

The lead cyclist twists my chin in his gloved fingers, forcing me to see cyclist 1. "I asked, did you do this?" And since I do not answer, the lead cyclist then roundhouses me, gloves scraping my jaw like sandpaper. "You answer when I ask you something? Hear me? My man Rex here, he told you the Aim Straight's a Spurtz bar, right? And you ain't Spurtz. You're—what? Kagyu, or something? Never heard of it. Never seen your colors around Denver, either. What are you, like a gang of dress-wearers?" He pulls his ski mask down. His nose is red, his eyes blue, and he sports a graying soul patch and a waxed twill mustache. "Territory is territory, Kagyu. Important. Territory tells us where we belong. Where we begin and where we end."

It sounds reasonable enough, in a Western kind of way, the way they define things. But it's their crowding me I take a disliking to. So instead of answering, I just stay quiet.

So that the lead cyclist continues. "I don't live far from here. My apartment, not far. Down Colfax a few blocks. My apartment's got ants. In the kitchen and the bathroom and the laundry room, ants. Say I go over to Rex's here…"—he shakes his broken-nosed compadre by the back of his neck— "…get some of his ants. He's got ants too. Say I go over his place, get one of *his* ants and bring it over my place, with my ants. You know what they'd do? They'd rip the shit of each other. That's all I'm saying. Territory. Who belongs, who doesn't. You Tibetans, you show up in Denver living your little émigré lives, talking about enlightenment, like you're better than us. Like your God's better than our God."

"We do not necessarily believe in God," I explain. "Although you can if you like. We have nothing against it."

"The point is, you don't know what I know, Kagyu. And that's your problem." He spits at the sidewalk, where it freezes limey green. "You come here, you want to fit in, that's fine. Let me do you a favor, make a deal. Because that's how we do it here in the West, we make deals. You want to make a deal? Huh?" He gloves my chin again, a little lighter this time. "How about, you find that dorje and bring it to me. It's worth four point nine million, you know? That's a heck of a deal. You bring it to me, and your world, my world, put them together. Make one world big enough for both of us."

"When I find the dorje," I tell him, "it will benefit all worlds. Yours, mine, everyone's."

"Yeah? Everyone's? Except this is the West, so I don't care about everyone. Just me. Bring that to us Spurtz boys, and we'll see it benefits those who deserve it to benefit. Without having to waste it on everyone."

"The dorje's value is not monetary like that," I tell him. "Not something that can be split in that way."

One of the cyclists in the crowd whips a bike chain against my legs. I can barely feel it. "Not monetary? What? You saying it's nothing?"

"I am just saying…" I say.

"Don't say anything," the lead tells me. "Just shut up and see things my way. There is no good, and there is no bad. There's whether you fit in, and whether you don't. You want to know why the insurance man was killed? Because that's what happened, that's all. Plain and simple. See what's in front of you. Forget the insurance man. Things have no meaning, so stop thinking about them like they do. You want to convince us of something? Something like enlightenment. Find the dorje. Bring it to us. Like you belong."

It is how they talk in the West. Friendly, but pushy. "Did you kill him?" I ask.

"Kill him? I didn't kill nobody. We all have our territories, Kagyu. Insurance men have theirs, we have ours, and Tibetans, they don't have anything. The question you got to ask—whose story you want to be a part of? Ours? Theirs? Whatever you choose, that's what you become. Ain't no going back from it."

"Ain't no going back," the bicyclists say. Then one by one, they rack their bikes in the bike rack outside the Aim Straight and Shoot. They gaggle inside. Cyclist 1 gaggles last, his neck bent and his head down. He points out something for the lead to see. A limo idling its engine curbside on Colfax.

The lead stares the limo down. "Being new here," he says to me, "you're going to find a lot of people trying to sell you something." He snorts through one nostril and spits to the sidewalk again. "But that dorje, you find it, you're going to want to talk to me first. Talk to my guy. Insurance guys talk a good game. But it's just talk."

"Did you kill Sonny Heller?" I ask again.

He snorts. "I didn't kill anybody. What about you? You kill anyone lately?" Then he leaves me and goes into the Aim Straight, so that a second or two later, it is as if he had never been here at all.

While the limo shivers curbside, its driver steps from behind its wheel to open its rear door. He tells me to climb inside, saying, "I believe you received our call. About the dorje."

The limo looks like Hellers's ride this morning down at the warehouse.

"Were they expecting something in the shipment?" I ask.

"Why don't you ask them yourself, officer."

Looking into the Aim Straight, I notice silhouettes watching me through dingy windows. Inside the limo, it feels warm and cushiony. Like what they call peace here in the West. Like how they sell cars on television.

By the time the driver assumes his seat at the wheel, I have already drifted into sleep. I dream of riding at the head of a vast niru army across the Tibetan plain, to rescue the Most Sacred of Objects. To liberate all mankind.

All beings, in fact. Whether men or not.

LESSON 11

Walk untouched. Unattached!

ELEVATOR DOORS OPEN. A RECEPTIONIST sits behind a wraparound desk with her cheeks rouged and a ring through her nose, wearing pink round glasses and an auburn ponytail. She smiles with big eyes and big plump lip-sticked lips.

"Well, look at you, all dressed in your Buddhist robes and all. Are you Buddhist?"

I look down at myself and see where the bicycle chain left a streak of grease on my robes. I look around the space where I am standing and notice the Heller Insurance reception area is decorated with cleanly angular furniture and crisp white walls. On the walls hang framed artifacts of old Tibet behind glass-covered displays. Prayer flags. Tingsha bells. Buddha stonework. Each with an index card loudly inscribed with the date of the object's Western discovery.

Life boxed as art. How the West decorates itself.

On a far wall, I see a silver sword tamped with jewels and the design of two battling yaks. Its index card says *Short Sword, used for administration of lingchi. Drepung, Lhasa, Tibet. 16th century.* In the glass's reflection I see the confusion on my face, staring at the sword's hilt speckled in blood, and a small lock keeping the case clamped shut.

I flick the lock with my finger. It swivels.

"Come on, tell me. Are you?" the receptionist pleads. "A Buddhist, I mean."

She stands now, tall, skinny, and framed in the light of a large picture window behind her. Her eyes pop like polka dots. Her dress too. Cream polka dots on a red background.

"Who owns this?" I point at the knife.

"The Hellers. They own all this stuff."

Glancing around, it makes sense now. The headline of the article on the insurance policy about icons of Drepung coming to visit Denver. Set up by Heller Insurance. Sonny killed with a lingchi blade. Maybe this one.

"Who has the key to these cases?"

"The Hellers. They have the key to all these cases, plus a tea cup collection and a collection of baseball cards and one of little tiny liquor bottles. Scotch mostly. Some Crown Royal, but mostly Scotch they get from airplanes when they go places." She pretends to hold one between her thumb and index finger, pinkie raised, and sip from it. "They are collectors."

I have heard of this American pastime, stockpiling stuff, calling it a collection. Possession obsession.

"All sorts of Buddhist stuff, they collect," the receptionist says. "More than what you see here. Some they keep someplace else. In a warehouse."

"On 33rd and Josephine?"

"Oh, I'm the wrong person to ask about that. I'm not good with addresses. So tell me. Are you Buddhist, or aren't you?"

I lean myself over her swooped ash wood desk, folding my hands, lowering my eyes, not out of respect or subservience, but more to read a claim she is working on. Four point nine million. Big number.

"I am Lama Rinzen Naraka of the Kagyu lineage." I reach inside my pocket and pull out a business card. It says *Detective,* but I hand it to her anyway. How I had gotten the card I cannot recall.

"Ooh, I knew it. A Buddhist. Me too."

"Have you worked here long, for the Hellers?"

"Freelance, yeah, like forever. Huey. Curly. They don't hire full-timers, because you know, insurance and benefits and all that. So I freelance."

"What about Sonny? Did you work for him?"

Her bubbliness bursts. "Horrible," she says, and she picks up a paper clip and unbends it, twirling its stem in her fingers. "Of all the three brothers, he's the nicest of them all. Every morning, *hello* he'd say. *Good night* when he left at night." She tries smiling, but is unable. "The place feels sad without Sonny here. You know what the Buddha says? Everything sucks."

"Everything is suffering," I correct her. "Not everything sucks. And even at that, he did not mean suffering. More of a dissatisfaction. Everything is dissatisfying."

"Yeah? Well, we do what we have to. Otherwise, why bother? That's what the Buddha should have said." She shrugs. "Somebody killed him." She spreads her elbows and props her cheeks between her fists. "Terrible." She lifts her glasses and rubs her eyes, and then an instant later, she effervesces once again, bubbling all over again. "Now, come on. I never met a lama before. So go ahead and tell me something."

"I just did. Everything is suffering, but really, it is more like dissatisfying."

"No, not that. Tell me something to make me feel better on such a sad day, with Sonny getting killed and all."

"Someone called me from here. I can tell you that. They asked that I come." I show her my cell phone.

She twists her face. "Come here about what?"

"The dorje."

"The dorje? What's that?"

"A kind of scepter. Beautiful to behold. Jeweled and magnificent and crafted of gold. Very Buddhist. The Most Sacred of Objects. Perhaps you have seen it, here amongst the collectables?"

"No. Not here. Maybe at the emporium."

Such an odd word. And yet I have now heard it twice in one day.

"The Madame Sun's Olde Tibetan Emporium and Meditation Center," she says. "The Hellers donate stuff over there all the time. They say it's good for business, but I think they just mean it's a tax write-off."

"There is no Madame Sun," I tell her flatly, without making much out of it.

"Oh, yes there is." Her fingers tap the policy on her desk. "She even filed a claim for four point nine million. Just this morning. I am trying to process it now with the Heller's Excess and Surplus insurer." She whispers, so that this next part is a little harder to hear. "The Hellers don't usually insure for that kind of money. You insure for that kind of money, you got to get your Excess and Surplus insurer on board. You know?"

"Madame Sun did not file a claim," I say. Still, four point nine million, the number reverberates inside my head. "What could be worth such an amount?"

"Buddha statues. A whole shipment of them. Made of plastic and all the way from Asia."

Four point nine million for plastic statues? "A bit extravagant," I suggest.

"I wouldn't know, lama…"—she looks at my card again— "… detective? Ooh, I like that, disguising yourself as a detective." She winks. "Especially when you're really a Buddhist. Do you know at home, Cassie my roommate and I have three little Buddhas on our windowsill where the cat sits. Hear No Evil, See No Evil, Speak No Evil. They're supposed to be monkeys, but instead they're Buddhas. Cute, huh? Yeah, Madame Sun, she insured the shipment for four point nine million. Forty-nine Buddha statues. Wow. You got to get your Excess and Surplus insurer to okay something like that. And you know, I don't think the Hellers did. You can ask them, if you like. Normally you couldn't, but today you're in luck. Normally, Curly doesn't come in so early, but today, yeah, he's here. They're both here. Curly and Huey. Can I ask you something, lama? Can we get a selfie maybe, me and you? I want to show Cassie. Here. Come closer, why don't you?" The receptionist leans across the desk and pulls me in, hugging me, and extending her phone in front of us, then flashing it. Bubbles of light douse my vision, blinding me. Inside the blindness, I hear floor tiles shifting. Someone walking toward us. The bubbles slowly burst.

"Detective." It sounds like a Heller. Huey, more specifically. He steps out from the bubbles, extending a hand at me. "Thank you. So good of you to come."

"He's a lama," the receptionist says.

"A lama?" Huey exclaims. "How nice. And your name, miss?"

"Mimi. Mimi the receptionist. I've been working here like forever. Freelancing."

Heller points a knuckle at her. "I like the enthusiasm, Mimi. And the attentiveness. A lama, you say?" He looks at me. "Well, lama, here at Heller Insurance we take pride in our freelancers. Good for us. Good for the economy. Good for everyone. *Ha hah hah.*" He laughs. "This way please. Follow me."

Before following I try reading the claim on Mimi's desk, looking for a signature or some verification, but the flash of her camera still bubbles my vision. I try focusing. Obviously the Hellers have called me here about the dorje. I need to get it from them. Before any more insurance claims get filed.

Spots of light burst my vision. I stumble after Huey. He walks slowly, turning to be sure I keep up, waving his arms about and speaking about the artifacts on the walls. "Our collection, quite extensive, lama. Quite interesting, but we love all this Buddha paraphernalia. At Heller Insurance, we appreciate the émigré and his travails. Culture is so important, won't you say, detective? Or should I address you as lama? Two jobs, so *de rigueur* these days, two jobs, lama and detective. Go for the gusto, I say. Make your millions while you're still young. How old are you? Let me ask, do the police provide your health insurance? I only ask because I'd like to know, that's all." He stops in front of a conference room and gestures me inside. "But how about we discuss that later. When Curly's not around." He waggles his head and index finger *no no no* with a puckered look on his face.

Inside the conference room its glass walls are frosted and framed inside stainless steel. Transparent, yet opaque, like so much of the West. On the other side of a large teak conference room table a picture window overlooks Denver. Equally as large as Mimi's window in the reception area, only with an alternate and seedier view of Denver's train yards and squat buildings and chimney stacks leaking fumes. Seated with his back to us, Curly Heller stares out at the view. I take a seat at the table across from him, smelling the room's mentholated radiator warmth. Curly swivels his chair to face me, his one hand on its armrest, the other clenching a folder he drops atop the tabletop. "We appreciate you joining us, officer." He glances at brother Huey. "Shameful, a fine insurance man like Sonny getting killed. As insurers, we so often provide service to the bereaved in their time of need. But who grieves for us when our time comes? Have you ever asked yourself that before, officer?"

"Not specifically, no."

A silence then settles in the room, as both brothers fidget with their thoughts. An uncomfortable silence.

"You called about the dorje?" I ask.

Curly stares at the file in front of him. "Dorje?"

"In the shipment?"

"Yes. Tell me, officer..."

"He is a lama," Huey interrupts.

"Tell me, lama. What is a dorje anyway?"

I look from one brother to the other. "It is the Most Sacred of Objects."

"Valuable?"

"In different ways, yes."

"You are asking about it being in the shipment? Because I assure you, it was not."

My chair is comfortably cushioned, but it now collapses a bit. Not from Curly's questioning. More his contention the dorje had not shipped. "How do you know?"

"It's not there, that's how we know."

"It was stolen."

"It was not stolen, lama. Damn thing doesn't even show up on the shipping manifesto. Buddha statues, yes, they're on the manifesto, forty-nine plastic figurines and each one safely arrived and standing in place down at the warehouse. But no dorje. We are collectors. We would know if something like the dorje shipped, and certainly would have been prepared for it. Frankly, I am not even sure such a thing exists. That is the case I will present to our Excess and Surplus insurer. It does not exist."

"It does exist."

"Not in the shipment, it doesn't. And the shipment is all Heller Insurance is responsible for. So in that manner, it does not exist."

What to hear? Denial. Shirked responsibility. What they do in the West. The inane contention that something cannot be real if not seen or touched or tasted or heard or smelled. Mere senses.

But what about the mind? Is that not a sense as well? In my mind, I hold the dorje's sensation, without a need to see, touch, or taste it. "It most certainly did ship," I say.

"Not according to the manifesto, it didn't. The policy clearly delineates we are only responsible for what shipped. Buddha statues, pure and simple. We will pay no claim for anything more."

"But I have not come to discuss claims."

"You will discuss this claim, lama. We've received a claim, and we will not pay it. Four point nine million dollars, can you imagine? From a Madame Sun. Do you know her?"

"There is no Madame Sun."

Heller seems surprised. "Well, let's hope not. Because we will not pay."

Huey takes the seat next to mine at the table, speaking more gently. "With scammers like this, it rarely is the name on the claim who is actually filing. Perhaps there is no Madame Sun, as you say. Or perhaps her identity's been stolen. Even more reason…"—he considers his words carefully, nodding them out to me— "…even more reason not to pay."

Curly lifts a glossy photo, the one of the girl at the warehouse, from his folder and lays it on the table. "What can you tell us about her?"

I do not look at it, even if in a vague way it does resemble Abril, who claims to have conjured me here. "I am here about the dorje," I state clearly, calmly, with only a slight strain of crackling in my words. "You called me. I came. Of course it shipped."

"Lama, if there is anything to understand about insurance, it's this. People file claims to which they are unentitled. All the time. Obviously, Sonny was not alone at the warehouse. The girl was there as well. Do you know her name? Anything about her?"

Perhaps it looks evasive, cloudy, unfocused on what is right there in front of me, but I push the photo aside. "Whoever killed Sonny," I suggest, "stole the dorje. We find it, we find his killer. It is as simple as that."

Huey, seated next to me, whispers, "Do you know her name, lama? That is all we are asking."

"Fiddlesticks," Curly booms. "Her name's Abril. She was a client of Sonny's. She requested a meeting at the warehouse. Perhaps I overstate saying she was a client. What I mean, she is an ex-client. Her file's in front of you. You can see her name there. A real story, this one. Everything about her."

He nudges the file to me while Huey drums his fingertips on the table top along either side of himself. "Let me confess, lama, I blame myself," Huey says. "We knew they were meeting. Sonny was a respected insurance man. Naturally, at a time like this, we hope you will keep our conversation confidential, and please tell us if she was only targeting Sonny, or if it's the business she's trying to destroy?"

"The business?"

"There are those who would like to tear insurance companies down," Curly says. "Perhaps we appear cold and ruthless, asking such a question. Sometimes in a family business, the emphasis winds up more on business than family. Sonny was a lonely man. A workaholic. We knew this about him. Not much we could do about it. And this Abril had a health policy that Sonny sold her. Later, he found she lied on her application. Naturally, we rescinded the policy. What else could we do?"

"Lying on an insurance application," Huey says, "who does such a thing?"

"What did she lie about?" I ask.

"Pre-existing conditions."

"All conditions pre-exist. You believe she killed him because of pre-existing conditions?"

"She wants to tear us down," Huey says. "That's why she killed him."

"Sonny was killed by lingchi. A Chinese form of execution. Where would a gweilo girl possibly learn such a thing?"

Curly twists in his seat. "Shouldn't you be asking her that? As we taxpayers pay you to do."

"She ran up a lot of bills," Huey says. "Medical bills. Which we are also under no obligation to pay."

"She is not even sick. Why do you believe she killed your brother?"

They appear uncomfortable. They squirm. "She broke into our offices," Curly confides. "She stole her rescinded policy like she meant to rub it in our faces."

"She stole her own policy? Is there any crime in that, particularly if it was rescinded?" It sounds odd to me. She said she had no insurance, and needed me to get it for her. I have the policy in my pocket. "Why would she do that?"

"To go to the insurance commission. File a complaint." Curly creaks forward in his chair. "We are a small business, trying to make a dollar. We don't need the insurance commission snooping around. Sonny said she told him to meet her at the warehouse, and she'd give it back. I believe he worked something out with her."

"So you did know Sonny would be there at the warehouse? When I asked earlier, you told me you didn't."

"I told you," Curly states. "We received a phone call."

"Why would she suggest meeting," I ask, "at a warehouse, where a shipment he insured was arriving?"

Curly opens the file and extracts a document labeled *Shipping Manifesto*. He turns it so I can see. *Contents of Delivery*: *49 Budai statues*. Nothing more. "You tell me," he says. "We called you, lama, because she killed our brother. It's your job to bring her in. Who is the lead full-timer on this case? Who do you report to?"

I have never been a detective before, but I understand how people bring down pressure. Their tone saying one thing, their words another. "Inspector Fernandez."

"Did he explain to you that Heller Insurance holds the policy on the precinct. On the entire police operation."

"I did not know that, no."

"Well, now that you do, what does it make you think?"

What should it make me think, I wonder. And what should it not? "It makes me think that if Sonny was such a fine insurance man, why would he insure a shipment of statues for four point nine million?" I push the manifesto toward Curly, floating it across the table until it rests within his reach. "Plastic statues, at that."

He steeples his fingertips together, resting them atop the bridge of his nose. "Our job is to deal with insurance claims. Yours, to arrest Sonny's killer. Focus, lama. Perhaps I should call Fernandez."

"No. Just a moment, brother. We called the detective here. Let me speak with him a moment." Huey takes my arm and helps me from the chair. "My brother does not mean to tell you your business, lama. But arresting her would be a big help." He stands me up and walks me to the hall, back toward reception. "He's upset. We both are. Sonny's death, and all. But Heller Insurance is a generous business. Our customers, they are practically family. I only ask that you consider this, when it comes to deciding your own insurance needs. Consider Heller Insurance. I'll see what I can do about Curly."

I have not been a detective for long, but I know the saccharin sound of being sold. I pull my elbow from his grip. "I do not need insurance."

"Oh." He winces. "I see," his eyes a pair of thin slits sizing me up. "Then for your sake, lama, ask her what was she doing there. Find out what she did with the policy she stole. And think about what we're saying. Perhaps Mimi can call you an elevator now." He snaps his fingers at the receptionist. "Mimi, right? That is your name?" Then he leaves the reception area without looking back.

Mimi sticks her tongue out at him, mimicking his words without repeating them. "Such an ass. Does the Buddha let me say that? That he's an ass."

In front of her, she is still working on the four point nine million dollar claim. Although I prefer to not discuss it, I point to it, "Madame Sun?" I ask.

"Her emporium."

It makes no sense. If Madame Sun had followed me, how could she have established an emporium so soon? And why follow me? She has no need. Plus, she does not exist.

"Tell me," I say to Mimi, "and I know this can be difficult for you at this time of Sonny's sudden demise, but did he have a meeting scheduled this morning at the warehouse? With a woman named Abril?"

"Oh, that's not difficult at all," she bubbles. "All I need do is check the computer." She mouses around the screen on her desk. "Yes. Abril. No last name. 8AM this morning."

"Where?"

She checks. "At the White House."

"The White House?"

"Says so right here. WH."

"The warehouse?" I ask.

"Oh, yeah, that's probably it. The warehouse. That's closer than the White House, isn't it, because like the White House, that's in Maryland, isn't it?"

Could the brothers be right? Abril indicated she did not know Sonny. "Meeting about what? Her policy?" I ask. "The one Sonny rescinded?"

"Well, to tell you the truth, Curly wanted it rescinded. Huey, too. But Sonny never did actually rescind it. He just said he did."

"And Abril knew this?"

"Yeah, she knew. Poor girl. How do you survive without insurance?" Mimi then turns the computer screen to hide her mouthing from anyone else seeing. "I think she was pregnant." Then she flexes her eyebrows in a you-know-what-I-mean kind of way. "You know what I mean, how expensive it is having a baby without insurance."

Abril says she did not know Sonny. She said she was not ill.

"Without insurance," I ask, "she could not have afforded it?"

Mimi winks at me. "Not a chance."

LESSON 12

Nothing exists alone.
All things only exist in relation to another.

THE GROUND FEELS SHIFTY, UNSETTLED beneath my feet. A jagged skyline cuts into the setting sun. Hot Cousin leaks from the jukebox inside the Aim Straight and Shoot. Outside bicycles are parked and chained in a row.

I climb the stairs to the apartments. What to see? Sonny was Abril's insurance man. The brothers say he rescinded her policy. Mimi says he did not.

The brothers say she killed him. But they do not mourn over it.

All effects have their cause. All conditions pre-exist. And yet, nothing seems predictable. Why rescind insurance because of pre-existing conditions? Why say he rescinded it, when he had not?

Where is the dorje?

A long climb up the stairs to the apartments, one step, then another. I pause to catch my breath. Moments flush over me. I sweat. It tastes of salt. I resume climbing, remembering now that I have not eaten since being reborn.

At the top on the landing, I knock on Abril's door.

A hollow sounding door. No answer.

I push on it. The door is unlocked. Inside the shower is running, the air steamy. The Buddha on his altar drips with condensation. The candles still burn, and the Buddha still smiles, but Daidyal now sweats inside his picture frame. In the picture, he seems younger than earlier in her apartment when he materialized. Which way does time move? In a straight line? In a swirl?

In Abril's front closet I find a puffed down coat, camo flak overalls, roller blades, a woolen cap, mittens, gloves, glove liners, and a Spurtz Granola jacket.

Who do they work for, this Spurtz gang? Abril? Someone else? Miss Desire, they called her.

In the kitchen her sink is piled with dishes. Her counters, cupboards, all smell of old fruit and rotting squash. On the refrigerator, a news article. *Icons of Drepung to Vist Denver.* In a smaller font—*Sponsored by Heller Insurance.* Sonny's business card on the counter.

She knew him. She had to. Why else would he not rescind her insurance? Why would she say he had?

Air from the heating grates rocks the baby crib slightly. I peak inside, and see two Tibetan monk dolls propped against a crocheted pillow. One holds a braided prayer wheel. The other a bead of rock sugar mala beads. Their robes are old and torn. One has the stuffing knocked out of him.

"You're back?"

She stands in the living room, rubbing a towel over herself.

"Yes."

"What are you, like a *mi casa, su casa* kinda guy now? Just walking in like that?"

"The door was open."

With one towel wrapped around her, and another drying the goosebumps on her arms, she looks at the door. "Yeah. It is. I knew you'd be back."

"You told me you did not know Sonny Heller?"

Her eyes narrow to see me better. "Your jaw's bleeding."

I touch it. It feels damp. "Your Spurtz pals, the jacket in your closet, they are looking for the dorje, too. They came at me. Where is it, Abril?"

She stops drying herself. "First of all, a jacket in the closet doesn't mean I'm with the Spurtz gang, okay? Just for your did-dley-doh, I stole that jacket." She steps closer to dab at my jaw with her drying towel.

"Second..."—she speaks softer now—"those asshole Spurtz guys don't know anything about the dorje. They're bicyclists. Jocks. Primpers and preeners and don't give a shit about anything but themselves. Like high priests, not bodhisattvas."

"You say you brought me here for insurance, and that you do not know Sonny Heller. He reinstated your insurance. You even have his card on the table in your kitchen. The article pinned to your insurance policy, it's on your refrigerator."

She pauses, behaving like someone stuck for how to answer. "He did not reinstate my insurance. Yeah, sure, he was my insurance man." She pushes the towel through her hair, so it squeaks. "He sold me shit. Doesn't mean I know him. It was just business. Like Abe Vigoda says in the *Godfather, Godfather 2*, I don't know which one. He was old and he says, *tell Al Pacino it was just business.*"

"You lied on your application."

"Yea-ah?" She says it in two syllables, like why am I even asking.

"You said someone's missing from your life. Who? Sonny?"

She takes my shoulders and turns my chin so I look at her. "You been talking to the brothers, haven't you? They're trying to sell you insurance, right? It's a trap, lama. Don't do it."

"Why do you have a baby crib?"

"It was my mother's. I told you, I know the bond of a mother and child. Actually, the crib's mine. I'm the one who slept in it. She bought it when I was a baby, and it's kinda stuck with me ever since."

She does not look at me now, but I know what she means. I recall my own father dying. Soon afterward I left for the Shedra, never seeing my mother again. The Buddha says we suffer because of our attachments. Me going to the Shedra was my mother's idea, to learn black magic from the abbot magician Daidyal of Drepung. So I might return and place a spell on my uncle, so we might get my mother's silver back. The things we once were, this is what we become. The things we lose, they never leave us.

"I didn't kill him, if that's what you're asking," Abril says. "I know the brothers say I did, but they're insurance men. They'll say anything."

I wrap her in her drying towel. Candle light makes her skin glow. We stand close enough I cannot see if she has a tattoo or not. "You two were lovers?" I ask.

She pushes me back. "What?"

"The photo of you naked at the warehouse, he had one in his briefcase. They were all over the floor. The police think you were there."

"The police? Right. Insurance men by another name." She goes over to a laundry basket, sifts through its clothing. She drops the towel she's wearning and pulls out a pair of undies, which she slips over her ankles and up her legs. "Look at the imagination on you, lama. What? You like asking questions, playing cop? Here's a question for you. Why did you kill your teacher?" She shakes a pair of jeans in the air and steps into them, twisting them up over her legs. "Huh? Tell me that. It's not like I'm the only one who needs to answer stuff."

"Daidyal was a renowned abbot. The abbot of Drepung," I confess. "But he allowed himself to be seduced. He stole the dorje from me. I have been searching for it ever since."

As I speak, Daidyal's thin form appears. "This way of speaking, lama, is this what you want to say to her?"

"I am not talking to you." I spit it out without Abril hearing.

"She asked why you killed me? Why not say?"

"It does not matter. She and Sonny met, at the warehouse, where the dorje arrived. He is dead, she is not. That is what I am asking."

"You are not asking, lama, you are needling. Like a prissy old detective. Gweilos do not know lingchi, you said so yourself. Why insinuate she did it?"

Abril asks, "Are you listening to me, lama? What do you call killing a teacher like that? Jealousy? Rivalry? Mitracide?"

"Purity," I say.

Daidyal laughs. "Purity? Oh, I like this word *purity*. So many meanings. So many ways to say it."

"Purity?" Abril questions. She snaps the button of her jeans. "One guy's purity is another guy's porn, you ever hear that?" She reaches inside my robe and pulls out the photo. She eyes it skeptically. "You think that's me? You think that's what I look like? I don't look anything like that. First thing, I don't have a tattoo on my ass." She digs her hands into her jeans pockets, stretching to fit into them better. When she pulls her hands back out, she holds two crumpled twenties, one wad each. She looks at them, puzzled. "What? Did I conjure you here without any money?" She sounds genuinely curious. "Silly of me. Here." She hands me a wad.

"You did not conjure me, Abril."

"You don't want the twenty?"

I hesitate. "That is not what I am saying." Because I know the West, what it takes to survive. Sure, I want the twenty. I take it from her.

"Look, this dorje. It's a collector's item, right?" She holds a tee shirt over her head, stretches it down her over arms and chest, its front emblazoned with an image of the Buddha. *Inquire Within* it says. "I'm just saying, a girl conjures up a lama, he's not always what she expects. Maybe I screwed up with you. I'm new at it. I never conjured anyone before, so maybe I confused you."

"Confusion is Hell," I tell her.

"I'm sorry. But you're here now and all we got is one another." She pulls on the same sweater from earlier, her head popping out its neck hole, her eyes crooked, her hair too. "I'll help you, lama. Like a team. But you got to help me. Help me get insurance."

"How can I do that?"

"Black magic."

"I do not do black magic."

"Tear down these Hellers. Find the dorje, if you have to."

"You think they have it?"

She walks into the kitchen, her voice trailing behind her. "Sure, they have it. They're insurance men. Insurance men have all sorts of shit. They're like collectors or something."

Maybe she is coming around. Maybe she is starting to make sense, too. The Hellers come to the warehouse, unconcerned about Sonny's killing, non-responsive when asked about the shipment. They do not even care if it was lingchi or not that killed him.

She comes back into the living room carrying a small wooden box with a mandala carved in its lid. "Of course, they have it." She pushes the box into my hands, opens its lid, and pulls out a strand of baubles, looking at them, then tossing them back. She pulls another strand, then tosses them back as well. "I'm going to help you, okay, lama. Just focus on that. I'll admit something to you. I was at the warehouse, but I did not kill him."

"You were there?"

"When I arrived, the shipment was there. Sonny had gone through it. He was upset. Something appeared to be missing." She picks up a necklace from the box, looks at it.

"What convinced him to give your policy back?"

"He never gave me my policy back. Maybe he wanted to, but he was preoccupied about the shipment. Look, I don't really know him. He's just my insurance guy. All I know he was acting like something was missing, and like it might cost a lot of money." She turns her back on me and lifts the business ends of the necklace over her shoulders. "Here. Make yourself useful, why don't you. Put this on me."

I place the mandala box down upon the table and step up closer behind her. I lift each end of the necklace in the pudgy, reptilian fingers I was reborn with in this lifetime, pulling its bauble against her larynx. "Did he say who might have it?" I fidget with the petite-ness of the necklace's lock.

"There is something you need to understand about insurance men. They deny what's expected. They behave like men unaware. Like businessmen, all right?"

The necklace clasps bury inside my finger fat. "You think one of the brothers has the dorje?"

"I believe all three arranged for it to ship here, and it never came."

"Of course, it came." I hold the necklace strands so they ripple side by side, as if in a stream, each ripple locking to the other. The necklace clasps fasten. Things come together.

Abril steps to the other side of the room, away from me. "I was at the warehouse the morning Sonny was killed. Sometimes in a family business, they emphasize business more than family. Sonny said that once." She pulls the necklace, straightening its bauble in front of her.

"When did he say that?" I walk up to her. "I mean, you say you did not know him? He was just your insurance man. So when have you heard him say something like that?"

"I don't know. One time when he was selling me insurance, I guess."

I make her face me. "How much insurance did you buy from him?" Looking at her now, I do not really care to know. Looking at her, I see the necklace around her neck sagging loosely at her chest.

Small and shiny.

I lift its bauble in my fingers, its gold plating. Its bits of sparkly glass.

"Where did you get this?" Sparkly glass jutting out at either end into orbs.

She answers without interest. "You like it?"

"This is the dorje."

"This old thing? This is what you're making all the fuss about? It cost me like a buck, maybe a buck fifty. I got it down at the *All Things Asian* emporium."

The words wring out of her wry and twisted. "Where?"

"Madame Sun's Olde Tibetan Emporium and Meditation Center. Down on Colfax. In the cathedral part of town. If you like it, maybe we can go there. See if she has any more."

She has a smirk on her face, like she knows exactly what she is saying. That in every lifetime it happens like this. Once, twice, three times someone mentions a name from the past. From many lifetimes ago. Then time shortens. Then my search for the dorje gets hurried. I need to find it more quickly.

Because no matter how much I deny it, and no matter how non-existent she may be, Madame Sun has followed me here. Even if not possible, she has followed me.

"There is no Madame Sun," I tell Abril.

"Sure there isn't. She's just a name on an emporium. There's no Little Debbie, either. But I sure eat her cakes."

Once I led a niru attack upon Drepung, storming its plaza. Daidyal mocked me. I ripped the necklace from his throat so hard, its charms and talismans spilled on stone and rolled away. I ponder this a long while, staring at the bauble that hangs from the chain around Abril's neck. Until she leaves the living room for the bathroom in back. From where I hear its faucet running, as I remain alone in the living room.

Something thumps her door.

It goes *thwack*.

An unrecognizable sound.

I peek through the door's peephole.

No one there.

I open the door. An arrow reverberates in it's jamb, having splintered it. Ribbons and feathers float from the arrow's tail.

At the bottom of the stairs, a shadow pushes the iced door open out onto the street. I slam down the stairs, catching the door just before it clasps closed. I push my way out onto the sidewalk.

Whiteness obfuscates the scene.

Otherwise, no one. No one there.

Otherwise, everyone. Early night drinkers pushing from bar to bar. Smokers hunched in door stoops. Elderlies. Gweilos. Tibetans and Hispanics, all manner of creature. All shadows, indistinct in their design.

Fresh snow on the sidewalk and street. And in the snow, a bike tire's imprint, stretching from where I stand, out into the deep darkness that runs along Colfax Avenue.

LESSON 13

Herons, cats, and burglars
Achieve their intentions,
Going silently unobserved.
- *Shantideva*

ABRIL STANDS BESIDE ME ON the sidewalk in a down jacket and furry pants, a jangle of keys in her mitten.

"Who are these bicyclists?" I point out the tire track. Snow is filling it in, making it more and more invisible.

"You're asking me?" She walks the curb and jabs a key into the passenger door of a '71 Plymouth Duster. "Come on, get in." The car's exterior glows disco orange beneath its coating of white. Abril walks around the car wiping snow from the car's glass. I help, using my sleeve to clear the passenger windows. Then I open the door and settle into the passenger side of the car's cold, vinyl bench seat, where I see a clipped advertisement for Madame Sun's.

My cell rings. I answer.

"Lama lama bo drama. I got news for you."

"Mimi?"

"Like I told you," the receptionist says. "Sonny reinstated her insurance. He gave it to her at the warehouse this morning when they met."

"Are you sure?" Because I find it impossible. Because I have it in my pocket, marked rescinded. "Is there a second copy? Is that what he brought to the warehouse?" I ask. "Are you sure she knew this?"

"Of course she knew it. He sent her an email. I'm looking at it right here, in his Sent folder. Even paid her first year's premium. Paid it himself, out of his own pocket."

I watch Abril leaning over the car, scraping ice off the windows.

"Sounds nice, but maybe not so nice. Curly and Huey told him to pay it. She didn't steal her policy, lama. She stole others. Ten of them. Life policies. Term life. She was blackmailing the brothers. She and Sonny were meeting at the warehouse so she could give them back, where Sonny was supposed to give her her policy paid up for a year. Weird, huh? First she has a policy. Then she doesn't. And then she does. The more we look at a thing, the less it becomes what it is, and the more our way of seeing it. Is that something the Buddha said?"

I hang up. Abril climbs into the car and adjusts the seat, adjusts the rear view. Flashing red and white lights curve around the corner behind us. A peloton of cyclists puffing up from behind. Abril starts the Duster, checks the side mirror and kicks into traffic, cutting off those bicyclists. Trying to stop, they tip over sideways and skid out spawling along the street.

I brace the passenger door holding myself upright. The car lurches over icy road ruts. Its interior smells like a hot spring full of rotten eggs. "What is that?"

"East coast. I bought the Duster back east." She slaps the dashboard. "The smell of ocean rot and salty roads. Slant six though." She slaps the dash again. "Put up with a lot of east coast for a slant six. Engine never dies."

The seat beneath my robes feels cold and hemorrhoidal. "Everything dies," I tell her.

"Plus, its paint job is Rally Red. Some say orange, but it's Rally Red, believe me. Can't find Rally Red anymore. A collector's color."

Everything in the West, a collector's something or other. Excuses for holding onto what they cannot let go of. "Could be just a car," I tell her. "Nothing more."

"Yeah. Car with a bitch-ass color. And a slant six."

We drive past pawn shops and the tinseled green windows of eateries and liquor stores and dispensaries, and a pornography arcade where elves blink in animated coitus made out of snow lights.

"This little dinky necklace," she asks, "this is the hot shit dorje you're looking for? Really?"

"The actual dorje is bigger than that."

"Yeah, well, the emporium, if they have the small size, they might have the bigger."

My thought precisely. But I am not considering that. I am considering why it is called Madame Sun's emporium. I am mulling over what Mimi told me. I watch Abril driving, staring into her profile. "Why are you helping me?" I ask her. "Why the sudden change of heart?"

"I brought you here. I feel responsible. Maybe I'm a bodhisattva too. Showing you how it's done. I don't know."

"You did not tell me Sonny paid up a year's premiums on your policy. Or that he reinstated it."

She hesitates before answering. "Yeah. How do you know he did? Black magic or something?"

"Black magic is a mistaken belief," I tell her, "hell-bent on controlling the world instead of opening to it. True magic—not black magic—true magic teaches us to accept the unforeseen. Without altering it."

"Yeah? Well, maybe I'm starting to believe you, lama. Because

he didn't reinstate nothing, and he sure as hell didn't pay for it."
She speaks breathlessly, chasing her words. "Look, lama, I Googled
you, all right. Google says Drepung's landlord was a dick, a real
dick. When Daidyal couldn't pay the rent, his landlord beat him.
Only one devoted student stood up for him and defended Daidyal
by casting down a stroke on the landlord, so his arms didn't work.
One arm he couldn't lift, the other he couldn't lower." She poses
over the steering wheel like a yeti in attack mode, displaying the
landlord's paralysis for me. "You, lama, you were that student.
Daidyal's most accomplished in the art of black magic. You say
you don't know it, but I'll tell you what—you deal with insurance
men as long as I have, you sure as hell would want to know it
then. I would. And you and me, we're not that different. Google
says the landlord never collected rent after that, not for a single
day. Says he couldn't use his arms anymore." Sweat beads her
forehead and upper lip.

"Do not talk like this, Abril. It does not make you look well."

"Is it true?"

"Perhaps… perhaps once it was true, a very long time ago.
Just once."

"Yeah? What do you mean, once?"

"An interesting question," Daidyal observes from the back
seat. "Insightful, isn't she? What do you mean, lama, when you
say you only used black magic once?"

"I do not see she is that insightful," I tell my teacher. Ex-teacher,
I should say.

"Well, consider," Daidyal tells me. "Does anyone ever really
do anything just once? Or is once a convention of linear thinking? A failure to realize all lifetimes occur in one single moment,
simultaneously? Boom. Cause and effect as one." He leans up behind my shoulder, touching the back of my seat. "Does not once
really mean forever? Is that not what she's asking?"

"The Buddha taught all things are impermanent. They start
and stop. Linearly. Sonny Heller was alive, then dead. One thing
after another."

"Ah, I see. You are a detective now. Seeking Heller's killer."

"So that I may find the dorje."

"So that you may find the dorje. Very noble." Daidyal shifts to my other shoulder. "Except, lama, when Buddha says *impermanent*, could he not mean that everything exists one time only, and that time is now, forever? Face it. Nobody knows what the Buddha was talking about. He was all questions, no answers. Maybe he just meant we should just listen and wonder. Tell me, lama, where are we going exactly? In this instant, in this car, where are we going?"

"Do you not already know? If all time is one, should we not already be there, and your question already answered?"

Daidyal leans back in his seat. "Very good, lama. You are progressing. If there is any such thing."

I focus on Abril. "He emailed you that he was reinstating your insurance. You say you conjured me here to get you insurance. Why meet him at the warehouse. Why not just meet him in his office?"

"He was checking a shipment. It is where he asked to meet me."

"Why was he checking a shipment?"

"It was worth a lot of money. Four point nine million, I think."

I re-position my left shoulder into the Duster's seat back to see her more directly. "He told you this? Four point nine million?"

"It's in their files. You can check, if you want."

"How do you know what is in their files?"

Abril slams the Duster curbside, into a parking spot between two plowed up ice mounds sprinkled with a dusting of snow. She kills the engine. "I looked," she tells me. And then she says, "And now we are here. The emporium."

Hearing her, I shiver. Out the front windshield, the emporium looms large between a *Pizza House for the Homeless* and a bicycle-repair-slash-coffee shop.

What to see?

A rain-stained altar cloth in the window rising up a stair-step riser.

No, not that.

A crack-faced statue of Lakshmi twisting her serpentine arms.

No, not that either. That is not what to see.

Gothic lettering, stenciled in gold across the front plate glass separating inside from out, the lettering reading…

Madame Sun's Olde Tibetan Emporium
and Meditation Center
All Things Asian

I feel a chill down my spine. Tired exhaustion.

"Come on." She opens the driver's door and steps out.

It takes a moment, but eventually I open the Duster's passenger door. Slowly.

"There's nothing to be afraid of, lama. Come on, let's go."

A moment after that, I follow her inside.

LESSON 14

Like a dream. Like an illusion.
That is how birth,
that is how living,
and that is how dying are taught to be.

THE BELL ABOVE THE SHOP'S door tinkles. A gweilo boy—
American, blond, flopped greasy hair, face full of pimples—
bangs at a computer keyboard while eying a big colorful Trinitron
display high up in the shop's corner above the cash register. The
Triniton blinks, its speakers pop as an imagined display of a small
metallic ball whistles and ricochets through a labyrinth of bells
and chimes. In the lower left of the Trinitron, a meter racks up
points. A game clock counts down. Electronic flippers deflect the
ball over digitized bumpers and pockets and rubberized corners,
boinging and springing in a noisy display.

No sign of Madame Sun in the shop, even with her name on
the window. Nothing particularly mysterious about the place, either. Just the gweilo and some dusty statues for sale. A reclining

Happy Buddha. A seated Happy Buddha. No dancing Buddhas. Not like at the warehouse.

An elderly proprietor slips from behind a curtain of hanging beads. "Coming," he calls in a thin, familiar voice. Surprise of all surprises, the proprietor looks up, I see him. He sees me, his teacher. The very man who accompanied me this morning.

"Choki?" I ask.

"Lama Rinzen." My lieutenant smiles, but then drops the smile—all in an instant—turning to the pinball display with its bells and whirly-gigs aflash and aglitter, and a cartoon monkey in the corner of the display jumping.

"You stop now," Choki tells the blond, embarrassed of him being there.

The teenager flips his head back, knocking the hair from his eyes. "I'm jacked, man. Numbering big." The boy slaps the side of the keyboard, focused and intent.

"No. No jack. Stop." Choki reaches down along the wall and pulls the Trinitron's plug. The display dies. The carnival music sputters to a conclusion. The kid bangs the keyboard harder, trying to resuscitate his action.

"What'cha doing, man?"

Choki ignores the boy.

"What the hell? What'cha doing?"

Choki focuses on me, tips his head, places his hands side by side before his lips, prayer-like in *angeli*. He bows. "I did not expect you, lama. Welcome."

"You did not tell me you owned an emporium."

From crouched position, Choki side-glances Abril. Then quickly he returns his gaze to the floor at my feet. "So grateful you have come to my small place of business. How was your visit with Inspector Fernandez? Did you find the dorje?"

Odd question. I watch him ask it, and then pace the emporium's aisles, surveying the shop's wares. "Should I have found it?" I ask. "The warehouse, is that where you had it shipped?"

Choki shrugs. "Me? No, lama, no. I did not have it shipped. No, no. It is what you have returned for, no? You went there looking for it."

I do not answer. I ask, "So this is *your* shop?"

"Hey, goom-ba goom-bas." The blond boy pulls his crotch, making a display of it. "What are you talking about? I paid good cash to play Monkey Mind. I want my score back."

"No," Choki seethes through clenched teeth, still hunched. "No score."

"How did you know it was Fernandez I was going to see?"

"The reason he's back is because I brought him back," Abril pants. She is panting. The snow and the cold tiring her.

Choki shrugs, bowing. "Perhaps you told me, lama, you were going to meet the inspector? Yes?"

"I did not tell you."

Choki shrugs again. "It is proper thinking. Logical. An insurance man killed. Sonny Heller." He shrugs again. "Killing such a man matters in the West. A gweilo. A big shot. Such an important murder most assuredly arouses a police investigation. Inspector Fernandez, he is full time with the police. Very few full-timers left. Had it been a Tibetan killed, perhaps only a part-timer would come. A freelancer. Perhaps no one. But for Heller, only the best. You, lama. You and Inspector Fernandez. The best."

"Who gives a whatsa?" the gweilo says. "Where's my score?"

I fix a gaze on the boy, the nuisance he is. Momentarily, the boy silences. I turn back to Choki. "They had it shipped here, to your emporium. The Hellers, didn't they?"

Abril pushes past the blond. She is sweating, still wrapped in her down jacket. "I brought him back. I conjured him here," she says.

Choki replies. "You, miss?"

"Yeah? He's looking for the dorje. Come on and give it up. Stop screwing around. Where's Madame Sun? Get her out here. Get this thing going." Her words slur.

"You did not tell me you own an emporium," I tell Choki. "Or that the warehouse shipment was intended for you."

Choki moves behind the counter, shuffling papers into piles, glancing through them. "I apologize, lama, for my shop's appearance." He folds a mandala cloth down over the Trinitron display. "This Monkey Mind game, so loud with confusion. In the West, children have money. So we sell what is trivial. Supply and demand. Cause and effect."

"Where's Madame Sun?" Abril repeats.

Choki looks at me, then tells her, "There is no Madame Sun. The lama can tell you that."

"The entire time we walked to the warehouse," I say to him, "you did not speak about your shipment inside. Why not?"

"Jorge's score is shit." The blond kid whines. "I had it beat. What you doing, pulling my plug? Pull my prick, why don't you."

"You go." Choki picks up a newspaper and swats the boy. "You go. You leave. You go."

"I want my money back!"

"Go! Go!"

"Slopey-eyed old coot. You're lucky I bring you my pinball business. I want my score posted. And I'm telling the other kids. This place is a rip-off."

Choki pushes him to the front door. "No, you go."

"You're the monkey mind, man. That game is the story of your life, you loser. You want to make me the loser, you're a loser. Jorge ain't beating my score." The kid swipes his arm across a shelf of Ganeshes, knocking them to the floor. "Chase your monkey mind, slope. Ah-hoo ah-hoo"—the boy jumps like a chimpanzee— "just to pay your stinking bills. Tear it down. You think you're so wise because what… you're from the East? Tear it down. Tell the sweaty chick what she's asking. Where's Madame Sun? I'm telling the other kids. I'm telling Madame Sun, this place is a rip-off."

Abril is dripping now, her face a pool of perspiration. I hold her shoulder. "What is wrong?" I whisper to her.

"Warm," she snaps. "Cold out. I feel warm."

Choki pushes the boy out of the shop, rattling the door closed behind him. He looks at us, his lips moving, perhaps adding up lost pinball revenue, or praying, or wondering what to say next.

"Lama, welcome."

The blond boy bangs on the outside glass. "Tear this shit down." He points to Abril. "Her. She'll tear it down."

Choki begs, "Please, lama, forgive this disturbance."

"How much did you insure the shipment for? It was not only Budais in those crates, was it?" Straight up, straight out, that's how I ask. Like how gweilos talk.

Choki's face contorts. "What do you say?"

I point to the front window, its letters stenciled in grime. From inside, they read s'nuS emadaM natebiT edlO muirormE. "What is the meaning of having such a name on your shop?"

Choki scans his shelves, searching for something to say.

Abril leans against a shelf, bracing herself. "He knows black magic. You want some bad shit karma, the lama can give you some bad shit karma. Turn this whole place into…"—she looks around, what to say— "…something dive-ier than it is."

Choki winces. "Please, lama. It is a name only. Madame Sun does not exist. You know this. You taught us. Consider Drepung. You and I, we rode together." Choki folds his hands in prayer. "I only mean to pay respect."

"The shipment included the dorje."

"I cannot say such a thing, no."

"The Buddha statues are there, but not the dorje. You placed this order."

"I cannot say such a thing," Choki repeats. "I cannot."

"You insured it for four point nine million dollars." The number hangs in the air, like a snowflake drifting. "I understand these ways of the West. Their inflated sense of value. But do you expect me to believe the price of plastic Budais has elevated to such an insurable level as four point nine million?"

"I do not, lama. No."

"What else shipped? You have it, do you not?"

"Lama. I do not." Choki's eyes puff round. His face tightens. He steps toward me, hands clasped and upright. "I did not insure the shipment for such an amount. I did not even know the dorje was here on Colfax until I saw you this morning. How could I have insured such a thing?"

How does it happen? How does a dorje just roll out of someone's life, and never return? I remember Daidyal and his monks in meditation. I reach for the Most Sacred of Objects to take if from him. The high plateau sun glints, blinding my reach. Rain breaks from the sky, clouding the sun. Beads of rain cascade down upon stone steps, flooding the plaza.

Behind Choki, the beaded doorway rattles. An old woman rolls out a handcart stacked three high with sealed brown boxes. Choki puts a hand on her shoulder. "My wife," he says. "Let me introduce you. Chodon is her name. So many lifetimes we have been together."

In the recesses of my mind, a Yellow Banner beats the wind. "Married?" Can I remember him married? Can I remember him at all?

"Married? Yet you take the name of the Great Seductress for your business."

The old woman brings the handcart to a stop. She slices open an upper parcel with a box cutter and mutters something in a high plains dialect I cannot understand.

Choki translates for me. "My wife, she says here in the West many businesses take the name of non-existents. Hello Kitty. Howard Johnson's. Bob's Big Boy." Chodon mutters further. Choki changes her words to English. "There is no such Bob. He is just a fat cartoon gweilo carrying hamburger meat on a plate." She mutters further, and Choki repeats it for us to understand. "Conjectured. Gweilos believe in such abstractions. Westerners are a superstitious bunch."

"Why did you name your shop after her?"

Choki hesitates. "She does not exist. No one to sue me for using her name. Plus, Westerners find it catchy, *Madame Sun's. All Things Asian*, they find that catchy, too."

I have studied the Dharma many lifetimes. *Catchy* is a lesson I have never learned. "You sell Budai statues, do you not?"

"The happy Buddha? Yes, I sell such things."

"And dorje necklaces?"

"Yes. When I first set up shop in Denver, it was Kocapelli figurines that were all the rage. But now I sell far more dorje necklaces and Budai statues than all the Kocapellis combined. And he is from this part of Colorado. The Arizona part. A local, so to speak. But Budais, oh so nice in American gardens. I buy them now in December, cheaper before lawn season. I get a good price. And dorje necklaces. Everybody likes a nice dorje necklace. Would you like one, lama?"

Chodon reaches inside the cut box and lifts out a Homer Simpson sculpture sitting cross-legged atop a donut-shaped gomden. She places him on an upper display shelf while a recording inside Homer chants, "Yummm," in the tone of a man salivating.

"If you did not insure the shipment for four point nine million, who did?"

Choki and his wife look at one another.

"Lama, we have no such four point nine million dollar insurance." He turns so as not to look at me. "This morning I saw you reborn. I said, *he comes for the benefit of all beings*, and my heart filled. I am saddened to see you once again suffering in Hell, but I am glad you are here." His words sound difficult to comprehend, but his intention rings pure. In this way, I understand. "I can help you, lama. More than the gweilo girl. Trust me."

His wife stops unpacking. She moves to the cash register and lifts out a folded sheath of paper, which she hands to Choki.

"Here. Here you see," Choki says. "Two thousand dollars. Yes, you see. A mere two-thousand-dollar policy with the Heller

Insurance Company for the shipment of Buddha statues. It is all I have."

I read it. Small print, tedious wording, written in the language of insurance.

"The Hellers sell many things," Choki says. "Health plans, housing insurance, whole life. I do not understand this whole life. Is it one life? Many lives? It confuses me. But in the West, everyone buys insurance. We conform, or face deportation back to some Lhasa Prison."

The policy reads, *In the event the shipment does not arrive safely, soundly, and of solid containment, the Heller Insurance Company, LLC will pay to Madame Sun's Olde Tibetan Emporium and Meditation Center the sum of two thousand dollars.*

I slip the policy inside my robe pocket.

"Lama, please. It is my only copy. The police keep my Budais. The gweilos will not play the Monkey Mind game. Please, do not take my insurance, too."

Abril shivers. "I'm cold." She looks pale. Her skin feels chilled and clammy. She stares at Chodon, who is lifting a copper figurine from its box. A beast in lama's garb holding a sword above a witch.

Choki points at Abril. "Lama, please. Your woman is sick. You brought a sick girl to my shop? The West is a contagious place."

"She needs a hospital," Choki's wife states flatly. She places the lama statue on the countertop. The monk—half bull, half human, fangs growing from his lower gums—wears a garland of severed heads and fingers. He lifts a sword in the air. His witch cowers. Her arms are nicked, her expression pained, the statue chinked with age. "Lingchi," Chodon says. With the box cutter she breaks down the empty box into something flat to carry down the aisle and lean against the wall.

"Not lingchi." I say. "A bodhisattva cutting through ignorance, seeking truth."

The old woman comes back at me. "Lingchi," she insists.

"Man slicing woman, like she is a prop for his pleasure." She looks at Abril, whose face has whitened. "She needs a hospital."

"A hospital, yes," Choki agrees. "But she will need insurance."

The stink of vomit on her policy rises from inside my pocket. Next to it, the cell phone rings. I lift it, look at it, but do not recognize its number. "Hello."

"Naraka? Fusco here. I hear you found her? Fernandez is asking, did you find her. Between you and me, let's hope not."

"I have found her, yes."

"Lama? I told you, be patient. Work it slow."

"I am with her now," I say. Outside the emporium, snow crystalizes in the air. "But she did not do it. She could not have."

"Yeah, well tell Fernandez that. He thinks she did. He wants to talk to you."

The phone shuffles, hand to hand. "Naraka. Fernandez. Nice work. You found the girl. She's our culprit."

"I do not think so, inspector. A girl like this could not possibly know lingchi."

"Oh, yeah, she could. She's our girl. They were lovers. Then Sonny takes her insurance away, so she kills him. Quick and easy. Keeps us on budget, ahead of schedule. Look at it any longer than this, that might change it. Nice work, lama, finding her like you did. On time. Under budget. The way I like it."

The phone sounds tinny. The inspector's voice repeats itself with each word he speaks.

"No," I tell him. "They were not lovers. He reinstated her insurance. That is all. Whoever has the dorje, that is who killed him. I am still investigating."

"Now, don't muddy things up, lama. A girl killing her lover, that's an easy conviction. You bring her in, so we can wrap this thing up."

Abril leans against the counter.

"They were not lovers," I say. "They hardly knew one another."

"Yeah, well, you listen to me, lama. Them being lovers, that's a good gossip factor. We'll see how it plays. Maybe we drop it, maybe it sells the whole story. We'll see. I told you about my father, right? Buying the Coupe de Ville?"

Chodon unbuttons Abril's coat. She lifts her sweater and tee shirt over her head so that her skin breathes. Her belly appears scaly and wet.

"He parks the Coupe de Ville in the street. Street parking, you know what happens with street parking, don't you? Somebody steals it. Maybe that's more plot than story, but I mean they just steal it right out from under the street lamp." His phone's mouthpiece scratches the inspector's pocked chin while Chodon soothes Abril's body with the flat of her palm, rubbing ointment on her.

"All the neighbors say my father's cursed. Cursed with bad fortune to have so fine a car, so new a car stolen like that. You know what my father says? He doesn't sway. He doesn't bobble. He says *We'll see*. You hear me, Naraka? We'll see. Bring her in. Maybe they weren't lovers. Doesn't mean she didn't do it. We'll see. Here, let me put Fusco back on."

Hand shuffling. The phone gets passed. "Short ass job, lama. You pooched it. He wants me to tell you to get back here. Pronto. And bring back the insurance policy you took from the evidence box."

"Why not tell me himself?"

"You shouldn't have solved it so fast. Bring back that insurance policy and finish going through the evidence boxes, he wants me to tell you that."

Something about what Fusco says does not sound right. "Why should I do that? If he thinks it is solved, why would he want me to go through the evidence boxes?"

"What difference does it make?" Fusco asks. "You should have dragged it out."

Abril convulses against the counter, her foot rapping its base. The herb ointment smells pungent against her skin.

"The dorje?" I ask. "Did they find it?"

A pause settles. The sound of Fusco losing interest. "Only one who found anything is you, lama. The girl. Too soon. You blew it. Now come on and get down here. I got to go. Got to start calling the freelance list. See if I can get me some spiff."

I hang up the phone. I slump to the floor beside Abril where Chodon speaks to her in an indecipherable dialect, soothing her. Indecipherable, except for its rhythm. "You should take care of her," Chodon tells me.

"She needs a doctor, lama," Choki says. "And insurance."

The policy in my pocket crinkles as I bend to lift her. "I will take her," I tell them.

"You, lama? You do not know how to drive?"

I have lived many lives in Hell. Once I drove a cab. In another, a semi.

Abril shakes. Her foot twists left and right thumping the counter base.

Thumping with the persistence of a long slow climb, never ending.

LESSON 15

There are as many perceptions as phenomena.

THE HOSPITAL DOORS SLIDE WIDE apart. I wheel-chair Abril in. At a desk at the far end of an echoing rotunda a fat man in a plaid suit points behind him. "Emergency room's in back." Abril appears ashen, her eyes sunken and dark and sweaty.

"Unzip your coat," I tell her.

"I don't want to be here, lama. A doctor sees me, next thing you know I have a pre-existing condition. Take me home."

I wheel her from the rotunda into the hospital itself, past radiology and obstetrics and vending machines that dispense prescriptions. Overhead lights bathe the corridors in a slow-maddening buzz. I push past frail gurneys and frail patients wearing frayed hospital gowns that open in back. I push her, not knowing where to go, while patients reach out to me.

Lama, please. I must call my son.

Lama, help. The television in my room only speaks Spanish.

Please, lama. The doctor speaks to me in ways I cannot understand.

I shake them off. I push Abril through hospital corridors, past surgical units and rolling IV canisters. A doctor walks by discussing a clipboard in the crook of her arm with a white-coated assistant. I read her name badge. *Whiner.*

"Doctor," I tell her. "This woman is sick."

The doctor looks at Abril, but without urgency or concern. "Give the nurse her information."

"It is urgent," I tell her.

The doctor wipes her eye. "What's wrong this time, Abril."

Abril hesitates, her eyes purple and shameful, and says, "I might be pregnant."

Perhaps I display some unease, because the doctor then asks, "Are you the father?"

I look to Abril.

"He doesn't know anything about it," she says. "We haven't discussed children."

"I am a lama of the Kagyu lineage," I explain.

Whiner and her white coat look at one another. Then the doctor says, "You've been in before with this kind of thing. But you have no insurance. It has been rescinded."

"Not rescinded," I say. Inside my pocket, next to Choki's two-thousand-dollar policy and his envelope of obituaries, I can smell her policy. It stinks. So much paperwork in the West. "She has insurance. It was reinstated. I can show you." I pat my chest.

"Please." Whiner puts her hand out. The white coat watches me, awaiting my next move.

I recite an incantation. One Daidyal taught me in the Shedra. I take the policy out and hand it to the doctor. She unfolds it and reads.

"Where did you get this?"

"Sonny Heller."

She hands the policy back to me. "The Hellers canceled her insurance. Pre-existing conditions. You shouldn't lie on insurance applications, Abril."

"All conditions pre-exist." I explain without smiling, without a frown. Just holding my gaze upon the doctor, steady.

She looks stumped. She takes the policy back from me and reads it once more. "The Hellers canceled her."

Abril's purple eyes look up. She straightens in her wheelchair. A bit ruddier now. "You don't want to mess with us, doc. My fellow here knows black magic. Don't you, lama?"

Whiner and the white coat look me over, my torn robes caked in street grime.

"I do not do black magic," I assure them. Whiner rubs a dry finger beneath the black rim of her horn rims, further studying the policy, her head tilted down, her chin and neck blobbing into one as dandruff dusts the shoulders of her scrubs. She has a faint tint of sideburns in front of her ears, and her hair is mussed with greasy mousse, her eyes puffed dry. She flips through the policy page by page, getting to where it's marked *Rescinded*, running her chewed fingernail under the word, lower lip folded. Warmth flows through me to her. "No deductible," the doctor comments, seemingly surprised by this. She points it out for the white coat to see.

The white coat takes the policy and holds it to the light. "Haven't seen a no-deductible in a while," he comments. They both appear oblivious to where it says *Rescinded*.

Abril rolls the wheelchair forward, then back, then forward again. "I just want to get some tests done," she says.

Whiner takes the policy back from the white coat and thumbs through it again. I hold my gaze on her. I can see she is not really reading it now, but simply stalling, before calling over a bobby-pinned nurse with brown chubby cheeks and spit curls. "Nurse. Prep this one here for an exam, will you please?"

"Told you he knew black magic," Abril gloats.

Whiner looks from Abril to me. "And phone Sonny Heller. Confirm her insurance has not been rescinded." Then she presses her lips into a phony smile.

"I do not do black magic," I tell her.

"You better not." She speaks as if in a daze. "This is a hospital." Then Whiner sniffs the policy and tells the nurse. "And sponge this thing off, will you please? It smells like bile."

The white coat nods. "Quite bile-ish."

* * *

I sink into a scooped-back plastic chair in the hospital waiting area, surrounded by other slippery chairs that lay about piled with yellowed newspapers and smiley-covered magazines. An elderly man snores. A janitor skates a mop over the floor, side to side, his movement hunched.

Across from me, a middle-aged woman of Japanese descent caresses a young man. Her adult son perhaps. The woman's face is scarred from acne dried long ago. Its pockmarks glisten in the overhead lighting from some application she's applied, some attempt to hide her scars. The young man bleeds from his face and arms. Not broad knife swipes of any sort. His wounds do not appear gang related, but instead smaller, tiny little nicks. Beneath his unbuttoned coat, blood dots his tee shirt.

My robes scratch against my body. The elderly man stops snoring. He awakens and says, "Today I die, lama. It was supposed to be yesterday, but they're behind schedule."

The Japanese woman fusses fingers through her companion's hair and kisses his scalp. Deeper kisses than a mother might. She lifts his wrists and kisses them too, displaying scabs on their fleshy undersides. The boy's eyes appear swollen. He has not been sleeping well, it seems.

Daidyal's lover once complimented me by saying I was a worthwhile student, even if my mother could not pay for my education. *You serve us well,* she said.

The janitor pushes his mop, swabbing beneath my chair. "Tell me, lama. Black magic. Is it different from other forms of manipulation? Money, politics, war, or seduction?"

I look up, and see Daidyal now dressed in a janitor's onesie. How unbecoming. How apt.

"Black magic begets impurity. Impurity does not allow for enlightenment," I say.

"But finding the dorje, won't that correct all that? Do you still look for it, lama? Here in this hospital. Or are you just wasting time?"

Doctor Whiner approaches. Behind her the white coat carries the clip board, its pages blank, or only lightly written on. "We couldn't reach Sonny," Whiner says, pausing, watching my reaction.

"The girl is sick," I tell her. "Not pregnant. Sick."

"But we did speak with Huey Heller," she continues. "He says it's okay. The policy's good."

I breathe. The Japanese woman sees me. Daidyal sashays the mop and its bucket on wheels around to the other side of my chair.

"So." Whiner takes the clip board, scans it, flips it over, writes *Insurance* and then puts a check mark next to it. She hands the clipboard back to the white coat. "I will examine her, but I assure you, lama, she is not sick. Nor pregnant. More of a... hypochondriac, really. She fixates on attracting attention to herself. On suffering and the dissatisfaction it creates."

I close my eyes. Dukkha. Another way of saying dissatisfaction. The West calls it suffering.

The white coat looks at his watch. "We're ready, doctor."

"Yes." Whiner turns abruptly to walk away, the white coat following. She stops at a water fountain on the wall and washes her hands beneath its kick-stream. "Don't go far, lama. You'll be driving her home soon. We'll come get you."

The white coat nods, then whispers something to Whiner.

"Oh, and one more thing," the doctor says. "Huey Heller asks that you call him." Then she and the white coat push through the swinging doors of the examination room, so that they *swoosh* behind them open and closed, open and closed, each *swoosh* shorter than the last.

* * *

I lean into my plastic chair. The Japanese woman's lover has now turned from her, leaning his head against her chest. Perhaps they are not lovers. Something else maybe. Their hue. Their facial structure. Their eyes. The way her cheeks break when she smiles upon him, flaking specks of makeup down on the sleeping boy, they could be mother and son. She looks at me, and without moving her lips she asks, "Are you a holy man, yet know the black arts? Are you someone good, doing bad? Or someone bad doing good? Is there a difference?"

I pray. Inside my prayer, I hear a stampede of niru ponies high on the Tibetan plateau. Daidyal speaks to me. "Tell her not to distinguish one thing from another," he says. "Two people speaking a single conversation, this is neither good nor bad. Just a natural occurrence." Sometimes Daidyal makes no sense.

The woman wraps her lover in a blanket. She hugs him like a son and lover. Daidyal's fingers gnaw the mop handle. His uniform sags from his body. He asks, "As a detective, why do you suppose Huey Heller vouched for the policy?"

The examination room doors swing, the white coat coming out, going back in.

"It is not my concern why, only that he did," I tell Daidyal.

"Do you think it was pure intention on his part?" Daidyal questions. "Or is purity no more than a dream we imagine while sleeping."

Sleeping? I should sleep. Reborn only this morning, listening to Daidyal's prattling, I should sleep. Rest and revive. See myself riding command of a dizzying army over a bridge over the ice floe waters of the Kyichu River. The bridge made of golden brick. Horse hooves clop, slow and tired. My legions sway in their saddles, the weight of an endless campaign. We carry the dorje, having defeated Drepung and its heretic Gelugpas. I see it in my dream. Beneath us the icy river cracks against the bridge's footings. The footing crumbles into nuggets. Its chinking loosens. Our horses stumble. They step upon nuggets of gold. They buck. The bridge twists from their bucking. The ice floes swell beneath us.

At the bridge's far end, toward where we advance, a snowy dust rises. Marauders on snorting ponies. They ride a steady pace. I assess our position, hemmed in by the bridge on two sides, stuck in its middle, only half-way to either end. The marauders ride toward us from the far end of the bridge. No place to turn. No place to retreat. Our escape seems far distant.

Choki's horse kicks up. *Give the command to run, lama. Our only hope.*

I study the advancing enemy. They hold no banner. They ride for no cause. Gelugpa, no doubt, coming at us for revenge. Gold crumbles into the Kyichu. These marauders appear naked, wearing only blue paint and wild hair. Their faces are bent.

I try drawing my niru into a circle. Instead my men retreat. "Fall in," I shout. My men ignore me. Arrows rise from the advancing marauders. They draw nearer. "What kind of Gelugpa are these?" I ask, and I pat down my chest, my robes, my pony's saddlebag probing for the dorje. To keep it hidden. Another of my horsemen, large and Nepalese, butts his horse up against mine as he retreats. A string of mala beads rips from his throat, rolling across the bridge's surface. Our horses slip on them, unsteadying.

"You've led us to a trap, lama," Choki yells.

Marauders advance. Arrows whistle. My niru fights. Some begin dropping into the Kyichu. Then an arrow punches my chest. My head drops loose, bobbing. My neck crimps in pain. I awaken. Mala beads collide like stones. The dorje drops from my saddle bag, rolling to the bridge's edge.

"Wake up, lama."

In my mind's view, the dorje rolls to the bridge's edge and down a long flight of steps to a plaza where monks meditate, like pebbles rolling across rock, or how a river's waves rise. Sameness, over and over. A repetition of cacophony, familiar. Like wind through the barley fields of Drepung.

My chair wrenches sideways. "Lama, wake up."

Daidyal and his lover say I crippled their landlord. Such karma. They banish me from studies at Drepung. *Revenge is black magic* my teacher says.

The chair beneath me twists. "Lama."

My eyes open.

"Lama, what are you doing here? Why do you come?"

Yoong kneels before me. He whispers, looking over his shoulder at the Japanese woman and her lover. Maybe her son. Yoong blocks the lighting behind him, so that he appears as a silhouette in shadow. "The West does not respect you, lama. Everything here used and spent."

I open my eyes, a slow process of awakening. "What are *you* doing here?"

"Please?" Yoong helps me stand. He places my hand out in front of me, pounds my arm to awaken me. I open my eyes.

"What kind of agent are you?" I ask. "What kind of policeman."

"I am not police. I am a countryman of yours. An agent from China." He pulls my left hand forward now, pummels its arm. Light touch repeated. Invigorating. Energy flowing through me once more. He pounds my arms to awaken it.

"Please, lama. Your search for Heller's killer. The inspector wants to know what you have found. The girl? Do you have her here?"

The China agent leans me back into sitting. He *tsks* at the poor curvature of the waiting room chairs. He pulls my foot to his chest, leans back, pushes in, stretching my leg. "You need to wake up, lama. The inspector wants to ask you questions." First one leg he pushes and pulls. Then the other.

"Do you think the girl killed the insurance man?" the China agent asks.

"I do not think it possible?"

"Nor do I." His voice does not raise above a whisper.

Then Fernandez steps around from behind the Chinaman, bearing down on me.

"You awake, lama?"

LESSON 16

Perception changes who we are
into a reflection
of what we perceive.

YOONG STEPS ASIDE. FERNANDEZ MOVES in, bowing. Not out
of respect or honor, but so he can speak without raising his voice.
"Where is she, lama?" He whispers.

I look around. I see the hospital waiting room. My throat tightens. I yawn. "Having tests," I say, a raspiness in my throat.

"Get him a glass of water, wouldn't you?" Fernandez says to
Yoong. Then he turns to me, flexes an eyebrow. "Tests? I do not
recall—perhaps you can enlighten me—I do not recall asking that
she have any tests?" His mouth thins at the corners. "In fact, I believe I told you to bring her in, did I not?"

Yoong hands me a Dixie Cup, half full. In a tone of supplication, he says, "Perhaps, Inspector Fernandez, the lama was bringing her in, after her tests." He winks at me, small, so the inspector
cannot see it.

Fernandez straightens himself up lanky tall. "Perhaps, Agent Yoong, you might wait in the hall while I speak with the lama here."

Yoong flaps a bit, eying me, not winking now. "Do you think that is wise, sir? He is a countryman of mine." He pours his mala back and forth, hand to hand.

"Yes. I do. Please. The hall."

The Chinese agent's face flattens. Reluctantly, he does as the inspector asks. He goes to the hall, where he watches us through a window, out of ear-shot.

The inspector and I alone now. The Japanese woman and her lover or son or whoever he is have relocated to a nursing station to argue insurance coverage. Fernandez asks, "You dream much, lama?"

"Perhaps this is a dream," I suggest. "How do we really know?"

"Yeah. I agree." The inspector nudges his chin over his shoulder at Yoong. "I dreamt someday someone from the East might come and infiltrate my work. Try and take it away from me. I've been a detective most of my career. A uniquely human occupation. No robot's taking my job. But a Chinaman... maybe a Chinaman might. The world's a small place. Wasn't always like that. Used to be when people talked about back east, I thought they meant New Jersey. Women in lipstick and tiger skin bikinis. T-shirts saying *In case of emergency pop this beer*. I never thought they meant the East east. The real East. Faraway."

The Chinaman paces the hall, watching us.

"Me neither," I say.

"Yeah," the inspector agrees. "Me neither. This freelance thing's a gimmick, you know. A story politicians tell like they're trimming expense. Embarrassing, the China agent seeing us like this, how we operate. Detective work isn't something you turn on or turn off. It's who you are, through and through, down in your gut like a heartbeat." The inspector forms a fist over his belt buckle, over his *dantian*. "Down here." He pats the low end of his bolo tie and rubs it. "Fusco tells me you're not just a freelancer. You have quite a story to tell."

"I am a Tibetan monk of the Kagyu lineage. Yes."

"So go ahead and tell me. Your story? Why not bring the girl in when I asked you? Unless of course, it's not your story at all. It's her story, and you're just some schmoe along for the ride."

I shrug. "She did not kill Heller. His death is from lingchi. Not something a gweilo might know. She is too weak. She could not have killed him. Not in her state. She needs tests."

Fernandez laughs without meaning it. "Weak? Who's not weak? They teach you this lingchi back in lama school? You went to lama school, didn't you? They teach it there?"

I sit straight so I might breathe more properly, more patiently under his questioning. "Everyone in Tibet has heard of lingchi. It does not mean that we are all practitioners. Lingchi is a Chinese punishment. Ancient."

"Against Buddhists?"

"Against those who speak truth. Against the unorthodox and those who violate the will of the state."

Fernandez settles into the scooped-back chair next to mine. "So then why Sonny Heller? Why lingchi him? I mean, it's ancient, but Sonny wasn't that old. He wasn't even Buddhist. How old are you when you're ancient, lama? How do you know if someone's Buddhist or not? Is it what they believe in?"

Lifetimes in Hell, questions sound so uncertain. Their answers more so. But this time it is different. I tell the inspector, "Buddhism is not something you believe. It is something you experience. And lingchi is not all that ancient. Even today the Chinese practice it in the work camps and prisons of Tibet against monks and nuns." In the hallway, I see Yoong pacing.

Fernandez interlaces his fingers, stretches his arms out long in front of him, cracking his knuckles. "So, if Abril is unable to commit lingchi herself, perhaps she had an Asian do it for her. An émigré, maybe? Some Tibetan?"

"A Chinese more than likely."

"Yes, well, Asian, anyway. Can we settle on that?"

"There are many forms of Asians."

"We only need the one, lama. Just one. You said it yourself. She couldn't have done it on her own. So she must have had help. Why would someone do that? Help her like that?"

"What do you know about the Spurtz bicycle gang? They do not seem fond of the Hellers."

"The Hellers are a prominent family here in Denver. Very successful. Those dedicated to leisure—bicyclists, that sort—they sometimes don't like people like the Hellers. But mostly they just ride around. Not really a threat. But Abril...Sonny being killed by this Abril makes sense."

"You have no evidence."

"Evidence? So, you're an evidence-based detective? Well, good for you, lama. Very heady approach. You get that from meditating?"

"Seeing things as they are. I get that from meditating."

"Yeah, well, me, I believe detective works comes from someplace lower. When you think about it, what is evidence anyway?"

"Every effect has its cause, inspector, which it carries inside itself. Look deeply enough, each crime conceals its own cause. Its own killer. I have looked at Heller's death. I do not see Abril in it."

"You have not been here long, lama. When you are, you will realize. The longer you look, the more you change what you're looking at. That's the thing about evidence. It can take on a story of its own. I don't mean to alarm you, but if you suspect police work is about justice, you're wrong. It's about order. Turning chaos into calmness. Your story, lama, needs to be that you found the girl, and she did what's most plausible. She killed her lover. *Boom!* End of story."

"She was not his lover."

"The Hellers are big men in this town. Too big to fall. We need a story that's simple, so people can understand. So we can have some order again." He cups his hand atop my knee. "I see a lot of freelancers. But you, you're different. You remind me of me. A true detective. Questioning. Always questioning. Why are we here? Well, let me tell you why. We're here for everyone else. Everyone who wants something they can depend on. So that for another day, another week, another year, another second, they can just keep on living. Tick tock. Continuity. Without any surprises. People don't have continuity to cling to, everything's chaos. Can't have chaos."

Daidyal tells me every lifetime has a lesson, and that Abril could be my teacher. What I hear now... can a teacher tell me whether it's true or not? I study the crags of the inspector's face, where his imperfection shows. I say, "The Buddha says there are two kinds of truth. Relative and absolute. Relative truth for day to day survival. How to get along. How to earn money. Pay bills. Mundane stuff. And absolute truth, which transcends all that. How we watch ourselves, without interfering. The story is not being the story we tell, but the one we observe. This is what the Buddha is talking about, when he talks about emptiness."

"Classy." Fernandez moves his hand from my knee to the back of my neck, squeezing. "That's what I wanted to say. That's why you got to bring the girl in. Don't second-guess it. Don't interfere. Just see yourself doing it. Unless there's something else you'd like to tell me. Like you told me about lingchi. And I believed you. And I believe she could not have done it alone. We all need help. I checked you out, lama. You're a helper. A natural born storyteller, too. This Buddha you talk about, he's quite the character, huh? Sounds like a detective to me. Like he's got *detective* deep down inside him. Absolute truth, that's something a detective might say. Without getting bogged down in whether it is real or not. Just that it happens. Justice takes a long time, lama. But order, sameness— that's something we can impose right away."

He sounds tired, a bit worn. Still, he continues. "There are some who tell me this dorje you're after is worth four point nine million dollars. But money's a relative truth. Whenever a thing becomes about money, it's not about the thing anymore. That's what the Buddha means when he talks about emptiness. Value standing in for the thing itself? Isn't that so?"

Silence settles. So much I can hear cockroaches crawling the walls and lights frizzling overhead, and doors swishing open and closed in the hallway.

"Did you figure out what her tattoo says?" Fernandez lifts up slightly from the chair, slaps his right butt cheek, and resettles. "*En su nalgas?*"

"She has no such marking."

"Really? You've seen it? Her *nalgas*? Quick work, lama. You made quick work of that." The inspector leans over himself, elbows to his knees, shrugging with his hands and chin. The waiting room clock's second hand ticks slowly around its face.

"She and Sonny were lovers. You may not like that, lama, but it's something you should know, before we go further. Yoong and I searched her place. Men's clothes hanging in the closet."

"Why did you search her apartment?" I ask. "To find what?"

"Nothing. Just seeing what's in front of us. Clothes in her closet. Suits, ties, sports coats, slacks. I don't want to put you in an awkward light here. You're a holy man. I don't know if you like hearing these things."

"Did you find the dorje?"

He cocks a quick look at me. "The four point nine million dollar dorje? You should forget about that, it never shipped. But here, let me show you what we did find." From inside the long sweep of his duster, the inspector pulls a blade. Familiar enough in appearance, debok to pommel. "Recognize it?" He holds the blade to the light. "Talk about lingchi, *toca la maraca*. Ding ding."

Plainly enough, I recognize it. Circa 1550. My blade, from my niru days. The very one with which I slayed Daidyal. The very blade used to cut away kleishas. I reach to take it from the inspector, but he pulls it back.

"It's the one she was holding in the art shot. Porno shot, some call it. How's that for evidence? Kept it in her apartment, with Sonny's clothes and a baby crib. Like they were planning a family together. Playing house. No kids. Just the crib. Sonny took away her insurance before she could have kids. You ever add up how much it costs to have a kid without insurance?"

"It could have been planted."

"The crib?"

"The sword."

"Yes, planted. Smart thinking. Very smart thinking." Fernandez stands the sword straight up between his chair and the one next to him, on the other side away from me. "But planting the sword complicates our story. Only makes it harder to follow. We need people to hear about the sword... know it is the murder weapon, and that's it. End of story." The inspector leans forward, elbow to knee. "Found in her apartment. Maybe we check it for prints. Find out who helped her. Now there's a story worth telling."

"What about the dorje?"

The inspector holds the sword in front of him, examining it. Absently, with his other hand he fishes inside his suit jacket. He extracts a sheet of paper and a pair of pince-nez from his jacket's front pocket. He pinches them to his nose and then flaps the paper to straighten it. "Packing slip." He lifts it for me to see. "That's what I have, the packing slip. Know what it says? Budai Statues. Forty-nine *en toto*." He turns the paper so I can see, but quickly pulls it back. "Just Buddha statues." He reads it again, his lower lip bent. "Forty-nine Buddha statues all the way from Asia? Why's someone do that?"

"It is not just statues. The shipment also contained the dorje."

"Not according to the packing slip, it didn't."

"Because the Hellers kept it off the packing slip for some reason."

"You need to understand, the Hellers do a lot for the émigré population. Forget about things that don't exist, lama. Better you and me... we work on finding who she partnered with."

Police work is a desirous profession. Desiring solutions. Of all the six realms, two are tainted by desire—Hell and the Realm of the Hungry Ghosts.

"We're here to restore order, lama. The sooner the better. So people go back to their sleepy lives." He raises the lid over his milky eye to adjust it, and then lifts his ball cap pushing his hair back. "I told you my dad bought a Coupe de Ville, didn't I? Got stolen. In front of the house. Of course, I told you."

He circles his finger in the air, like he's taking the room's temperature. He stands and shakes out his legs. "Patience. That's the lesson we need to learn. Whoever stole that Coupe de Ville, it took patience. Then they brought it back. Parked it right out in front of the house. My dad goes out, he opens the trunk—big, big trunk. You know what he sees? Twenties. A trunkful of twenties. Andrew Jacksons—a great, great president, Andrew Jackson—all in the trunk. Shakedown money? Drug money? Lottery money, who knows? Twenty-dollar bills, right there in front of him. Stuffed in every corner, crevice, wheel-well and cranny. And you know Coupe de Villes. They are known for their trunk space. *Papa,* I say. *You hit it big.* My father, all he says is *We'll see.*"

Fernandez looks at the examining room doors, both still remaining still and un-moving. No one going in. No one coming out. "Watch yourself, lama. When she finishes her tests, why don't you bring her in. So I can ask her why she loved Sonny so much, and who helped her kill him." He flicks his fingers from himself to me, me to himself. "Together, we can solve this thing, me and you. You'll see."

He winks his good eye, and in that wink he disappears out into the hallway where Yoong still paces.

While I sit alone in the waiting room, with its hard-edged seating and dirt-mopped floors.

LESSON 17

Enemies cannot harm us.
Only our unguarded thoughts do that.

THROUGH THE TRAPEZOIDAL CHICKEN WIRE glass separating me from the hallway, I watch Fernandez count out on his fingers to Yoong what he is saying. *One, two, three.*

Reading the inspector's lips, he does not mention Abril. He has an *All Things Asian* catalog he waves at Yoong. His lips do not form the word dorje.

What is he saying?

Nothing, now. He turns and abruptly buttons his duster, lifts its collar around his neck, and leaves. He walks out toward the hospital rotunda, to the revolving doors that go outside.

Once gone, Yoong checks his left, right, sees that nobody is looking, and then takes out his cell, and dials it.

Nobody looking but me.

My phone rings. I answer.

"Lama. You must leave now. Fernandez, he thinks you did it. For Abril."

"I just spoke with him."

"You should leave. Hide. He believes the girl brought you here to get her insurance back. And that maybe you are the Tibetan who helped her kill Sonny Heller."

"I just spoke with him. He did not say that." Cause and effect. Whatever you believe, you bring it into what you do.

Fernandez told me the dorje does not exist. Why then would he suddenly suspect me? So I hide. So I do not interfere with his finding the dorje for himself.

I waste no time.

I make my way to the revolving doors out onto the hospital's wraparound drive. Out into the cold. Snow squeaks with each step. I look for footprints, tire tracks. I look for any sign where Fernandez might have gone.

What to see?

Christmas lights slap the hospital's archway entrance. Faded, plastic choirboys silently glow from the inside out. A plywood Santa carries a sack on his back. White-wire reindeer bow to a doll dressed like Jesus in his crèche.

I walk the wraparound out to the street. Snow rains down in a heavy curtain of white. A limo sits at the curb, idling, chugging exhaust. A figure wrapped in wool and synthetics leans against it.

"Get in, Lama. I will drive you away from here." His voice muffles beneath his muffler pulled up to his nose. His clothing weighs him down. He resembles this morning's driver, only chillier. The temperature dropped along with the sunset. Snowflakes drop too, woven out of water and air and emptiness.

"Who are you?" I ask. "How did you know where I was?"

The driver straightens. "Get in the car, why don't you?" He sweeps open the limo's rear door.

"Are you with the Hellers?"

"Lama, please. You talk too much. Listen to the snow around

you. So peaceful it sounds. What Westerners call still."

"I just ask. Do the Hellers have the dorje or do they not?"

"Ask them yourself. Let me drive you."

His muffler ices to his mouth. His words are barely decipherable. But the limo appears cushiony and warm. I climb in. Its wipers rub across glass. The driver gets in, behind the wheel. He does not look back to see if I am there or not. He begins driving. Out the window I watch Denver pass by, its buildings and flat storefronts, and the way snow forms into outlines along the fences and bike racks and passing bus benches.

Until the limo slows.

Its headlights reflect a slithering in the darkness in front of us. An indistinct shape. We stop. The rear limo door opposite me opens. The sliver climbs inside. I push back into my side of the car, watching this darkness take form right before me. A pale, ashen, wintry display of Huey Heller. He brushes snow from his coat sleeves. He smells like damp wool.

"Good evening, Mister Heller." The driver turns, removing his cap and muffler. He beams a crooked row of teeth. He is Tibetan.

"Evening evening evening." Heller grudgingly answers. "Shit weather. Shit. Car freshly cleaned and waxed, always brings shit weather. Pure shit." He pulls off his gloves, slapping them against the upholstery while twisting his smile at me. "Detective. You've come. Thank you. Thank you very much. Not a night for business, I understand..." but then he gets straight to the point. "I've prepared an insurance quote for you. No obligation, simply an estimate of value versus expense. Whatever you're doing for insurance nowadays, I assure you we at Heller Insurance can do better. Much better. Offering you the complete package. Health. Life. Umbrella. Plus, some long-term and short-term disability. Everything you need. You're a policeman, are you not? Dangerous work. You're going to want insurance. Everybody does, sooner or later ."

"I am freelance," I inform him.

"Yes, freelance. More dangerous. Nobody has your back when you're freelance. You work for Fernandez. Nice fellow. But don't trust him. You probably understand what I'm saying."

The car's heat tightens my skin. His sales pitch, too. "I do not need insurance," I tell Heller. I hold my gaze, and watch snowflakes spin from the sky outside the window behind him. Each flake dissipating, growing absent of itself. Falling into a blanket of white over the street. Indistinct boundaries.

Heller adjusts in his seat. "It is quite an attractive quote, I promise. We would love your business, lama. Quite frankly I'd be doing you a disservice if I didn't sell you insurance."

"I do not need insurance," I repeat.

"Do you feel different than everyone else? Or do you consider yourself more of the same?"

"No, not the same," I explain. "Different, but insignificantly so."

"Exactly. There are those who belong, and those who don't. And those who belong deserve insurance."

The limo bumps over light rail tracks.

"Belong to what?"

Heller smirks, like I already know the answer without seeing it. We approach an intersection. The driver stops for a red light, where we idle. While waiting for the light, a stick figure *knocks* up against the limo, at Heller's window. A bicyclist. He leans there against the car, looking in at us.

Then another against the driver's door up front. Then more, thumping my side of the limo, and against the trunk and the hood, until soon bicyclists have surrounded and engulfed the entire vehicle, their silhouettes darkening our view of the snow outside, in their knob-headed helmets, each of them gloving the car while pedaling upright stand-stills, waiting for the light to change.

"Get off my wax job." Heller bangs at his window.

The rider at Heller's window peers at us through teardrop goggles and gives us a gloved middle finger.

Heller opens his door, then slams it shut again. He knocks back the bicyclist, knocking him into another bicyclist, who then knocks another, until one by one the cyclists begin falling like dominoes.

The driver revs the engine spitting exhaust out over them.

The light turns green. The limo slips forward. Any cyclists still leaning on it now flit off like doves rising in flight.

Heller repositions in his seat. "Spurtz hooligans."

"Why are they after you?" I ask.

"Me?" Heller eyes sag, dipping his chin to his chest. "Why should they be after me? You gave her the policy, didn't you? Yes, yes, don't say it's me. The hospital called. They inquired about you and that policy. I thought Curly and I made it perfectly clear, you were to arrest her, not give her the policy back. It says *Rescinded* right on it."

I re-frame my thoughts. "You said she stole it. Yet Sonny had it, right there in his briefcase."

Heller exhales. "Listen, lama. I notice you fail to recognize how much good Heller Insurance does for people. Not only do we collect Tibetan artifacts, but we're philathropists as well. These Spurtz Granola Snax. A damn good snack, but their bicyclists, I just don't know. You must see what I see. Everyday Tibetans de-bark planes, come to Denver and crowd streets and sidewalks. And these bicyclists...all they can see is more cars on the road, more traffic with each new arrival. They feel hemmed in, so they hem in émigrés. Heller Insurance, we like the émigré business. Sixty, sixty-one percent of our clientele is now Tibetan." He nods, like it's true. "The cyclists, they have their lanes, and we have ours. But I will tell you something. They lean on my wax job, I'll knock them down." He pulls a briefcase up onto his lap and opens it. "Let's take a look at your insurance quote, shall we?"

"I cannot afford insurance."

"Oh, don't let price be an objection. We have ways of apply-ing future payouts to current premiums. A little something Heller

Insurance worked up for the newly arrived. Did I mention how important insurance can be in your life?"

"Why did Sonny meet Abril at the warehouse?"

"Why?" He seems surprised at my asking. He looks over the insurance papers, fingering them nervously. "Because Heller Insurance cares, that's why. Sonny, he cared especially hard. A good insurance man. He belonged in insurance. A bit like you, lama. And he was a collector. A tribute to the past. You know if there really was a dorje, Sonny would have found it, I can tell you that. I envy him, really. Except his being dead. Curly runs the business, did I tell you that? Very hard-nosed about it. Without Curly, we would have closed up shop long ago. Still, there's something Sonny knew. He knew how to sell insurance, by caring about people. By listening. Sonny sold a lot, but maybe he listened too much. Heard too much. Tell me something, lama. What can I do to get you into a policy tonight?"

"Why did he meet her there?"

"Why?" Heller coughs. "I really don't know. But answer me this. Do you consider yourself likeable? Someone people like?"

"Many lifetimes, all so short, it never matters whether people like me or not."

"Well, that's a blessing. Consider yourself lucky. Being liked is hard. But it pays dividends. That's one of the first things we tell the Tibetans when they come over. We like them, and we like to sell insurance. And that we'll work hard for them."

The limo crosses Colfax, its wipers still pushing snow. I widen my knees, spreading the hem of my robes for the floor heat to rise up. The buildings along 11th Street close in around us.

"You came out on a night like this to sell insurance?" I ask. "Is that why I am here?"

Heller leans toward me. "I don't see you as just another Tibetan." He pauses. "Curly and I are concerned that you have not arrested the girl. She stole a policy from us. Her policy."

"Not her policy."

"She lied on the application. She killed Sonny, and threatened our business. She's inscrutable. Probably even told you she's pregnant with his child, I would suspect. Oh, the things she says. Threatened to go to the commission and say that Sonny had taken advantage of her."

I wait before asking, "They were lovers?"

"Lovers? I can assure you, they were not lovers. Took advantage of her by selling her insurance. Abril is the kind of girl who likes being looked at. Seen. Hers is not the only policy she stole. Do you know this? There were others. Ten others exactly. Whole life policies. I have the names right here."

Heller presents me a sheet of paper, nicely typed. I read it, its list of names. Its names all gweilo. Collins, Garrett, Nelson, Patrix. Matheny. Rogers, Dupree, Michaels, Klein and Klingoffer.

"There are no Tibetans on this list," I remark.

"No. No Tibetans," he confirms. "She did not steal Tibetan policies."

"Sixty percent of your customers are émigrés. Yet these are all American names."

"Yes, well, these are old policies. They have been long paid, the insured all dead, with payouts rendered. Still, for the sake of the commission, we need the policies back. Sonny met her at the warehouse. He believed he had talked some sense into her, and she was supposed to return them."

"He reinstated her policy."

"Oh, good God, he would never do that. She lied on her application."

What to hear? Her policy in his briefcase. Sonny was going to return it to her. Even though it is marked *Rescinded*. Then he gets killed. Abril says she was at the warehouse, but did not do it. Except he un-rescinded her policy without giving it to her. Who has the other ten? Who does things this way, by stealing insurance policies?

"We need those policies back, lama. Not just hers. All of them."

"What about the dorje?"

"There is no dorje. It never shipped. She stole policies from us. She was supposed to return them, but she never did. It's why you're here. It's how you can help us."

The limo turns onto Colfax, coming from the south now. I recognize the place. Heller stoops down in his seat to look out the window. "Here." He punches the back of the driver's seat, telling him to stop.

We pull to the curb at the Aim Straight and Shoot, now closed. Colfax as quiet as a snowflake.

"I need you to go to her apartment, lama, find those policies, and bring them down to me."

"Break in?"

"It is not breaking in. You're police. And I am an insurance man. I can vouch for you."

I look out the limo window. The building appears cold, its glass door still iced. I step from the car, while Heller and the driver wait inside.

There are no policies in the apartment. I open the iced door. The staircase grins at me, step after step. I climb. At the top I hunch over, hands to knees, trying to catch my breath. I hack a little, phlegm in my throat. I lean against her door jamb where the arrow shattered it. I touch her door. It opens. I step inside.

Everything about the place looks the same, only eerier in her absence.

What to see? What should I see? No sign of policies anywhere. No sign of anything different than before.

The Buddha statue. Candles burning. My cushion collapsed, still holding the impression of where I sat on it and meditated. All moments are dreams. Every moment a meditation.

I look to the table where Daidyal sat. The catalog, *All Things Asian*. It is opened to a page with a crudely drawn ad. Drawn in pencil. *Dorje for Sale. The Most Sacred of Objects. $4.9M.*

There comes a moment, no matter how often you relive it,

no matter how many times you relived it before, there come moments that distinguish themselves from all the rest. Moments of realization. With clear and present obviousness.

The ad in the catalog shows a phone number. Written in Chinese. That is how to find the dorje. Call the ad. Arrange to meet with whoever is selling it. Then—whatever it takes—take it from them. And hold it close, so we may all be enlightened.

My path.

Perhaps a trap. It could be whoever followed me here is using this ad as a trap.

But is not everything a trap? A way to get stuck and stagnant and never move on.

I extract the cell phone from my pocket. It has rung so often, I now need to puzzle a moment over how to dial it. I punch the phone number from the ad into its keypad, its Chinese country code and the numbers that come after.

In the phone's earpiece, I hear ringing, like a warbler calling his mate. A moment later, in a long and trilling treble, the phone beneath the baby crib calls back.

It repeats.

First, the phone in my hand. Then the ringing beneath the crib. The phone in my hand. Then beneath the crib.

No dorje ever shipped, they say. Except Abril. She says she will help me find it. And now, when I dial the number in the catalog, her phone rings.

Like it rang when I met her. Over and over, and she yelled at me to answer. She said it could be important, but I let it ring too long.

I hang up my phone, and the room falls silent.

The phone beneath the crib stops ringing.

LESSON 18

We lose the things we cling to,
as surely as first touch
fades into oblivion.

BY THE TIME I TRUDGE the stairs back down to Colfax the limo is gone. Heller has left, without the policies he asked me to retrieve. Another diversion. The West is full of them.

I walk frozen sidewalks past neighborhoods that developers call *promising*, where neon signs spell *Coors* behind caged barroom windows. A juke box thumps through the cold. I follow the sound into a bar. Stepping inside I stomp my mukluks on the barroom's welcome mat, my toes feeling like they might shatter. Shatter like lost hope.

When you dial the number in the dorje ad, Abril's phone rings. She says she is the reason I am here. For the dorje, and she says she will help. Daidyal says she is a teacher. Is this what the Buddha talks about when he talks about emptiness? The trust I placed in her, only to now discover she has been lying all along?

Inside the bar and all around me people are living it up on their cell phones, LOLing and OMGing with pinched and stoic faces, wearing emotionless expressions disassociated from the messages they send and receive. Disconnected from one another, what do you call such people? Émigrés?

I settle into the synthetic leather of a seating booth. Sensation slowly comes back into my frozen fingers and toes. They itch. I worm my fingers inside my robe pocket feeling for Choki's envelope, which I lay on the table, poking through its clippings. Each clipping smells Xeroxed, like freshly baked bread. Each an obituary for some slain Tibetan. Ten of them.

Choling Dolma, 37. Heart stabbed. Kidneys cut. Throat skewered. Fingers and toes gone.

Jamyang Cering, age 52. Skin whittled. Stomach excised. Appendages severed and piled in a pile to the side of the torso.

Dharey Duga, 67. Ears gone. Nose and eyes empty holes, gaping.

One after the other, I read them. Each Tibetan gruesomely slain. Each obituary notated, *investigation pending*. Each with an oval-shaped stamp in the margin, and the obituary's file number bordered by the words *Heller Insurance*.

We do a lot of business with the émigré population, one of them told me.

I turn the obituaries over, but their backsides are blank. I turn them back and read the death dates. Each more than forty-nine days old, killed by lingchi. In my mind, I hear the pop, pop, flick flick of skin ripping from muscle. The sound of lingchi, if you're standing close enough.

I take Heller's neatly typed list of stolen policies from my pocket and read its names. Also ten in number. All gweilos. I place his list next to the obituaries, side by side on the tabletop. The Tibetans killed by lingchi. The gweilos dead of Western causes. Heart attack, cancer, cirrhosis, gunshots. Alzheimer's, kidney disease, influenza and suicide.

The barroom door blasts open. The obituaries and the Heller list ruffle in the cold air. Yoong steps through wearing a puffed parka, his Eskimo hood drawn up tight to his face and his glasses fogged. He waits for the glasses to clear, and then scans the room. He sees me.

"Lama. Such good fortune, finding you here." He crashes down heavy into the booth's bench seat across from me. He spreads himself wide, his feet stretching down the length of the seat, his back wedged against the wall. "Such a day, such a horrid day. And this place, horrid, as well. Why are you here, lama?"

I don't flinch. "Detective work."

"Yes, detective work. We share that, you and I."

He exudes chumminess. More than exudes, he pushes it on me.

"What kind of agent are you?" I ask. "What is it exactly you are doing here?"

Yoong removes his glasses, wipes them in a napkin he pulls from a tabletop canister. He breathes on the lenses and wipes again. "Detective work, lama. Certainly you see the police, the methodology they use in the West. How would you say—they work from their stomachs. Their gut. Missionaries, not bureaucrats. I am here to learn from that."

"You flatter them." I scoop together the obituaries, removing them from his view.

Yoong defends himself. "They are our hosts. I only try to learn. I admire the West. Ours is a culture of respect for elders. The West takes a more natural approach, protecting its young. In nature, have you observed, how the cry of a distressed yearling arouses the herd into action? So it is here in the West. A culture only survives by seeing to the safety of its young."

That kind of agent. Maudlin. "I understand you and Fernandez searched her apartment."

"Yes."

"What did you find?"

"Perhaps it would be better if you discussed such matters with the inspector. I am simply a guest here."

"We are all guests, wherever we go. All émigrés. Why not just tell me?"

"Westerners have sensitive egos, lama, you must see this about them. Their survival depends upon it, their continuance of self. They obsess over imaginary fears, and fly into irrational rages. Perhaps I am not being honest, perhaps not just Westerners. Perhaps we all behave this way, struggling to survive. Have you noticed how the cry of a human child continually changes pitch and cadence and rhythm? Not easy to ignore, such constant change. It makes itself annoying. The West is like that. Not wanting to be ignored. Like children."

"The West ignores plenty. Like how they ignore émigrés in the streets, letting them be killed like that, forced to relive lifetime after lifetime in Hell. Lingchi."

"You blame that on the dorje not being found, don't you? I wish I could help."

He mocks me. His smug tone, it mocks me. "You know where it is?" I ask. "Did you find it when you searched her apartment? Or the warehouse perhaps?"

His mouth opens, closes, and quickly he says, "No." Then he sits in still life, his expression suggesting that what I ask is silly, simply silly, and should not have been asked.

"Life in the West seems obsessed about money, Agent Yoong. Surely you see this. Once a thing becomes about money, it no longer resembles itself any longer. I do not seek the dorje for its value. Only for its blessing."

"And yet, you have not found it." He holds his glasses above his belly, staring down through their lenses, inspecting their frames. "I must say you startled Fernandez with all your talk of lingchi. What made you bring it up? You never did tell me." Cheerily he asks, but with a slight needling to his tone.

"The body was severed. Pared of its skin. Why did *you* not mention it?"

"Because I know better. Because Westerners are pragmatic. And pragmatism is a way of defining things already understood. Lingchi is not something a Westerner might comprehend. Still, you avoid my question. Why mention it?"

"I am Tibetan. It needed to be said. Dead Tibetans in the streets and alleys of Denver, and the way Beijing has imposed lingchi on my people for so many lifetimes."

Yoong wraps the wire of his glasses around his ears. He adjusts their lenses on the bridge of his nose, squinting, smiling. "1956, lama. Tibetans, Mandarins, we are all Chinese now, and stronger for it. You, me. Our presence is now being felt in the West. Plus, lingchi has been outlawed. For well over a century, so why even discuss it any longer?"

"Yet still practiced inside Drapchi Prison."

"Ah, there it is." Yoong smiles wider. "Drapchi. So many lifetimes, it never fails, I can count the moments before some Steppe-dweller such as yourself mentions Drapchi. Yes, horrible, horrible. Agreed, horrible. But Drapchi is a world away. This is America, with its bang bang shoot 'em up, guns, guns, guns. People here do not have time to execute the long, slow, methodical practice of lingchi. Here, it is quick-shot and whisk pain away under the rug. Like it does not exist. They kill their enemies secretly from out of the sky, while they snack on cookies and buttered sandwiches."

"They have their superstitions."

"And we have ours." Yoong pulls the mala beads from around his wrist, fidgeting with them, placing his feet to the floor and folding his mala-enwrapped hands atop the table, leaning into them, leaning toward me. "When did you first suspect the dorje might be here?"

Could it be? A moment of admission from Yoong? His saying he is interested in the Most Sacred of Objects? "Why do you ask?"

"Because many lifetimes ago amongst the merchants and traders of the Silk Road, there was a lama who preached that the dorje could bring all to enlightenment. The merchants and traders boiled him in his own fat. Have you heard this story?"

"Yes, I have heard it." Once it was told to me during a lesson on impermanence. Another time I heard it from Madame Sun.

"I am trying to protect you, lama. As your countryman. Promises in the West are no more than tricks of survival that do not come true. Westerners like to say, *Wait. Not now. Sometime later, we'll see*, ascribing all things a value, a price to be paid. What price have they ascribed the dorje? Do you know?"

I unfold the copy of *All Things Asian* I lifted from Abril's. I open to its dorje ad and the Chinese phone number.

Yoong looks at it solemnly. "You should have brought the girl in. You could have saved yourself some concern. You could have realized, the dorje never shipped, and that it was simply a game she played to get you here. A way of attracting you to her, like they do in the West when they are trying to sell you. As is their karma."

He sits solemnly, not changing expression, not changing position. He sits with his chest leaned out over his fat fingers entwined inside their mala.

"No," I tell him. "It shipped. I am certain of it. Abril is trying to sell it, I know this now. And Fernandez, the Hellers, perhaps even the emporium, they are all trying to buy it from her, but they do not want to say. Because in the West, no matter if you have strived, no matter if you deserve or do not deserve, not matter if you are a bodhisattva or not, one feels entitled to the Most Sacred of Objects simply because they can pay for it. I am here to end such thinking, and to bring all to enlightenment."

"Lama. See what's in front of you. All things have two truths, not one. Relative truth. You and I as detectives. Natural seekers. And absolute truth, in which there are no answers. Only distractions. You should have brought the girl in. You would know all this by now."

"For what? She did not kill Sonny Heller. She is simply just one more confused gweilo, only this one trying to sell the dorje. I will find her. I will take it from her. Then I will hold it, and we will all achieve enlightenment, and the whole mess will be over with. And none too soon."

From the next booth over, I can hear Daidyal say, "Why repeat yourself, lama? You said all this before back in Drepung."

Yoong settles back into his bench and sprawls his arms wide along its back. "Perhaps." He wags his jowly face. "Perhaps she did not kill Sonny, and perhaps she never could. Imagine, a gweilo understanding a ritual such as lingchi. But she did steal policies from the Hellers. You know about this. And even though I am only a guest here, the inspector has asked that I inform you, he has taken you off the case. You are to make no more contact with the girl. We will bring her in ourselves. He and I."

My scalp itches. Sweat scratches hair follicles, and my ears flush warm and red. "What kind of agent are you, telling me this?"

"Please, lama. I feel your shame. Believe me, I do. As your countryman, I feel for you." He unfolds his hands. "But the Hellers are insurance people. They like things certain, risk free. Curly expressed concern to the inspector. Curly found you uncertain. There was nothing that could be done. He complained about you."

I do not understood insurance, but I know the hearts of those who sell it.

Yoong averts his eyes, refusing to look at me. His teeth smile crooked. He snaps his fingers at the barman. "Izze, please. Ice." Seeing the nervous way in which he sits there, there is something false about the Chinaman. Like he is not a man thirsty for Izze, but more like someone nervous, needing something, anything, a cup maybe, to hold onto.

The bartender plops down a plastic bucket. Ice crackles in a sea of orange soda. The China agent slurps, sheepishly repeating, "Had you brought the girl in...," but then he only burps, without continuing.

"These stolen policies Heller claims Abril has, they are gweilo policies? Fernandez says an Asian helped her with the lingchi. But

I ask myself, why? What Asian is wronged by her stealing gweilo policies?"

Yoong slurps through his straw, three quick sips. "You are conflating one thing with another, lama. And failing to see what is directly in front of you."

"What is in front of me, Yoong?"

"You yourself learned lingchi, did you not? At Drepung? Part of your black magic studies?"

I twist in my seat, seeing how round and peepish his eyes are behind his glasses. I watch him open his puffed down coat and bring out a lithograph that he places on the table between us. I look at the sketch. A replica of the sword-slaying monk cutting through obscuration, the same as the statue that Chodon unboxed at the emporium. The obscuration's hands are tied behind her back, her shoulders taut and bony. The monk's sword tip against her flesh.

I pray the story may pause here, but it does not. I pray I should mention to Yoong, once I had been the captain of a great niru army, who led a raid against Daidyal, enslaved to his captor seductress, and how my army slayed false monks and destroyed much heresy. But in the end, I failed to rescue the Most Sacred of Objects. So I return, from one lifetime to another. Which is why I am here now.

Yoong asks, "Disobeying the inspector's order could be considered a transgression worthy of lingchi. Could it not? You should have brought her in."

At other tables men lift drinks. Beyond them women stand lined up before dart boards. Each in their own conversation or game. All oblivious to Yoong's and my talking. Outside on the streets, snow falls. Dogs scavenge leaky alleyway dumpsters. Where I sit, the Chinaman slurps Izze. Upon finishing it, he stands large in his puffed down parka, looking down upon me with small eyes and jowly cheeks.

"I tried to help you, lama. Wherever I could, I tried to help. I have failed you, I know, and I am sorry." The flab of his chin and neck is doughy. He steps from the booth to the bar's front door. "You should have just brought her in. We could have ended her story right then and there. You'd be a hero now. A bodhisattva."

He opens the door. A cold wind swirls inside the bar after him, where it lingers long after Yoong has left.

LESSON 19

Our problem is that we think there is time.

OUT ON COLFAX, COLD PULLS tight across my face.

"Some kinda something, that one, huh? A Chinese agent talking to you like a gweilo."

"Quiet."

"You let him speak to you that way?"

"Quiet."

"He cannot take you off the case, lama. He is not even from the West. As your former teacher, whom you once listened to, I insist you speak with Fernandez before accepting anything a China agent says."

"That is just your sort of diversion, Daidyal. Abril has the dorje. I must find *her*. Not Fernandez."

He singsongs it out, one note each syllable. "To get the dorje from her."

"To protect her from others trying to get it for themselves."

"Really? To protect her? Perhaps I have taught you something after all."

"You teach nothing. You are like all the others—you dismiss the dorje's importance."

"Perhaps I have been wrong. Perhaps you have converted me to its cause. Let me ask, why are you here?"

"To find the dorje and bring all beings…"

"No, no, forget that. In a more relative sense, why are you here?"

I look around me, the street where I stand, the snow's silence, the thing to say. "To find Heller's killer."

"And the brothers? Why did they mysteriously come to the warehouse this morning?"

"To find Sonny."

"And why was Sonny there?"

"To find the dorje. Even though his brothers say it does not exist."

"How does one search for what does not exist? Is this not what the Buddha talks about when he talks about emptiness? Seeking what isn't, yet anticipating it is. Anticipating is far more engaging than actually finding a thing."

"Are you now saying the dorje is here?"

"Indeed. And yet not here."

"Why not?"

"Because I watch you, lama, and I see that every step you take on Colfax, it is not you moving toward the dorje, but instead you running from it. You prefer the anticipation of finding it, rather than the actual discovery. You fear giving up the thrill of chasing it for the banality of actually holding it in your hand."

"But it will bring me enlightenment."

"Yes, yes. Of course, it will. It will bring all of us enlightenment. And what will that be like? Do you know? Or do you prefer the surety of remaining here in Hell, searching for the dorje always over the unknown state of actually being enlightened? Causing you to run from enlightenment, and not towards it?"

"You are a fine one to talk about running. Madame Sun's man. I am not running."

"Let me ask it this way. Can a being be both a bodhisattva and a loner? Can he desire to help others, without first accepting help himself? What are you afraid of, lama?"

"Help from whom?"

"From Abril."

"She is trying to sell the dorje."

"And?"

"And I must help her. By taking it from her, and bringing her to enlightenment."

"Is this your way of helping? By keeping her from what you believe she is trying to achieve. Is this how you acknowledge her? By failing to see how she may be helping you?"

His words thunder down on top of me. An echoing thud pauses the story and lifts me from the moment, like a bardo. I stop walking. I stoop to the sidewalk with its freshly fallen snow, and I observe its whiteness. I touch it. I run my finger through the snow's particles, painting out a picture of occurrences. Huey Heller sends me up to her apartment to hunt down missing insurance policies. They are not there. He does not wait for me to return. He says there is no dorje. Yet how can he know what does not exist without first knowing what it is. In its existence?

Yearning and anticipation, these are the ways the absent becomes present. Hell is a desire realm. Desire the lesson it teaches.

Lifting snow from the sidewalk, I see it break apart in my hand. The mind works this way, too. Never knowing everything without seeing anything. A whole comprised of snippets. Pieces missing. Emptiness.

"I taught at the Shedra," Daidyal says. "I taught how our minds trick us into seeing what we already see. Seeing such illusions creates confusion, which we repeat from lifetime to lifetime."

I squeeze the snowy granules in my hand into a ball. I killed my teacher once, in an attempt to rescue the dorje from his withered, womanly hands. I failed. The dorje rolled away from me.

"When you run from a thing, lama, you lose focus on where you are headed. The more you run, the more focus you lose."

"Huey Heller left me at her apartment. Why, if he thought she had the dorje, would he send me there in the first place? When he is trying to capture the Most Sacred of Objects for himself. Is that what you are saying? I should hunt down Huey Heller?"

"If that is what your running mind tells you, yes. But not Huey. No. Curly is the one who convinced Fernandez to take you off the case. That is what the Chinaman said. Why not go see Curly first?"

Lesson 20

To the deluded,
mind and the natural world are separate.
To the enlightened they are one.
- *Dongshan and the Practice of Suchness*

TIME MOVES.

Around midnight I arrive at Curly Heller's Cherry Creek Denver Square with its long stone porch and Grecian urns strung with Christmas lights, holly and ivy dripping from their lips. The front door is carved into stag heads. A deep, rich Ravenna brick climbs the façade of the house from porch to Mansard roof. Imported brick. Rugged.

The doorbell glows dim. I stand on the porch. How did I get here? I rehearse the act of ringing the bell, stepping out from sight of the door's peephole, listening for someone to answer. When he answers, I will toe-tap the door's kick plate, forcing the answerer to lower their attention. So I can then barge in, without them expecting me.

How did I get here? How might the door open? Should I slam it, push my way in narco-style? Like something I had seen in another lifetime, or on TV, or once read in one of those PM Nugent Jersey Shore mysteries.

I push the bell. Its dim light haloes around my shriveled fingertip.

I step to the door's hinged side, flat to the brick. On the street a ruckus arises. Bicyclists pedaling past. Inside the house, a lamp lights. An upstairs window brightens. Fumbling, fiddling, someone awakens.

A moment or two later, I hear footsteps padding down the stairs. The stairs sound carpeted, and the footsteps about the weight and gait of a man of Curly Heller's size and demeanor.

He wanted me off the case. Why? I taste the dryness of the cold night air, and I press against the brick, out of view of the upstairs window.

The door's peephole opens. It casts a dull gray beam into the darkness. Then, it darkens. Someone looking out.

"Who's there?" the peep hole asks.

I slow my breath. I squat into earth energy, strong-legged and springy. With my toe, I tap the door's kick plate. I wait for Heller's attention to look down.

Nothing.

No reaction.

The door does not even crack, nor does its handle display any jiggle. I thumb its latch, and find the door unlocked. How odd, an insurance man sleeping with his door unlocked. Had he been expecting me?

I step inside the vestibule. No one there. Whoever came is gone. The chandelier glows weakly beneath a harlequin shade, and its crystal tinkles in the cold breeze that follows me in. A secretary desk leans against a wood paneled wall. The desk's lip has been folded open. On the lip rests a lingchi sword.

I approach it. The blade feels hollow. Like a tawdry

reproduction. No blood on its blade. No strength in its feel. The handle is screwed on loosely. A child's weapon, almost.

Upstairs, I hear shuffling. Someone rummaging, searching. I feel my way up the stairway bannister. It smells of pine spray. I sniff my fingers. Yes, pine spray. I walk without putting much weight into the stairs, so the wood doesn't creak and give me away. All the way to the top, the staircase's paneled wall displays photos of the Hellers.

Teenagers in swimwear at a Nebraska lakefront.

Young men in suits pointing to a store marquee saying *Heller Insurance.*

Sonny getting an award.

Curly catching a fish.

Huey leaning back in a desk chair, his head relaxed in cupped hands, his elbows wide. He laughs.

Each photo hangs like a moment in time. One of Sonny and Abril holding champagne flutes at a gala.

What had she called him? Her insurance man, with whom she drinks champagne out of flute glasses?

The bannister turns left. I turn with it. At the top of the stairs I hear rummaging rattling from down the hall. I enter a side room and hide, where a green desk lamp with a cut-glass shade sits atop a base of carved jade. The jade is shaped into a depiction of a monk slaying his mistress, cutting through obscuration. He has his sword to her skin. The lamp holds a cardboard placard scripted in ink that says *Late 1500's depiction of a Kagyu monk, Lama...*but then the ink goes blotchy from water stains. I look up to see drops splashing down from a sweating radiator pipe overhead. The pipe elbows its way into the ceiling. A fresh droplet falls. I reach out to catch it. It burns.

On the wall a Felix the Cat clock shifts its eyes and tail left, then right, then left. On the desk an appointment book is opened to December. Each date—Monday through Sunday—with a To-do task written in.

Make money today.
Make money today.
Make money today.
… like a mantra.

Next to it, an *All Things Asian* catalog is opened to the dorje ad and its Chinese phone number. Beneath the ad, another phone number written in red ink and circled. The circle underlined. The underline with a smiley face at one end. I pick up the desk phone and dial the circled number. It rings three times before anyone answers.

"She's at the hospital," it says. A man's voice. He speaks secretly so not to be recognized. "Have you forgotten about her?"

It is true. Abril, she is still at the hospital. I try to keep him talking. "Forgotten about whom?" I ask.

"What do you mean, *whom*? Have you found what you're looking for?"

"The dorje."

"Why are you calling me?" The phone clicks dead. The man's voice, now gone, echoes inside the receiver.

In the hall, the stairwell creaks. I get up from the chair and step toward the door. No one there. I step out into the hall, my eyes adjusting to the dark. Nothing. And then, something. Heller at the top of those stairs, waving to me. "Why are you here, detective?"

My eyes try adjusting. What to see? Heller, no doubt. Standing tall. He holds the child's lingchi blade from the secretary's desk downstairs. He steps one foot forward, and brings the blade hand back behind his shoulder. Then he brings the blade forward. He flings it at me.

Something wrong. Upon release, Heller's shadow bends, grasping his blade hand.

The blade clangs to the floor.

Its handle keeps flying through the air, straight at me, knocking me dead center in my forehead.

Sparkles. Confusion descends. The hallway goes dark. I stumble.

LESSON 21

Relax! Nothing is in control.

MY FOREHEAD THROBS. I TOUCH it and feel a knotted bulge.

The hallway is now empty. The lingchi blade lay in pieces on the floor. I touch my face and robes, but find no blood. I pull my-self up into standing, reeling a bit, making my way back into the room with the desk and the Felix clock. The catalog, the number I dialed, they are no longer there. I think back. I am unable to place the voice on the phone, who's it might be.

Only what it said. *She's at the hospital.*

Which is probably where Heller went. Plus, whoever's num-ber I called. They are probably at the hospital, looking for Abril.

* * *

At the swooped reception desk with spot-lit lighting, inside the echo of the hospital lobby's domed rotunda, I ask, "Where is Abril?"

The rotunda man—pencil-thin mustache, pencil-thin tie, and a massively gray plaid sports coat—speaks in a stuffy, over-weight snit. "Where have *you* been?" He stands unbuttoning the sports coat and smoothing its plaid sleeves.

"She was supposed to call me."

"Call you? She's in a hospital. *Comprendes?* Sorry for your inconvenience, but perhaps she was unable to call you. Have you considered that?"

"Then you should have."

"*Moi?*" The rotunda man palms his cherry cheeks. "I am the receptionist. I receive calls. I do not make them. Says so in the job title." He sounds bored, but then with obvious reluctance and ill-concern says, "Sixth floor solarium. Elevators to your right."

Westerners behave that way. Like they are living beneath their station in life. I walk to the elevator.

"Wait!" The rotunda man stops me. "You have to sign in." He turns a loose leaf note book at me. I write down my name, which the rotunda man reads, feeling smug. "Thank you, Lama *scribble scribble,* whatever you wrote here. Terrible penmanship. Sixth floor. Elevators to your right."

I ride up. The doors open. Another reception desk, this one less ornate. The overhead sign reads, *Nurses' Station*.

"I am looking for Abril."

A squat pumpkin-ish nurse pushes up from her chair. She opens the nurses' station half-door and walks toward me, her chin and mouth squashed up toward her nose, her forehead and eyebrows too big for her face. A compressed woman, in her forties. Maybe fifty. Wide and short. "I'm Head Nurse Flowers." She speaks like snapped elastic. "We wondered when you'd get here. Girls were taking bets."

A petite Vietnamese nurse waves money in the air. "I bet you'd come two minutes past one in the morning, and now look at you. You arrive."

"Someone should have called me."

"Called you?" The nurses exchange looks. "You didn't leave a phone number."

I un-pocket my cell and look at it. What number would they have even called? "I do not know the number," I confess. "I do not know where I even got this phone."

Nurse Flowers squints like I am saying something odd. The Vietnamese nurse suggests, "Maybe someone planted it on you. I saw a show on TV, somebody tracking somebody by their phone. A game show, I think it was. No, a housewife show. Yes, a housewife show, where they hire hitmen."

Nurse Flowers grinds her teeth, top mandible over lower. "I cannot help you with learning your phone number," she says. "Follow me." She rocks side to side walking down the hall. "Your Abril, she may be sleeping. In which case I will not disturb her."

"Sleeping? It was just tests. Is something wrong?"

She stops and faces me. "That is for a doctor to say. I am not a doctor. You want to know what a doctor knows, you should ask a doctor."

She continues up a slight up-ramp and down its other side. She bobs her head inside a door, and then back out. "As suspected, she is sleeping. We'll discharge her when she wakes. Until then, you will need to wait."

"No. I cannot wait. We have to go. Have there been others to see her?"

And then, as if answering the very question I ask, a commotion erupts. Curly Heller at the far end of the hall, walking toward us. His hand is bandaged. "Detective?" he calls. "What are you doing here?"

Then more commotion. The Chinese agent stepping from inside Abril's room. "Out of the way, lama. You're not on the case anymore."

Nurse Flowers appears flabbergasted. She scolds Yoong. "Where did you come from? Guests must stop at the nurses' station before seeing the patients."

Yoong pushes her out of the way, advancing toward Heller, grabbing the insurance man by his arm and swinging him around to face the wall, where he cuffs him.

"Officer, please," she scolds. "There are patients sleeping."

"He's after Abril, lama. Luckily we are here to stop it, even if you are off the case. The best thing to do, take the little nurse here and have her start the paperwork to get Abril released. Then drive her away from this place. Far away."

"You want me to take her?" I ask.

"The paperwork, first. It can be cumbersome in the West, so please hurry. I'll take care of Heller."

I look at the door where inside Abril is sleeping. I look at Heller in cuffs and at Yoong. There is something not right. Nurse Flowers motions to me, "Yes, yes. Let's get her dismissed. She has been here long enough."

I follow the nurse down the hallway, stepping up my pace.

"You'll still need to speak with Doctor Whiner before Abril can be released", she tells me. Then Nurse Flowers squawks into her cell phone like a walkie talkie. "Doctor Whiner. He's here to check her out. We will be at the nursing station."

"We should hurry," I say. "I must bring all beings to enlightenment."

"Not so quick. We have procedures." Nurse Flowers pushes through the swinging half door into the nurses' station, holding it open for me to pass. "The doctor always meets with the family before releasing a patient." She points at a plastic chair molded around a metal frame, just like those in the waiting area. "Take a seat."

I slide into it.

Flowers says to the Vietnamese nurse, "Rosie, bring me the girl in the solarium's patient file, please. She may be leaving with the detective here."

"Detective?" Rosie asks. "Is she under arrest?"

"Are you arresting her?" Nurse Flowers asks.

A bit of quick thinking, a bit of not knowing what to say, until I say, "If I must."

"Really? You did not tell me you were here to arrest her."

"Well, actually, I am not."

Nurse Flowers picks up the phone. She dials.

"Who are you calling?"

"If you ask me," she tells me, "there are way too many free-lancers arresting way too many people these days."

"Who are you calling?"

Nurse Flowers leans back in her chair. In the cup of her ear, I hear the echo of a phone ringing. Between rings, Nurse Flowers explains, "Far too many freelancers come in asking about the pa-tients for me not to check if you're legitimate or not."

Rosie approaches Nurse Flowers with an opened file, pointing to something. Flowers reads it. The phone inside her ear clicks. "Fernandez." I hear him say it, a dull and sleepy voice at the other end of the phone. Not good. He sounds like she woke him.

Just as suddenly as Fernandez answers, Nurse Flowers hangs up and closes the file. "You're Naraka?"

"Yes."

"Her husband?"

"Does it matter?"

"If you're her husband? Yes, it matters. If you're her husband, we can't stop you from taking her. You'd be next of kin. If you're here to arrest her, that's something I will need to discuss with Gus Fernandez."

"Her..." I stumble. "I...I only mean husband is perhaps too specific a word for how I think of myself."

She lifts the file. "Says so right here in the paperwork. You two are married."

"I..." —how do you word such a thing— "I consider her more as someone who helps me," I say. "When I look for things. In that way we are married, yes."

Doctor Whiner enters the nurses' station, carrying her

clipboard—its pages scribbled in small and indistinct penmanship. The white coat is not with her.

"So you've returned? I thought I asked that you wait for her."

"Something came up." People say this in the West, whenever they act irresponsibly. Something came up.

"I see." Whiner looks at the file. "How long have you known her, lama?" The doctor settles into a plastic chair, her hair uncombed and greasy and her face patchy with liver spots I had not noticed earlier. She yawns, while I contemplate—*How long? What is long?* When exactly on time's spectrum does *short* turn into being *long*? And known her *how* exactly?

"Hardly at all," I say.

"Really?" Whiner fans her fingertips over her cheek. "Yet you're married. And she knows so much about you. I thought perhaps..." Whiner tries stifling a yawn, interrupting herself, rolling her hand around her wrist, "vice versa. When did you meet?"

"This morning."

"And you're married?" The doctor clicks her ballpoint pen so that its nib comes out, goes in, comes out. She draws a line on the clipboard, back and forth, ripping its paper into a scar of warm ink. The nursing station clock ticks. Whiner thumbs the clip board's papers. Over her shoulder a poster shows a cartoon dog washing before bedtime.

"If our being married means I could take her with me, then yes. In that way, we are married," I say.

Whiner lifts her glasses, fingering sleep from her eye. "She says you do magic. You're a magician?"

"She should not believe everything she reads on the Internet."

"Is that where you met? On the Internet." She unclips some glossy photographs—eight by tens—from the clipboard. She lays them on a nursing station table. Each photo a bit queasy. Each a little pornographic.

A woman's naked body. Her breasts bleeding. Her thighs, her shoulder, buttocks, her back—all scarred and ripped and bleeding. Thin nicks of skin. Some older than others and healing. Others newer, glossier, and more open.

On her upper gluteal, I see a tattoo. I touch it, and her photographed wounds. I outline the precision of their cuts, seeing her body as a canvass of life's pain. Each of us a victim in Hell. Lingchi.

"Most patients like Abril keep their scarification hidden," Doctor Whiner says. "As a way of surviving, keeping it secret. But Abril shows her wounds out in the open, on display, the way she cuts herself."

"Cuts herself?" The wall clock slices the quiet second by second. Tick. Tick. Tick.

"I confess, I do not understand Buddhism, but your wife…"

"She is not my wife."

"Your fiancé, her Buddhism…"

"She is not Buddhist."

"She lives in a state of dissatisfaction, lama. NSSI."

"Nissi? What are you saying? She is Japanese?"

"Non-Suicidal Self Injury. She cuts herself." The doctor touches the glossies while keeping her distance. "How long has she done this sort of thing?"

I did not see it. When she stood naked in her apartment or in the photo from the warehouse, I did not see it, nor her tattoo. Had I not allowed myself to see her? Her suffering? Should I have, as a bodhisattva might?

"She says the Buddha says everything's a pain," Whiner tells me.

"Everything is suffering," I correct her. "Dukkha."

"Precisely. Is that why she cuts herself?"

"She does not do this. A gweilo such as she is. Lingchi is administered by the strong upon the weak. The Buddha says we suffer because of attachment, seeing two as one. For this reason, many others, I would not know. Can I see her, at least?"

"What do you mean by this word *lingchi*?"

I feel tingling in my skin. I wonder now, why is Yoong here, and Heller. Both down the hall with Abril. How did Yoong know Heller was coming, or that Abril was still in the hospital? And why has Nurse Flowers allowed them to stay in the hall outside the room where Abril sleeps. I wonder about me here, and Yoong and Heller out there moving freely about the hospital. I stand to see if I can see around the corner from the nurses' station.

"Sit down," Doctor Whiner tells me.

I do not. "What are they doing to her?" I ask, and I shoot a glare at the doctor, causing her chair to slide back against the nursing station wall, with her sitting in it. She struggles, but remains pinned in her seat. The half-door unlatches and opens without anyone touching its handle. Nurse Flowers, Rosie, they see it happen. They watch me get up and disappear into the hallway, toward the solarium where Abril is sleeping. Where I hear the steady pulse of footsteps echoing. I move up the ramp, and down its other side to her room. A starched-white nurse in high heels is coming at me. She carries a tray above her shoulder from the far end of the hall. Pills in bottles. Medicines and rubbing alcohol. The nurse walks with elegance, like a waitress carrying a platter of entrees.

I look inside the solarium, but cannot see Abril. Its door is locked. The nurse keeps coming, never dropping stride, never altering her expression, nor her tray. She just keeps walking.

"Where is she?" I call.

The nurse does not answer. Out the corner of my eye, Abril now springs from the solarium's doorway, sparkling like electricity, pushing me aside. She is dressed in pajama bottoms, boots, her sweater and puffed down jacket. She ricochets against the wall, momentarily blocking my view of the nurse coming toward us. A moment later, Yoong bolts from the room, a hefty jolt of aliveness. He wields a blade. He sees me. "Grab her! She's medicated!"

"What did you do with Heller?" I ask.

Yoong comes at me, jabbing with the knife as if to prod me

into action. "Get her, lama. Do you want to be on the case or not?"

But the way he swings the blade, no, I do not get her. I jump, my full body lifting into the air, and then dropping down atop Yoong's arm.

The nurse's heels click atop the linoleum. Time slows. I fly up once more, and then come down on Yoong's arm again so that the blade now falls. Abril swoops in under us and catches the blade before it hits the floor.

The nurse keeps walking.

Abril slices the blade through the air, pushing Yoong back. The nurse gets closer, never breaking stride while Yoong whirls at Abril and she kicks at him, forcing him to collide into the nurse, making her dump her pills and bottles and rubbing alcohol from the tray. The hall smells like spilled raksi.

Abril swings the blade once more, this time ripping Yoong's cheek. Blood spurts. He paws it. The elevator opens. Curly Heller holds its door, car keys in his hand. "Come on," he yells. "Get her and let's go."

Only then does he see Yoong bent over himself, and do I see that the car keys in his hand belong to the Duster.

I sense that.

Abril runs for the elevator, pushing Heller back.

I scoop up the spilled alcohol vial and douse Yoong's face so that his knife cut smolders. He rubs it hard trying to make it stop. I run to join Abril at the elevator. With the knife she forces Heller out of the elevator into the hall. She gets in and begins hitting the elevator's buttons to escape.

I grab the car keys from Heller, and I pull Abril from the elevator into a stairwell that leads to the lobby.

"Oh, what, now you want to help?" She says. "Now, finally?"

We take the stairs one at a time in rapid descent. We cross the lobby toward the wraparound drive, the receptionist yelling behind us, "Hey, where are you going? You have to sign out!"

We do not sign out.
We rush into the wraparound where the Duster's parked.
We climb into the car.
We escape.

LESSON 22

Man steps slowly. The ground remains patient.

TRAFFIC LIGHTS ON THE FRITZ. They flicker red overhead. I skid into an icy intersection, nothing to hold onto. I yell at Abril. I hear myself saying the same thing over and over again. "What are you doing to yourself?"

"What are you doing, lama?" Daidyal asks. "Slow down. Where did you learn to drive?"

Abril kicks the dash. "What did you tell those cops? You were supposed to wait for me. I didn't even know where you were. You just up and go. Then the cops show up." She swats my arm. "Where were you?"

Daidyal sighs. "What's the play here, lama? You and she, driving off into the snow cover of midnight? Do you think you can escape this way? Where'd you learn to drive?"

"I drive, okay. I just drive," I snap at him.

"Don't talk to me like that." She swats my arm again. "It's my car. Everything, it's mine. You're here because I asked you here."

Daidyal leans closer, clutching my seatback. "The police want her. You want her. The Hellers want her. She's a very popular girl."

"I do not want her. I want the dorje, pure and simple."

"Oh. Is that where we are going? Finally, to get the dorje?"

The lights of Colfax flicker amber and red. The Duster's tires slip over the road.

"She has it," I tell him. "Call the ad in the catalog, her phone rings. I am protecting her. So I can get it from her myself."

"See things as you like to, lama."

"I see things as they are. With pure intention."

My cell phone rings. "Lama Naraka. Nurse Flowers. You did not complete the paperwork. Plus, there's a problem with Abril's insurance." I shut the phone. I throw it to the back seat.

Abril punches my shoulder, forcing me to jostle the Duster into oncoming traffic. "What?" she says. "Now you're not talking to me? See it for what it is, lama? The Hellers, the police, they're one and the same. Tear this shit down. I'm not fooling about that either."

I right the Duster back to its proper lane. "What are you doing to yourself, Abril. Lingchi, all over your body."

"What do you care?"

"Ooh," Daidyal says. "Watch yourself, lama. She is not nearly as fragile as you think, except maybe a bit."

"You should not do that to yourself."

"It's just cutting. It's just me, trying to feel something. Okay?" She kicks the dash again. "Maybe you ought to try it. Try feeling something for once in your life."

"I feel. This moment here, I feel it. I am protecting you, am I not?"

"Protecting me? Or this crazy dorje you're after?"

"Protecting her, lama?" Daidyal asks. "I suspect she might be better at protecting you."

"I don't need your protection," she says. "I need you to open your eyes. See what's true. There is no dorje." She says it breathlessly. Just like everyone else. "And you're supposed to help me get insurance. And now the hospital's calling, because there's a problem, right?"

"You and Sonny were lovers."

She scratches a woolen mitten beneath her eye. "You don't understand. You're not from Colfax." Her voice sounds dribbly, like maybe she might cry. "So what, we were lovers. Not really. We didn't care for one another or anything. Just trying to survive." She lifts her hands in the air, like ta-da or voila or some other collection of syllables Westerners say when stating the obvious or the embarrassing. "Life stinks, but at least I survive. I needed insurance, he's an insurance guy. He needed to make quota. Everything's a horse trade in the West. Transactional. That's how we act civilized, everything with its price. You want to call it a relationship, sure, go ahead, call it a relationship. I call it what it was. Blasé. Boring. A lot of watching TV, sitting on the couch, getting up off the couch, necking on the couch, but not really. We were a million miles apart. The whole time. I needed insurance. He needed to make quota. That's all it was."

"You stole insurance policies from him. Ten of them."

"What? Those Tibetan policies. Sonny gave them to me."

The Duster rattles over a pothole covered in a mound of snow. "Do not lie to me. They were not Tibetan policies. They are gweilo."

"They sound Tibetan. I can't pronounce any of their names, so they sound Tibetan. Look, lama. Sonny texts me, says we should meet at the warehouse. Make things right. Says he has something for me. I thought he was going to give me my insurance back."

A car turns onto Colfax, its headlights lighting Abril up.

"I go to the warehouse, okay? Sonny's there. He's scared. Sonny wasn't a guy for getting scared, he's an insurance man. It freaked me out. Plus, he doesn't give me my insurance back. I say,

What the hell? Instead he gives me these old, paid-up Tibetan life policies. Says it's better than insurance, and I should hold onto them for safekeeping. Says his brothers will pay gold to get them back. Instead, they don't give me shit. They think they're gods, these insurance men. Like they're masters and we're just little puppets whose claims they deny. Who do they think they are?"

"You say you brought me here. Why? You and Sonny were lovers. He could have straightened your insurance for you."

"Yeah, we were lovers. Sex maybe, sure. But not lovers. Not really." She stares blank-faced, crossed eyed, with unwashed hair and a freckled-brown nose. These things she does not see about herself.

"I know that the missing policies are not Tibetan," I tell her. "I have a list."

"Jeese, listen to me, why don't you? They're Tibetan."

Such conversation. Me a lama, her not. Why does she not listen to me? "Let me see them," I say. "Let me read their names and see if they are Tibetan or not."

The Duster passes sidewalk cigarette smokers, gaunt like hungry ghosts.

"That what a bodhisattva does. Doubt everything I say? Jeese, lama. You want to do something a bodhisattva might do? Buy me a cup of coffee? How's that? You want me to think you're a nice guy? Get me a coffee." She kicks the dash once more. "Two blocks down. Pete's Diner." She wags her head. "First time out with a girl, least you can do is buy her a cup of coffee, why don't you?" She turns to the window. "Like you're at least pretending to be a bodhisattva."

Lesson 23

Live in the moment
by not trying to live in the moment.
Let it just be.

THE COFFEE TASTES WEAK, MORE water than bean, but the mug feels warm on my fingers.

We sit in a front booth next to the window. Abril's insistence. She says she wants to watch the night go by.

The counter man shuffles over, drops down our ordered-up plates of biscuits and gravy. Gelatinous pasty flour atop hardened biscuit-y flour. American dining. Bloated, nutritionally light, cooked to keep you hungry, wanting more, ordering more, spending more. That's how they eat in the West.

I unfurl the rolled-up paper napkin. A fork and knife clang out of it onto the table top. I pick up the fork and push it around my plate, checking the gravy's viscosity and drag. Abril shakes pepper over hers, then stabs some up and chews. She gulps coffee to break down the biscuit. The plate glass window next to our booth shivers against the cold.

"Do not tell me the dorje does not exist," I tell her. I pull a copy of *All Things Asian* from my inner robe pocket. "Why when I call the number in the ad does your phone ring?"

Abril looks it over, twisty faced, like she has not seen this ad before. "That's not my phone number. It's Chinese."

"It rings in your apartment."

"Really?" She shakes more pepper onto her gravy and lifts the catalog to read more closely. "Is that really what the dorje looks like?" She points at its crude rendition, pencil and ink. "It says right here, Madame Sun's Emporium. You want to find it, go back there for it. I'm not going." She tosses *All Things Asian* back at me. It sloshes coffee from my cup down onto the ad. "Where'd you get that catalog?"

"In your apartment."

"*My* apartment? I've never seen it before."

"Dial the number in the ad and your phone rings. Yes, your apartment. You have the dorje. You might as well tell me, Abril. You are trying to sell it. Heller, the Chinese agent, they came to the hospital to get it from you. And Fernandez, he is trying to pin you with Sonny's murder."

She bites some biscuit while digging hard for some excuse to tell me. "That explains it. The nuisance calls I keep getting. Look, lama, I admit. You're not the first to ask about the dorje. I get phone calls, day and night. They started a few weeks ago. I thought maybe Sonny had something to do with it."

"You told me you know nothing about the dorje."

"I don't. Up until seeing it in this catalog it was just a word I heard. I don't know what it means. Just something people say. Like what the Buddha means when he talks about emptiness. A word without meaning."

"Where is the dorje, Abril?"

"There it is again. You saying it, that word." She reaches for the catalog. "Madame Sun's emporium. That's where it says here. Not me. I got nothing to do with it. Go back and ask that old couple. Maybe they're the ones keeping it from you?"

Diversions. She is good at them. "Choki was once my trusted lieutenant."

"Really? I didn't know you trusted anyone."

"He tells me he was, and I trust him." I turn to watch the counter man leafing through his newspaper. Never on any one page too long. Just the three of us here, the only ones in the place. "What do you know about lingchi?" I ask. "Anything?"

She laughs. She forks up more biscuit and gravy. "I thought we were talking about emptiness." She waves her fork about the diner. "Like this place. Empty."

"Quiet, I would say, more than empty."

"No. Not quiet," she tells me. "Empty. This time of night, this place should be jumping. Bar kids and junkies and night-shifters and old couples scoping out early bird breakfast specials."

"It is too cold for any of that."

"Yeah. Just you and me. Plus, the counter man. In all the time I been coming here, I ain't ever seen him before." She nods. "That counter man's new. And he's blind." She stabs more biscuit onto her fork, points it at him. "That sound right? A blind man working the counter?"

I watch him leaf through his newspaper. "He is not blind. He is reading. How can he be blind?"

"Same way anyone acts like someone they're not. He's pretending."

"Pretending? Then why not pretend to read Braille, with his fingers, if he is pretending?" The counter man turns another page. A light, greasy breeze wafts from the page over his face. The counterman tastes its freshness on his lips.

"I'm telling you, he's blind," Abril says. "I've never seen him before. What's he doing here? Those cops you sic'd on me, maybe they put him here to watch us."

"How can he watch us, if he is blind?"

"You bet he's blind. Here, watch this." She waves her cup in the air without saying anything.

The counter man looks up. "You all want more coffee?"

"See that? He is not blind," I mutter beneath my breath.

The counterman shrugs. "Don't make no matter to me. You get free warm ups, so I pour you more if you want. Comes with the biscuits and the gravy. Says so, right there next to the sugar shaker. Right there on your table."

"Not blind, huh? Look." Abril points at our table's collection of condiments. "No sugar shaker, sugar," she says. "He's blind."

The counter man shuffles over. "Coffee it is. Coffee's good tonight. A good night for coffee." He stands over us with the pot in his hand, heat rising from its spout, his gaze wandering a bit, unfocused. He picks up my cup with a finger against its lip and pours. Steam dampens his cracked knuckles while the he bobs his head in time to the rising warmth. Then he takes up Abril's, doing the same.

"You're blind, aren't you?" she says.

"Yes, girl, I am," the counter man tells her. "If it makes you curious, yes, I am."

She dumps Coffee Mate into her warm up and swizzles it. I sip mine, staying quiet. "I never seen you here before," she says.

"Well, I never seen you, neither." The counter man laughs. "Not sure who you are. The regular crew, too cold for them outside. So I come in." He shuffles back to his newspaper, laughing, feeling his way with his feet.

"Told you he's blind. Doesn't work here either. Not regular. Told you that too." Her voice echoes a bit loudly inside the diner's glass and the glass's aluminum window frame. Outside a bicyclist pedals past wearing a Spurtz jacket. Just a diversion.

"Why when you dial the ad's number does your phone ring?"

Abril puts her cup on its saucer. "You're a do-gooder, right, lama? A bodhisattva wannabe. You ever get phone calls you can't explain. Telemarketers? People selling shit, you don't know what it is. Nuisance calls. I don't know why anybody calls my phone. But I get all these nuisance calls all the time about the dorje. That's how I knew to conjure you. Somebody called. Said if I wanted you back, I should take an ad in the catalog. Okay? Said the ad should say I had the dorje for sale. Then you'd come running."

"Who told you this?"

"A woman. On the phone."

"She told you to place the ad in the catalog?"

"Yeah. But I didn't do it. I Googled you instead. Then I conjured you up."

I push myself back into my seat. "Who are you working with?"

"Nobody. I'm gainfully unemployed. All this time you been here, what? You haven't seen me go to work, have you? Or complain about my boss? Or bitch about somebody in the next cubicle, have I? Working's a way they trap you, lama. I don't do that shit."

I lean toward her, toward her side of the table and I whisper, "Madame Sun?"

"Madame Sun?" She laughs. "There is no Madame Sun. You told me that." She takes my hand in hers. "Forget about Madame Sun. She's nothing to you anymore. See what's in front of you, lama. Me, sitting right here."

I take my hand back. I take up my mug, sipping from it, smelling burnt coffee on my fingers, and the smell of the burlap in which the beans shipped. And the sweat of its harvesters. The clamminess of its soil. Each sip holding the complete fullness of its many lives. When I place the mug back on its saucer, its porcelain rings like a bell fading after being struck. Sounding like emptiness.

"Lama." She scooches forward. "What if I was to tell you, I can't help you find the dorje? Would you think any less of me?" Asking me this, her one eye looks at me larger than the other.

"You said you would help me."

"You know what I learned about insurance, lama? It does not last. Once you use it, that's a pre-existing condition. Obsolete." The bicyclist rides past. "What do you think that nurse on the phone meant, there's a problem with my insurance? Some pre-existing condition, right? So why should I help you if you can't help me? You, who can't even help yourself, can't even find the dorje. There is no Madame Sun, just like you say. But her emporium is there. The old couple, you sure they're not playing you?"

Choki. My niru lieutenant. Together we rode upon Drepung. He never wavered. Or so he tells me.

"I am a bodhisattva," I say. "People bring me their desires. Like I can make them come true." I take Choki's envelope from my pocket, sprinkling its obituaries onto the tabletop. "Hell is a desire realm." I sift the obituaries through my fingers, picking them up, dropping them one by one. "He asks I pray for these unfortunates. All killed by lingchi. If I do, will they be any different than how they are now? What good are prayers, except to convince us what's missing in our lives? But with the dorje, I can bring all enlightenment. I swear I can. Without the need to pray or believe. It will just do it, all by itself."

"Ahh, so sweet." She mocks me. She picks up a handful of obituaries and lets them flutter, mocking me. "You look for certainty, lama. That's the mistake you make. No matter how diligently you peruse a thing, you never quite see it. Certainty's an excuse. Certainty is what we blindly convince ourselves of."

The bicyclist circles back, passing us the other way. Abril folds her elbows atop the clippings. "The Hellers said I stole those Tibetans' policies, but I didn't. Why do you suppose they say I did?"

"They are not Tibetan, Abril. They are gweilo policies."

"They're Tibetan." She picks up an obituary and reads it. "Like this name here. Tibetan sounding." The bicyclist rides the other side of the street. She picks up another obituary and reads it. "Where did you get these? You see how they're all stamped *Heller Insurance*? What did you say, the emporium guy, he gave them to you?"

"Yes."

"Listen." She reads one to me. "*Choling Dolma. Skin sheared. Appendages detached. His family scheduled for deportation to China, unable to demonstrate an assured means of on-going support.*"

"Lingchi," I say.

"Choling Dolma. I know this name." She reads another. "This one too. Dawa Ema. I know these names, from the Tibetan policies Sonny gave me." She reads one more. "This one too. Their families all being deported. All because of *lack of verifiable funds.*"

"The West is an unwelcoming place," I tell her.

"No. These are the names on the life insurance policies. They had life insurance. Sonny said the policies were all paid out when they died. Their families should all have verifiable funds. Not be getting deported."

The Spurtz cyclist rides closer, up our side of the street, barely pedaling now, moving slowly. As he draws near, Abril stands. She folds the obituaries into their envelope and puts the envelope inside her coat pocket. "Come on. We need to get out of here."

"I will need those obituaries, to pray for those men," I say.

"Come on. Get up. Let's go. Those policies Sonny gave me, I think these are them."

It sounds odd. Heller's list was all gweilo names. I stand, but when I do the counter man takes my arm and holds me from following Abril.

"Well now, that's fine. Sounds like you two had a nice conversation, nice breakfast, nice morning. Deciding now to leave. That's fine. I don't mind having the company, I don't mind don't having it neither. But you got to pay. Oh, yeah. You're leaving like you are—sounds like you are—you got to pay. That's all."

He hands me a bill. Greasy feeling, so that it slips from my fingers to the floor. I stoop to get it. While stooping, Abril shouts, "Lama, watch out."

The plate glass above me pops. I look up and see a hole dimple through the glass. A shattering little pop-hole, where I had been sitting just moments earlier.

I turn to the wall opposite the plate glass, and see its paneling splintered from an arrow that now sticks out of the diner's health code certificate tacked on the wall.

I crawl to the booth. The shrill wail of the night whistles in through the freshly popped arrow hole. Around it, the glass has spider-webbed. I cannot see a thing outside. I lean an eye to the hole, and see now the Spurtz cyclist pedaling away down Colfax.

I look to the door to be sure Abril is okay. And quickly I figure, yes, she must be.

Because the door to Pete's diner now flaps open in the cold. And in the snow outside I see footsteps of her running from the diner. Leaving me here alone, holding the counter man's bill in my hand, while she has taken the obituaries and fled.

LESSON 24

The sensations of pleasure and pain lay the groundwork for attachment and aversion. This is how conflict is created.

SHE LEFT. TOOK THE OBITUARIES and left. Left the car keys behind, right there next to the sugar shaker. Other than that, she left.

"Ain't really blind," the counter man says while making change of my twenty. "I like saying I am, but I ain't."

I run outside. I climb into the Duster and drive over ice-covered Colfax to the Aim Straight and Shoot. No traffic lights flicker now. No amber or red. No stop signs. I park and see the Aim Straight's shackled, closed up, and dark.

I step from the Duster and tread the snowy, sanded sidewalk. I climb those long, slow stairs up to the apartments feeling warmth rush down upon me. Not a heat kind of warmth, like a radiator's or steam pipe's. More an angry hot, with a whiff of human perspiration.

Light shines through where the arrow cracked Abril's door jamb. Inside the apartment, the baby crib is smashed into pieces. Dishes lay smashed on the floor. Overhead lighting dangles from thin wires. Altar candles still burn, but are tipped onto their sides. The Buddha statue too, smiling over on its side, a chipped plaster gash running down its cheek.

The place has been ransacked. I kick my way through the debris calling for her. "Abril."

On the altar lay a packet of insurance policies tied in ribbon the color of candy canes.

I page through them. Each reads the same as the other. One for Choling Dolma. One for Dawa Ema. One for each of the obituaries Choki gave me. Ten in all. Huey Heller said they were gweilo. Why lie about a thing like that?

I pick one up. Dawa's. I read it, and notice something peculiar in the paragraph headlined *Beneficiary* …

Upon death, benefit will be paid in memorium to Madame Sun's Olde Tibetan Emporium and Meditation Center in the sum of fifty thousand dollars ($50,000).

Norbu's policy.

Upon death, benefit will be paid in memorium to Madame Sun's Olde Tibetan Emporium and Meditation Center in the sum of fifty thousand dollars ($50,000).

I check each one, and draw a conclusion. Abril was right. Choki has duped me. These Tibetans, he duped them too. He and his emporium are the beneficiaries of their policies. They die, killed by lingchi, and he collects the insurance money. Not their families.

He lied to me. He told me he did not have the dorje.

I shuffle through the policies, each the same as another. Even the last policy. The most curious policy of all…

Should shipment not arrive in its totality and in solid condition and sound shape, benefit will be paid to Madame Sun's Olde Tibetan Emporium and Meditation Center in the sum of four *million nine hundred thousand dollars ($4,900,000).*

Some say nothing exists without value. Everything is worth some amount of money. Perhaps Choki said it while we walked to the warehouse. Perhaps someone else. I cannot recall.

From the back of the apartment, Abril's bedroom door creaks. I pocket the policies and step toward it. Lightly I push the door so that it opens. Inside, clothes and belongings are strewn every which way throughout the room. What to see?

On the night table, a Princess phone and a lamp.

On the lamp, a Post-it note.

On the Post-it, glitter writing. It says *Calls for the Dorje I Received,* and an arrow points from the Post-it to a spiral notepad. Names and phone numbers written in columns. One right after the other, pages and pages. She called them nuisance calls. Why write them down?

I skip through the spiral notebook pages, seeing a name I recognize. *Sonny Heller,* circled in red.

Skipping further, another name. Also circled.

Curly Heller.

The Hellers called her about the dorje.

The Princess phone then blushes pink while the phone in the living room trills beneath the smashed baby crib. The Princess blushing, the baby crib trilling, they happen simultaneously. I lift the Princess receiver. A voice says, "Abril. Warehouse. 7:30."

"Doesn't anyone say *hello* anymore?" I ask.

The phone does not answer. It hangs up.

Lesson 25

Sensation arises, passes,
Arises, passes.
We live in flux, in the same way we breathe.

THE WAREHOUSE LAWN TREES BEND with ice. Inside Budais stand seven by seven, arms in the air, laughing. Heller and his Shaker chair have been removed. The stink of death lingers, but not its presence.

I walk the maze of Budais. Each step a new statue blocks my way. Some I kick from my path so that they skitter across the floor sounding empty.

"Yoong. Heller," I call. I sense their presence. I walk among the statues. My step upon the floorboards causes some statues to warble and others to fall. When they fall, they roll with the sound of hollow emptiness on their fat bellies, before eventually coming to a standstill.

Except one statue. The last one to fall. The one closest to the warehouse sanctuary. This one does not sound hollow. Inside it, I hear raindrops, sounding like mala beads pinging on stone.

I reach for the statue, just out of reach. I try lifting it, but cannot. Something pulls me back. A hand on my shoulder. "The inspector wants a word with you, lama." I turn and see Yoong. He holds me. He turns me to face him, and then steps aside so that I now see Fernandez.

"What are you doing here, lama?" He wears his duster like a cape across his shoulders, unbuttoned. He walks around me, with the hem of the duster swishing the floorboards. "I believe the agent here explained to you, you're off the case. So why come back?"

The beading sound inside the Budai plinks now into silence. "I do not report to the Chinese agent," I say. "I am Tibetan, and I report to you, inspector."

I hear him breathing as he circles behind me. "*Reported* to me, lama. *Pasado*."

"Why *pasado*? Because Curly Heller said so?" I nod at Yoong. See his cheek slashed by Abril in the hospital dribbling blood. "Who do you work for, inspector?"

The inspector still circles, coming around now in front of me. "Watch yourself, lama. I thought maybe I'd ask the questions here, if that's all right with you. I thought maybe I'd ask...why are you here?"

"To meet someone."

"To meet someone?"

"A suspect."

"A suspect? Does this suspect have a name?"

"Curly Heller."

"Ah. Curly Heller. One of the insurance brothers?"

I watch their reactions. "He has the dorje," I say. "Or expects to soon."

"He called you and told you this?"

"In a manner of speaking. Perhaps you should ask Agent Yoong. He can say."

Fernandez glances at the agent, but talks to me. "Funny thing. Curly Heller calling you. Because, you know, he called me too. Says you broke into his house last night."

"The door was unlocked."

"Really? An insurance man, leaving his doors unlocked?" Fernandez shrugs. "Why would he do that?"

"Ask Yoong." I nod over at the Chinese agent, but I am talking about Heller. "He knows more than he is telling you."

Fernandez holds his hands together in front of him. "Seems everybody knows more than they say these days. Agent Yoong, please, check the lama here for weapons."

"What are you doing?" I ask. "We are wasting time. Heller has the dorje."

Yoong approaches solemnly. "I am sorry, lama. I must search you now." He pats my robes, up and down.

"Ask the agent why he was at the hospital?" I shout. "Ask him what he was doing there with Heller."

Yoong finishes patting me. He steps to my side, and in a swift, unanticipated move, chops into my ribcage, fingertips first. "The inspector said he will ask the questions, lama. You and I, we are guests of his. Please allow him."

"Why did you break into Heller's?" Fernandez asks.

"The door was unlocked," I cringe. I am folded over slightly from the suddenness of the blow. "I suspected trouble inside, so I investigated."

"What kind of trouble?" The inspector stands tall on one leg, like a bird in the swamp, while the sole of his other foot scuffs the floor, back and forth.

The jab to my ribcage, I can barely squeeze the words out. "Sonny…" Plus, seeing the world as it is, this also holds my words back. "Sonny was killed because Curly wanted the dorje."

Fernandez's face twists. "You're saying Curly killed his brother? How? He does not know lingchi."

"Ask the China agent. Lingchi is a Chinese form of torture."

Fernandez, with his tongue stuck in the sac of one cheek, says, "Suppose I was to tell you... Yoong's status as an international guest precludes me from asking him anything? Meaning out of the two of you, you're the only one I can ask?"

"He is here for the dorje. He and Curly, they were trying to steal it from Abril."

"So she has it, you're saying? Even though it never shipped, and doesn't exist?"

I can hear the clap of thunder outside, awakening me. I hear hail cascading atop the roof and Fernandez scuffing the floor with his shoe—back and forth—in a rhythm as steady as jewels inside a Buddha statue. "It did ship," I say.

He stops scuffing. "There's something I'd like to show you, lama. Get your opinion, if I might."

But then the inspector doesn't move. Like he is expecting me to show him something, and not the other way around as he suggested.

"If you will not question the Chinese agent," I say, "bring Curly in. Let him tell you." Yoong's wound has opened more, so blood now pools down his cheek.

Fernandez knocks me at the shoulder. "That's precisely what I wanted your opinion about." He nudges me to follow him back inside the warehouse, toward its sanctuary, where I see now an illusion of sorts. A half-wall, eight feet up, painted a perfectly matched color as the wall behind it. One looking like the other, so that when you see them from inside the warehouse, they appear like one wall at the back of the building. Even though between them, they create an un-ceilinged room. A sacristy within a sanctuary, from its Catholic days.

We walk the blood-stained floor where Sonny bled out. We enter the hidden room through one of its two un-walled ends. I see now at the exterior wall an iron door clamped closed. A metal, fireproof door, painted identically to the wall surrounding it.

"Parking lot outside," Fernandez says casually. "Overgrown.

Dead stalks growing through asphalt. Go ahead. Open the door. Take a look, if you'd like."

Yoong and Fernandez step back, waiting for me to pull the door's handle. When I do, cold rushes into the sanctuary, and I see it is no longer hailing, and I hear the door clang with a heavy weight as it bangs open.

In the parking lot, snow and crystals of frozen fallen ice. Among the crystals, arms and feet and fingers. The snow dyed with blood.

On the door's outside, hung like a Christmas wreath, Curly Heller suspends from a hook.

What is left of him.

I gag. *O mane Padma hum.* My prayer gags with the smell of biscuits and gravy.

The inspector raps his knuckles on the door's iron. "Lingchi," he says. "Just like his brother before him."

LESSON 26

Feelings are not planned.

DOWN AT THE PRECINCT FERNANDEZ steers me to an interrogation room. A boxy little confinement. The same type room where Garcia brought me earlier, only this one with better furniture. Nicer chairs to sit in.

Fernandez points me into one. "A lot of freelancers don't cut it, lama. It takes a subtle skillset to be a freelancer. A skillset to be and not be at the same time. You're not really a cop, and you're not really not a cop. Fusco should have told you that, when he dialed you on the freelance list. He should have told you the way you succeed being freelance is by seeing things like I see them."

It is just the two of us. Me sitting in an interrogation room chair, the inspector hiking a foot up atop the chair next to me, brushing scuff marks from his Zelli Avianos. "I perfectly well understand why she brought you here to kill Sonny, they were lovers.

But why Curly? Why kill him? You ran a little amok there, didn't you, lama?"

I have heard this sort of accusation before. "I did not kill anyone."

"You went to her place unaccompanied. You answered a call about meeting Curly Heller at the warehouse. Just like she set you up to do. To trap him? To trap you? Both of you?"

"You ransacked her apartment."

"I ransacked nothing. I executed a warrant. Let's just leave it at that."

"What were you looking for?"

"You." The room echoes when he says it. "I thought you'd be there. Then I got a call from Pete's Diner about a bicyclist nuisance."

"A bicyclist attacked me. One of the Spurtz gang."

"The Spurtz gang," he laughs. "Please, lama, they're bicyclists. They just like wearing Lycra, that's all. I understand this Lycra-wearer shot an arrow and broke Pete's window. The counterman saw the whole thing. Says she left you there, so you went looking for her at her apartment. And what did *you* find? Stolen Tibetan policies all tied up in a bow, right out in plain sight. Like she wanted you to find them. Like she tricked you into finding them. She's stringing you along, lama." He brushes the last of the dirt from his shoes and stands straight now, both feet to the floor. He stretches up on his toes, heels to the air, so that he towers over me even more than normal, and then flattens his heels to the ground. He stretches once more, up on his toes, down. Some western yoga working his calf muscles, it seems. "She's pinning it on you, lama, and she's doing a damn good job, because so far you're all I got. And this case is starting to exceed budget. And we're going to need to wrap it up soon, and you're all we got. She got you here on false pretenses, to pin Sonny's murder on you. You fell into her trap. That's a plausible story to tell. You're not even from around here. People don't like strangers, you know."

"Yoong and Curley Heller, they came to the hospital after her."

"Curly's dead. Sonny, too. Their names circled on her nightstand. Why do you think she picked on you? Because you know lingchi?"

"Lingchi is a Chinese form of execution. Speak with Yoong about it."

"Yoong's a guest. Why'd you bring lingchi up in the first place, if you didn't want to get caught?"

Intention, desire–these things do not always come from consciousness. Sometimes they come from someplace deeper. That is what the inspector is asking. "She has the dorje. It is why they are after her," I say.

"We've searched her place. Executed a warrant. We did not find any dorje."

"But you went there looking for it, did you not? Twice. Looking for what you did not find."

He stops his yoga exercise. His shoulders slump. "The dorje did not ship. Probably doesn't exist. But if it does, and if it did ship, I am under obligation to return it to our guest. To the PRC, for them to return it to its display in the Lhasa Museum. And all this talk of yours about the dorje, it diverts valuable resources, chewing up the budget, and so far you're all I got."

"So you admit it. The dorje is missing from the Lhasa Museum."

"She brought you here, lama. She played you. Oldest story in the West. Damsel in distress brings a gunslinger to town to save her. Only once she's saved, just one problem left. Got to get rid of the gunslinger. Cover her tracks. She brought you here to tear it all down. Two Hellers dead. What more does she need from you? She told the China agent at the hospital, you willfully agreed to help her."

It rings false. "She would not use such words as *willfully agreed*, inspector. And she did not summon me here. I came of my own volition. To bring enlightenment to all."

"Yeah. So you say. But let's face it, this talk of enlightenment, it's really just a distraction from everyday life, isn't it? From doing the things we have to do."

"I did not kill anyone. Sonny died before I was even reborn, and Curly while I was in Abril's apartment."

"Maybe that's true. Maybe it's not. The thing you need to understand, lama, detective work makes pictures out of things. Right or wrong, it doesn't matter. As long it's easy enough to understand, and on time, and under budget, and makes a nice picture. You want to know the picture I see? She lured you here with talk of the dorje. You did what she wanted. You're an assassin, from way back when. We are the things we do."

"She did not conjure me."

"Before there was any such thing as lingchi here on Colfax, before it started, I can't find a single record of you even existing. Only once you showed up did the trouble begin."

"I do not commit lingchi."

Fernandez stares at his fingers, cracked from the dry and cold. He looks at one, then the one next to it. Then all five in a row. "Where do you come from, lama?"

"The warehouse. You brought me here, just now."

"Before the warehouse?"

"Abril's apartment."

The inspector sits, elbows the table, resting one arm upright, leaning his cheek against its two raised fingers. "You're like a nobody. An émigré stranger. Someone to be discarded. There's no record of you. Not until the killings began."

Yoong comes into the room, *click clacking* his mala beads, hands behind his back.

"Why is he here?" I ask.

The inspector shifts in his chair. "He's a guest of mine." Two whitened finger imprints run down his cheek. He turns to Yoong, who from behind his back produces a statue of a monk slaying ignorance. Identical to the base of the lamp at Curly's home office, and what Chodon pulled from the box at the emporium. "He's your countryman, and he showed me this. See what it says there, what they call this statue. *A Kagyu Monk Killing his Mistress.*"

"A monk cutting through kleshas," I clarify.

"That...what you say right there, that is superstition," Fernandez says. "A way to avoid seeing what is in front of you." Then he says her name out loud. "Madame Sun. The woman in the statue, that's who she is, isn't it? Like the name on the emporium. A Gelugpa sorceress, killed by a Kagyu lingchi master. That's the story they tell."

"I only come to help," I say.

"And that's very nice of you. But Madame Sun was killed by lingchi. Back in the day." He flaps open a folder he has placed on the table, fanning out photographs from inside. An array of angles. All from the warehouse photo shoot. All of Abril holding the knife, naked. Little nicks in her skin. The photos black and white. What Westerners call art. Relics of the deeply seeded mind.

"Perhaps you did not kill these men. Perhaps she brought you here to show her how to kill them herself, as your apprentice. It's a story I can tell downtown, and they'll believe it."

I see the photos. Abril naked, her back to the camera.

"Photos capture moments," the inspector says. He points to her butt smudge. "Read what it says there."

"It is just a birthmark. Nothing more."

Fernandez turns the photo so he might see it better. "Agent Yoong. Is this a birthmark?"

"It is a word, sir, tattooed on her skin. An English word."

"And what does it say?"

"It says *Desire*, sir. *Miss Desire.*"

The inspector turns the photo back toward me. "Mean anything to you? *Desire?*"

The photo stares at me, a moment frozen in time. A break in life's continuum.

"Huey Heller called early this morning. Says Curly didn't show for work. He was supposed to meet Abril at a warehouse, except she didn't show. Instead you did, lama."

"It is a lie. Curly does not come to work this early. Ask the receptionist. Mimi."

"I'd like you to stand, if you would."

"Why?"

Fernandez hangs his face sad now, like a puppy dog, feeling misunderstood and offended. "Because I asked you to."

Agent Yoong comes up behind me and helps me from the chair. With soft hands, he pulls my right wrist behind my back and cuffs it. Then my left hand. He cuffs it too. Both hands gripped as one. "You should have seen things as the inspector does," he breathes into my ear. Then he steps back.

"I need to find the dorje," I say. "For the good of all, you must free me."

"Ah, yes, free," Fernandez says. "How important it is to feel free in this country? You know the way to be free? Learn how not to be free. That's how you do it.

Yoong leads me from the room, while the inspector continues talking. "To be free, I tell prisoners when I book them, to be free you must accept the fact we are not free. That's a lesson I teach. Something I can teach you, lama. Something you can learn from. Starting right now."

LESSON 27

To change the world,
change your mind.
Then it is done.

CARDBOARD BOXES ARE STACKED ALONG the walls of my jail cell, hemming me in. I pace the thin pathway between them and the bars. One of the stacked boxes juts out shoulder high, jabbing me as I pass. I try pushing it back into the stack in line with the others, but the boxes cram too tightly, and the cell space proves too narrow for me to get much leverage.

When was it? Another lifetime, reincarnated as a fighting animal shackled in leg irons in an encampment of carnivores? The shackle's teeth ripped my coat and bone. I bled. I chewed at my leg for nourishment until it severed. Then I hobbled off free.

Only when we see the good and bad of a thing do we see it whole. Only by breaking a part of ourselves away, do we see ourselves at all.

The cell squeezes. Two walkable feet wide, no more. Magic

Marker odor stings the air, scribbled on boxes, labeling their contents. Discarded office junk. Stencil duplicators and carbon paper and adding machines and handheld chalk boards and files.

All that the West creates best. The obsolescence of its stuff.

Fusco strides the hall outside rattling a walking stick through cell bars. "Keep your hands off those boxes," he cries. "Just because the department runs out of storage doesn't make it yours." He snorts through his crimped nose. "Judge shows up, hears you been in any of those boxes..." he leans close toward my cell, his breath sugary from alcohol ... "Not very friendly, the judge isn't."

He walks on, telling the next cell. "Keep your hands off those boxes. Judge shows up..."

I squeeze past the boxes and cell bars to the freestanding toilet in the corner, seeing its flush handle wedged between one box and another stacked above it, handle unable to move. I sit upon the bunk's scratchy mattress. The toilet smells of putrid black gas and discolored piss. I try un-wedging the flush handle, but the boxes squeeze too tightly. It does not budge.

I sit again and brace my back against the bunk's back wall, pushing my feet against the stack. It stays still, keeping the handle fixed in place. Toilet water trickles in the basin.

I kick at that stack until the soles of my feet throb black and blue. Bits of cardboard—paper dust really—flake in the air. My knees ache. The cell block whispers a dusty silence. I kick again, seeing the target box dimple slightly. I claw at the dimple, scratching. A thin rip opens. I pull at it, opening a slight glimpse to the inside of the box.

Files. This box is crammed with files. I stand atop the toilet's rim, balancing for a better grip. Water sloshes in the basin. The basin smells of extinguished cigarettes.

Lama.

The water sloshes more quietly now. More still.

Lama.

My feet ache. My fingers bleed. I listen.

Is it you, lama?

A voice from a distant cell.

I step off the toilet. Water drips, pinging the unwashed odor. "Who is it?"

No answer. Then, "Lama, is it you?" A lone voice. Indistinct in accent, age, or sex. Then another. "Are you with us, lama?" And another. "Lama, have you come to help us?"

On and on they go, dispossessed in the dark. I press my face to the cell's bars. Inside the lock-up's dank space, in other darkened and barred enclosures, I sense shadows shifting. Forms in motion.

"Who is it? Who are you?" I ask.

"Refugees," one man says. "The newly arrived and discarded. Arrested and imprisoned, living our lives in Hell."

"Why arrested?"

They speak with shame. "I was caught standing on a street corner, and was accused of loitering."

Another confesses, "I stole dumplings from a dumpster to which a nonprofit had already laid claim."

"I asked for the time of day, and was sold a stolen watch."

"I was poor. I was indigent. Gweilos feared for their children and reported me."

Voices roll atop one another, confused, yet eager to confess.

"I own more credit cards than I should be allowed."

"My car leaks pollution."

"I told someone a joke and they did not laugh."

"I opened a box in my cell," one admits. "It was filled with junk, and I told them so."

Grievance upon grievance, until silence settles in once more.

I look at the box stacks around me. Collectibles. Stuff unused, but held onto.

One of the voices asks, "Why you, lama? Why are you here?"

I wait for silence to settle, and then I tell them, "I seek the dorje."

"The dorje," they pray without inflection or intonation. "You have not yet found it?"

"The gweilos hide it from me."

"Gweilos," the voices chant.

"Choki, too. He holds insurance, and had the dorje shipped to him. To the emporium, his place of business."

"No, lama. Choki is a worthy lieutenant of whom you should be proud."

How gullible they sound. How trusting. How disrespectful that they do not trust me.

"Choki introduced us to the Hellers in the first place," one of the voices says. "Lost inside this new land, he introduced us so the Hellers could sell us health insurance. Without health insurance, no one survives the West."

"Yes, the Hellers keep it affordable. Every health plan comes with a $50,000 life policy attached, from which we pay our monthly premiums as a convenience. In the West, dreams are achieved by such wise use of money. The Hellers told us that. You need never pay for anything in the West. All you need do is borrow."

I do not understand insurance, nor how it works. Life policies? Choki as beneficiary?

"All life is an abstraction, lama. In the West, abstractions are made of money. When we die, our policies pay $50,000 to Madame Sun's Olde Tibetan Emporium and Meditation Center. Minus any money previously advanced for payment of our health premiums."

"What about your families? Dawa, Norbu, these men were murdered by lingchi. They had these life policies, but their families received no money. Only Choki. His emporium."

Wind stirs through the cinder block walls of the jail block. Toilet water drips in my toilet's basin.

"Choki is your lieutenant, lama. Should you be speaking of him this way? Like how a policeman speaks about émigrés?"

I sink onto my cot. Its metal frame zings as I land upon it, its molecules shifting.

"You have sought the dorje a very long, lama, and never found it. Perhaps insurance is a better way."

And then—having never heard a gandharva sing in any lifetime before or after—I hear now the sweet cherub invocation of a child's voice. "Why, lama? Why seek the dorje?"

"For truth." I lie upon my cot, listening, and I see how the cardboard box I ripped now bulges, a file sticking out, exposed.

"Relative truth, or absolute truth?" the gandharva child asks.

"Don't you be going through any of those boxes." Fusco's voice echoes from down the hall.

"Absolute truth," I tell the boy. "So all may find enlightenment."

"Enlightenment?" the gandharva replies. "What is it? Have you found it yet?"

"No. Only hints of its existence." I stand and pull at the folder hanging from the torn box. I pull until it emerges. I see a business card stapled to its face. *Life is Hell*, it says. *When you don't have insurance.*

"But is not absolute truth built on relative truth," the child asks. "Just like bicycles need wheels, does enlightenment not need to embrace life moment by moment in the relative world?"

I open the folder, and find inside a deed and a bill of sale.

"Why seek the dorje, lama?"

I read the deed. I read the bill of sale. Wordy documents. Multi-paged.

In consideration for cancelling all insurance premiums as yet unpaid or to be paid to Heller Insurance by their insured Choki Golda (hereafter referred to as SELLER), Choki Golda and Heller Insurance (hereafter referred to as PURCHASER) agree to the transfer of Madame Sun's Olde Tibetan Emporium and Meditation Center, including its stock and inventory, debts and receivables, insurance and protections, from Choki Golda to Heller Insurance for the additional consideration of one (1) dollar.

"Does it not seem odd?" the child asks.

Cut through all the bill of sale language, and it answers it. The Hellers, not Choki, own the emporium. I breathe these words to myself. I watch them fog before my lips, where I can read them once again. Then I recite them for all to hear. "The Hellers own the emporium. Not Choki."

"Yes, lama?" the gandharva sings. "But why? Why should the Hellers take out a policy against their own company? To pay themselves four point nine million dollars? For a dorje that's missing, or never shipped, and yet still they behave as if believing it is here on Colfax?"

Lesson 28

Laughter erupts from nowhere,
and yet does.

I ABANDON MYSELF TO SLEEP. Beneath a thin blanket. The cell block feels cold. I shiver. I toss. I notice my cell door unlatched. I rise from my cot and step from the box stacks into the corridor. I look inside the other cells, and see that they are empty.

Abandonment comes without warning. I walk the cell block down into a large hexagonal atrium, with elevated windows just beneath its ceiling, the windows darkened from snow piled outside them. The snow casts a gray dullness down upon me.

At the atrium's far wall, I see a door. Its pane of glass a darker gray than the windows above. I pull at the door to open it, and on its other side find a wall of snow etched in a bas relief design of the door's exterior.

The wall stretches up taller than the door frame. I punch into it. The powdery snow absorbs me. Deeper and deeper, I punch.

As I do, the snow above loosens and avalanches into the atrium. Punching up into it I can now see the sky. It is filled with falling snow, so that I know now, I am in a crevasse. The cell block is in the cellar of police headquarters. To escape I will have to climb up the snowy crevasse to ground level above. I punch harder, stepping into the wall of snow so that it now fully swallows me. Beneath my mukluks a stairway rises. I punch further, stepping up those stairs atop rounded footsteps of snow. As I climb up through it, the snow changes from soft to crusty, and then becomes slippery with ice. I use my knees, my hands, my head to punch through and rise above it. Clouds blind the sky. I climb steep and angled. A long push up into cold and weighty snow. Engulfed in its whiteness I muscle my way through, my robes wet and weighed down. The crevasse rises steep. I stumble. I fall. Eventually, I ascend and emerge up out of the snow. A vast white field awaits me.

"Om mane Padma hum." My voice cracks dry. Swallowed in the space that engulfs me, I can no longer distinguish where I am from where I have been, nor in which direction I am heading. Whiteness all around, all I see.

They say enlightenment brightens a mind. They say brightness can burn so bright it keeps us from seeing what is right there before us.

I cup my vision with my hand. I listen to the sound of my breathing, large and loud.

If I was to step outside myself, and look down upon me trudging the snow, I might seem no more than a speck inside a vast white emptiness. Nothing more than the sound of my breathing. Nothing more than the wind's breath moving across the Tibetan plains. Snow reaching from the ground to absorb a descending sky, touching it lightly, whitening it.

As if it is nothing.

LESSON 29

Reality is an illusion,
although a persistent one.
- Albert Einstein

WITH ITS EMERGENCY FLASHERS FLASHING and its Rally Red luminescence, the Duster stands out in the whitening blizzard like an ember burning inside smoke. I push toward the car. Arriving, I shake snow from my robes and climb inside.

Abril sits behind the wheel.

"This dorje gets you in a lot of trouble, doesn't it? They arrested you, lama?" She speaks with fatigue and disappointment. A distancing tone.

"They did not arrest me because of the dorje," I correct her. "Curly Heller is dead."

She cocks her head. "They think you killed him?"

"Let us clear the air, Abril. I think I believe you now. You do not have the dorje."

Resting upon the steering wheel, Abril tilts her face toward me. "Thank you," she says.

"It does not show up on the manifesto."

"That can only mean one thing, lama. It did not ship."

"No. It did ship. And is at the warehouse. Hidden inside one of the Buddha statues, I am certain of it."

"The warehouse?"

I listen to the quiet of the snow outside, and feel how it tires me. The Duster feels stuffy. I say, "There still is one thing, Abril. The Tibetan policies, I found them. Wrapped in a bow in your apartment."

"My apartment?"

"They match the names in Choki's obituaries. And I also found the notepad by your bed, with Sonny's and Curley's names in it. Did you kill them? With lingchi?"

"Like how you killed your teacher? How could I do that?"

"Fernandez thinks you did."

"That's why I have you, lama. For your black magic."

Can I tell her, if only it was true, I do not do black magic? "Drive," I say. "To the warehouse."

She looks at me, uncertain. "You want to go back there?" She leans back in her seat, shakes her head, turns the key, puts the Duster into gear, and drives in silence, the Duster climbing over snow. She slows for intersections and snowplows. For one brief moment, she says, "You know your problem, lama. You need a new story. You been telling this one too long." Then silence again and the Duster twists and careens until turning onto Josephine, its wipers squeaking, the snow momentarily abating.

When the warehouse nears, I signal for her to slow down and hold the Duster back a block. We stare out the windshield, seeing the commotion that plays out before us.

"I'm afraid we're too late, lama," she says.

There at the front of the warehouse, a conglomeration of part-time police are gathered. They wear mismatched uniforms, and file in and out of the warehouse pulling Budai statues out by their arms and legs and throwing them into a heap beneath the twisted, bare-limbed weed trees of the warehouse's front lawn.

Fernandez stands on the portico, his cowboy coat flowing to its floor. He oversees the proceedings, standing close to the portico's edge. The brim of his ball cap shadows his eyes. To his right Huey Heller paces nervously as he watches the Buddhas pile up.

Yoong stands amid the trampled snow on level ground while ten to twelve part-timers and cyclists file past him in procession, Buddha statues bouncing against their knees as they carry them. No one talks. No one says anything.

The China agent pulls one part-timer from the parade. The flap-eared cop who stood guard on the portico, now dressed in vanilla flannel with wide black stripes that run up, down, left, right across his chest and sleeves. Holmes slumps to attention in front of Yoong. The agent points at the Buddha pile. Holmes lifts the topmost Budai from the pile and stands it upright. He steadies the statue with the tip of his index finger, holding it atop the Budai's up-reached hands.

Yoong nods at another flannelled part-timer, arms and chest a patchwork of itchy, crisscrossed design. Garcia. The patrolman who drove me to headquarters. He swings a mallet in a pendulum arc atop the snowy ground. With two hands, he lifts the mallet to his chest and steps in front of Holmes, studying the finger-balanced Budai, its fixed and frozen grin.

I sense how inside his mind, part-timer Garcia is thinking of his Marie, with whom he spoke earlier on the phone, and whose face he now envisions. The wrinkle of her eyes. Her hands calloused from working other people's jobs, and her belly soft and round and warm. I sense how he remembers his last time lying with her. Children asleep on the floor or in their beds. I watch him adjust the mallet in his grip, knowing this job he does, it would be nothing if not for Marie and their family. These are the reasons he works. Plus, for the insurance.

Garcia spits into his chapped palms. He grips the mallet and lifts it above his head, tip-toe high, stretching its weight back.

The mallet pulls the breath out of him and strains the flannelled muscles inside their shirt sleeves. Holmes's eyes close. He turns from Garcia, his index finger trembling atop the Budai. The Budai teeters. Sweat pinches his view. Garcia sucks in his hips, sticks out his *culo* and swings the mallet, full swing, down in front, down atop the smiling face of the Laughing Budai.

Holmes quickly pulls his finger back, sucking it in his mouth.

The mallet hits. The Buddha cracks. It splits. Plastic explodes in an insurrection of arms and cheeks and ear pieces loosely flying and sprinkling to the ground. Where once wobbled the laughing Buddha, now lies a collection of its parts. Plastic shards in the snow.

Garcia wipes sweat from his face. Yoong pushes Holmes down to his knees to sift the shards. The part-timer pours crystals of snow and plastic through his gloved fingers, looking for something not there. Yoong lifts what's left of the statue, holding it upside down by its foot and shaking out any remains. Nothing.

On the portico, Huey Heller paces.

"What do we do?" Abril asks. "Just sit here?"

On the ground, Garcia places his hand on his heart, steadying its rhythm. Holmes lifts another statue from the pile and balances it upright. Taking a breath, Garcia flexes his flannel once more, stepping forward. He spits on raw and cracked fingers, and lifts the mallet.

Heller fidgets, looking down from the portico.

The second Buddha splinters. Holmes sifts through it. Nothing.

One by one, each statue opens up, as the snow slows and eventually stops. A bit of sun even breaks through from behind clouds. *Nubeluz.* Sweat freezes the inside of Garcia's shirt, chilling him. He continues shattering the statues with loud cracks of thunder. The Budais fly apart into arms and legs and other parts, revealing no hint of the dorje. Garcia surveys the destruction, unable now to determine which Budai finger connects to which severed hand. Which shoulder with which arm. Which smile with which cheek.

Snow drizzle returns, light and sideways. Abril restarts the windshield wipers. Three statues remain. Part-timers squeeze around Garcia to see. They know they are getting close to discovery. One of these remaining statues holds the dorje. Any second now.

In the distance, I see a commotion rolling up 33rd. An elderly Tibetan coming from the east, pushing past cops and cyclists on the sidewalk. Pushing up to Garcia, pulling him from his task. He carries an insurance policy, which flaps sideways in the falling snow.

Yoong slaps the intruder back. Garcia lifts one foot, then the other, trying to warm them. Three statues remain. Snow settles upon them, dusting little moustaches atop their smiles.

"That's your lieutenant." Abril says. "From the emporium."

And although unrecognizable in his tightened denim coat and face-covering scarf, I am familiar with the way he gestures, and the way Choki jumps about while gesturing.

Yoong, in big puffed mittens and puffed-up coat, pushes Choki away. Part timers grab the old man and hold him. Yoong lifts the forty-seventh Buddha from the remaining three, and I see that this Budai pulls a bit differently and stands a skoosh heavier when upright. And inside it sloshes with the sound of rain falling. "This one." I wipe breath from the windshield. I lean toward the dash to see.

The Budai smiles. Just like those before him, not giving himself away.

Yoong pushes this new statue at Holmes. Garcia leans upon the mallet's handle, sweat shivering his body.

A single index finger extended, Holmes balances the forty-seventh Budai. Garcia gasps for strength. He stretches his shoulders and neck, rolling them. He raises the mallet. Part-timers hold Choki back, but they focus on the Buddha, their grip softening.

Garcia swings. The mallet falls. As it does, Choki kicks one of the part-timers, knocking himself free. Holmes steps back. The statue tips to its side. Choki lurches forward and grabs the fallen Budai, tucking its bulbous form beneath his armpit and bounding through the snow toward Josephine.

The part-timers watch as Choki runs up an alley, quite quickly for such an old man.

Yoong flaps short arms, beating the part-timers into action. "Chase him! Chase him!"

But the part-timers only yawn, like men at the end of their shifts, working part-time and poorly paid. One of them even points at Choki and says, "There he goes."

I slap the dash. "Quick. Down that alley. He has the statue. He has the dorje."

Abril responds, jumping the Duster out onto 33rd, steering straight at him.

The part-timers hang back, but Yoong chases Choki. Abril honks and tries swerving around the Chinese agent. He zig zags to block her passing. She slips the Duster up alongside him, then throws opens her driver's door and knocks him into a snow bank.

Over a bullhorn from the portico, Fernandez squawks. "Do not follow him, Naraka! You're still under arrest!"

But no patrol cars follow. No one in pursuit. Yoong pulls himself from the snow pile, hands to his knees, and bent over he watches us disappear down the alley, which now swirls with snow and late afternoon shadows.

Lesson 30

If you think reality is taught by teachers,
you have not learned to not see yourself as real.

- *Buddha*

DOWN WHERE EAST COLFAX LAY perpendicular to streets like
Colorado, Monaco, and Quebec, in the sprawl of flat-roofed
motels and businesses no more than a story high, where telephone
wires sag inside the skyline—there sits Tibet Town.

A Shangri-La hideaway unseen by gweilos. A ramshackle of
snowy streets dusted in grime and the sand-blasted housing from
Colorado's mining days, air now tinged with the savory scent
of buttered tea and momo grease. Bonfires burn in the median
strips. The ghosts of past émigrés—Mexicans and Jews—hide in
its streets and alleyways.

I point out where Abril should turn and how to get where we
are going. Never having been here, I am uncertain how I can do
this. She glides the Duster past sizzling pyres of wood and piles
of trash and packs of sidewalk dogs. Past snow-laden vendor carts

lining the curb. The carts smell of potatoes and steamed squash.

Abril pulls the Duster to the curb and stops. We step out onto a street called Pontiac. Its fires cast shadows of dancing telephone poles and street posts across long lawns holding small bungalows. The streets as wide as those in Lhasa. I look up to the rooftops for any sign of neighborhood protectors, but see none. Everything just snow.

A sudden wind splits the night, carrying with it the whump whump sound of drumming and the yip of coyotes. And cackling women. And men celebrating city blocks deep inside Tibet Town.

"What's that?" Abril asks.

I say nothing. I could not have answered if I wanted to. I take her hand and together we walk toward the ruckus. When it momentarily dies, we stop in our tracks to guess from where the silence had settled. Then the yipping and drumming resume again, and we continue toward it, and the fermented scent of chhaang and raksi.

"A celebration?" Abril wonders.

Blocks later, we come upon a mansion—now an abandoned community center—in a park. The park stretches a city block wide, less than that deep, and on either side stand a line of women clapping. Between them a gaggle of men hooting and lifting jars of raksi at one another. All of them Tibetan. The women too. The men straddle their archer's bows as if riding ponies. Not the short bows of a niru cavalry, but longer seven-foot bows for firing from an upright infantry stance on level ground.

In the park's distance I see a pyramid of dirt pushed up three feet high and molded narrow up top, with a wooden arrow shaft running the length of its face, the arrow's tip pointing to the sky.

An archery target.

On either side torches burn. Their light illuminates an array of spent arrows stuck in the triangle's face, or in the trampled snow around it.

Embedded in the pyramid, at the tip of the target arrow,

something protrudes. Something dazzling and bejeweled.

I step closer to see. A man wearing dark glasses intercepts me and steps me back to the others. "Please, lama. We must maintain a clear path for the contestants."

Another man in worker's cap and unbuttoned denim, hunched slightly and feeble, a surgical mask across his mouth, assumes a position in front of the crowd. He carries his bow erect and vertical before his chest, ceremoniously.

Some boo. Some push or swat the man's shoulders as he takes his stance. The archer does not flinch. The man in dark glasses bellows with the yowl of a dying cat, "Chiiru!"

The crowd silences. The archer stands alone. The man in dark glasses holds out a quiver, and the archer draws a silver-tailed arrow, notches it into his bowstring and steadies its shaft in his grip. He fixes his gaze on the target. He breathes in. He breathes out. He lifts the bow, aligns his sight and focuses on the distant glitter of the pyramid.

Spectators back off. They murmur.

The archer stands as still as the target itself. He pulls back the bowstring, coated in beeswax and resin. The bow's belly bends. He lifts his aim, tension shaking his arms. He steadies. He quiets, soft like descending snow. He unfolds his fingers. The bow snaps into shape. The arrow splits through the darkness, tail feathers whistling with the familiar shriek that makes armies flee.

Moments collapse into one. Then, a puff of dust rises from the pyramid, just beneath the glitter. Someone catcalls. Another man yodels. *Fine shot*. Money passes hands. High near the top of the pyramid, the silver tailed arrow stands erect, three inches of shaft swallowed in dirt.

A fine shot indeed. I look to the archer, but between his wrappings and the darkness I do not recognize him.

Men erupt into jackal cackling. They whoop. They dance out of the crowd and high step into the center of the snowy lawn like boys on imaginary ponies, ga-lump, galumphing from side to side, their arms outstretched. Women clap and call to their men, nattering at them with come-ons and insults. The men ignore them, dancing in a circle around the pyramid as they pony ride their bows, woohooing, circling in, circling out, before breaking and muttering and walking slowly to their places back in the crowd. Back to their jars of raksi.

A small gathering of men remains at the pyramid, laughing with the archer, pointing to his arrow. I push through the drunken crowd. I keep focus on the pyramid's glittering pinnacle above the arrow's shaft, and the men gathered there.

"Just like old days, is it not, lama?" Someone tugs my sleeve.

I pay it no mind. I push on to the target. Abril follows me, but gets caught in a tangle of spectators who playfully pull down their masks to laugh monkey laughs at her. Women serve up warm and salty ladles of hot buttered tea. Men pass jars of raksi. In the crowd at the pyramid, I see the archer who fired the winning shot being backslapped and congratulated, his mask now removed. His face plain.

Choki.

"Hey!" Choki reels a bit upon seeing me. "Where is the dorje?" Someone grabs me by the shoulder.

"Old days, indeed, lama. Such excitement." The words hang in the air. Men dance around me. I feel dizzy. I watch Choki climb up and balance himself atop a seesaw. No longer moving so old or feebly, he smiles to the crowd. Much less timid now. More of a lieutenant. More in command.

I go up to the seesaw and call out, "Where is it?"

He reaches for me to join him. The seesaw teeters as I do, and as Choki lifts my arm to the sky and announces for all to hear, "Lama Rinzen has returned."

The crowd silences and bows with folded hands. Some kneel. Women step close. Children in snowsuits and pudgy red faces stare. "Lama Rinzen," the light voice of a child says, and now the crowd hurrahs and the children stomp their feet so that their snow boot buckles ring like bells.

Choki steps down from the seesaw, pulling me with him. He bends to a child and whispers in his ear. The lad turns and runs to the pyramid target. He climbs up its dirt face and dislodges the target arrow. The boy returns to Choki and presents it to him, pointy end up. Choki accepts it with grace, and then turns to me standing as upright and straight as a soldier can, his face now younger and handsomer. His smile shinier, though rugged. The arrow drips with red, black and gold ribbons tied at its tail, its four-pronged arrowhead embedded with beadwork the color of rubies and sapphires. Choki bows. "Old days, indeed," and with each end of it in either of his hands, Choki presents me the arrow.

Taking it, I feel the chill of night in the arrow's shaft. My mind flashes with remembrance of placing just such an arrow in a pyramid of pure Tibetan soil on the high plateau. Perhaps this very arrow. This I remember.

"As fine a target as we practiced on outside Qinghai, in the year the Great Fifth scoured demons from our land. You practiced us well, lama."

I scan their faces seeing they expect me to speak and say something warm.

"We practiced for purity," I tell them. "For a campaign well fought."

"The campaign." Men thrust their bows in the air, punching the sky. With raised cheekbones and pulled skin, I see now how Drepung's marauders have wrinkled from so many lifetimes in Hell. Serfs, field men, strugglers. They once rode under the Yellow Banner, drilled in the skills of conquerors. To kill your enemy, you must be your enemy. I trained them this way. With bows steady and minds focused, seeing their arrows pierce their targets. Feeling their enemy's pain at the arrow's piercing, as if they themselves were the ones shot. Tear it all down.

Cold air puffs from beneath their masks and mustaches.

"Why did we ride?" one calls.

I call back. "We rode for the dorje. Against Gelugpa lords."

They cheer, and as they do I cast a watchful eye on Choki, expecting him now to bestow the Most Sacred of Objects upon me, as would be fitting, this humblest of lieutenants, who served at my behest. Such a lifetime here on Colfax, this must be the moment. This must be the lifetime I recover the dorje.

"The dorje," men mutter, their voices hoarse with the tight squeeze of raksi in their throats.

"We rode to avenge the Great Fifth," I call.

"The Great Fifth," they cheer.

"We rode against Daidyal, my fallen teacher, with his obsequious hands, and I killed him."

"Chiiru!"

Women bang copper pots and light cigarettes that sparkle in their lips. Children run with ropes burning, swinging circles of fire and chasing and falling upon one another and rolling on the ground like cats at play. All the while, snow floats wistfully from the sky, stinging down upon icy ground.

Choki stands steadfast on the outskirts of the crowd near a statue of Baron von Richthofen, beaming but silent, as if not only is he pleased I am here, but he takes pride in it too.

I clamor on, "I return now to you, my army, my students, I return now for the dorje." Then I pause, so my words might settle. "Tonight. Here. This evening, so I may receive it from you." Then I speak no more.

Choki steps from beneath the baron's statue, his bow in his hand and his quiver dangling from his belt. He lifts a foot atop the baron's knee and says, "Lama, so pleased we are you are here among us. But surely you know you yourself have the dorje, which you captured at Drepung. It is you who must bring it to us."

"Yeah," the crowd says. "You bring it to us. Not the other way around."

I do not understand. I saw Choki take it. The Budai statue, at the warehouse. I scan the faces in the crowd. They seem as confused as I am.

"You return, lama," Choki bellows, his words aged and hoarse. "To take us from Colfax into enlightenment. It is your mission, is it not?"

The crowd murmurs, "Yes, yes. Your mission, lama?" They murmur in a dialect I find hard to comprehend. I walk among them, inspecting their faces, one by one.

"If I truly had such a thing would I now be seeking it?" I ask. When I reach the fountain, I pause before Choki and say, "We rode with our guru upon Lhasa. Serfs and slaves and concubines of Daidyal's Drepung cheered our arrival with a welcoming gong. Like a wind horse sweeping upon them, we pinned the enemy down. You brave archers circled the fallen Gelugpa monks. We spared the blood of innocents that day, while I..."—I scan the crowd now—" ... while I freed the dorje from the corrupt grip of the fallen Daidyal."

"Daidyal," they chant, reclaiming frenzy. "Daidyal. Daidyal. Daidyal."

Until a child with teeth larger than his mouth steps forward and asks, "Who is this Daidyal you mention?"

The ground beneath me freezes. I slip on its ice without falling. I look at the boy, snow obscuring my vision of him. His cheekbones bubble with droplets. "In the year of the Fire-bird, 1657, locusts came upon our barley fields, feeding with greed and hunger. Drepung confiscated all you had. Men cried. Women played the acquiescers. Black magic fell upon us. This is what the Great Fifth came to rid us of."

"Yeah, but who is Daidyal?" a voice from the back calls out. "And what did you do with the dorje?"

"The Great Fifth sent armies to rid Tibet of a bewitching gyalpo. A perfidious presence, great in power, haunting Drepung. The Great Seductress, who craved craving itself, who instilled in Daidyal, the abbot of Drepung, a craving for black magic as well. He fell under her spell. He took the Most Sacred of Objects from us. Surely you remember Daidyal." I speak loudly enough that my voice echoes from the walls of the community center and bungalows. "The fallen abbot of the Monastery of White Rice."

The crowd whispers among themselves, one saying, "I never heard of this Daidyal. Perhaps you have a snapshot. Something we could look upon and remember?"

"Yes, a snapshot," they cheer in unison.

"No. No snapshots. It was the 1600's, no photography at all. The Great Seductress swallowed his soul. His name was Daidyal. You must remember him?"

Choki leans on his bow, its camber moaning beneath his weight. He addresses me. "Our captain. Our lama. We rode against the Gelugpa under the banner of the Great Fifth, did we not?"

"Yes."

"But, lama. You taught us the Great Fifth was of the Gelug school. As are all Dalai Lamas, before and since, all Gelugpa. No?"

How does he speak to me like this? He is a lieutenant. I, his captain. I ignore the question. Not because it is unworthy of response, but because of Choki's tone and impertinence. "Please," I say. "Stop all this. Just give me the dorje. You have it."

"You are Kagyu, lama," Choki says. "One of the Emperor of Thang's men, whose armies burned the Gelugpa libraries. You say you carried the banner of the Great Fifth, a Gelugpa himself. And this Daidyal? Such a curious name. Tell me, how could your teacher, presumably a Kagyu, be abbot of a Gelugpa monastery? It doesn't make sense, the way you tell it."

My jaw tenses. My eyes grow small and focused. "She seduced him, that is why."

"Seduced him?" Choki twists the words, as if spitting them at me. "We rode upon Drepung, as a rag tag army of thieves. Does it not make sense the Dalai Lama would have given the dorje to a monastery of his own lineage? Why free a thing from where it belongs?"

"Yeah," another in the crowd says. "I wonder that myself. What were we even doing in Drepung? Why did you take us there?"

Snow drifts. The ground pitters beneath its touch. I explain, "A student observes his teacher to see his faults. To strip them away. I sliced Daidyal so his hide fell from his bone, clean and pure."

"Then where's the dorje?" Choki asks. "If you sliced him like you say, you should have taken it, should you not?"

"You know where it is. You have it. In Drepung, it slipped from my fingers. It fell down the steps. It rolled away."

"Rolled away?" Choki leans upon his bow, his breath gray in the night air. "How could it do that, lama? It being such a long-shaped thing, and not round. How could it roll away?"

I grow impatient. "We rode for enlightenment, that is all you need know. Not only ours, but for all sentient beings. For the drab souls of Colfax, and the dead Tibetans in the alleys. For these, I have selflessly returned, and to lead you from this Hell. But first, give me the dorje. You have kept it from me too long as it is." I put my palm out in a gesture of emptiness, and begging, and supplication, and need.

The crowds' eyes shift, so not to stare at me too long. I turn to Choki. "You took it from the warehouse. Inside a Buddha statue. I saw you."

He appears wounded at my accusation. "No, lama. At any time in any life, what do we see? The world, or the reflection of our own desperation? Who exactly did you kill in Drepung?"

I was a niru captain once. In a lifetime after that, a cabbie. In another, a prostitute. Once an emperor. Once an emperor's servant. A highwayman, an inventor, a composer of radio jingles. A wife, a child, a saint. A priest. A killer of priests. All these many lifetimes in Hell.

"You seek the dorje still, do you?" Choki asks. "But do you truly believe I can just hand it over? You taught us to be stronger than that." He turns to the man in dark glasses and speaks in a foreign dialect. The man takes the multi-feathered arrow from my hand, returns it to the boy, who returns to the pyramid and embeds it back in the dirt. Its arrow tip glimmers skyward as the torches burn around it.

Abril steps from the crowd. "We should leave, lama."

The man in dark glasses takes an arrow from his quiver. He rests its tip over his right set of fingers, its streaming tail of green ribbon over his left, extending it to Choki, who takes it and braces it in his bow.

"One shot, lama. You a niru captain. I, your lieutenant. You taught us well. I humbly propose a contest. If I the servant surpass you the teacher, the dorje stays hidden. But should your arrow come closer to the target's tip, you will have earned what you seek and the respect of all of us gathered, and I will then lead you to it, so you may free us from the Hell to which you condemned us."

A cashier, a banker, a nurse, a painter of houses and a beggar in the streets. These are the lifetimes I have lived. These versions of myself are the lives I must rescue. But in no such life had I ever been an archer before. I led a niru of them, yes. But I was never one myself.

"I have not fired the bow in some time," I say.

"Do as I do," Choki tells me.

Bystanders place bets, long odds against me. Choki assumes his stance. He pulls back the string, subtle and taut, his eye fixed down the arrow's shaft, taking the target inside his frail body. In one swift motion, he lifts the arrow's tip to the sky and unfolds his fingers. The arrow leaves its bow, whistling, and for some time during its ascent, it appears as if there is no arrow at all. Until the dirt mound puffs, and the torchlights dance over the display of the target arrow, with Choki's arrow directly touching its tip.

The crowd cheers. A near perfect shot. Choki appears smug as men slap his back and offer him raksi from their jars. Women clap. Children step forward, throwing stones, trying to hit Choki's arrow.

The man in dark glasses calls *Chiiru!* He takes an arrow from the quiver and lifts it to me. The crowd quiets. Choki passes me his bow.

I take it. I assume position and look at Choki's shot, the way its shaft sticks upright blocking any clear view of the target arrow's head. Its ribbons fluttering in the falling snow.

The man in dark glasses supervises as I notch my arrow. I check the target, torchlight wavering over its triangular mound, dancing and rippling the target's shape and position. Snow balls roll down the pyramid's face. Choki's arrow has puffed away a small circle of snow where it landed, no more than a silver dollar wide, exposing dirt. A clear patch of darkness. That will be my aim. My intention.

Fidgeting, I re-notch my arrow once more, testing the bow's suppleness. I hold its twine in index and middle fingers. I pull my hand back to the cup of my ear, feeling the arrow's strength. The bow trembles in my grip. I inhale. Slowly, I let my breath out. The trembling subsides. The black dirt encircles Choki's arrow tip. A very thin shot.

Perhaps I should drop the bow, the arrow, drop the contest and insist here and now that Choki bestow the dorje upon me, as I deserve, being a lama and his captain.

Instead, I hold steady. I see the light drift of falling snow settle upon the shaft of his arrow.

I arch back. I look to the sky, pivoting, adjusting my aim, up, down, left. Then, as if one, I release my grip from where the twine creases the skin of my fingers. Silence rises with the arrow's ascent. Torchlight shimmers across the target's surface. Eternity evolves. A split second of it. Had I missed? Had my arrow gotten lost in the sky?

Crack.

An explosion of shredded green ribbon. The crowd bends forward, looking. Choki's once erect arrow now split, one side of it bending limply, then falling to the ground.

"Halved," the man in dark glasses announces. "The lama's arrow split Choki's arrow in half, its arrowhead severing the target!" He lifts my arm in the air. "Chiiru!"

The crowd cheers. Men pass raksi. The child who placed the arrow now scoots off to one of the booths for a cup of hot buttered tea, which he balances in small fingertips while walking back toward me, careful not to spill it. He offers me the cup.

But I do not take it. Instead, I scan the sea of celebrating faces for any sign of Choki.

Finding no hint of him.

LESSON 31

Confidence requires no sense of self.

"TEA, LAMA?" THE BOY STANDS before me, chattering in the cold with his obnoxiously large teeth.

I knock the cup from his hand. "Where is he?" I scan the crowd for Choki. All ruckus and drunken rumble, but no sign of the deceiver. I grab the boy's sleeve. "Where did he go?"

The child waves his steaming fingers in the air, scalded. "Who, lama? Who?"

Men in a nearby crowd laugh at the boy, and tip their raksi cups to me. All except one fellow in a rainbow skull cap. He breaks from the men. "Lama, please." He looks over his shoulder to ensure no one is watching. He takes the boy's hand in his, rubbing the child's fingers. "You should not draw attention to yourself, lama."

"I just won the contest," I say. "Choki owes me the dorje. I am here to bring all beings to enlightenment," I protest.

"Yes, yes, and so happy we are you have come. Now, please. Follow me."

He gives the boy a piece of hard candy from his pocket. With sugared fingers he then takes my hand, pulling me to follow him, turning back and smiling as he pulls, his front teeth outlined in gold, his woolen rainbow skull cap dangling an orange tassel.

I pull away. "I have had enough." I point to the pyramid. "I won the contest. Choki must present me the dorje. A deal is a deal. Here, now, fair and square. I severed his arrow, just as wisdom severs ignorance with the heat of Manjushri's blade. I am here to collect the dorje, and rid myself of this Hell, this Colfax Avenue."

The rainbow man steps toward me and leans to my right ear. "You mean, so that *we all* may be rid of this Hell Realm, do you not?" He holds his gaze on me, without relenting.

"Where is he?" I ask. "It is a soldier's honor to congratulate his victor. Not to flee."

He lowers his voice and secretly says. "He has not fled. Now quickly, come with me."

"No." I brace my feet to the earth, so that not even the falling snow might shake or shiver them loose. "Where is he?"

Rainbow lifts his eyebrows, but not his gaze "You are making a mistake, lama. We can never be sure they are not watching. The contest was a diversion, meant to give Choki cover to slip away. Yes, he has captured the dorje. And there are many who seek it. So few who deserve it. You must know this."

"What are you talking about? I deserve it. Me." I look about the gathering, up to the rooftops, down the whitened streets. "Who is watching? What do they see?"

"They are watching you," the rainbow man says. "Do you not see your own behavior? Niru armies move with stealth. You taught us this in Drepung. Yet here you come vainglorious in robes, hiding from no one other than yourself. You do not need to keep telling us you are here for our enlightenment. You just need to do it."

Rainbow cups his palm around the nape of my neck leaning our foreheads together. "When they kill in the West, it is over and done with. But you and I, we soldiers of Drepung, we know how death stays with us from one lifetime to the next. All moments in time. No one ever dies and gets away with it."

He loosens his grip, pushing me back, and he wades into the crowd backward while looking back and watching me.

A commotion arises on the street. In the park I see Abril drinking raksi, and men laughing. Abril, too, laughing. And snow falling, floating down upon the dirt pyramid and the street. I hear the ruckus of bicyclists pedaling through the crowd. They pedal slowly, as if looking for someone. The crowd jeers. Men throw raksi at the cyclists. Someone fires an errant arrow into the statue of Baron von Richthofen. To my left, Rainbow's orange tassel is being swallowed into the night.

"What about Abril?" I call to him.

"They are not after her. Now come."

I follow, looking back at Abril laughing and drinking raksi, and I marvel at how I have never seen it before, her laughing like this. Perhaps that is what the Buddha talks about when he talks about emptiness. Moments unshared.

I follow Rainbow, venturing deeper into Tibet Town. In the distance, I hear mumbling voices echoing inside the maze of streets. I smell the musty stench of my mukluks, the stink and sweat of my robes. I kick snow following Rainbow's path, until we come to an open door from which light spills out. The door to a barroom.

Rainbow steps to its entrance and waves me inside.

Inside, there are no windows. Its space appears barely large enough for its few bone-wood tables and thatch chairs or the crowd settled into them. The walls are carved bookshelves ceiling to floor, and the bookshelves crammed tight with catalogs. A library of catalogs.

Overhead a fan swirls gray smoke about the room. A dung fire burns in the corner. The air chokes with raksi and drunkenness.

As I enter, the room quiets. Men huddle inside oily sweaters clutching dirty glasses in their dirty, sundrenched fingers. Their eyes stare bloodshot. The catalog bindings indicate they are each from the same printing, all the same year. The same width and height. *All Things Asian.*

An elder shuffles from behind a fold-down plank of plywood that serves as the bar. He pours clear liquid from a dingy bottle into a rusty-lipped metal cup, neatly to its brim nearly spilling it. He pushes the cup at me. "Raksi. You drink."

The men watch. With the vigilance of an infantry, they watch. I take the cup and lift it to my lips. I sip. Dead microorganisms strain through my teeth, and my nose hairs singe with the scent of smoked rice and millet, stinging at first, but then slipping ever so smoothly down my throat, velvety and warm. Inside, my stomach throbs. When had I last eaten? I try to remember. The raksi tastes strong. I stumble into a spindle chair, reaching to steady my descent, grabbing a catalog shelf so that one of the catalogs pulls out and falls down on top of me.

As I land in the chair, Rainbow tips a cup to me. "You like?" He points at the opened catalog plopped in my lap. "None of it exists, you know?" I give him a curious look, or at least feel my face twisting oddly. He continues by saying, *"All Things Asian* my ass. They make that shit in Secaucus, and then stamp it *Made in China* so it sounds exotic. They love buying Chinese stuff in the West. Chopsticks, little rickshaws. It makes them feel exotic."

And even though he is talking, I need to twist myself to see him through the smoky haze of the dung fire, so that my chair creaks as I pivot.

An eruption at the door. "Cyclists," someone says. The Tibetans strike casual poses slouched against walls or down into their seats. One of them points at me. "Quick. Tell us a story. A story of Drepung."

"No. No stories." Rainbow leans between us. "Inconspicuous."

He pushes me deeper in my seat while the Spurtz boys push in and look around the bar. One looks at me, but not for long. The smoke makes them cough, and then leave. "Air polluters," they say.

"Gweilos." A Tibetan leans in on me and nudges the catalog in my lap. "They shop mail-order souvenirs all day, these gwei-los." His words sound phlegmy. "Tack it up on their walls. I seen them do it."

I sip more raksi. The bar door closes kicking up a breeze, so that the catalog pages now flip in my lap one by one, each page with the same ad. *Dorje for sale, Dorje for sale, Dorje for sale.* No matter which page it is, you call the number, Abril's phone rings.

"Yeah." A young Tibetan reels into my face, jittering as he speaks. "You know how gweilos are. One wants the dorje, they all want the dorje. It's what they do."

Another one, bleary-eyed, drapes his arm across my shoulder with his jowls down upon my table, pointing at my jar. "More raksi, lama?"

I lift my rusty cup.

Rainbow scrunches into the spindle seat beside me and pours. He raises his own jar and clinks my cup. I ask, "Did you pour it half empty, or half full?" I see now where my robes have stained, where I spilled some. On my mukluks, where I spilled some, too.

"So much better than the swill in the park," Rainbow announces, his wool cap pilling with sweat. He fingers his jar, two handed, holding it sacred.

I show him the catalog. "It sells the dorje." I point at its pages.

Rainbow pulls off his hat and floats it around his fingertips like a circus act in a cheap circus. "They sell anything." His words fall out more slowly than it takes to hear them. "Frankly, I don't think there is a dorje."

"Yes." I try standing, but find it only sinks me lower in my seat. "Yes. I heard it. In the Buddha statue Choki stole." My eyeballs leak grit. I scratch them with my knuckle. Men's faces seated around me fold in on themselves. Slack lips and lazy eyes, and cheeks and chins and features like you find on men's faces. My cup feels hollow. My stomach warm. Rainbow towers above me. "These Hellers." He tosses the *All Things Asian* catalog in the air. "You sliced them, lama. Slicey slice, like they slice émigrés to collect insurance money. How can they lose?"

My eyes feel hard to open, my breathing difficult. "I see...," I say. "No, not I see, I say... the Hellers kill their brothers."

But actually I don't say anything. My words come out garbled.

"Gweilos do not know lingchi," another says. "If it is not you who killed them, who else? You killed Daidyal, didn't you?"

I stare into the eyes of my accuser. "Daidyal?"

"Daidyal." They laugh. They chant at me, "Daidyal, Daidyal, Daidyal, you talk so much of Daidyal."

"Lama, please, let me ask," Rainbow says. "A thief goes into an empty house to steal what? What is there to steal? A lama slays a non-existent teacher, but who has he killed? The teacher or himself?"

"Daidyal." My teacher's name slips into the sound I make. "I killed him for the dorje."

"Lingchi." Rainbow clinks my cup. It shatters to the floor. No. It falls and then shatters. No, it is tin. It clangs. More like a bell.

"Who did you kill, lama, during your great niru ride?"

The chair where I sit creaks. The bartender hands me a fresh dollop of raksi floating with squabble and bugs. I lean over it to sip, but the glass is too far from my lips. "All Lhasa rode," I say. "Gandarvas blew conches. Monks banged their gongs. The city gates widened, opening our path. To the Mound of White Rice we rode, where Gelugpas sat in meditation. In sunlight. Heaven opened to our archers' arrows. The corrupt Abbot Daidyal on his throne."

"Daidyal." Men slam their jar bottoms onto table tops, over and over.

"Daidyal, holding the Most Precious of Objects," I recite. "I drew my sword. Earth and sky thundered." In a dark corner of the barroom, I see its space as empty. "I placed my sword to the abbot's throat to take the dorje. It slipped away. Down stone steps. The sound of rain falling on fields."

"Slipped away?" one asks. "How odd."

I have grown tired of the telling. I say no more.

Rainbow turns a chair, sits in it backwards so that he may be close. "We love the story, lama. Every time you tell it, we love it. Such mystery. So now, perhaps you can tell us—who is this Daidyal?"

Need I say? Daidyal is here. He hovers over me, like a garuda, only more round shouldered and stooped.

"There is no Daidyal, is there? And the Monastery of White Rice, it was a Gelugpa abbey, was it not?" Rainbow asks. "Why would you, a Kagyu, have a Gelug teacher? And ride upon Drepung? And perform such an act as lingchi?"

On the steps of Drepung, sun sears my vision and wind slices my view. The abbess' robes cover her. She sits upon her cushion, her face hidden from mine, and she holds the dorje. Rain crackles from the sky upon stone steps.

I tip her headdress back. Her hair cut short. Her eyes reddened. She bleeds.

Rainbow speaks from a distance. "We wrap ourselves in a story, which we relive, even if only in our minds. You in yours, she in hers, all overlapping. This story of self, is this what the Buddha means when he talks about emptiness? How the story we tell of self is never quite true? How we survive through its distortion? How we obsess over it, failing to see the part we play in another's story? Losing our way, wondering which is mine to tell, which is hers? And why do we do the things we do to one another, without seeing how we do the same to ourselves?"

Rainbow gulps his raksi. It sloshes and he wipes his lips, saying, "Hell is when we fail to see what lay before us." His eyes glow bright. "Madame Sun was a Gelugpa teacher. Presented the dorje by the Great Fifth himself in recognition of the magnificence of her teachings. A gwalpo, to whom you could neither resist nor submit. You stole the dorje from her. And you haven't escaped it since, attaching to what you don't have. Is that what the Buddha calls emptiness?"

I do not listen to what he asks. Instead, I recall a teaching long forgotten. A lesson Daidyal taught… or someone… about how intention creates the world, setting our focus. In this way we see, hear, smell, taste and touch in ways that make it familiar. Creating our realms. Hell, Hungry Ghosts, Animal and Human. The Formless Realms, too. Warring Titans and Gods. These are the ways we abide on Colfax. Elsewhere. Nothing beyond what we already know, just as we intended.

Daidyal taught that.

Somebody did.

LESSON 32

The forms of earth, water, wind, and fire create
seeing, hearing, smelling, tasting, and touch.
Each such interplay of cause and result creates energy.

OF COURSE, NONE OF IT is true. All just drunken rambling, as in a dream.

We come into life as mysteries. We solve mysteries by making them predictable. What diverts from our predictions, we label misfortune inflicted by another. Murders to be solved. Crimes against the state. Failures to conform.

There are no true lives, but merely uniforms we wear, which we believe project a proper image of who we are.

Lives do not occur how we see them. They happen more like this. I am reborn inside a Colfax shithole, confused, without sleep, jetlagged maybe. Disoriented. Self-pitying.

What to learn? That I should sleep more? Worry less?

Or that lives are no more than dreams sneaking through the night, unsettling us, but never so much that we run from them. Because we need not run. Because in a dream, each moment changes scene to scene. Before we ever get a chance to remember it.

Is this what the Buddha talks about when he talks about emptiness?

Many students studied at the Shedra, but in my dreams I was the only one.

While others busied themselves with chores and classes, I stretched. While young monks slept alone in their cave-cold cells inside the earth of Drepung's hallways, I stretched the usual student-teacher relationship. While novices huddled before their tea stoves for warmth, its flame swallowed inside the night, I walked Drepung's halls to the chambers of the abbess, Madame Sun.

My teacher called me to do so.

I ventured up rickety stairs crackling with a glow that smelled like struck matches.

No, scratch that.

Not the smell of struck matches.

I ventured up rickety stairs, the air tangy with the *taste* of struck matches. Sulfur tickling my throat. Hallway walls bright with illumination. I lifted my arms to the warmth, and then saw I walked sleeveless. And then saw I walked naked. No gown at all.

What to feel?

The hallway's warmth. So unlike Colfax this time of year.

What to hear? Abril saying, "I found something, lama," without deterring me from my dream.

I walk to where the hallway bends and I turn to follow it, and at the end of the turn my teacher's room blazes in the distance, burning, its door a crackling inferno and its transom licking flames.

I sweat from the fire's heat. The slipperiness of my damp skin, I sweat. I hear the cries of my teacher inside her room. I lather myself with sweat and walk through those flames to save her. Is that not what a bodhisattva does? Save people?

My hair and skin singe. I inhale. My wangizmo warms. My teacher sits upon her cushion, lotus seated, her yoni in the shape of a heart between her legs, the way she shaves herself.

"We should leave," I tell her. "This is no way to survive."

She rakes hair back from her forehead, sitting still and pale, as if dead and ascended to Nirvana.

"There is no here and there is no there. Neither this nor that," she tells me.

"What are you saying?"

"There is nothing you are and nothing you are not. What good would leaving do, if there is no escape?"

"Madame Sun, we do not have time for this right now. The abbey is burning. We must leave."

Abril says. "I have learned something, lama. There is no Madame Sun."

"We will suffocate if we do not leave," I say.

"All beings die. Some in battle, some in punishment, some in sleep," Madame Sun tells me. "No one way better than another. Each with a lesson. Tell me, are you sleeping right now?" Flames cast light and shadow across her skin. I feel myself leaving her. Not from intention. Because she will not come.

"We have to go."

"Why? Because you killed our landlord."

"The monastery is burning. And the landlord was going to evict you. We have to go." I cup my wangizmo, shielding it from the heat.

"Years from now in another lifetime, lama, you will find your-self asking who killed a man. Maybe two men. You will only know the answer once you see inside yourself. There is no place to go."

"I did not kill these men. It is just that it is Hell, and we are burning."

"Do not focus on burning, or you will never let it go. Have you ever asked yourself why you, a Kagyu, study inside a Gelug monastery?"

"Why should I? It is an awkward question."

"You seem troubled, lama. Can you not awaken?"

"How can I? If you do not hear me? We must leave."

And then I do. I awaken. In a bed, inside the raksi bar, I awaken. Abril lying alongside me. Unblanketed, naked, exposed to the cold. She stirs awake, sleepy-talking. "Forget Madame Sun, she does not exist. I am the one who brought you here. You're in my story, lama. And in my story, there is no Madame Sun. In my story, it's just you and me, and neither of us real. All that's real is what we share."

I feel the empty space between us, the warmth it holds.

"No you, no me, no here, no that, none of it," she says. "Only what's in-between."

Abril moves her hand to me. "In my story, when the Buddha talks about emptiness, he's talking about what we create moment to moment, passing one to another, and then gone."

She pulls herself up in the bed—more of a rolled-out couch, really—surrounded by the reek of last night's raksi. I feel myself disrobed and disheveled. In the corner of the bar, a Buddha altar has collapsed, and the room's spindly tables and chairs, they have all collapsed and fallen as well. The place appears ransacked. Catalogs lean drunkenly against one another, spilling from shelves.

The space inside my head pulsates. The weave of the mattress chews inside my lower back, gnawing at me like a hungry ghost. My head feels drilled to the pillow. My breathing is shallow, warm, and stale. Numb and dead. My robes hang from a chandelier built from sticks above us. I touch my wangizmo, its hair cloyed and wadded.

"Why are we here?"

"Because I found something, lama. I found where Choki lives, and where he is keeping the dorje."

On the floor Tibetans sleep with their hands wrapped around empty raksi jars. Faraway, a superintendent yells, "This is no way to be rid of yak poop, burning fires on the floor. No no." His yelling rattles the bar's plywood, which in turn rattles the empty glasses lined atop it.

Abril rolls to her hip facing me, her arm pinning my chest, making me wonder who was it who told me once—Daidyal maybe, or someone—*we are at the beginning. The Hell Realm once more. Let us begin.*

"Did you seduce me?" I ask.

"You're a bodhisattva, lama. You have come to help. How can you help others if you don't let others help you?"

I do not understand. I do not look at her. I fixate on the ceiling fan, considering how much older she appears than me. Like a teacher.

"I found something, lama. The story I tell, about you and the Hellers and the cops—you all fit into it very nicely. Even Choki, he fits in. And his wife. But the Chinaman? How did he get here? What kind of agent is he? Do you know?"

"I do not."

"I asked around. He's a customs agent, that's what. Preserving customs. And he worked with the Hellers to ship the dorje here. It was some kind of insurance scam they were working."

The Tibetans around us stir. Bones creak. Raksi jars spill. Someone from the East, I consider, infiltrating the inspector's case. Fernandez told me that.

"How do you know this?"

She rolls to her side, reaching beneath the couch so that its coils creak. On her upper glute, I read where it says *Desire*, and I touch it.

"Don't start that again." She rolls back pushing me flat, and one by one she drops Bodhi seeds made of bone down upon my chest. They feel warm from her holding them.

"I found these at the warehouse. They match the beads on the Chinese agent's rosary. He was there, at the warehouse when Sonny was killed."

"That is not possible. You said you left before Sonny was killed. How could you have found them, if Yoong had not yet come to kill him?"

She picks up the beads, dropping them one by one to my chest. "Because time is not linear. That is just the way our mind sees it. Plus, he's Chinese. He knows lingchi. You said so yourself."

Whatever she says, I do not hear it as much as feel it between us.

"We should get going to Choki's, find that dorje," she says. "Before the Chinaman does."

LESSON 33

Do not depend on the hope of results.

- Thomas Merton

THE LOBBY OF CHOKI'S TENEMENT building teems with green leafy plants so lush you might think them fake. At its elevator I push the UP button, the letters faded from years of fingermarks. Hoist cables snap. The car locks. It shimmies down to us in the lobby, where it opens, and we step inside.

I check the directory for Choki's apartment and push the button for floor 43.

Abril leans against the wall, her head tilted, her eyes closed. She beams a bit. She rolls her head massaging her neck. "How did you find those mala beads?" I ask her. "If Yoong was there to kill him, and you were there before Sonny was killed, how did you find the mala beads Yoong left behind?"

I notice in the West, the expressions people make when questioned like this. Bardo expressions. Brief moments between asked and responding, when they raise an isolated eyebrow or twitch a corner of their nose, signaling that soon she may cry, or laugh, or blurt out an obscenity to reprimand me.

"You think I'm lying? You think I sent Yoong in after me to kill Sonny?"

"I..." It is her nose that twitches, where little short hairs grow invisibly inside it. "I do not know."

"Sonny was my lover. Why would I do that? No matter how much I hated him, he was my lover. Look, I'm working hard here trying to find you the dorje, and I don't even have good insurance yet. A deal's a deal, huh? Stop asking so many questions. We get this dorje, you still need to get me insurance, remember."

She makes it sound innocent, making me wonder if I see her properly, or only see what she wants me to see. Still, she is the only one since being reborn I can truly talk to. Is that not itself a skewed perspective?

The elevator stops. It opens. In front of us an apartment door gleams with fresh paint and bronzed numbers. Choki's apartment number. Dust mites drift across the hall carpet. I step over them and knock on the door, hoping I am not too late and that Choki answers.

The door opens. Chodon appears. She says to Abril, "How do you feel?" Without any urgency. Just calm, courtesy, and concern.

"I feel churn-y inside, kinda."

"You drank much raksi last night. You need chai." Then acknowledging me, Chodon says, "Lama Rinzen. Welcome. Choki tells me you won the archery contest. Very fine. Very fine, indeed. You honor us so." She steps aside and widens the door for our passing.

"We are only here to get the dorje, which he promised me."

"Yes, yes, yes. Please, lama, come in, come in." She points into an apartment laid out like a long railroad boxcar, poorly lit. Candles burn at a hallway shrine with photos of today's Dalai Lama tacked to the shrine wall. Other lineage holders too, from lifetimes gone past. Gelugpas, all. Chodon escorts us as we pass one empty bedroom and then another. At the hall's far end, it empties into a narrow kitchenette. To the right before the kitchenette, I see a living room. Choki in a La-Z-Boy, buried beneath a green and red knit blanket. Half-crescent glasses perched on his nose. He reads the Denver Post, and in his glasses and the La-Z-Boy, he appears feebler than at the contest. Less spry. Older.

We enter the living room and Choki adjusts his chair. "Ah, Lama Rinzen. You found your way. Very good. Very good. I was trusting you'd come. How does your head feel? Like raksi, does it not? With such hangovers, we awaken. Bardo moments. But also we feel dead, both at once. Death and awakening in one moment. Such wisdom hangovers bring." He folds the newspaper aside and places it atop a three-drawer bedroom night table oddly placed alongside an unmade daybed crammed next to a sunken loveseat, which sits in front of an array of kitchen chairs and a kitchen table. Living, dining, sleeping, all assembled together in one space, much like a high plains yurt—everything one and cluttered together. "You are here about the dorje, aren't you?"

He tries standing, but is suddenly seized by a spell of coughing. "Winter phlegm. Bad in the West." He shakes his head, props up in the chair by his elbows. "The contest did not help. Very cold out, very cold. As in Drepung. Are you angry I did not give you the dorje last night? Have you come to kill me, lama?"

"No," I tell him. "I have not come to kill you."

"Of course not," He laughs. "Nor do I believe you would. Although, you did embarrass me some, winning that contest. You have always been a brave captain. But so fine an archer, this surprised me."

"A lesson in uncertainty," I tell him. "Perhaps now you might give me the dorje, so we can leave."

"Oh, now you cannot leave, lama. You have just arrived. We must savor the moment. Let us have chai."

"No chai is necessary," I tell him. "The dorje will suffice."

Abril intervenes. "Don't be ungrateful, lama. Let us have chai. So he can explain to us why the Tibetans' death policies all paid their benefits to Madame Sun's emporium, and not the deserving families of the deceased."

Choki holds his smile. "Not death policies, miss. Life policies, for when you die. As you know, everything a matter of how you say it in the West. To which I say, I received no money from those policies. Let us have chai, shall we?"

Choki seeps deeper into the La-Z-Boy. "Let me explain. The Hellers claim to be friends of the émigré. We come to a strange land, Chodon and I. The Hellers at the plane, they greet us. They hang mala beads around our necks. I don't know why. Something they saw in Hawaii once, I imagine. They say we are free now that we have arrived here, and we should make business. An emporium and meditation center. It will require insurance, but not to worry. The policy's premium pays itself from future payouts. Then when we die, the remaining proceeds go to the emporium as a donation. Not just me, they say this to, but to all the newly arrived. Selling them life policies. For when we die. They say this to us, but the paperwork does not. The paperwork says something different. That the payments are a loan from Heller Insurance. Which they can call upon for repayment at any time. Buried inside paperwork too cumbersome to read. Paperwork kills slowly in the West. Like lingchi."

"The West needs enlightenment," I say. "I am sorry for your troubles, Choki. As your teacher, as your niru captain, I am so sorry. But you must listen. Yoong, Fernandez, the Hellers, they are all after the dorje. For your own safekeeping you must give it to me. Yoong has already killed two insurance men, and perhaps the Tibetans in the alley. He will kill you too, unless you give it to me now. After all, I won the contest fair and square."

His face twists. "You believe this, lama? The dorje can save us from someone like Yoong? An agent of the People's Republic of China? I know you mean well, as when we rode on Drepung. I saw how mercifully you slaughtered its monks. Bringing an army as you did, you honor your victims with glory."

"He knows black magic," Abril tells Choki. "He could take it from you if he wanted."

"These lamas can do anything they want, miss," Choki tells her. "Filled with their magic and their years in the Shedra." He adjusts the La-Z-Boy, notching himself more upright. He points to the loveseat, not entirely wide enough for the both of us, and he says, "Please, sit. Chodon will make us the chai."

Choki then snaps at his wife. "He once commanded a vast niru army, you know. I served as an archer of moderate skill. But a strong captain like Lama Rinzen..., a strong captain can strengthen any soldier." He thumps his chest, one-fisted, twice in rapid succession. "The lama made me brave."

"Yes, well, thank you," I tell him, "but we really cannot stay."

"No, let's," Abril suggests. I do not know why, so then she adds, "I have never had chai made by an actual Tibetan before. I imagine it's scrumptious."

"We cannot stay," I tell her. "You know this. We are here for the dorje, to bring all to enlightenment."

"Oh, no, please, sit first, lama." Choki points to the loveseat laden in pillows and frilly knittings. Abril settles into it, and then pulls me down to join her. Squeezed together tight, our elbows knock one another for position. First hers on top, then mine, then hers on mine—until finally she leans forward and me back, making room.

"A quick cup," Abril says. "And then we must take the dorje and leave."

Choki leans toward us. "Before administering the dorje, I must first ask. In this lifetime here on Colfax, what have you found, lama?"

I do not hesitate to answer. "You. A follower. A student. A man of devotion who now holds the dorje, inside its Buddha statue. Which will bring the end to so many Hells."

"Yes, yes," Choki says. "But no, lama. I ask not what you have achieved. I ask what you have found. I, for instance, find that there are two kinds of seriousness in the West. First, the seriousness of greed. Its pursuit of craving. Its disappointment with never finding what it craves. And second, the seriousness of stinginess, forever clinging to what little they do find. What about you? Which have you found? The first—the seriousness of valuing life above all else? Or the second—valuing life more than it merits?"

"I find the more I look, the more confusing the search," I tell him.

Choki nods, agreement slowly dawning. "Yes, quite true." He laughs now. "You have found much. Just as one needle completes being threaded, another needs threading. Very wise."

Chodon re-emerges carrying a tray with four steaming cups, each cup on a saucer, and each saucer adorned with ginger snaps. The tray smells of warmed honey, cinnamon, cloves, and milk. Choki proudly beams at the presentation, praising Chodon in a chirruping Tibetan dialect I am unfamiliar with, but speaking of what they have between them. What they share.

Chodon hands me my cup and saucer adorned with two ginger cookies, and then Abril hers with one, and then she passes Choki both remaining saucers, hers and his, each with half a cookie. She carries one of the kitchen chairs to the La-Z-Boy to sit next to her husband, taking her tea from him and resting it on her lap.

I sip first, lifting my cup, savoring the warmth of fresh yak milk and cloves.

Only then do Choki and his woman lift their own cups to sip. Only then do they snack upon their cookie halves. "I am sure I need not tell you," Choki says sounding cheery, "but in Zen – I am not Zen, but I mention it—in Zen there is an expression. If you see the Buddha on the road, kill him." He laughs, so that bits of cookie drop from his teeth. "Kill him. That is funny, no? The Buddha." He laughs some more, and then his mood turns more solemn. "Because no Buddha can be your teacher. No lama. Only you can teach yourself. The Buddha inside, that is your teacher. To have another is an act of dualism. These lamas can do anything, miss," he tells Abril. "Trick us in these ways. Do you remember this lesson, lama? This teaching you gave?" He opens his arms to emphasize what he is saying, dripping tea over the lip of his cup. "No Buddha exists, except the Buddha inside each of us. No teachers. No guru. To believe anything less is Lamaism. Medieval."

Squeezed tight in the loveseat, I squirm before answering, hoping to soon be rid of the cookies and the niceties and get straight down to the business of the dorje. "I do not recall teaching about the falseness of the Buddha. No."

"Oh." Choki slumps low, ashamed with himself.

Chodon smirks. "I have lived with Choki many lifetimes. He sulks like this when corrected, lama. Please. Let us sit quietly and enjoy our chai."

This cheers him. Choki flutters his feet. "Yes, yes, many lifetimes together, Chodon and I. So she teaches me, lama, she teaches me much. Together, we two are one. Yab-yum. Too much loneliness in the West. But Chodon and I have been married many lifetimes. As with you and me, lama, riding together, the sun glaring so brightly as we rode upon the Monastery of White Rice. Your instruction to us, beware of false teachings and black magic, and the Buddha on the road who will divert us. You do not remember this? You killed your teacher that day, as she stood in your path. You do not remember such a teaching?"

"Married many lifetimes," Chodon says. "I remember this."

"Although not every lifetime married," Choki laughs. "In some I married her sister. A skinny girl. Not so sweet. Of course, this did not keep Chodon from acting my wife from time to time, in those moments we found ourselves alone."

Chodon blushes. "Do not say."

Abril balances her saucer and cookie on her knee, leaning forward. "Imagine such a thing. You two are lovers, as well as husband and wife?"

"We have not time for imagining such things," I say. "Yoong is coming."

"Of course, lama. Of course, he is coming. He is an assassin from the East. Do you believe we should run from him?" Choki bites down upon his last bite of ginger snap, savoring it with each chew. "In the West many pretend to be individuals, but then cling to conformity. In Tibet, we live more collectively, neighbor knowing neighbor, more homogenous. In this way, we each pursue our own path. In the West, each covets what another has, trying to be the same. It's what they mistake as freedom."

Choki then places his cup of chai atop its saucer.

"The dorje, Choki, I need it now. I won the contest, fair and square."

"I am afraid it is too late, lama," he tells me. "Too late, except for me to ask why you never found it. A lama, such as yourself." He stares into his chai, not looking at me. "So many lifetimes you told us of its magic. So many lifetimes I believed you. Yet I carried it all the way here from von Richthofen Park. I broke the statue open, and found the dorje inside wrapped in burlap. I unwrapped the burlap, and lifted the Most Sacred of Objects in my hands." He holds his hands above himself.

Chodon tells me, "You should have found it, lama, long before this, if that is your mission." She stands and takes my plate and saucer, and Choki's, and Abril's, and she leaves the room.

"In my hands, lama," Choki says. "I held it. And yet I did not achieve enlightenment. I sense it is too late. Whatever was once special about it has worn off. Whatever magic it had, perhaps it is gone." Choki opens a drawer next to him. He lifts out a burlap sack folded and wrapped. "See for yourself. Nothing." He presents it to me, a crudely wrapped parcel.

His words do not deter me. "It must be held by a lama," I instruct him, "in order to be effective."

I hold the burlap in both my hands. Its cloth rough, but the sacredness inside as light as birds in flight. I savor the moment. In the hallway, Chodon speaks without my recognizing her words. Another voice joins her, speaking back, but I do not focus on what they say. Slowly, I begin unraveling the burlap, only to be interrupted as she and her companion enter the living room. Chodon, first. Behind her, Agent Yoong. He holds a knife on the old woman, and the rip in his cheek where Abril sliced him earlier has newly opened, appearing shiny red like fish guts.

"I see we are all together," the Chinese agent says. "Finishing your chai, so nice." The lingchi knife is slightly curved and rusty. He walks the room, passing each of us before coming up on Abril. He stares her down, but he speaks to me. "Leave it in the bag, lama. Easier for me to carry that way."

"It is not yours," I tell him. "It is a sacred object of the Tibetan people."

"The Chinese people, you mean? Who conquered your medieval ways and freed Tibetans from their bondage to old and superstitious thinking."

"What are you doing here, Yoong? How do you even fit in?" Abril asks.

"I am here to retrieve the dorje, as an agent of the PRC, to return to its rightful place in the Lhasa Museum. To display behind glass, as a display of what it is. Art. Nothing better. A collection of gold and jewels, done up in the form of a scepter. Imbued with Western superstitions of wealth, and ancient Eastern beliefs about power. I am here to ensure that the lamas no longer dangle it like a fetish over their people, in the way that Westerners dangle insurance. I am here to render it a relic, and nothing more. Like the lamas themselves are relics of time gone past."

Through the coarse burlap, I can still feel the dorje's sacredness, after all these many lifetimes. Slowly, I resume unraveling, to free it into my bare hands, to bring all beings to enlightenment.

Abril tries standing. "Go back to where you came from," she tells Yoong. "You're not wanted here."

I unfold the burlap slowly, so Yoong may not see while Abril distracts him.

Yoong's nose contorts. "Gweilos never mind émigrés who come over and acquiesce. I imagine a PRC agent is a little too non-compliant for your taste. I am sorry. But I must say, you play your part well, miss. I only need to ask, did you really need to slice me?" He touches his cheek where it bleeds. "To make your deception of the lama appear any truer?"

I stop unraveling. I see Abril looking at me. "What is he saying?"

"He's lying."

"Am I?" the Chinese agent asks. "Is there any such thing as lying? Or is it all just misunderstanding what you hope to not see? Understand this, lama. The West is a place of singular vision. Even if she did *love* you, as you crave, how would she know how?"

"I did not deceive you," she says. "Look, I brought you to the dorje."

Yoong looks at the bundled burlap in my lap, my fingers unfurling it. "Watch what you're doing there, lama." He grabs the sack from me.

Abril un-squeezes from the loveseat. "You can't take it. The lama won it, fair and square."

Yoong holds the knife between them. "You assaulted me once already, miss. Step back. Or I will gladly repay you in kind."

"Leave her alone," I demand.

"Really, lama? Chivalry is not your form of medievalism." Blood dribbles down his cheek.

Hearing his words, and what he says about her, and seeing his grip upon the dorje, I stand. Fire rises inside me. Black magic, maybe. Who knows? As a swooping crane, I fold down atop the burlap and pull it from Yoong's hand. He swipes at me with his blade, knocking the dorje to the floor. I swoop in once more, but Abril moves faster. She and I collide. The dorje falls, bouncing. Once. Then twice.

Yoong comes in after it. I ram my shoulder to his chest, pushing him up and away. Abril sweeps in beneath and catches the dorje on its third bounce, scooping up the burlap and running to the kitchen.

Yoong follows.

Me too. I grab Yoong to slow him, but he proves too large. He pulls me along behind him. I am hanging from his back. He pulls into the narrow kitchen of two parallel walls lined with a sink and a refrigerator and a dishwasher and stove, and with Abril boxed at its far end. Yoong approaches her slowly, me behind. She opens the kitchen's window and sits upon its sill. I signal to her, pointing behind me. "Throw it," I yell. "I have a clear exit! Throw me the dorje."

Yoong elbows my ribs, knocking me back. I fall to the floor. I lunge for his ankles. I try to topple him, but instead he kicks me in the face.

"Throw it," I cry, although on the floor, I know I do not make a good target. Yoong lifts me and slams me down atop the yellowed Formica countertop.

I hit hard.

I feel dazed. I reel to my feet and look about the kitchen.

It's empty. Just Yoong and me.

No sign of Abril.

Just a cold chill blowing in from the kitchen's far window, and a window shade flapping in its chill.

Yoong sticks his head out the window. I join him. Side by side we squeeze together staring at the ground, where I see no sign of her. No sign of the dorje.

I twist up to look at the roof. Had she climbed?

Unlikely.

No gutter spout to shimmy. The building frozen with ice. The roof too high.

Falling snow stings my eyes. Despite this, I see it plainly.

Abril is gone.

Yoong pulls himself back inside.

I linger a moment longer, checking one last time, leaning

farther and more unbalanced out the window.

She is gone, as if never here. What had Yoong said about her? Had she only hurt the Chinese agent to make her deception appear truer?

I squirm into the kitchen, but Yoong boots me back, out farther onto the sill. I grab the window's frame, either side, bracing myself. I balance. I try bending back up, lifting my head first. At the kitchen's far end, Yoong flings his lingchi blade. Bad trajectory. The knife shatters the upper pane of the window and flies off out onto the lawn. Glass sprinkles down on me. I slip further, and I hang onto the window's frame that way, unbalanced. Cuts and scrapes dotting my face and hands. Snow falling from the sky into my eyes.

Inside, I hear commotion. I feel dizzy. Exhaustion weighs on top of me. Sleet and glass fall. I shake my head to rid myself of it. I recall all I have seen. Moments ago in the yard below me.

Nothing.

No Abril.

No sign of the dorje.

Just the shadow of Yoong running through snow to find her.

Lesson 34

If we look at a single jewel, we see all jewels.
If we look at all jewels, we see but one. In this way,
the universe is nothing more than reflection.

WEIGHTLESS IN A SLIPPERY GRIP. Let go.

Dropping, drifting, ungrounded. Let go.

Cling to belief, uncertain whether it is real or not, let go. Let each moment change you.

Chatter drifts from the kitchen. Someone talking about me? Outside the window, the ground is blanketed in snow, fluffy. Let go. Let the snow catch me. My fingers loosen on the window frame. I try to hold on.

Gotcha.

Thoughts drifting through me like dreams. Like meditation.

Gotcha.

I feel unbalanced. Someone swings me up, yanking me. Squeezing my wrists, hoisting me forward through the window.

"Steady, hombre. *Te tengo a ti.*" My head bangs the upper sash as he pulls. Shards of glass loosen and fall on top of me. He yanks me into a sitting position on the window sill. Someone holding me.

"Can you hear me, lama? I am Part-timer Garcia. Do you know what I say?" He snaps fingers in my face. His other hand cups the back of my neck. "Tell me your name, lama? Do you know where you are. Tell me your name."

The kitchen appears dizzy, askew.

A wooly man in flannel. He malleted Budai statues at the warehouse. He drove me to the precinct. "What is your name, lama?"

"You know my name."

"Si. But can you tell me please?"

I rub where my head hit the sash, where the raksi still throbs. "You know my name."

In a turned-away voice, Garcia calls, "Inspector, please. He will not tell me his name. I think he hit his head outside."

I try standing, try pulling myself into the kitchen, but the room stumbles and I fall. Garcia catches me. "*Un momento,* lama. Not so fast." He points to the shattered glass in the window's upper pane, then chops the blade of his hand against his neck. "You are lucky. Glass could have sliced you." He leans me against the wall and helps me to slide to the floor, where I roll onto my side among food crumbs and dust. In this tilted view, I see the hem of a duster float toward me. Tipping my head up, I see it is Fernandez's duster. Looking past Fernandez, Choki lies dead-eyed on the living room floor.

Fernandez stands over me removing a pair of rubberized gloves that *swack* as they pull off. He steps behind me opening up my view of Chodon on the floor next to Choki. Both knife-sliced. Both dead.

"Yoong," my throat croaks.

The inspector leans against a cutting board butcher block of a table, hacked and gritty with butter knife slices. He looks down upon me on the floor. His good eye droops. He rubs his neck. He asks Garcia, "How's he doing?"

"Nonreasonable," Garcia says, and then grimaces at saying it wrong. "Nonresponsive, I mean."

The inspector pulls me upright into a sitting position on the floor. "Not lingchi this time, huh, lama?" He sweeps his fingernails back and forth again across the front of his neck. "Single cut. You're changing style." He points to the window. "What was that? You trying to escape?"

I gasp for air. Cold air from the broken window. Its remaining shards rattle as the air passes over them. I see a second part-timer in the living room flapping a blanket in the air, letting it float down atop Choki and Chodon.

"They are dead?" I ask.

Fernandez looks at them, then at the window, then at me. "What happened here, Naraka?"

Chai and cookies. Choki and Chodon. Yoong and Abril. One of them has the dorje. One of them is chasing it.

"I know you were helping her," he says.

Slowly, weakly, I pull myself into standing. I look in upon Choki and his wife of many lifetimes. "He killed them."

"He? Who he?"

I spit grit from my teeth into the sink. "Yoong. Abril has the dorje. He came here to take it, but she has it now. He killed the Hellers. The Tibetans, too."

Fernandez nods. "All that?"

I lean against the sink and shake myself off. I turn on its faucet and wash debris from my hands and neck. My fingers itch from the water's warm flow, its many drops cascading. "Choki took the dorje from the warehouse. You saw him do it. Yoong came to get it from him. But Abril took it instead, then disappeared."

Fernandez takes the bar of soap from my hand and washes his own fingers. Lifting a dishtowel from the refrigerator's door handle he dries himself.

"Abril. You're saying she ran off?"

No, I consider saying. *She didn't run. She left me. She encouraged Choki and Chodon's little chai party, giving time for Yoong to show up.* That is what I should say.

I point to the window. "What I mean is—she disappeared. Black magic, somewhere out there, with the dorje."

The inspector re-racks the towel. He bends his lower lip. "We've been through this, lama. There is no dorje. It never shipped. What I found—me, who has been working this case—is Choki here was supposed to order it for the Hellers' traveling artifact show, but he didn't. Instead he took out a two-thousand-dollar policy on it to make it look like he ordered it. So he could collect when it didn't arrive. Insurance fraud. That's serious business."

Live in Hell long enough, facts distort into ideas our minds just cannot catch up to. Harder and harder to comprehend. "It did ship," I tell him. "I saw it. I held it."

Fernandez leans against the counter, folds his arms. "You held it? What did it feel like?"

"Burlap."

"Burlap? The Most Precious of Objects feels like burlap?"

"It was wrapped in burlap."

"So did you hold it? Or something shaped like it made out of burlap?"

"It shipped to the warehouse, inside a Budai statue. You saw it."

"It never shipped." He flaps the shipping manifesto at me. "No dorje listed."

Part of Western pragmatism is the way paperwork allows them to not see what is true. "Yoong is a customs agent," I tell the inspector. "Working with the Hellers to bring the dorje here, so he might kill them and steal it back. Would he do something like that if the dorje did not ship?"

"Give it to them, so he can steal it back?" Fernandez lifts his hand to my shoulder. "You're going too far with this dorje story, lama. See life more simply, why don't you. You are an assassin.

You killed Madame Sun back in Asia. There were no lingchi murders on Colfax until you showed up. Your lover, your wife, your accomplice, she's the one who brought you here. She had a falling out with her boyfriend, Sonny Heller, and she wanted him dead. Knew you were just the patsy to do it. All with your signature style. Lingchi. She promised you the dorje, and that's how she got you to do it. Except there never was a dorje. Never will be."

I laugh at the silliness of what he says, and also at the way he says it. "I did not kill anyone," I tell him.

"You wouldn't be the first guilty man to say that. Who are you, lama? I've been doing detective work longer than you've even been here on Colfax. I know how it's done. I know how to find who did what. Look for the one who denies it. Who thinks he's something he's not. Watch it slowly dawn on him, the thing he thinks he's not—is actually who he is. Watch his deception become real. Then arrest him."

He takes a statue from atop a kitchen shelf and places it down on the butcher block counter. A monk slaying his mistress, sword in hand. "You and this Madame Sun go way back a long ways, don't you?"

I know how it must look to him. To a detective. "We are the things we do, inspector. As well as what we intend. I seek the dorje to benefit all. Madame Sun keeps me from it. She keeps us all from enlightenment by denying it to me. Every lifetime, it happens like this."

"I thought you said she doesn't exist."

When had I told him this? What had I told anyone here in Hell on Colfax? Only what I needed to say to survive. What I needed to go on living in Hell. This is the deceit I play. Not on others, but on myself.

Fernandez now lifts a spatula from a kitchen carafe and rolls its handle this way and that between his hands. "You say she disappeared. That's too bad, lama. Because we're just about out of budget, and I got to bring somebody in. You know about detective work. It's never about who's guilty. It's about who's in front of you when the budget runs out. You got one girl, Madame Sun… she doesn't exist. You got another, she's non-existent too. Disappeared. That leaves just you." He nods at the monk slaying his mistress. "A lingchi monk who killed many enemies back in the day, and who's now trying to pull the same shit on Colfax. We are the things we do, lama. What you do—it's not too good."

He drops the spatula into the sink. "Part-timer Garcia, cuff this man. I'll call the coroner. Have him pull some DNA from the bodies in the living room. Wrap this up. On time, under budget."

"Inspector," I say. "I suspect Yoong means to do Abril harm. Like he did Choki and Chodon, and the Tibetans."

"Yeah, well I wouldn't worry too much," Fernandez says. "From what I see, she can take care of herself. After all, she disappeared, didn't she? Left you here to take the fall. Like my Coupe de Ville story. Car disappears, leaves my dad all alone. Then suddenly it comes back with a trunkful of cash. Did I say what happened after that? Did I tell you? Goons show up to question my father. Big ape-men. They want their money. They want the car. They want it all. Why are you any better, lama?"

Garcia steps up behind me, tippy-toes, whispering in my ear, "Do not need to listen, lama. Just relax, please. So I do not pinch you putting the cuffs on." He speaks like a man with very little sleep, only being paid part-time for all the hours he puts in. Yet still, he takes the time to see that the handcuffs do not pinch.

Intention informs cause.

Cause creates effect.

But is it like this?

* * *

Garcia cannot tell why the inspector prattles on like he does. Like he always does, he prattles on. Pompous. Pretensioso, con una lengua inflada. While he prattles, Garcia looks at Fernandez and dutifully nods, Si, inspector, si. Like with Maria when she cries through her telenovelas.

Then, pinch. Garcia feels his fingers pinch. He looks to the task at hand, and sees he is no longer cuffing the lama. He sees that the lama is no longer in the room with him.

He looks about the kitchen while the inspector continues his recitation in the living room. He goes to the kitchen window, its curtain still flapping, and he looks out. "Inspector," he calls.

Fernandez comes to the kitchen and looks about, bewildered. "Where'd he go?"

Garcia nods to the snow down in the yard, footprints trampled through it. "Disappeared."

The inspector looks out the window, and then leans back inside against the counter top, picking the spatula up from the sink. "When? Before or after my Coupe de Ville story?"

But Garcia cannot say when. "I do not know, inspector. I was not listening."

LESSON 35

Once we feel anger,
we have ceased seeking truth,
and instead seek ourselves.

I RIDE THE ELEVATOR UP the Heller office tower. In the Heller lobby, Mimi sits behind her reception desk beneath the light of a single lamp.

Seeing me, she stands. "Well, hello, lama." She comes around to the front of the desk. "You are back," and she smiles a big-lipped smile. "I knew you'd be back."

She looks different. Her hair has been pigtailed and dyed Christmas tree green. Her eyeglass lenses too, tinted avocado green and framed inside green moss-colored frames. She wears a plaid sleeveless tunic, pleated right down to her knees. Its plaid is predominantly green.

"I am looking for Huey Heller," I say.

"Is he expecting you?"

"I do not know."

"He's expecting somebody." She nods down the corridor. "Back there, in his office."

The corridor is dark. Nothing to see.

"He's nervous, lama. Curly's dead now too. Maybe I should be nervous. Soon it may just be me working here at Heller Insurance, and then how do I get paid? What will happen to my insurance?"

"What do you mean he is *nervous*?"

"I think there's a problem paying Madame Sun her money. Four point nine million, that's a lot of moolah." She points to the display case where the lingchi knife once hung. "He's taken the knife with him, and told me to hold his calls. You can go back and see, if you want. I just can't call him to say you're coming."

He has the lingchi blade. It seems there are too many of them in the world. "Has anyone else been here?"

Mimi wags her head. "Just me. Now you." She nods to the offices. "And him. I'd walk you back, but I don't want to, okay? He is acting too nervous."

Staring once again into the unlit hall, I see no distinction between its walls and the darkness inside them. Is this what the Buddha means by emptiness? Space without edges.

I walk into that darkness. I pass a door with *Sonny Heller* etched on its nameplate. I open it and see inside the room is empty. No cabinets, no desk, no chair, no lamp, no standing lamp, no notepads. Nothing.

Down the hall farther, I open Curly's door. The same. No time wasted sweeping up after the dead here at Heller Insurance.

Down even farther, Huey's closed door emits a thin sliver of light beneath its frame. Inside, I hear tapping, like a tree branch against glass, or fingers drumming a desktop, or metal chinking metal. I put my ear to the door, listening, wondering whether to knock or just barge in.

"Who is it?"

It takes a moment, but I realize the voice on the door's other side is asking me. "Who's out there?" it says.

I open the door. Inside Heller sits behind his desk with the lingchi knife in his hand, which he stabs over and over again into a gouge he has made in the desktop's metal.

"You?" He pauses long enough to point the blade at me, more in recognition than threat. The desk is sparsely adorned. A lamp. A laptop. A pair of spongy dice that say *Atlantic City*, one pink, one blue. An insurance policy for four point nine million dollars stretched out before him, and a claim letter from Madame Sun's Olde Tibetan Emporium and Meditation Center.

"You work with Yoong, don't you?" Heller asks.

"Yoong is a killer."

"She works with him too, doesn't she?"

Like what he has said about her all along. His brothers, too. Abril is the killer, maybe working with Yoong. "I do not know that for sure, no. Maybe."

"But they're coming, right?" The insurance man goes back to jabbing the desk. "I know what *you* are, lama. You're a freelancer. An émigré. No loyalty to our way of life here in the West, and all the hard work we put into building our company. Plus, you're a dorje snob, like we don't deserve it. Because we're Westerners. You've done this kind of thing before, haven't you?"

"What sort of thing?"

"Killed someone for the Most Sacred of Objects. Well, let me tell you something. I don't have it. Never did. It never shipped."

"It did ship. I held it."

"Don't lie to me, lama. If you held it, you'd be enlightened by now. Not stuck here on Colfax."

"It was wrapped inside a burlap sack when I held it."

"Well, you should have unwrapped it." He stabs the blade at the desk more furiously.

"Please, Mister Heller, we have limited time. Yoong and Abril, they are coming. Yoong, at least. Hopefully Abril. We must be ready."

"Abril? The application liar? What's she got to do with it?"

"You said she killed Sonny. Because he took her insurance away."

Heller folds in on himself, smaller. "Don't play me like a fool, lama. Insurance is a tough business, and I'm not that gullible. There's risk all around. Insurance is supposed to manage that risk. But that doesn't take away its risk. You never know where your next paycheck's coming from when you work insurance. And the dorje never shipped. It never left its museum in Lhasa. We never intended it to."

Maybe it is the glare of the desk lamp, the way its glare splits the room into light and dark. Maybe that is why I am not sure I heard him right.

"What do you mean, not intend it to ship?"

The knife pings the desktop over and over, while Heller stares into the hole it creates. "It was Yoong's idea. The Chinese agent. A customs agent, he told us. The way he talks… these Chinese customs agents can do anything. He says take an ad out in the *All Things Asian* catalog for the dorje. Four point nine million, he says, because it's sacred. To me it looked a little cheesy, like a Five 'n Dime flyer they stick in people's mailboxes. Yoong says we should pick a number out of the phone book to put in the ad. He says it doesn't matter which one, he'll make it look Chinese, so nobody knows. Turns out, we mistakenly picked out an ex-client's number. Abril. We just placed the ad, I swear. All the rest of it was Yoong."

"But Abril is coming here? Is that what you are saying?"

"Why would she?"

"You ordered the dorje from her? From the catalog? She is bringing it to you."

"No, not really. We just made it *look* like we ordered it. Took out an insurance policy on it, but never really ordered the thing. It was all Yoong's idea. We don't order it, you see, so the dorje never shows. So we collect on its insurance policy. Split it four ways. Two ways now. Sonny and Curly are dead." He looks into space.

"Soon, maybe just one way. Yoong gets it all. I never trusted him really. These Chinese, they're cunning. In the West, we talk about a work ethic, but we don't want to work. We just want to make money. The Chinese know this about us. Insurance is a hard business. Sell a policy one day, wake up the next day, and you got to sell another. Never ends. Day after day, you just have to make a living. It wears you down, making money. It's a long, slow death."

I try clarifying, "Yes, but the dorje, it is here, is it not? You ordered it from someone. Even if not from the catalog."

"No, not really. We wanted people to think that, but no. Sonny goes to the warehouse, to *discover*—I use the word loosely—to *discover* the dorje didn't arrive. He calls us—was supposed to call us—tell Curly and me *hurry, come down to the warehouse, the dorje's not here*. So we can go down and say *yeah you're right* and file a claim with our Excess and Surplus insurer. Except Sonny never calls. So, I call him. No answer. So we go down, and the police are there. You. You say Sonny's dead. You say the dorje got stolen. Except we never ordered it, so we know it's not stolen. You say it's lingchi..." He whimpers. "It should have been obvious. We return to the office, and there's a claim. Madame Sun's Emporium, signed by Madame Sun. We own Madame Sun's emporium. There is no Madame Sun. Then we realize, Yoong played us. The Chinese are smart. They're taking over the world. They even bought up our Excess and Surplus insurer. That's who Yoong's an agent for. We never knew."

"Yes, yes, maybe so...but the dorje, I held it in my hands. I held it in my hands."

"The claim letter says it is, but it's not. The claim letter says if we don't give it back and surrender our license, Yoong will demonstrate another display of lingchi for us. That's when Curly was killed."

"But Abril has it. The dorje exists. You say she has nothing to do with it, but she has the dorje. She is bringing it to you, is she not?"

"No, not really. Why would she bring it to me? She lied on her application and we canceled her insurance, that's how much she thinks of Heller Insurance."

Heller stabs his desk and twists the knife so that the gouged metal shines. The laptop atop his desk pings. An app he has installed. An intercom app, Mimi's voice over the PC's speakers. "Mister Heller. I know I am not supposed to call you, but there's an agent here. A Chinese agent. He says you're expecting him."

The computer pauses. Heller pauses too. No more knife stabbing.

Mimi speaks once more. "He has some bicyclists with him."

I look to the door. I close the laptop's screen to extinguish its light. Yoong I could handle, but bicyclists...that confuses things. Like Abril confuses things. Her having the dorje, but not bringing it here. Heller saying it did not ship. "Is there another way out?" I ask.

He sits immobilized. Nervous. "No. No way out."

"There must be. There is always a way out."

Deep down the hall, I hear footsteps. I reach across the desk and flick off its lamp, darkening the office. I lift the insurance man by his shoulders, the full weight of him. He resists. "No way out," he says. I pull him into the hall. At the hallway's far end, toward Mimi's desk, I can make out a silhouette of Yoong and the bicyclists advancing toward us.

"You there. Heller?" Yoong yells. "I'm looking for Heller. Who are you?"

I recall my days at the Shedra, and what Daidyal...somebody... taught me. Holding onto Heller, I make ourselves unseen.

I pull him down the hall away from Yoong, the two of us now unseen. I silently unlatch door after door in search of an escape, a way out. I see a dully lit plastic sign saying *Emergency.* I open its door and we step inside.

Before us lay a long, lit, cinder-blocked stairwell coiling downward to street level. A fire escape. We begin our descent, landing by landing, Heller resisting, me pulling his weighty, whimpering body. "No escape," he gurgles. "He's going to kill us. He is going to kill me."

We manage to put five flights between us and the door above before it opens and the bicyclists flood in. Sensing our presence, but still unable to detect where we are, they sneak down landing by landing, pausing every now and again to fire an arrow in our suspected direction, trying to flush us out. We hug our backs to the cinderblocks, keeping too severe an angle between us and them for the arrows to hit, leaving us vulnerable only when we cross the landings from one side of the stairwell to the other.

We move quickly. Arrows shatter against the flooring at our heels but come no closer. Six landings, seven, eight, maybe more, we make it.

But with each crossing, the bicyclists' aim gets more accurate, and our forms begin to materialize for them to see. One arrow even nicks the sole of my mukluk, momentarily pinning me in place. This next crossing, I know, it could be our last.

I pull Heller into a cubbyhole. We catch our breath. Above us, cyclists keep descending. Across from the cubby I notice an exit door. Much like the door through which we entered. It juts out, slightly exposed. An easy target, indeed, once the archers see it open. They keep coming toward us, step by step, a tad more slowly, more cautiously now. Like they know where we are.

I push Heller. "We are going through that door," I tell him.

"No." He's hyperventilating. "No way out. It's a security door. Locked. You can't get onto a floor you're not supposed to be on."

The bicyclists whisper closer.

"We have no choice." I throw him at the door and then push up against him, releasing the door's release bar. It opens. We spill into a hallway of cubicles. We wade through them, each no different, one cubicle the same as another.

At an intersection, I spot an over-sized maintenance closet with plumbing pipes and light bulbs and air filters stored inside cardboard boxes. We slam inside. "You wait here," I say. "When I step out, lock the door behind me."

"Where you going?"

"To create a diversion. They will come after me, not you."

"You're a bodhisattva, lama. You're supposed to protect me."

Yes. Protect him and all creatures. "Just breathe," I tell him. "I will be back for you."

I step into the hall and continue through the cubicle maze. Here, there, this way and that, until finally I find a mail chute in one of the walls. Package-sized. Beyond the chute, the hallway dead-ends. Climbing into the mail chute, I bang its walls. I tip over a stamp machine. I shimmy down into the mail chute, pressing my feet and fingers against it to hold myself in place.

Darkness and silence. Bicyclists search above. I can hear them. I brace.

"He came down here," one says.

"Where'd he go?" another asks.

No one opens the chute. I hold steady.

Then, Yoong's voice calling. "Lama. Come, lama. Even the best leaders fall. Just as Tibet has fallen. We are all Chinese now, your people liberated from feudal monkish monarchies. You and I, we are no longer different. Except I am a victor. You not. And so, I must take the dorje from you to bring back to Lhasa. Has she given it to you? Is she here with you?"

I hold in place. Time elapses. Eventually, where Yoong's voice once echoed above me, I now hear only whispers of silence.

The sound of them leaving.

Shuffling from the hallway, they leave.

Is it a trap? Is it a diversion?

I hold myself suspended, struggling to balance my desire to stay hidden with my desire to escape. Will they find Heller? Can they?

Advance or retreat? What should I do?

This or that.

LESSON 36

Clinging to things as existent is empty.

WHAT TO SEE? DARKNESS.

What to touch? Empty space around me.

What to feel? The draft of the mail chute's chill air.

What to smell or taste? Only myself.

What to listen for? Nothing. No sound. None above. None below. The bicyclists have left. Yoong with them. Why?

I should find Heller. I should find Abril, as well. What had he said about her? *What does she have to do with it?* If not her, who?

I pull myself up the chute and out into the hall. It's empty, no one there.

I wade through the cubicle maze to the maintenance room. No Heller.

No indication of a skirmish.

He escaped. There is always a way out.

I take the stairs to the lobby. I slip out the building onto the street. I walk, my mind lost in Denver's urban mosaic. What had the bicyclists whispered? What had Yoong said? Something about the dorje, no doubt? Something about Abril, maybe?

I stand on the warehouse front lawn, bottom step to the portico. I sense a presence inside. I walk up the steps. I go inside.

Candles burn on the warehouse's window sills as little dots of light inside its darkness. Candles burn on the floor around its perimeter. Candles climb up the steps of the riser to the apse. They melt atop filing cabinets and empty packing crates, casting shadows like long-dead ghosts, flickering and bending. Distorting the warehouse's walls.

Candlelight casts a dimness on a burlap sack at the center of the warehouse's floor. I approach. I kneel. I lift and touch its warmth. Over my shoulder, something creaks. A small sound. I slowly and solemnly unwrap the burlap, twist by twist. Again, I hear the creak. Very small, but thunderous inside the warehouse's silence.

I look over my shoulder and see a chair. In its bony Shaker design Huey Heller sits slumped, trussed, lifeless. Sheared of all form.

A moment of emptiness. A bardo moment passes. It catches in my throat. A diversion, settled between the moment before and the moment after. This moment now, when I realize I had not protected Heller at all, and that Yoong found him. And killed him, like he did his brothers, and then dragged him here.

No. That would have been too messy.

He dragged him here, then killed him. Only why had I not heard any commotion, back in Heller's office tower? Certainly death changes an environment, even if many cubicles and a mail chute away.

Heller sits without moving. What they call peace here in the West. Stillness. Candles burn. A breeze stirs about the room.

Someone has followed me. The burlap slips from my fingers. It rolls to the warehouse's edge.

"Hello, lover."

Her words crackle, like bad AM radio. Echoed and clipped. "I have been expecting you, lama."

In the darkness, her form shimmers. Her whitened face glows around waxy glossed lips and eyes the shape of almonds. Golden robes flow down her body, she sits upon a gomden. She shimmers, but otherwise remains perfectly still. Like waiting in ambush.

I bow, averting my eyes from her. "Madame Sun."

She says nothing. "You have returned?" I say.

"Returning is such a linear concept, is it not?" Madame Sun asks. "Another way to observe it might be—I have been here the whole time, but you failed to see me."

I bow more deeply now, staring at the warehouse floor, its nicks and wheel-cart scratches, and the outline where pews were once bolted in its Catholic days.

"I mean no disrespect," I say. "I only meant… you are enlightened. So why return at all? You are moved on. Beyond Hell."

"To be enlightened is not to move on, lama. To be enlightened is to live with life as it is, without resisting it. Live within Hell, and you will progress beyond Hell. Your mind will make it a different place. Do you believe that?" Her voice creaks, like an unoiled door slowly opening.

"You held the dorje. In Drepung. I saw you. I tried taking it from you. Certainly, you are enlightened. It slipped from my hands. You held it so tightly." My fingers strangle their grip of one another as I bow. "You took it from me."

"Poor poor lama. Everything taken, nothing received. Sit, why don't you." She nods at a cushion on the floor. "Sit so I may see you, and you can tell me…what have you seen?"

I sink into a lotus position, onto the cushion. I glance at where the dorje sack rolled. The room's silence brightens.

After some time, Madame Sun speaks, which she does in this way, saying...

Madame Sun: You suffer, lama, pursuing this dorje of yours. And you despoil it by chasing it so.

Rinzen: The dorje denies me. Far too many lifetimes in Hell.

Madame Sun: You despoil yourself by chasing yourself. Feeling bad about what you have done in your lives.

Rinzen: You taught me in the Shedra, to not focus on past lives. To only see now.

Madame Sun: In every *now* the past is hidden. Cause and effect married as one.

Snow falls outside the warehouse unseen, untasted, untouched.

Rinzen: I suffer because of my devotion to bring all beings to enlightenment, Madame Sun.

Madame Sun: Yes. In a relative way, you suffer from not finding the dorje, as you say. But in an absolute way, you do not find the dorje because you suffer. Allowing yourself to suffer, it is an obsession of yours. An excuse to which you've grown accustomed.

Rinzen: To bring all beings to enlightenment.

Madame Sun: Are all beings not already enlightened? Do they need you? Does anyone?

Rinzen: I come for their benefit, as a bodhisattva.

Madame Sun: Why? Because *bodhisattva* is a word that entertains you? A word that gives hope you may entertain others, so that they need you?

Rinzen: If all beings are enlightened already, I would know it, would I not? Because then I too would be enlightened. As a bodhisattva, I enlighten once all others have. Yet still, I grovel. Here in Hell. Others grovel with me. Waiting on me to lead them. It is what I do.

Madame Sun: Words well spoken, lama. With inflection, and intention, and the importance with which you believe them. Still, words are like scabs atop wounds. Pick at them long enough, the wounds beneath them bleed once more. What do you really mean to say? Please, tell me.

Rinzen: I say the things I think are true. Because what I think is who I am. And who I am is the intention I bring to my actions. Others seek the dorje, but without the purity of my intention.

Madame Sun: Very dualistic, lama. Calling yourself well-intentioned because comparatively *the other* is not. The question you should ask…is your intention benevolent?

Rinzen: I am benevolent.

Madame Sun: You oppress no one.

Rinzen: I oppress no one.

Madame Sun: Except by expectation that they see you as a bodhisattva.

Rinzen: For their own benefit.

Madame Sun: For their own benefit, they should acknowledge you in a way that conforms to your self-image. Is that not oppression?

Rinzen: My sacrifice…is for all sentient beings. They should see this about me.

Madame Sun: To bring all to the realization of enlightenment?

Rinzen: Yes.

Madame Sun: To some strange faraway fantasy world, where it is magical, and someplace far into the future? In the *out-there*? Not here now.

You are not so good with promises, I have noticed, lama. Not good at seeing enlightenment lasts no more than a moment. No more than a lightning flash. Enlightenment experiences all time in a single instant, for no longer than it takes to snap a picture.

See these Hellers. They lived outside the moment, struggling to balance past accumulation against future desire. Each one, past and future, disappointing the other. Neither accomplished, neither satisfied. They died this way. Lingchi. Stripped of the *who* they never allowed themselves to be.

Rinzen: Yoong killed these men. Seeking the dorje, he killed them. An assassin.

Madame Sun: And you have come to discover this about him, have you not? As a freelance policeman. What will you do now that you know Yoong is the killer for some large corporate Chinese Excess and Surplus insurance conglomerate? Assassinate him?

Rinzen: I kill no one.

Madame Sun: You killed me once. For every effect, its cause, lama.

I do not look at her.

Rinzen: Killing you was not my intention. You should have given me the dorje when I asked. Forgive me, please. I expected you would just hand it over. And I felt that just holding it once, as you held it, I could be enlightened. Forgive me. You were my teacher. Had I not challenged you, had I been a better student, it could all be different now. You must forgive me, please, so that now I may finally escape this Hell.

Madame Sun: Your actions are not mine to forgive. Only you can do that. My path is not yours to follow.

Why do you suppose in this lifetime you pursue the Hellers' killer? To face a killer, or to see yourself?

As a bodhisattva must see himself, to find that he is empty of self? Not defined by the good deeds he does, but by the selflessness that allows them to be done.

Consider all truths. Think how relatively speaking, you slayed me with lingchi. Think second, how in an absolute way, long before lifting your blade, you killed me with your expectation of who I should be. Someone you could follow. Someone you could conform to your expectation. Someone who rejected your following me. Someone you thought would get you to enlightenment, like a Buddha on the road.

Someone who should behave according to your expectation.

Within the confined perspective you built for yourself, so you could say I was behaving properly and as you expect me to behave.

Or otherwise, you might slay me.

Rinzen: You were my teacher. I respected you that way.

Madame Sun: Yes, your teacher. But an unreliable teacher, at that. See these Hellers. Who would not want to kill them? What value did they find in themselves? The more we see a thing, lama, the more it changes into what we expect it should be, and not what it is. Just as the more we pay for something, the more we suspect it is valuable.

Rinzen: Please, the dorje, Madame Sun? For one second—no more—may I hold it? So I might know what you know. So, I might explain.

Madame Sun: You desire that?

Rinzen: Yes.

Madame Sun: But desire is a habit, lama. An expectation that never lasts long enough. Flying off—*flit, flit, flit*—like birds from a telephone wire. Desire creates order from chaos, to which we cling.

Rinzen: I desire the dorje, only so we all may leave Hell.

Madame Sun: Sounds hea-ven-ly. Yum yum, delicious delicious, lama. Is this what you desire?

Rinzen: Yes.

Madame Sun: *You?*

Rinzen: Yes.

Madame Sun: What *you*? What is *you*? A fixed, solid, unwavering mind. The hero of a story you tell yourself.

Rinzen: I am a bodhisattva.

Madame Sun: Exactly. A made-up word.

Rinzen: I seek the dorje to benefit all. How else can I escape this Hell?

Madame Sun: By not escaping. By finding enlightenment in this moment, here, now, without escaping.

There is no *you*, lama. Only your moments of interaction with the world around you. You live in Hell, because you desire Hell. Desire is how you define yourself. Who *you* are. She brought you here, lama. Do not ignore that.

Rinzen: Who?

Madame Sun: She Googled you all week. You two are not that different. Do you know what the Buddha talks about when he talks about emptiness? Seeing yourself in another's story. Even if just a small part you play in it. A walk-on, maybe. Someone she can do shtick with, or tell her troubles to. Without lines of your own, maybe. In most of her story, you may not even be there.

An energy rises up my body. Then back down again.

Madame Sun: Someday you will hold the dorje, and your quest will end. Someone may try to take it from you, but they will fail. Because you will hold it inside you, in all its many parts, and your quest will end. Go now. Go there into the darkness and pick it up.

I can barely discern its shape, nor exactly where it lay. Nor how to see it. Nor what to expect.

Madame Sun: Pick it up. Carry it into her story. Protect her with it.

Rinzen: Protect her how?

Madame Sun: By seeing inside yourself.

Madame Sun unfolds her gown, showing she is naked, showing her scars from lingchi. An emptiness, as if not there. She pulls a lingchi blade from beneath her gown, and tosses it to the warehouse floor, where it clangs.

Madame Sun: Watch yourself, lama. Watch the things you do.

Watch yourself without interfering with yourself. It is your story to observe. But not to tell anymore.

* * *

A moment passes.

Another.

Madame Sun lowers her eyes and enfolds herself inside her gown. I rise from my cushion. I lift up the blade she has thrown me and carry it. At the edge of the warehouse, I pick up the dorje and unwrap its burlap.

I behold it.

I caress its tarnished, dull, jewel-fallen shaft. Its dust-caked crevices of gold. I feel where its manufacturer's seam chinks along the edge. It feels weightless, as if made out of tin.

"It is nothing," I tell her.

But when I do... Madame Sun is no longer there to hear me.

Lesson 37

We do not say because things are empty they do not exist;
we say that because things exist they are empty.

I MOVE TO THE WAREHOUSE door, lingchi blade in hand and
the dorje inside my robe's back pocket. I pull the deadbolt, pull
the door open. Winter pinches in. The blade ices in my grip. The
snow outside lay before me smooth and untracked, and above it,
a halo of fog settles on the buildings around 33rd and Josephine,
floating above them, as in a dream.

I close the door, but before it completely shuts I hear something. The door pushes in on me. Abril enters, knocking me to the
floor, where I land on the dorje.

"Where you going?" She secures the dead bolt behind her and
looks at me. She looks at the dead Heller in the apse, and then at
the blade in my hand. "You do that?"

"He was dead when I got here."

She looks at him, then again at the blade. She offers me an

arm to pull me up, hand to wrist, but as she does she strips me of the blade and looks it over. "Where'd you get this?"

"Madame Sun." I say. "She gave it to me."

"Madame Sun? For someone who doesn't exist, you sure talk about her a lot."

She picks up one of the burning candles and illuminates the blade's edge. "No blood. No inscription." She turns it one side up, then down, then over, flashing it in the candlelight. She uses it to point at the dorje sagging inside my robes. "What's that?"

My back spasms where I fell on the Most Sacred of Objects. I limp over to show it to her, its lifeless chipped surface and fallen jewels, and the way its one orbed end now bends where I landed on it. "All these lifetimes, I did not even know what it looked like exactly," I tell her.

Abril rolls her hand around its surface, examining its feel from all angles. "Doesn't look like much." She hands it back and cracks the door open again. "Did you hear it out there? That kinda grinding sound, like bees swarming." Her face glows. Red even. Ruddy. "Bicyclists are coming."

"I heard something. Are you feeling better? You look better. Your complexion, it looks healthy."

"Yeah. Thanks. I am better." She says it like something she is hiding.

"You are not sick anymore?"

"No. Pregnant, that's all."

The dorje drops from my hand to the floor, rolling. "Whiner says you can't be pregnant."

"Whiner's a doctor. What does she know?" She eyes me up and down. "A woman knows when she's pregnant. What? Maybe a little happiness maybe, huh, lama? A little *rah rah*. You and me. Pregnant. Hoo-ray."

"You and *me*? We..."

"Last night. The raksi bar."

"But that is too soon to be pregnant."

"No. Believe me, a woman knows these things."

My mind tries pulling apart its web of raksi and fog. Outside, the chattering whine now rises and sounds more constant and unchanging, *swoosh swoosh*, getting closer. The sound of bicyclists pedaling. Metal on metal. Abril cracks the door and peeks out.

"They sound like cicadas," she says.

I lean out behind her. Cyclists pedal in full stance, leaned atop handlebars and circling the intersection of Josephine and 33rd. Three, four, six times they circle before jumping the curb and gaggling up onto the warehouse's front lawn. Ice shakes from the weed trees down upon them and their tires thunder kicking up snow. One by one, they stop, forming an arc of bicycles in front of the warehouse. They dismount and drop their kickstands. They line up, their bows cocked and aimed at us in the warehouse doorway.

"Watch," I whisper. "They are going to file right and encircle the building." And at that moment they do so. Bowlegged, side by side, they clomp the snow and take positions beneath the stained glass on either side of the warehouse.

"Send her out, lama. We know she has it." The lead cyclist calls to me. I remain quiet. I say nothing.

But a quiet mind arouses nagging thoughts. "What do you mean, pregnant?" I ask.

She says, "Quiet. How many do you think there are?" She is talking about the bicyclists. "I'm guessing thirty, forty tops." I can hear them now, boosting one another up onto the outer stained glass window sills all around us.

"What do we do?" she says.

"Come."

We move to one side of the warehouse, beneath the windows. To the archers hoisting to the windows above us, we are all too close for them to get an angle on. To those opposite, we are an open shot. Split their army. Render one half ineffective. I remember this from my niru days, and I pray the archers above us attack first.

"Send her out, lama!" Not the lead cyclist. Yoong calls. Short-tempered and blaring.

Abril's eyes question me.

"She has nothing," I call back. "The dorje is nothing." Then I realize, what foolishness, yelling like that to let them know where we are. Shadowy silhouettes hover like gargoyles in the windows opposite us. Assuming position, lying in wait they knock their bows. Above us, I hear breathing.

"That is not yours to say, lama." Yoong bellows. "She sliced me. She stole the dorje. Send her out. It is only her I want. You can return to wherever you came from, I have no need for you. But the dorje is Chinese now."

Silence, again. Still mind. I see what is plain enough to see. How this is Abril's story, not mine. They do not want me, even though I feel properly reborn here on Colfax.

I squeeze her hand. Together we squeeze tight to the wall. Suddenly, arrows punch through above us, pulverizing the stained glass into dusty colorful shards that rain down upon us. Arrows pass overhead, hitting mid-warehouse, harmlessly.

Then the opposite line of stained glass opens up. More troublesome.

"Shield yourself," I tell her. I take the dorje from my pocket, its clawed orbs blunt and jagged. As cyclists above bridge the windows, I pound the Most Sacred of Object at them, and then grab their shoulders and somersault them out into the warehouse as shields for their compadres' arrows to pulverize, their carcasses flattening to the floor.

"Use the blade," I tell her. Cyclists still perched on window above try gaining balance to jump in. Abril runs window to window stabbing and slashing, driving them to the kill zone in the middle of the warehouse.

The front door thunders. A battering ram. "Send her out, lama."

Archers breeching the far windows now see us, giving them a clear shot. Archers above us pour in, ripping their Lycra on shards of stained glass, jumping down on us.

Then, with no understanding why, the left flank stops firing. Those on the right, too. The door rattles, ready to splinter. Cyclists slip down off the sills of the shattered Old and New Testament depictions, making their way in. Dropping their bows, they pull lingchi blades and come at us. All of them, blades out. Coming at us.

Abril slides across the floor and slices one through his Achilles. Another she stabs in his throat. A third up the stomach, ripping his Spurtz logo in half.

I swing the dorje like a baseball bat, smashing flesh, fascia, muscle, and bone.

The battering at the door continues. I can hear the hinges weakening.

"Go," I tell her. "A door in back. Go. They are not after me. They are coming for you. Go."

"No, lama. You have the dorje. That's what they are after." She continues swinging the blade, not leaving. Bicyclists still climb in, their faces blackened in ski masks and war wax.

The door lets loose. Its hinges explode. Yoong enters, sucking in more Spurtz cyclists behind him. He thunders across the warehouse floorboards to the apse where Abril and I stand. He slices the air with lingchi slashes. Wounded cyclists lay about. Others surround us, their blades and arrows aimed and ready.

"Stay close." I say to Abril, lifting a flap of my robe to shield her.

Yoong wears his parka hood squeeze-tied tight to his face hiding the scar she inflicted. The squeeze-tie keeps his gaze stiff, so that in order to look around he must turn his entire body, like a tin man.

Beneath my robe Abril grips my waist. An ache throbs in my side where she grabs me. More than a throb. A sharp pain.

Here, her story stops...

As it should. So she might question, is it real, or a dream? Bicyclists attacking a warehouse that once housed Catholics in prayer? These things do not happen.

Dying bicyclists carrying bows and a Chinaman swinging a sword. In what such world could such a thing occur? Why begrudge Chinamen? There are so many of them, and surely Yoong is just one of many, many Chinese agents.

And why deride bicyclists, even if they are rude in traffic wearing their gaudy outfits plastered in free advertising?

We are many different people living many different lives, each with our own story to tell. But our stories do not tell everything. Not who we are moment to moment. Not the part we play in another's story. Someone we may know or not know.

Sentient beings fall through life like shattered glass, once one thing, and now another. Once an Old or New Testament depiction, but now just dust. We fall into emptiness. Each and every waking moment.

This is what the Buddha talks about. This being unfixed and forever evolving. Living one moment, so brief, it is empty of self.

As Abril and I are. We empty ourselves, as a diversion. We disappear.

And when we do, bicyclists lower their heads and squint through their goggles to find us. Yoong slashes his blade through space, like a defeated Vajrakilaya.

Slashing at nothing.

* * *

"Where are we?"

Her story does not end. It continues, with a chill now passing through it. Colfax moves with traffic. The Aim Straight and Shoot's Christmas wreath devolves into a spindly entanglement of sticks wrapped in a sun-bleached bow. Beneath the wreath, a cardboard sign taped to the saloon door says *Closed in Honor of Pawnbroker's Day*. With a gummy sticker attached. *Make love to me, I'm a pawnbroker.*

"Where are we?" Abril looks Colfax up and down. I do not

know I can even answer. A breeze passes through me, empty.

"At the beginning," I tell her. But seeing it does not help. I say, "Here come. Follow me."

I take her hand. I lead her to the glass door going up to the apartments, the stairwell now narrower and steeper and longer than I recall. Inside, the door closes behind us, ushering in a blast of cold. I touch beneath my robe where an arrow protrudes from inside me, where once I had worn a scabbard for my ling-chi sword back in the niru days. I try untangling the arrow, but it snags. I listen for someone coming. Someone who might have followed us here.

At the landing where Daidyal once sat, Abril says to me, "Sit, lama. Rest. You're hurt." She leans me to the wall and sweeps a hand over my face, closing my eyes. "And you're cold."

She presses my side. An arrowhead presses back.

"I am fine," I say.

She does not hear me. Above us, her apartment door rests slightly ajar, its jamb splintered, light slithering out. Fernandez and Garcia stand atop the landing looking down on us. The other part-timer too, who says, "That's the girl with the tattoo on her ass. We don't talk about her much anymore. Not like I once hoped we might."

The inspector steps down the stairs. Garcia follows. "Don't move," the inspector says.

I lean against the wall. Abril rips my robe open where the arrow protrudes. When the inspector arrives I tell him, "We are already not moving."

"Give me the dorje," he says.

"Look at him, inspector," Abril cries. "He's dying." Then more loudly, "Do you hear me? He's dying."

For my part, I can feel the arrow snapped inside me. Something burning.

Fernandez and Garcia step closer. The other part-timer stays on the landing above.

"I need the dorje," Fernandez says. "The Chinese are very upset that it is even here."

Abril pushes him back. "You don't even believe in it."

"I believe in its value. Its importance to international relations and the country's debt."

My face drips sweat. "There is no dorje," I sputter. "It is nothing."

Garcia tells the inspector, "I will call for backup, sir. An ambulance." He dials.

"You look cold," Fernandez tells me, and then he fingers where my robes are ripped and have dampened shadowy red. He touches something gnarled and chinked and badly tarnished. Forcefully, he pulls at it. Something snaps. Not an arrow. A jagged edge of the dorje. It catches in a threaded tangle of my robes, not pulling free.

"Apply pressure," Fernandez says to Abril. "We need to get him to the precinct. We can take care of it there."

She slaps the inspector's hand off the dorje. He does not react. He pauses. He listens to something outside on the street.

"He won't make it to the precinct," Abril says. "He's bleeding. Do something now."

He does not. He just listens. He raises a finger, and a curious look. "Do you hear that?" We all listen. "Who followed you here?" he asks. He points to the glass door at the bottom of the stairs. To something outside.

My breathing grows heavier. My mouth tastes of blood. "Om mane Padma Hum." My words feel harder to say than breathe. My robes heavy, the dorje weighing them down.

Then in a crash, the glass door bangs open. Bicyclists swarm the stairs below, lining their way up to us step by step while strapping their bows. Yoong ascends through them with his lingchi blade drawn.

"I have this, Agent Yoong," Fernandez announces. "Seems we have found the dorje after all."

Yoong stops mid-ascent. His eyes hold steady, but his mind moves. "Give it to me."

"I am afraid it is not that easy. One of your archers pierced it, dislodging a bit of shrapnel into the lama here. We're taking him downtown to have it extracted."

"Not going downtown."

Yoong says it just once. He doesn't say it a second time. Instead he takes an arrowed bow from the cyclist next to him and fires it through the left lapel of the inspector's duster, so that his cacao striped suit and coffee colored shirt rip and darken just outside his heart, collapsing Fernandez down atop his Zelli Avianos.

"Whoa, what's this shit?" Holmes steps back on the landing, tries disappearing into Abril's apartment, but instead takes an arrow to the neck, another to the back, one to the side. "Whoa." He staggers, the word spilling out of him.

Immediately, Garcia kicks his heel into the cyclist closest to him, creating a domino effect, tumbling them end over end down the stairs while a bevy of arrows lets loose from down by the glass door. Garcia leans in taking incoming to his shoulders, arms and legs. None doing harm. I huddle over Abril, weakly burying her inside my blood-soaked robes. As the bicyclists reload, Yoong charges. When just about on us, Abril swoops from beneath my cover, slashing at the China agent with her blade. He parries, his sword knocking the blade from her grip.

It falls to the steps. End over end, it descends downward, settling on the next lowest landing.

We watch it fall, and we see Yoong raise his blade above us, forming a right angle to the sky, his sword aimed at Abril. He holds position, a priest over his sacrifice.

If you see the Buddha on the road, kill him. Any teacher other than yourself is false. A bodhisattva once freed himself by slaying his father called Ignorance and his mother Desire. But a true bodhisattva does not take life like that. He gives. He takes on the suffering of others and gives himself to their story, acting out a role empty of self.

I step between Abril and Yoong. Breath flows in. A bardo moment. Then exhale, wind energy. Without even touching him, Yoong falls back, wildly swinging his arms in the air seeking balance, swinging his blade aimlessly.

I stand firmly in place. Yoong's sword and I meet. Its stillness cuts me, as if in all my lives I have existed only in this one moment.

As he tries to pull his sword from me, Yoong's footing slips. He tumbles backward, colliding into bicyclists on his path down the stairwell. Their arrows fire this way and that, into the ceiling or back down on themselves. One catches Yoong in his larynx.

And then the cops show. Garcia chases the cyclists down the stairwell, while a wall of part-timers push in from the street and crowd them up. Together, Garcia and the others corral the Spurtz gang, tying their wrists in rags of ripped Lycra.

Abril reaches, keeps me from slumping. Arrows pin me to the wall. Yoong's sword hangs from where I once wore a scabbard for my lingchi blade during the niru days. My body sags. I have been severed. Lingchi.

A channel of energy breathes outside my form. Colors swirl through my vision.

Spirit flows away from me. My view of Abril grows smaller.

I feel the dorje snagged where an arrow hit it, and now where Yoong's sword pierced it stripping me of obscuration, shattering the dorje into shards inside me where it no longer feels whole. Just pieces, working through me, clogging my inner flow. Its gold and gems circulating inside.

"Don't, lama." Abril's voice. That is what it sounds like she says. *Don't.* And like she is the reason I am here, so I cannot leave her. The way she says these things, her voice sounds buried inside a gray, smoky light. Like a voice I had not heard before. Not in her story.

Like in a dream.

Dull yellow, my vision clouds. Cold rushes the stairwell. It rushes over the dead. Particles and shards of the Most Precious

Object rip inside me, chafing like the cold waters of Kyichu. Each drop a particle. All particles a flow.

Here and gone.

Empty.

I see Abril's gaze transfixed. Transfixed, as if seeing the stairwell anew, and as it is. Without police, or archers. Without Yoong. Without me. No superintendent yelling at her.

She stands there. She stares. As if staring might bring me back.

Which it cannot. Because all appearances are empty.

Daidyal taught me that.

Someone did.

Lama Rinzen in the Realm of the Hungry Ghosts

HEAD WEST. SHAKE OFF KANSAS behind me.

I am a doctor in this lifetime. Doctor Rinzen Naraka. A lama still, true. But a doctor. And I am running. Hungry, thirsty, I need to escape.

Rebirth is suspension. A way of moving from formless into form. In this lifetime, I am a relief doctor, running from place to place to cover the practices of established practitioners who find themselves in need of vacation, or a research sabbatical, or an extended drug and alcohol rehab. That is when a relief doctor fills in. In those transitory moments. Three months, six months, however long they will be away.

And when it ends, I run again. Another town, another hospital. Another place I do not belong, just transitioning through, from where eventually I escape.

Where to now? The Colorado plains. Saint Colman's. One hundred beds and fewer than 4,000 admissions per year. Should be quiet. A small-town doctor, that is what I will be. All lifetimes are just a form we assume.

Without form, we have no breath.

Without breath, we have no rhythm.

Without rhythm, we have no flow.

Without flow, we have no direction.

Without direction, we have no path.

Without path, we have no self.

Without self, we are empty.

That is how we progress.

I feel a blizzard coming. Clouds in the sky, moisture in the air, moving down from British Columbia. Need to make Saint Colman's before the storm, but I am hungry and thirsty and craving someplace to stop along the way.

I drive by rest stops. All closed and dark with winter gloom. Hungry Ghosts follow me, chasing me down. I keep driving, hungry.

I stay on the road to where I am going.

To escape where I am coming from.

49 Buddhas Glossary

Angeli
A colloquial term for showing reverent respect to a teacher or enlightened being.

Bodhisattva
In Mahayana Buddhism, a person who compassionately delays achieving enlightenment in order to help other beings do so first.

Bodhi seeds
The 108 beads strung together to make a mala, or Buddhist rosary. *Bodhi* translates as enlightened. The beads used in malas are typically one solid unpolished color, allowing their ridges and imperfections to show.

Budai
Sometimes called the Laughing Buddha, and considered the second Buddha after Siddhartha. The image of Budai is based upon a Chinese monk.

Chaang	Alcoholic beverage popular in eastern parts of the Himalayas.
Chiruu	As used in *49 Buddhas,* an expression meaning *Hey, listen up.*
Dantian	Loosely translated as "Energy Field", the Dantian is considered a source of the body's energy located in the lower belly.
Dorje	Sometimes referred to as "Vajra", a ritual object that represents the thunderbolt of enlightenment and the abrupt change in human consciousness when we realize that all beings are empty of self. Although *49 Buddhas* speaks of one Sacred Dorje, the dorje (vajra) is a common instrument used in many Tibetan Buddhist rituals.
Drepung	Translating from the Tibetan to mean "Rice Heap", Drepung in the Tibetan city Lhasa is considered one of the three great monasteries of the Gelugpa school of Tibetan Buddhism. Gelug is the lineage from which the Dalai Lamas emanate.
Dukkha	A Buddhist term for our condition of suffering that defines all sentient beings. Dukkha is also the Buddha's First Noble Truth—Everything is suffering, referring to both physical and mental afflictions. In the case of mental afflictions, a better translation may be dissatisfaction. We exist in a state of dissatisfaction because our kleishas (afflictions) distort our perception of self and the world around us.

Émigré   A person who has left their own country for another, usually for political reasons.

Fungo   A light weight baseball bat used in practice for hitting fly balls to fielders.

Fungtow   A Tibetan word for storm, and used in *49 Buddhas* in the term "fungtow troopers", a name referring to similar beings in a certain obscure science fiction movie series.

Gandharva   In Hinduism and Buddhism, a term used for heavenly beings, such as angels. In Indian classical music the term is also used to refer to skilled singers.

Garuda   A large humanoid bird that appears in Hindu and Buddhist legends.

Gelugpa   Considered the youngest and most wide-spread school of Tibetan Buddhism in today's world, the Gelug school was founded by Je Tsongkhapa (1357-1419), one of Tibet's greatest scholars. It is sometimes referred to as the Yellow Hat School, and is the lineage of the Dalai Lamas.

Gomden   A rectangular, box-like cushion upon which one sits for meditation.

Gwalpo   A slang term for a witch.

Gweilo   A Cantonese derogatory slang for Westerners, particularly those of European descent.

Izze   A brand of delicious sparkling fruit drink, like soda.

Kagyu	A school of Tibetan Buddhism that traces its lineage back to Shakyamuni, and whose teachings are based on the Indian yogi Tilopa (988-1069). The lineage includes such luminary teachers as Naropa, Marpa the Translator, and Milarepa (considered the greatest yogi of Tibet), and Gampopa, whose coming was foreseen by the Buddha.
Kleisha	In Buddhist thinking, the kleishas are afflictions that distort our perceptions and effect how we think, act, and feel. In this way they create the suffering (dukkha) we experience, and keep us stuck within the Six Realms.
Lingchi	Sometimes translated as Death by a Thousand Cuts, the Slow Process, the Long Climb to the Mountaintop, or Slow Slicing, lingchi is a form of torture and execution practiced in China from 900 until it was banned in 1905. In lingchi, an executioner used a knife to slowly and methodically remove parts of the victim's body over a period of time, eventually resulting in death and an afterlife in which the victim is disfigured and no longer a complete being. Lingchi was used to punish crimes against the state or against one's parents.
Mala	A string of beads used in meditation to assist in counting mantras or as a silent reflection on the sense of touch.
Manjushri	In Mahayana Buddhism, a bodhisattva associated with Insight.
Niru	Term for an army division.

Om Mane Padma Om
A mantra to be recited silently or aloud that unites method (path) and wisdom, thus transforming an ordinary being into the pure body, speech, and mind of the Buddha. It translates as the Six Paramitas or Purities of Buddhism: Generosity, Ethics, Patience, Diligence, Renunciation, and Wisdom. These six are meant to counteract the impure behaviors of Aggression, Greed, Ignorance, Passion, Jealousy, and Egotistical Pride.

Paragate
Pronounced as four syllables (Par-a-ga-tee), it means "Be Gone". Literally it means "Be gone to the farthest shore", or to the shore opposite the shore where the speaker currently stands.

The Path
There are three paths a Tibetan Buddhist practitioner may walk to achieve enlightenment:

Hinayana—the path of personal enlightenment,

Mahayana—the path of the bodhisattva, who seeks enlightenment for all,

Vajrayana—a path of magic and ritual practice, in which the practitioner follows a specific teacher as his/her spiritual guide. Vajrayana is said to allow a being to achieve enlightenment in a single lifetime. It is sometimes referred to as lamaism.

Raksi
A distilled alcoholic beverage in Nepal and Tibet often made at home. A form of moonshine.

| Shedra | A Tibetan word meaning "Place of Teaching", it refers to the educational system in Tibetan Buddhist monasteries. |

| Six Realms | The Six Realms of existence are the lessons beings must learn in order to progress toward enlightenment. They also can be thought of as the lives we live, whether in individual lives or on a daily basis. The six realms can be considered to be "learned" by practicing the Six Paramitas (see *Om Mane Padma Om*) |

The Six Realms are:

The Hell Realm—Aggression and confusion, tamed by the Paramita of Patience,

The Hungry Ghost Realm—the Greed of continual Hunger and Thirst, tamed by the Paramita of Generosity,

The Animal Realm—the Ignorance of acting instinctively without intention, tamed by the Paramita of Ethical behavior,

The Human Realm—Life based on Passion/ Desire, tamed by the Paramita of Diligence,

The Warring Titan Realm—Jealousy, tamed by the Paramita of Renunciation,

The God Realm—Egotistical Pride, tamed by the Paramita of Wisdom.

| Sukhavati | In Tibetan Buddhism, a Vajrajana (see *The Path*) rite of chanting for one who has died. |

Three Jewels	The three jewels of Buddhism are the Buddha, the Dharma, and the Sangha. These three serve as our guides to enlightenment. The Buddha refers not just to the enlightened Buddha Siddhartha, but to all enlightened beings. The Dharma refers to both the Buddha's teachings and to the world in which we live. The Sangha is the community with which we practice, as well as the lineage of our family, teachers, and guides.
Tonglen	The meditation of giving and receiving for the benefit of ourselves and all suffering beings. With each in-breath, we take on the suffering experienced by ourselves, our friends and family, our enemies, and the world. With each out-breath we instill compassion and good thought to each of these recipients.
Vajrakilaya	A Wrathful Deity who powerfully assists sentient beings in destroying forces that deny our cultivation of compassion.
Wangizmo	A slang term for male genitalia.
Yab-yum	A common depiction in Tibetan and Nepalese art of a male and female Buddha in sexual union, depicting the union of Wisdom and Compassion.
Yoni	A term for female genitalia.

ACKNOWLEDGMENTS

Book writing is lonely. There are many I want to thank for helping me through it, with their friendship, conversation, and advice. I hope you all stay with me as I continue the series. I particularly appreciate Bruce T. Martin for sharing the artist's way with me for so many years. His photography inspires me. I thank my Buddhist friends, Todd Ansted and Gabriela de Anda, for helping me see and for listening to me question. I thank the teachers I carry with me—Lama Tenpa, Lhoppon Rinpoche, and Zenki Christian Dillo.

I thank Susie Schaefer for her patience and guidance through the process, James Hallman for the conversation and direction, and Virginia Wolf for the wonderful cover design. To my friends and community at Lighthouse Writer's Workshop, I owe you all something special. Particularly, Andrea Dupree and Mike Henry. And many more. Cathy Spader, Mary Walewski, Corrinda Campbell, Melissa Johnson—thank you all.

But most of all, my readers. This book is about you. I hope you enjoy.

ABOUT THE AUTHOR

As a 20+ year practitioner of Buddhism and as a fan of detective fiction, Jim finds profound similarity between the Buddha's teachings to see the world as it is and the detective's challenge to focus only on the facts of the case. Both Buddhist and detective struggle to experience what it plainly there in front of them, without the overlay of prejudice, presumption, or ego.

Besides the *Lama Rinzen Mysteries,* Jim authors the *WritingLikeaBuddha.com* blog, offering meditations and writing exercises to help followers appreciate the small moments of meaning in our daily lives. He previously published the "sales-horror" novel *Wolf,* and lives with his Tibetan Terrier, Rascal, in rural Colorado.

Jim also edits and advises for the on-line publication, *Reader's Life Magazine.*

Jim is available for speaking engagements on Buddhism and mystery writing, as well as Skype discussions and book club meet-ups. To invite Jim to speak at your next event, please visit www.jimringel.com.

56530857R00198

Made in the USA
Columbia, SC
27 April 2019